**WHEN TODAY IS ALL THERE IS AND TOMORROW MAY NEVER COME, LOVE TEACHES A WOMAN. . . .**

*EMILY McROSS*—As a gray-eyed girl she had thought one love was meant to last forever. She never dreamed she would claim the hearts of three unforgettable men. . . .

*ALEJANDRO DE BARBILLON*—In his eyes burned all the proud passion of the Andalusian sun. As magnificent as the Spanish society he dominated, he would become a soldier fighting for his land and his life before he could make Emily his bride.

*DERMOT KILPATRICK*—Son of an Irish earl, heir to Castle Keene, his laughter and charm lured Emily from the depths of sorrow. A dashing RAF Squadron Leader, he gave Emily his heart forever, but his future rode on the perilous winds of war.

*SAM TREADWELL*—A handsome British soldier, he found opportunities in war he would have been denied in peace. He taunted Emily as a woman of privilege, but not even his anger at her world could keep him from loving her, or challenging her mind and heart as no man had dared to do before.

*THE
HEART SPEAKS
MANY WAYS*

# THE
# *HEART SPEAKS MANY WAYS*

*Madeleine A. Polland*

A DELL BOOK

Published by
Dell Publishing Co., Inc.
1 Dag Hammarskjold Plaza
New York, New York 10017

Dell ® TM 681510, Dell Publishing Co., Inc.

ISBN: 0-440-13629-6

Reprinted by arrangement with Delacorte Press
Printed in the United States of America
First Dell printing—December 1983

*For our Man on Islay*

## AUTHOR'S NOTE

Of course RAF Darlowe existed. I have excellent memories of it, and made lifelong friends there.

But anyone who was there will realize that no character in this book represents any one person. Rather is it the best I can do to recollect us all, and to recollect the Station under its assumed name.

I have to say thank you again to all the people to whom in the interests of this book I said, "Do you remember?" They all answered with great kindness and in great detail.

MADELEINE A. POLLAND

# ONE

"Stop the motor, Luis."

Don Rafael spoke abruptly to the driver, and laid a hand on his wife's arm to stop her flow of talk.

In the hot silence they looked back and listened from the bright crest of the hill; staring back at the white city of Málaga, which lay between them and the far, dark blue sea, all of them straining for the sound of gunshot. The two girls looked at each other with raised fearful eyebrows, but there was nothing more than the wind singing in the grass and the endless rasp of the cicadas, the column of smoke above the city rising in dark silence.

Emily McRoss, the Irish girl, listened and looked with an anxiety as great as any of the Spaniards', for to her every such incident was an immediate threat. Not of the civil war that everybody feared, for that seemed too impossible and remote; something that belonged to the grown-ups alone. But if it got too difficult or dangerous, she would have to leave Spain. For two years she had been living here in the home of Don Rafael and Doña Serafina, companion to their daughter Remedios, who sat beside her now, twitching with irritation that they should stop for something so trivial as a column of smoke. Her father sensed her impatience.

"*Hija*," he said. "Daughter. One day it may be your home."

Emily did not want to go back to Ireland yet. She wanted her third year in Spain, which she had grown to love. When they were both young, Doña Serafina and her own mother had been at school together in Madrid, deeply fond of each other. When Doña Serafina had first written to ask if Emily could come and spend three years with Remedios, the isolated youngest of a big family, she had not wanted to leave Ireland. Now Andalusia was embedded in her heart and mind.

Emily knew that Remedios was only concerned about the column of smoke because it had delayed them even a few moments on a journey that filled her with pleasure and excitement;

and she had lived through enough uncertainty as to whether the father would allow them to come at all. It would be the last journey for the summer, and even Remedios knew the faint cool chill of wondering if it would be the last journey at all—out to the finca, the olive farm and country estate of Don Rafael, for a day-long picnic the likes of which might well never be seen again. Don Rafael had been doubtful all the week: there had been rumors of bands of Communists ranging the hills and the countryside beyond Málaga, and sporadic violence crackled even in the streets of the city itself. In the end he had given way to the tears and pleas of his adored youngest child. Remedios was never so happy as in the country, and cherished the summer days at the Finca de los Angeles like the golden beads on her rosary.

"Very well," he said in the end. "It is allowed."

Maybe for the last time.

The invitations had been raced on horseback through the hot countryside, and for just one more day they would all gather as they had always done, and pretend there would be no war.

In the unaccustomed silence of Doña Serafina, whose normal habit was to drench companions, no matter whom, in a tide of inconsequential conversation, Emily had begun to think of something else that had happened that week. Strange. Rather nice, but really extraordinary.

They had gone back to school, in the still hot, golden sun of Spanish September, and there had been a new girl. Even that was strange, for they were not daring to take many new pupils in the convent, which by order of the Republican government was stripped of every crucifix and every holy picture and outward sign of religion: the poor nuns shamed and embarrassed in ordinary clothes so long foreign to bodies that had forgotten everything other than a lifetime in the habit. Miss, now, not Sister.

But there had been this new girl, that first day at school, and the nuns were eager and excited to introduce her to Emily: delighted to have two Irish girls who would no doubt be company for each other.

"But I'm not new really," the girl had said, after the introductions. "I came here as a little girl, staying with my grandmother, out on Gibralfaro. I knew Remedios then."

Remedios had nodded vigorously, beaming, only half understanding their English, a long strand of hair falling loose from the smooth shining cap of her head. Every day the old *dueña* brushed it until it shone, and drew it tightly into a long beautiful cascade down the girl's back. Every evening, Remedios came home a drift of whisps and tangles, as often as not her ribbon in her pocket.

The new girl had a short, gleaming cap of fair hair that was almost gold, and looked as if it would never loosen from its place. She smiled at Emily with dark blue eyes, long-lashed. She was quiet-looking and extremely poised.

"The poor Sister—I mean Miss," she said as she held out a hand, "wasn't very clear. I'm Anna Kilpatrick."

Emily took the offered hand.

"Castle Keene?" she said, astonished.

Anna nodded.

"But," said Emily, "we must have lived all our lives no more than twenty miles apart. A good day's hunting."

This must be the Lady Anna Kilpatrick, no less, who lived in the grand gray house that could just be seen across its green parkland, off the road between Emily's home and Galway. They had never met, although she remembered seeing them at the Meets of the Blazers when they were younger. Two fair-haired boys and this immaculate little sister. Always with beautiful horses, and the handsomest parents.

"How strange," she said, "we never met. So close."

"I was away in school in England," Anna said. "And my parents traveled a lot, too, and I went with them. I was here a lot, of course."

"I was at school in England too," said Emily.

"Anna," said Remedios, speaking English for good manners and pushing back her wandering hair, "is piece Spanish."

Anna smiled at her affectionately, as everybody smiled at Remedios.

"We had an ancestor," she said, "who fought with Wellington, and for a reward he got given a bit of land out near Loja. So we've been a bit intermarried ever since. It's my father's mother who lives on Gibralfaro."

In the old cloistered patio, with the jasmine and bougainvillaea hanging off the walls, and the flowerbeds around the greening fountain still rich with roses, they had talked then of far-off Galway and of home.

"And how long," Emily had asked her, "will you be here?"

"A year," Anna said. "They want me to polish up my Spanish. That is," she added, "if there is not a war first."

Emily nodded soberly, and it was Remedios who tossed her dark head in disbelief, unwilling to accept that her beloved country could be so foolish.

Now as they drove away from the threatening column of smoke above the city, Remedios spoke first, looking for reassurance.

"It is nothing, is it, Papa? In Málaga? But José—I heard José saying to a friend in the Horse Patio that Madrid is terrible and Barcelona is a . . ."

She stopped and her soft olive face went scarlet, caught with shame that she should have used the servant's own word for Barcelona. Before her parents. But Don Rafael only smiled below his long moustache, and Doña Serafina had not heard, already immersed in the far more important thoughts of all the housekeeping arrangements for the weekend ahead, and all the hospitality.

Little of it was real to her or to Remedios in their gentle sheltered life: the civil war had not yet come that was to ravage the ancient town where they had both been born, spilling the blood of their friends, and leaving the proud family dead or homeless. At the moment it was still no more to them than a threat to a country picnic, like the first incalculable rain of autumn.

Emily was more uneasy, wondering always if she would have to leave.

Conscientiously she did her best to understand what threatened her, and the country she had grown to love, going to Rafaelito, since she found Don Rafael, in all his kindness, rather remote and unapproachable.

"Tell me, please, Rafaelito, what exactly is happening in Spain? Everybody seems to be fighting everybody else and I don't understand."

Rafaelito smiled, his long narrow face so like his father's.

"Indeed, *chica*," he said. "I think you are quite right, but I will try and make it clear to you."

Even with his patient explanation, she still found it very confusing.

"They put away the king," she said. "I know that."

Every week, still, Doña Serafina took out and shook and refolded the blue and gold flag that lay in the chest on the front landing, waiting for the day when the king would come back and it would hang proudly again from the white flagpole on the balcony. But even Emily understood that few other than Doña Serafina hoped now for this day.

"Now," said Rafaelito, "the country is a republic. But not a safe or stable one. It is threatened by the people who want a king back, and by the Falangistas, who want power for themselves."

The Falangistas. She had seen them. Rich young men from the old families, the old families of power, screaming through the city in their big black motors, hats drawn low over their eyes, and the sun on the barrels of their guns.

She had heard the machine guns stuttering in the hot, dark nights.

"Falangistas," Remedios would whisper and bless herself, awake and alert with fear, for although they were of the same political belief as her father, they were still terrifying. Wild. Unpredictable and uncontrollable.

"And then, of course," said Rafaelito, "there are battles on the side between the Anarchists and Communists, who hate each other even more than they hate the so-called rich oppressors."

"Poor Spain."

"Poor Spain indeed. But the ultimate battle will be between the Army and the Republicans who hold the country now. There is talk of an Army uprising for the Nationalists. Any time. The Army is gathering in North Africa. Waiting for the order to rise against the Republic."

"Would that be the end of it?"

"That would be the beginning of it. That would be the civil war we are all afraid of. The ultimate lineup. Republicans against Nationalists. And the Army would be on the side of the Nationalists. Is that better? Do you understand?"

Emily nodded.

"And we are Nationalists?"

He smiled to hear her identify herself with the family. Please God, before anything serious occurred she would be safe home in Ireland. "Do not molest yourself, Emilia. You will not be able to stay here, and we will get you home. And you know that Remedios does not concern herself about the war."

"It's not going to drive her away," said Emily.

Rafaelito looked at her then, his face unbearably sad and grave, and did not answer for a long moment.

"Who knows," he said somberly. "Who knows."

She had grown to love dearly the vague, affectionate Remedios, and the whole family loaded her with endless kindness. A year was such a short time in Spain, the turning of the seasons so sharply marked, not only by the weather but by the chain of ferias and festivals that hung the months like lights.

October, with the first rains, would see the end of the ferias and the bullfights and the picnics. The rains would come then and the winds, and gradually the dark cozy nights of winter, when she and Remedios would gossip by a bright, sweet-smelling fire of olive wood, the charcoal brazier warm under their table: listening to the wind howling in from the east across the harbor, hissing in the dry fronds of the palm trees and hammering at the shutters. Through the brilliant, glass-clear weather of December, they watched the snow sparkling on the high peaks of the Sierra Nevada; waiting for the turn of the winter and all the festivals of the New Year. Then the Feast of the Three Kings for the children, and more celebrations. In no time at all Easter would be coming, the rains over and the sun out again and all the shutters open; somewhere always the sound of a plucked guitar or a hoarse voice from the kitchen patio tossing a snatch of some Sevillana. After the week-long mournful processions of the penitents through Holy Week, there would be the first of the bullfights on Resurrection Sunday, everyone greeting each other as though they had been in hibernation all the long winter, which was indeed so short. Summer again, and the dry, languorous heat, and the flowers, and all the ladies up to Carratraca in June to take the waters, the whole clamorous pack of the family children with them, filling the entire echoing hotel with bedlam. Remedios always with a discreet and careful eye out for the boys.

"For what else, my dearest Emilia," she said one time when Emily was shocked by some outrageous piece of behavior. "What else is life all about? You are too English, pretending that they don't exist."

"I'm not English. I'm Irish."

Remedios shrugged.

"*Es igual*. It is the same."

And Emily was left wondering a little unhappily if it was she who was wrong. Seventeen, and yet what Remedios said was still substantially true. For her, as yet, the boys scarcely existed. Except in dreams and ideals that had nothing to do with the handsome Spanish boys who bowed over her hand and exclaimed with open pleasure at her freckles. Always the freckles. Even the *piropos* from the street corners on the way home from school always mentioned the freckles. But as yet, none of it was real.

Emily watched Remedios with affection. The increasingly rare visits to the country meant so much to her, whose effervescent spirit seemed sapped by the dust-laden streets of the city.

Emily herself loved the weekends when they went out to the finca near Alhaurín el Grande, some twenty kilometers of winding, beautiful dusty roads to the north of Málaga. The drenching light of the Andalusian sun poured down as far as one could see, there. On the gray trembling leaves of olives, or the thin foliage of almonds, that at the end of winter filled the gentle valleys with pale leafless blossom. Behind it all, in the far distance, the blue mountains lay hard against the sky, the sun carving pitted shadows on the high flanks. Deep in the trees, in its own circle of tall, fronded palms, was the sprawling white house, doors and windows bordered in the old style with yellow ocher. The drive between clipped cypress led to the long echoing archway where hooves took on a hollow clatter, then into an outer patio draped with jasmine and rich swags of bougainvillaea. Beyond the house, the stables for the horses were Don Rafael's pride. The whole gathering the next day was for the viewing of a new foal, and the choosing of its name.

Beside the stables was the *picadero*, the small private bullring in whose red-walled circle great matadors would kill in private for Don Rafael and his guests, or the fine horses circle through their flawless paces, ridden by the family and their friends. Curiously enough, one of the most skilled and elegant on horseback was the untidy and clumsy Remedios. Once she mounted, she seemed half the size, and immaculately tidy. On horseback, she came into her own. Or dancing.

The wild oats blew along the roadside banks, translucent in the sun, and the olives stretched like a gray-green sea, rising and falling with the hills, flattening at last into the plain beyond Alhaurín, the finca like an island in its sheltering palms, dark blue mountains of the Sierra de Ronda away beyond it, sharp against the enameled sky.

They were almost the last to come—all the family and most of

their guests were there before them, clustering and chattering in
the patio or the shuttered coolness of the salon, countless shrieking children racing in and out among the indifferent grown-ups.
The arrival of Doña Serafina set off a tide of kissing that even
after two years left Emily shy, and when it was all over, she
heard Remedios sigh with gusty relief beside her.

"There, the duties are over. Now, *por Dios*, let's go and see
who's here."

Emily grinned at her. To Remedios that meant a careful and
discreet survey of all the young men who had been invited,
chosen for their behavior with both the horses and the girls; to try
Don Rafael's magnificent horses in the little ring. Or cape a
young bull on fiestas; and to treat his daughter with the propriety
and respect that was expected. Remedios wandered idly, an
innocent expression on her face behind the gentle fluttering of her
fan, greeting her girl cousins and carefully assessing the young
men where they stood grouped together at a distance, beside the
barrels of fino on the long tables in the patio; fiercely handsome
and proud in their Andalusian *traje*, calf-length riding trousers
and brief, velvet-collared jackets molded to their fine short figures;
Cordoban hats tilted down over their noses; the sun gold in their
wineglasses; dark eyes as carefully estimating the girls as they
were being estimated themselves. Remedios accepted without
rancor or dismay that in a year or two her parents would choose
one of them without consulting her, to be her husband, as they
had chosen for her elder sisters. Usually it would work out very
well. For the moment she might flash soft bright glances around
her fan, and pretend that she could choose.

She seated herself on the edge of the fountain, in her white
dress, sedately crossing her slender ankles, lace fan fluttering
before her face, whispering wickedly behind it to Emily.

"Antonio Angel de la Sierra! What a pair of legs in *traje*! He
is tall, too, for an Andalusian. But I do not care for his face. He
could be cruel. Ah, but *Madre mia*, look how Sebastian Diaz has
grown up! Regard that mouth, Emilia. There is something. Would
you not like to be kissed by that? He would be a lover!"

"Remedios!"

Emily had been in Spain long enough to know the pattern, and
found most difficult this pretense by Remedios that she was free
to fall in love. It seemed to her all the more impossible when the
time came for Remedios to marry to her parents' wishes. Never,

she thought, could she accept an arranged marriage such as all these girls would have. With no time first to know her own heart, and be sure the man was one she would want for all her life. It might do for these sheltered girls who had grown to the idea from childhood, but never for her. Never.

The sheltered girls, meanwhile, were humming like bees at swarm; shaking out the flounces of their dresses; straightening each other's collars, shining heads together, giggling behind their fans, passing quick critical remarks, and correctly looking at every green corner of the huge patio, except the one where the young men grouped beside the wine barrels.

Remedios shot Emily a glance above her fan. Her adored Emilia always wanted to pretend that she did not know what it was all about. She glanced down at the decorously crossed ankles and the fine hands that told of the beautiful woman she would one day become. Of course, they all pretended that they knew nothing. It was all part of the whole subtle and exciting arrangement. But there was no Spanish girl of her age who was as innocent as *cariña* Emilia seemed to be. It was all a deep and grave design, holding the young people apart so long, like a child gazing at the sugared almonds at the feria; speculating on the whole business, speculating on each other and who might be chosen for them. Holding them apart with just enough contact, so that by the time they were allowed to marry they were wild for it, and almost anyone would do. These marriages were nearly always successful.

Remedios shrugged. Of course, later it was necessary to accept the other women. The mistresses that the husband would have in his wider life, leaving the girl at home to raise the endless babies. What of it? It eased the tiresome burden of a too demanding husband.

Emilia, on the other hand, seemed to think that marriage was a love for life, and there should be no other women. *Caramba!* when would she ever have her bed to herself? Or even the chance of a lover if things went that way.

The Spanish way was better. Everybody knew the rules, and there was less likely to be pain.

Emily was not as uninterested as Remedios thought, taking discreet and careful glances at the young men. How handsome they were; and how proud and sure of themselves. All a little short by her standards, but then this was Andalusia and they

made up for it by some natural grace and dignity, moving
elegantly around; talking and laughing a little overloud, well
aware that they were on parade. How Spanish, she thought. All
the girls together in one group, the young men at a safe distance
across the flowering patio. In the salon, the older women comfortably grouped with their heads together, talking of children and
childbirth and the running of their houses. The older men had all
vanished with Don Rafael into his dark office, where they spoke,
grave-faced, of many things, but inevitably of the coming war;
safe here among their own kind, to set out their loyalties and
proclaim themselves for what they were. Only the children were
allowed to run without question between all groups, like a flock
of little colored birds, welcome with their shrilling and chattering
wherever they should go: until their neat young nursemaids in
pink and blue dresses would come to claim them for siesta when
the long business of lunch was over.

Rich. Secure. Rooted in the patterns of their mores; their high
self-confidence only beginning to be threatened by the dogs of
war that howled beyond their high green hedges.

Emily was thinking only of the boys and girls. It was not really
so very different at home in Ireland, except that theirs was a bit
of a female household with the father dead, and no men to root
themselves in the back parlor with the whiskey, as in other
houses. But at least you'd be allowed to get to know the fellow
you'd want to marry and choose him for yourself. How could
Remedios face being given a husband on a plate like that? And
soon. Almost straight out of school. She'd be married before she
was eighteen.

The sun moved around and the top table at the end of the patio
fell into shadow. The servants were moving about, putting down
plates in between the bottles of manzanilla and anis, and the big
stone flagons of red wine. Huge platters of tender *lomo*, and dark
garlic sausage in fine slices; the best of olives; tomatoes and
pickled cucumber; strips of *serrano* ham from plump Jabugo pigs
from the hills of Huelva, and uncut loaves of hard-crusted bread
that would be broken on the tables to their soft fresh centers.
From the house, some of the older women were drifting out, still
talking, in groups of two or three, every one of them in the
mourning black that pursued most Spanish women through their
lives. Sharply, without seeming to move an eye, they assessed
the girls for their behavior and the boys for their eligibility.

*"Madre mia,"* said Remedios suddenly at Emily's side. "Whom have we here? The day begins to improve." Emily could hear the rise of excitement in her voice.

A young man had paused at the end of the long archway, just out of the black shadow and into the sun, looking for a long moment over the huge patio—the lemon trees and the hibiscus, and the tall palms, their roots set in beds of brilliant flowers; the tables laid with white cloths—and at the girls, all staring at him, bright and untouched as the flowers themselves. He had the look of breathing it all in and savoring it, and then he smiled, and with a gesture of greeting that included all of them, he turned for the house, and his hosts.

"My cousin," breathed Remedios. "Would you believe it? My cousin. Alejandro de Barbillon. He has been in England studying something, and I haven't seen him often. His parents live in Madrid, but they have a small finca over there toward Coín. He is my second or third cousin or something like that. Not too close."

Not too close. Emily knew she meant, for marriage. The endless preoccupation. But he certainly was handsome. And tall.

"Is he not something, Emilia?" her friend rattled on happily. "Did you see those eyes? We will see to it that for luncheon he is at our table. After all, he is my cousin. Do you think he will notice me? He is so *tall*."

Like all Andalusians she was obsessed by height; conscious always of her own lack of height. Emily smiled at her affectionately. Her excitement was already loosening her hair, and her olive cheeks were flushed with rose, her fine eyes brilliant. Who could not notice her, Emily thought without jealousy. Awkward and untidy, she still held some quality of unfathomable beauty.

She said it out loud.

"Who could not notice you, *chica*?" And Remedios glowed. But Emily's own hand had moved instinctively to her soft red-gold curls, cut short in the English fashion, touching them into place, and she had stirred to shake the creases from her blue silk dress. The girls around her were seething decorously, but never would she enter into competition, even with Remedios, by admitting the tremor that had run through her as those grave dark eyes across the width of the patio had unerringly picked out the only stranger in the company; a small pause in the glance, which was like a promise. And then he had smiled and was gone. Tall even by her standards, and with a bearing that could still get attention in this world of proud and self-assured men. No grays or greens for him. His clothes were formal black, pale boots gleaming below the calf-length riding *traje*, the strap of his Cordoban hat framing a long strong chin.

You are as bad as Remedios, or any of them, she reproached herself. It was only because she was a redhead. All Spaniards were attracted by her hair. La Rubia, they called her. The fair one. It was no more than that. As her mother would say, she stuck out in that company like a sore thumb.

"Twenty-two, he would be by now," breathed Remedios, who had been working at her memories.

"Marriageable" was what she meant.

The servants were hurrying out now with the hot food as the guests began to crowd the patio. Great iron pots steaming with chicken and rabbit stew, and flat two-handled pans of paella, yellow with saffron, black with mussels, and scarlet with cigalas' claws. The men were drifting from the house with their huge cigars, their faces carefully benign. The rest of the day for the family, anxiety and responsibility set aside.

Remedios was beside herself. For the meal the boys and girls were allowed to mix under the watchful eyes of the grown-ups, with fierce discreet jockeying for the company of their choice. Setting the pattern for the long exciting afternoon around the stables and the practice ring, while the older ones were snoring in the shadowed rooms.

"I cannot bear it," she said to Emily, and there were actually tears on her heavy lashes. "I cannot bear it if he doesn't sit with us. When he comes out I shall go and kiss him, and invite him. He is after all my cousin," she repeated. "I have known him since we were babies. And my Mama is his hostess. That would be quite correct, would it not?"

Emily laughed at her and pretended to be indifferent, but could not help wondering with a faint tremor of excitement whether her discreet and disapproved-of touch of lipstick was still in place.

Emily was always to remember that brilliant day as both an end and a beginning. Although she didn't know it, it was to be the last time she would see the finca, until after the holocaust of European war, when she would stop her car and stand with her own growing children at the familiar gates. Watching strange owners come and go, and peopling the place, for her children, with those whom she had loved.

They were all coming to the end of their pretenses that there was little to fear, and that the old safe, ordered life could be preserved for anyone. At Don Rafael's hospitable table that day were several men in heavily braided uniforms, come with dark serious faces from the talk in the paneled study. Ready now, like everybody else, to set aside if only for an hour or two the tension lying over the sundrenched valley, and the calm order of their lives. And over all of Spain.

In the face of all the rumors of violence and arson and bloodshed running through the city in the past months like wind through summer corn, Emily had often wondered why they still kept her there; indeed, why they had ever let her come. In July, her mother and eldest brother had wanted to take her home, but Remedios had been distraught with tears, and Doña Serafina had looked aghast that they should so distress her. In the comparative calm of Málaga, where little violence had yet fallen, she was still determined to convince herself it was all a passing threat; to keep her determined mind only on her well-conducted household, touched as yet with neither hardship nor anxiety: the well-being of her adored grandchildren far more important to her than which government had fallen last. If she thought of it at all, she would not believe that there was any danger to such as herself, from a rabble of ill-armed *Comunistas*, soon to be sent packing back to where they had come from, wherever that might be. The Spain she knew had stood too long. In no time it would all blow over, and the blue and gold flag unfolded, to be smoothed again with proud hands, over the railings of the balcony. Her husband, Don Rafael, would protect her as he had protected her from every anxiety throughout their married life.

She found nothing to fear. No reason for Emilia to go home and her darling Remedios to be made unhappy. By the end of next summer their daughter would be old enough for them to arrange her betrothal, and the parting with Emilia would be easier. Sometimes in her benign responsibility for all who entered her loved world, she felt she should arrange a marriage for Emilia also, to some young man of good Spanish family. Then she would sigh, aware that in the proper time Emilia must go home, and find her husband there, where they did things differently.

But in the proper time, she told Don Rafael, repeating herself endlessly and unsuitably to his patient face. Not helter-skelter because they had burned a church in Barcelona or fought bloody battles in the streets of Santander or snatched the estates of the nobility in Estremadura. These things were not here. Firmly she had kissed her old friend, Emilia's mother, and told her on a tide of talk not to molest herself, that no harm should come to the child if she stayed. Her mind was already on the supper party in the patio, which she was giving that night to say good-bye, and in the next sentence she was wondering if José had remembered to go to San Pedro to get the *langostinos*.

Doña Serafina presided normally over her household from her favorite tapestried chair in the salon, usually a dark-eyed baby in her lap clawing at her pearls. A comfortably large lady who had given Remedios her enchanting smile, it was her custom from this chair to dictate the lives of her entire family and all the affairs of her household by means of a remorseless tide of conversation in her high Castilian Spanish, which wore down opposition or independence more surely than any argument. She would smile lovingly from one daughter or daughter-in-law to the other, and tinkled on benignly against any efforts to interrupt her, coming back always after endless deviations to the point that had been her original decision. Family and servants were brought to an unheeding daze, barely able to remember on what grounds they had first disagreed; bewildered out of reason by all the divergences.

It was the dictatorship of a generous and loving heart, and all her household had taught themselves to think or even talk of other things, letting the tide pass over them, knowing that whatever emerged at the end of it all would probably be right.

Her housekeeping was impeccable and her family and servants loving and content, knowing, from the husband down to the girl who scrubbed the kitchens and to the little donkey boy, that she was thinking always of them and never of herself.

Emily had grown both to respect her and to love her.

Emily's brother John was not so easily satisfied, and went quietly to Don Rafael.

"My mother is concerned, Don Rafael. Even frightened. Has she reason to be? Will Emily be in any danger?"

Don Rafael looked grave and sad, stroking the long moustache that to Emily made him look like all the portraits of medieval Spaniards she had seen.

"There will be trouble," he said at last. "Great trouble. There will be war. My poor country will be in a far worse state before it sees better."

He was a mild-mannered man, marked by a great sense of presence even in his stillness, deep-set dark eyes full of intelligence. He looked tired and careworn.

"Then we should take Emily home?"

"Does she want to go?"

His English was impeccable.

John was honest, his long freckled face sober with the decision he must make. No good leaving it to his mother.

"Quite honestly, no. She feels this last year of Spain is very precious. There is all the rest of her life for Ireland, she says. She has fallen in love with your beautiful country, Don Rafael."

Don Rafael smiled and inclined his head as if the compliment had been for him. In the small moment of silence the cathedral bell boomed softly across the city in the hot evening.

"Then, I think, she need not go," he said. "Not yet. Just yet. I give you and your mother my promise that if the situation should grow threatening, I will get her home at once. One of the young men of the family can escort her, and my friends are such that I would never lack place on a ship. I do not find these airplanes dependable."

John hid his smile.

"We could always meet her, perhaps in Marseilles."

"Or Genoa. It would be ideal."

John looked at him, wondering whether to express his lingering doubt. The Spaniard seemed so sure of himself, so much in touch with the situation, that it would seem almost rude, and one must be very careful always of offending these proud people.

"There is no danger of the situation, Señor, going up in flames without warning?"

The older man looked at him gravely, his dark eyes quiet and somber, full of sad knowledge.

"There will be warning, Señor Juan," he said. "We will get her out."

They had been standing at the head of one curve of the staircase in the Málaga house, below them the vast patio where once the carriages had wheeled. Even Remedios remembered the stables being there when she was a little girl, below the great sweep of the stairs. The Horse Patio, they still tended to call it, even though the horses had long left, and the rich warm smell of those days was replaced by *gasolina* from Don Rafael's black Buick, and dogs and cats and goats and chickens and children no longer rambled freely between the wheels.

Up at the top of the stairways were the galleries, all of them opening to the central patio, with long narrow windows to give light from the high roof of greenish glass, on which the rain drummed in winter like an attacking army. The house was built around the patio, so that the family in wet weather had been able to come dry-shod from salon or library or bedroom, down the great stairs to the stables or the carriages, or the dark traveling coach encrusted with its coat of arms.

Now the Buick was there, and the Hispano Suiza that Don Rafael used when he was being formal; and the servants' three-wheeled pickup for the markets; and all the forgotten bicycles and boats and roller skates of Remedios's brothers. A couple of donkeys that never seemed to reach the new stables, and in the nights a few carefully hidden goats, for how else could the señora have fresh milk for her breakfast. Beyond it all lay the teeming warrens of the kitchen patios, with the ancient lift screeching up into the paneled dining room.

Even John on so short a visit could feel the strong sense of family and permanence and security.

After that conversation, with a feeling of living on borrowed time, Emily had kissed her brother good-bye, torn between him and his anxiety, and this country that had grown so twined into her mind, and indeed her heart; kaleidoscope of sun and dead black shadow: flowers and dust and music and sharp blue skies. She told him and her mother not to worry and watched the wide, comfortable train rolling softly to gather speed down the long length of Málaga station. She waved and blew them kisses for as long as she could see. Then she turned back to Remedios and her father, and José, who had driven them all in the big Buick through the airless evening. At the end of the station she could see through into the street, to the plane trees dark with their weight of dusty leaves. The evening sun fell through them in gold patches, and beyond, the sky was almost navy blue.

## TWO

Another year. *Si Dios quiere*. Please God.

She savored every day of it; and knew herself that day at the *finca* to be savoring it with even more tangible delight. As though she touched every moment to mark it in its passing. Looking back, when she was once more beside the winter fire in Galway, with the Atlantic wind lashing the rain against the windows under a sky of sodden gray, she felt she must have known that day was special.

An end and a beginning.

"Ooh," cried Remedios at her side. "There are the *padres* of Alejandro. They must have gone straight into the house. I will go and make my respects."

With the delicate grace so odd in her plump body, she sped away across the patio, and Emily noticed with a smile that one long strand of hair had already wandered from the bow at the back of her neck.

"Tia Angelica! Tio Pedro!" Sweetly she kissed her aunt and uncle, and was warmly kissed in return.

"Not really aunt and uncle," she said to Emily later, "but one must call them something, and in the family everyone is Tio."

"*Chica*," her aunt said now. "You are so grown. And so *guapa*. So pretty. You are well?"

"*Sí, sí*. I am enchanted to see you. It has been a long time."

Even more enchanted, she thought wickedly, to see Alejandro. "Have you seen Alejandro?"

Her aunt pushed back the wandering strand of hair, slightly prominent gray eyes assessing rapidly. The *chica* was developing well. Thinning a little, and would thin more, with a promise of great beauty. Mentally she docked up confirmation of a long-held plan. Remedios would do very well for Alejandro, when the madness in the country was settled down.

"I saw him only passing," Remedios said demurely.

Her aunt smiled benignly.

"Well, you will see more of him now, yes?"

Don Pedro, having made his affectionate gestures toward the girl, went to join the other men at the top table. Behind them the radio blared flamenco through the empty house.

"Yes?" Remedios wondered what she had been missing, but did not dare to ask.

"You did not know he is coming to work with your father?"

Remedios stared at her wide-eyed, stunned by the enchanting possibility, delicious visions racing through her mind.

"He has finished his studies for the moment, and his father wants him to work for two years or three with your Papa before he takes his degree. If God wills," she added, as did everybody at the moment who thought to make plans for a doubtful future.

"He will live with us?"

Why had Mama said nothing about this most exciting thing?

"No, *chica*, that would not be suitable." Not, she thought, with what I have in mind. "No, he will live with the Ramiro cousins out at Limonar." She named a fashionable outer district of Málaga.

"Aiee. That will not be far away."

Her aunt smiled at her transparency, benignly foreseeing an easy success for all her plans. At that moment Alejandro himself came from the house, and under the approving eyes of his mother, Remedios was free to kiss him prettily and ask him to sit with her and her friend for lunch. With affectionate courtesy the young man agreed. He had been away so long, he was a little strange among the enormous family, and Remedios would do as well as any other for the way back in. From a little distance Emily watched Remedios with a wry affection. She would never blunder pink-faced into situations, as would Emily herself. No matter how excited, Remedios never lost the careful manners to which she had been trained.

Her eyes turned then to the young man, who hat in hand, was making small pleasantries to Remedios. She had met him before, of course, in the first summer she had been there, heedless of him as anything more than one of the flock of family boys. In that summer, she and Remedios had cared for nothing but the horses. Last summer, he may have been here, but there had been a flare of violence in Málaga, and she and Remedios had been packed off to the wide safe spaces of a bull ranch up near Cádiz, owned by yet another branch of the family.

She had watched his mother go away across the patio, threading her way between the tables in a drift of black, a certain satisfaction in her manner.

Two years. Was it indeed he who had so changed? Or was the change in her, staring at him now in something close to astonishment; conscious of the same physical tremor as when she had first met his eyes. Some deep and blithely unconscious part of her being stirring into almost painful life. A sensation of feeling as well as merely seeing the matured young face under the glossy, lightly curling hair. Not regularly handsome, the nose a little strong; generous mouth smiling over beautiful white teeth, but what was that, for what Spaniard did not have them. Over Remedios's head she caught again the same sudden arrested stare of brilliant and embarrassingly observant eyes. Tall for an Andalusian. Taller than she, and not many of them were that.

She realized that both of them turned their eyes away, with difficulty, locked in the same astonishment. Remedios whirled around, her lovely face radiant.

"Emilia! Alejandro, do you remember my English friend Emilia?"

"Irish," said Emily, and Remedios pouted prettily.

"I never remember there is a difference," she said.

"That," said Alejandro, "is what they have been fighting about for years. As we are about to do."

He spoke before he even gave her a greeting. What was serious to him must come first. Then he smiled a little and moved forward, his face grave, as if he did something of great importance. He took Emily's hand, and bent over it, sun gleaming in his thick black hair, to leave a kiss just short of it.

"Of course I recall the señorita," he said, and smiled his full disarming smile. "It seems to me," he said, "she has grown more Spanish. But she is as enchantingly *rubia* as ever. And all the little spots."

Red hair and freckles.

As common as the bogs in Ireland, but here they drew the men like a cockfight. She knew she was stared at in the streets. Heard the *piropos* from dark doorways. She stood, feeling dumb and foolish and very un-Spanish, for no Spanish girl was ever at a loss, and she was searching desperately for something to say, other than "Yes, I remember you too" and "But you weren't half so handsome."

*"Gracias,"* she said inadequately, and *"Encantada."*

"I'm delighted to meet you."

"Can I arrange you some food?" he asked them then. "Where are we to sit, Remedios?"

The trestle tables with their enormous white cloths were already filling up, beneath the palms, the patio growing deafening with the noise of these voluble people, delighting in each other's company; all miraculously capable of eating copiously without ever slackening their tide of talk. White-shirted servants and the older children were circling the tables with bowls of the chicken stew, deliciously mixed in with pigs' feet and lumps of pork, *garbanzos* and potatoes and a rich toss of garlic. The gorgeous smell reached Emily, and she knew suddenly that she was wild with hunger. Hunger and some strange new deep excitement that she couldn't measure.

"There's no room left to sit together now," she said. "Remedios, you sit with your cousin and I'll sit with the Aunts."

The Aunts. The common Tias of all the family. *Por Dios*, to sit with them now would be an anticlimax to break the heart. Two aging relatives, one fat, one thin, that no one could quite place, living on the generosity of Don Rafael, doing all the duller jobs of the household that everybody else would wriggle out of; the inevitable dependents of any big Spanish family, where no one, no matter how old or dull or stupid, was ever left to face the world alone.

"You will do nothing of the sort," the young man said firmly, and swept over to a table full of children, who were banished, plates and all, to eat where they might find room. The interminable meal was the excitement of the day. At the long tables where the flirting and the giggling held a certain touch of the hysteria of the segregated, envious glances were being shot at Emily and Remedios, who had clearly landed the big catch. Remedios tossed her untidy head as if to allow that they were right, and Alejandro moved to rearrange their table and bring the servants running with spoons and forks and wine and bread. Remedios looks at him, thought Emily, as if he were Michael and all the Archangels rolled splendidly into one. She wondered again if she should sit somewhere else, and realized at once that if she did so, one of the aunts or cousins or even mothers would move over to join them. Even she and Remedios alone with the young man were not being quite correct. Only as affianced *novios* might they eat alone together, even in public. Smiling then, willing to take what the day had brought, she moved over to where Alejandro stood waiting for her, holding out a chair.

It is ridiculous, she told herself as the same shock ran along her nerves, knowing that he would not have moved the chair for her until she met his eyes. Ridiculous. She had only just met him. It is more than foolish shyness, she thought, because none of them have looked at me quite like this. Although she had been long enough in Andalusia to recognize the warm hypnotic charm of Spanish men. The magic of compelling liquid eyes. They had it when they were little boys, and they never let it go. It lay still in the tired intelligent eyes of Don Rafael, and in the thin, teasing smile of the old grandfather who sat among the men in his special chair in the shadow of a palm, enjoying nothing so much as to have about him the loveliest of the girls.

Reluctantly she admitted to herself, pretending to give all her attention to her steaming bowl of stew, that this young man had more than his fair share of it all, even for Spain. Looks. Magnetism. The beautiful confidence born of complete self-certainty. But he would be for Remedios. She had been able to see that in the mother's eye.

Remedios thought so. She was glowing and ecstatic, flashing her fine eyes and thrusting back her falling hair with her long beautiful hands, tossing out a waterfall of talk, so that for long periods there was nothing for the other two to do but to sit silent; and try to avoid each other's eyes. She kicked Emily under the table until her shins were sore, to be quite sure she understood the splendor of the young man they had succeeded in trapping, and Emily, scarlet to the edges of her hair, knew him aware of every kick, and what it conveyed. Sighing, she drew in her feet, and knew it had only begun. When they went to bed that night, he would be assessed and dissected down to the last button on his braided jacket and the last hair of his thick black lashes. The endless fascination of forbidden fruit.

It began when the long, embarrassing meal was over, and they went upstairs to change into their riding habits; Remedios reluctant to let go even for a moment. Emily took out the short close-waisted Andalusian jacket, frogged and braided, the long, looped skirt over the heavy horse boots. At first she had had great trouble, for she had only ridden sidesaddle once, for a joke, on an old saddle of her mother's from the stables.

"What do you think?" Remedios asked her breathlessly, wrestling herself into the dark green skirt, her frilled blouse sideways and her fingers grappling for the wrong buttons. Emily swore that somehow the moment she was on a horse, even her clothes came right by magic. "Is he not *magnífico*?" she cried now. "*Qué guapo*. Did you observe his eyes? And he is so tall. And so, so *simpático*."

Emily had noticed all these things, and didn't know how to answer, for the first time ever feeling, with a small shock of sadness, a reservation toward her friend. She was aware that across the bright flirtation with Remedios, and all the flashing glances and quick answers, much had been left unsaid between her and Alejandro. She knew, a little tremulously, that in due course it would all be said. The generous and gentle Remedios must never be hurt. At the same time, shadows of something like the Inquisition crossed her mind, as the penalties for stealing the young man of a girl of good Spanish family.

She smiled teasingly at Remedios now.

"But, *niña*," she said. "I thought you were forever in love with Antonio José Fernandez."

He was out there today, always a little aloof, surrounded by his own charisma. One of the famous matadors of Spain, cherishing his anonymity even here, below a pulled-down cap; flashing fine eyes and an enchanting diffident smile at those he knew to be his friends.

Remedios giggled, grimaced and shrugged, and eased the strap of her hat below her chin. With a careless foot she pushed aside the clothes she had taken off, for the servants to pick up.

"I am," she said. "Oh, I am. Who would not be? But Alejandro is more—more possible."

Through the late hot afternoon, when not even the palm leaves rustled in the stillness, the ladies retired to the bedrooms for the siesta and more gossip, the younger children with them.

Don Rafael and the gentlemen led the pilgrimage to the square white block of the stables, the little practice ring beyond through an archway, and farther on the sea of olives washing up below it like a tide. There was first the new foal, in a small special pasture, to be admired and exclaimed over, and discussed; standing long-legged beside his mother in the shade of the eucalyptus trees, drowsy in the heavy heat.

Four of Don Rafael's horses were already saddled, sidling with slight hostility among the visitors who had come mounted. Splendid in the brass and silver mountings of harness and high Andalusian saddles, heavy iron stirrups dangling, manes plaited with green and white ribbons.

One by one the young men and some of the girls took their turns in the ring, putting the beautiful horses through their paces. The crowd of handsome and strong-faced people watched almost in silence as each highly trained horse went through the delicate routine of its schooling, dust rising up to haze the sun. Timeless world where fear and violence and the threat of war were no more than a memory of nightmare.

But Emily noticed suddenly that the men in uniform were gone.

She gave her attention back to the ring, never failing to be enthralled, coming as she did herself from a land of highbred horses. But never schooled like this, except a few of them for showing. A stable lad now was plucking at a guitar, each note falling separate against the heat, and a dapple gray with red ribbons in its mane and tail circled the ring, following the music with careful and deliberate precision.

Emily felt alone and very still, oppressed with the need to take time by the hands and halt it; a sense of the perfection of a pattern about to break; that might never be remade again. Would even the cicadas ever sing again so loud, or the plangent notes of the guitar echo so perfectly in the silence over the long valley; the coats of the horses shine so in the light; or the dark faces of her friends ever be so fine. She felt the sun on her face and her boots in the dusty soil, and knew a grief for Spain that was never to touch her again so bitterly, even when the worst of terrors had engulfed them all. She drew a long deep breath and knew herself close to senseless tears.

"You have good horses in your country too, Señorita. I have been there. To the Horse Show in Dublin."

She was taken by surprise, enthralled by the exhibition in the ring, and shaken by her formless sense of loss. The young man, Alejandro, was beside her, his eyes on her with an intensity too great for his simple remark. She came back abruptly to the untouched present.

"Oh, yes," she said. She reminded herself firmly that such intensity of gaze was stock in trade, yet for a few moments her

Spanish maddeningly deserted her, and she fumbled even to find the word for yes.

"We can speak English if you prefer it," he said. His words were correct, exact, but his accent terrible, as though he had learned his English from a book.

"I have enough Spanish," she said, annoyed with herself for being short with him. Why was she being such a fool. All Spaniards thought "English" girls were awkward and uncouth, and here she was, setting out to prove it.

"Tell me of your horses," Alejandro asked, smiling gently, as if to give her another chance.

Remedios was in the ring, amazingly immaculate in her green habit with the yellow facings, her lovely face intent, drawing *olés* from her friends with her perfect performance.

"Bravo," cried Emily, "bravo, Remedios." In her pleasure for her friend she forgot her awkwardness.

"Oh, yes," she said then to the young man beside her, and did not realize how her enthusiasm transformed her fine features. "We have magnificent horses in Ireland. But only a few of them are schooled like this. We hunt with them, and jump them and race them. They are for harder work. Not delicate like this."

"*Qué barbaridad!*"

He was grinning at her now, perfect teeth gleaming, and she could not but smile back. "I have heard of your, how do you call it, hunting. Where you charge all over the *campo* like soldiers at battle, chasing a fox, and everybody falls off, and all the women are huge and strong and come home dirty and wet with rain to eat the English tea. That is it, no?"

Her eyes were on Remedios, but she laughed.

"Near enough," she said. "You must come," she said then, without thinking, as she would say it at home to any young man who was a friend of the family. "You must come some time and visit my home, and we will take you hunting. You would enjoy it. Look at Remedios. She is superb."

"Ah, yes," he said. "The little one." And threw one indulgent glance at the ring. "She does very well."

Emily turned her big gray eyes then and looked at him fully. His amiable disinterest touched her suddenly with a sad premonition of sorrow and disappointment for poor Remedios; and in the clear glance that would not relinquish hers, she saw with shock the first astonishing hint that she herself might be the one responsible.

Oh, no, she thought, and as she had thought before, ridiculous. I have only just met him. He is simply playing the Spanish game. No girl must be let go past without this gallantry; this suggestion of something special.

He gave her a small and slightly formal bow.

"I hope indeed," he said, "that someday your parents will invite me to your home."

"My mother," she said. "My father is dead."

"I am sorry."

He was so correct.

"It was a long time ago," she said. "I remember him only a little."

"Tell me about this home where I am coming to visit."

He was moving too fast for her. When you just made a casual invitation like that, you didn't expect the fellow to be arranging to be on the doorstep next day. Yet she told him. With a pang of nostalgia that took her by surprise, for she had thought herself unwilling to go back. Told him of the square gray house set back behind the cottages at the end of the village, its very gates between the last two of them. Buried in its bower of trees so that all the rooms were a little dark. The tangled flower garden on the other side going down to a few acres of park where they pastured the horses. The old gray stable block away out to one side.

"Nothing much," she said, and he glanced at her and smiled.

They began to talk then easily, suddenly, of their lives and homes.

"We have a small finca the other side of Alhaurín. Only a summer house. But my father has estates in Catalonia, and a house in Madrid."

His handsome young face grew grave. "It is not good now in either Catalonia or Madrid," he said. "I would prefer them to stay down here."

Her gray eyes roamed his face as if he were the ultimate authority.

"There will be a war?"

"There must be."

Silence fell between them like a cloud over the bright day.

"Don Rafael promised my brother he would send me home before there was any actual danger."

Alejandro glanced somberly across the ring to where Don Rafael leaned on the wooden railing among his friends, Cordoban hat so low on his nose that it almost rested on his long cigar. Emily thought of the braided officers who had been there before lunch, and then thought of all the lovely horses and wondered if they would take them if there was a war. Was that why they had been there? The thought of the horses going made it all more frighteningly real, and she knew it was stupid. What of all the boys who would go with them?

"Don Rafael will know," said Alejandro then.

He turned around and leaned backwards with his elbows on the top rail, trying not to stare too obviously at the girl so close beside him. He found it difficult to keep his eyes from the short silky red-gold curls, crisping under the black rim of her hat; the enormous wide gray eyes with the dark lashes that didn't match the hair. And *por Dios*, the little spots. What was it they called them? Freckles. He was fascinated by the shocking forwardness that had her asking him to her home when they were barely met; completely contradicted by the clear and steady innocence of the gray eyes. A Spanish girl of her age would have long lost that charming innocence.

"It could be soon," he added, keeping his thoughts to himself; speaking only of the war and of her going away; unable to keep the note of regret from his voice. They looked at each other, fully forgetting all the rules and conventions, aware that something startling had begun between them in the short hours since they had met. Aware that all of it, unspoken, barely thought of, had little hope against what might overtake them.

They went riding then, in the first lengthening shadows of the evening, as many of them as could be mounted, the younger married girls as duennas. The cavalcade strung out along the dusty paths between the olives and the aloes, and it was not difficult for Alejandro in the end to work his way along beside her. But he was discreet and rode as much with Remedios, joining Emily only on the way home after they had stopped for a *copa* at a small cantina in a dusty clearing in the olives, littered with white pecking chickens and patrolled by a brace of rangy, evil-looking dogs. The horses jostled and sidled in the pale lamplight from the windows of the small white house, lambent in the first dusk, and voices and laughter carried in the lonely silence. They called good-bye, exchanging blessings with the family, leaving them to their dusty isolation, and the young man rode home beside her through a limpid dusk that she had never found so lovely; filled with the twittering of birds and the scrape of cicadas, the darkening air as soft and tangible as silk; smoke from small isolated chimneys rising straight into the windless evening. They talked of themselves and their homes and their lives, almost all question and answer, groping through the first steps of getting to know each other, the familiar scene edged with unfamiliar excitement.

Behind them some of the young men were singing the songs of Our Lady of Rocio, and others were clapping; the hard, staccato rhythm of flamenco. There was a wonder in the air for Emily, sharpening all the old magic that had already bound her to Spain. Yet when afterwards she tried to remember Alejandro, she could conjure up nothing except the shadow of his face below his hat and the gleam of his fine teeth when he smiled; the indolent grace of his seat on the horse. All so vague that he might have been no more than part of the exquisite evening.

She was barely aware of supper. The swarming children were cheerful and noisy, refreshed by their siesta, the whole company exhilarated by the coolness after the day's heat. There were guitars and singing and clapping, and the young ones dancing the Sevillana. Alejandro looked over at her and told her with his eyes that he would not ask her; he had singled her out already as much as was proper for today. There was no disappointment. Enough had already happened for her to be longing to go away and think about it, with some astonished certainty that it was important.

He danced with Remedios, and she smiled with pure pleasure to watch them. Every child was taught the weaving grace of the Sevillana before it was even steady on its feet. Like her mother when they were all small, teaching them in their London house all the steps of the old jigs and reels. The heritage of a country. But the jigs and reels, she remembered, were really war dances, the fierce leapings of men going off to battle. Like all flamenco, this was a dance of courtship and pursuit, endless preoccupation of a passionate people. She was aware that it had some deep new message for her, but she was too tired, too full already of new sensation and experience to accept it: watching with a pang of guilt and concern the exquisite grace of Remedios, and the transparent adoration with which she lifted her eyes to the young man whose boots clattered on the floor beside her spinning feet.

At last the visitors began to drift away, scooping sleepy children off the sofas and even off the floor, full of affectionate thanks and warm good-byes, touched with the sharp edge of sorrow that none of them knew when they might meet so again. But they cried, "*Hasta la vista*," and made plans that might never come to pass, and rode and drove away into the misty moonlight, their voices coming back out of the darkness when they had long vanished, as though they were already ghosts.

When Alejandro went, he did his round of good-byes, no more to one than to another. He was riding home, and then off to lunch somewhere else tomorrow. She could find no more than courteous correctness in his bow above her hand, and his "*Hasta luego*."

The day was over. She listened to the hoofbeats of his horse, echoing through the long archway and then losing themselves in the dust of the drive, and visualized him riding away between the shadowed cypress trees, and knew a chill certainty of disappointment. She had attached too much to it. Caught again by Spanish charm.

In their cool high-raftered bedroom, with the lamp turned out, Remedios sat on the chest beside the window, looking out at the moon beginning to sink above the olives, and the last lights of the village pricking up the side of the mountain. She was too excited to go to bed.

"Did you not think he was handsome, Emilia?"

No need to ask whom she meant.

"Oh, yes."

But not handsome exactly. Something more valuable than merely handsome. She wished Remedios would shut up and come to bed, and allow her to take out the day and pass the hours through her mind as she would pass her rosary through her fingers. Examining every word and gesture for meaning. Savoring again the sun on his brown face as he was talking; and all the other things that had belonged to today. The horses and the sun on the turning leaves of the olives and the great moon shouldering its way up around the hills.

Remedios was babbling happily on. Down below they were still banging pots and pans in the kitchen and talking with that special emphasis and urgency of Spain that had once made her think people were always quarreling.

"He asked *me* to dance," she said. "That was very public."
She laid her head against the window frame, her long black hair
streaming down over her white nightdress. Heavily she sighed.
"But that could be only politeness. I wonder when we will see
him again."

Emily's eyes shot wide in the darkness.

"But I understood he was coming to work with your father.
And that he is your cousin."

"So?"

Emily was so astonished that she sat up, swept by sick
disappointment, shorn of what she thought of as the one certainty.

"Well . . ." she said. At home, any young man working in the
family like that would be forever in the house. Especially if there
were daughters. Or even sons, come to that. He'd be a family
friend, especially if he was related, like Alejandro. What a
tedious and complicated country Spain was.

"If he's working for your father," she said carefully, "won't
he be coming to the house? And a cousin at that?"

"Only a very distant cousin," said Remedios. "Distant enough
to marry, and that makes a difference. Oh, yes, he may call on
Mama to pay his respects occasionally, and they would always
ask him on a day like this, but with this miserable war, how
many more days will we have."

"But . . ." Emily's mind was still on her home, always full of
young people coming and going to all sorts of things, the ones
that were special to each other pairing off; her sisters' boyfriends
never out of the house.

"But . . . can't he just come around and see you?"

She thought of her mother counting heads every Sunday before
she would arrange the lunch.

The pale oval of Remedios's face turned sharply, and Emily
could see her shock.

"Oh, no. That would be most improper."

"Improper? In your own home?"

"Oh, yes, if a young man should call like that, then it would
mean he wished to marry me. No man can call until he is your
*novio*."

"Well where do you get to know him?"

Remedios shrugged.

"No one bothers about that. It is the parents that must know
him."

Emily gaped at her.

"No matter how old you are?"

She could sense that the other girl thought the question stupid.

"We do not grow old unmarried in Spain," she said smugly, and Emily realized that that was true.

"And what if you don't like the young man your parents have chosen?"

Remedios shrugged again.

"It is God's will," she said. She spoke with Spanish resignation, which covered every sorrow that could wither life, hugging herself against the sudden cool of the night breeze. Then she giggled.

"But I will do all I can," she said, "to see that God's will is Alejandro. It would be entirely suitable."

Emily looked out past her at the sinking moon, and felt herself growing small with disappointment, no less because she had no reality about which to be disappointed. Was she really never to see him again, other than as the *novio* of Remedios, their marriage arranged? She slid down on her hard pillow, suddenly and irrationally homesick, as she had not been since she first came from Ireland.

As far as she could understand it in the cocoon of ignorance on which Don Rafael insisted, the government of Spain changed almost weekly through the beautiful autumn, when the dust of summer was laid by the first short rains, and the air stretched clear as glass to the Sierras, the wind holding, even in the heat of the sun, the chill smell of the first snows.

Over the gray city lay an air of tension and unease, although little happened to break the ordinary run of life to which Doña Serafina so desperately clung. There were outbursts of violence between Anarchists and Communists.

"If only," said Remedios's brother Ramon cynically, "they would kill enough of each other, then our troubles would be over. They do not seem to be able to decide who is the enemy."

It was no more to the family than a stuttering of machine-gun fire and the sharp crack of rifles in some distant barrio, or a pall of smoke hanging black behind the twin towers of the cathedral. The Falangistas were more in evidence, screaming trigger-happy through the narrow streets. The people turned to watch them pass and blessed themselves, for the tales of their violence were terrible, horrifying even those who knew that when the time came, they would have to fight with them.

"They cause trouble they are not yet ready to control," said Don Rafael in one of his rare pronouncements over the evening table, Doña Serafina ruthlessly pressing the tide of her conversation against him in more harmless directions. Secretly they terrified her as much as the *Comunistas* and *Anarquistas*, and she could see nothing to choose between them.

All over Spain, through the golden days of that autumn, under the threat of terror that was so soon to come, the old life struggled to continue; the last of the ferias and the last corridas, all the festivals of high summer were over, and as people closed the shutters for the first time against the chilling winds, facing the hibernation of their winter, they wondered, with a fear as cold as the winds, what spring would bring.

Emily watched Don Rafael for some sign of anxiety, some indication that he was thinking of sending her home, and found nothing in his calm face. He came and went to his office overlooking the fountain at the end of Larios, and in the late quiet evenings, his friends came purposefully up the long staircase from the outer patio, José carefully closing the Judas door behind them, to sit with him in his paneled study, their deep voices rumbling late into the nights.

She would not have cared now if the ancient cannons up on Gibralfaro had managed to be loaded with their monstrous shot and fired into the town. It would have been no more than an infuriating nuisance that might drive her back to Ireland. War and the threat of war had receded from her mind, and she sighed with relief each day when Don Rafael's thin face showed no more than its usual intelligent urbanity. Then, against the barrage of conversation around the table, she would drift back to the only thing she wanted now to think of.

She was in love. Astonishingly, she told herself, ecstatically, and deeply, embarrassingly, in love. It had happened to her. This mystic thing that the Spanish girls were always talking of. Or did they know the truth of it, who were not free to choose for themselves? How could they feel as she did?

When they had driven back through the moon-drenched dusk after the weekend at the finca, everyone, even Doña Serafina, was silent, touched by the fear of what might pass before they should go there again. Emily had felt seared by some sweet special grief, marking each known character of her world with poignant and unbearable beauty. The moon larger and more yellow than it had ever been before; the leaning yuccas etched with painful beauty against the fading sky; every light gleaming from a cottage door filled with some tender message of security and love.

Beside her, Remedios began to chatter of the weekend, unable to be depressed for long by something she did not really believe in. Wars were for her father and his friends. No concern of hers. The future was hers and all her happy certain plans for marriage. Emily crushed the sour impulses of disappointment and gave way in the beautiful evening to the grandeur of the might-have-been, seeing again against the indigo sky every remembered detail of his face, and the manner of his talking; the execrably accented English and the long fine hands so expert with the horse; the whites of his eyes brilliant in his dark brown face.

When the girls had gone back to school after the weekend, they had found the nuns in fresh distressful turmoil over new threats against their freedom and safety. All of them were trying desperately to seem worldly, as though the chill discipline of vows had never touched them, the big double door standing wide open to the hot street, refuting any idea of enclosure. The crosses carved into the two panels of the outer doors had been defaced with hatchets.

"I can see you and me soon on a boat," Anna, the other Irish girl, said to Emily, ambling up to her as they ate their *merienda* in the middle of the morning. Chorizo, garlic sausage, sandwiched in the pale hard-crusted Spanish bread. Emily looked at her, trying always to assess the real extent of danger.

"Is your father anxious?" she asked her.

Anna smiled.

"He doesn't know much about it," she said. "You should hear my grandmother. It is no more than a small passing inconvenience."

"Doña Serafina is the same," said Emily. "But I think that Don Rafael keeps her like that deliberately. He doesn't want her to worry before she has to."

"It will be all the worse for them when it comes. But I think my grandmother understands very clearly, really. She just doesn't want to give in."

"You think it is coming?"

"All the servants say so, and they always seem to know everything."

Emily was silent, thinking of all the sad and terrible stories she had heard of their own civil war in Ireland. Brother against brother. Father against son. Would it be as bad? Or worse?

Curiosity and the sense of missing out on some epic excitement battled in her mind with plain fear. She was grateful that the choice in the end wouldn't lie in her hands. The bell rang for class, and she swallowed her last piece of crust and followed Anna inside. If Don Rafael said so then she must go, and her mother was probably already having stitches about what there was in the English papers. There was nothing, she thought with painful sadness, other than her affection for Remedios to keep her in Spain. Alejandro would never be for her.

She relinquished him then as utterly as if he had existed only on the finca, vanishing into the world of fable when he rode away between the cypresses.

So determinedly did she banish him from her mind, that she stood and stared with shock when he was waiting outside the cathedral after the one permitted Low Mass on the following Sunday morning. Yet so deeply was he printed on her memory in his black formal *traje*, that it jolted her to see him in a gray pinstriped flannel suit, with a wide blue tie, his soft felt hat in his hand, the sun catching the gleaming brushed-back hair. Coldly he ignored the rabble of rough youths who hung around the cathedral steps to jeer and shout at the faithful who were still brave enough to go to Mass. At the edge of the pavement a little way along the road, a light blue sports car with rich upholstery of red leather was standing, open to the sun. Rich and different and special. She knew at once it would be his.

Perhaps she and Remedios would go home in that!

She had to curb the impulse to race down and say hello, physically dizzy with the sudden pleasure. To her astonishment, Remedios did not rush down to greet him either.

"*Madre de Dios,*" was all she said, her great eyes glittering, and a hand going up to smooth the mitered edge of her mantilla.

"*Madre de Dios,* but this one is forward." Then she devoted herself prettily to speaking to her mother's friends, while the driver eased the car to the foot of the steps so that Doña Serafina and the girls could get quickly into it, away from the jeers and catcalls.

Doña Serafina paused a moment in the shadow of the big car, and held out a hand to be kissed by the young man with his hat in his hand.

"You have been to Mass, Cousin Alejandro?" she asked him, and a flicker of wise amusement touched her brown eyes.

"I have been to Mass, Señora," he said firmly, and it was like a message of some sort, for the mother gave a small satisfied grunt that was not quite a laugh.

"You will come and take a *copa* with us before the meal?"

Alejandro had turned to bow over the hands of Remedios and Emily, whose Irish informality still felt a little embarrassed at the gesture. Again to her surprise, Remedios merely fluttered her downcast lashes, as if she barely knew him.

"Cousin Alejandro. *Encantada*." she murmured, and no more.

Emily was about to relieve, as she thought, the awkward moment with some small conversation when she realized Doña Serafina was waiting for her to follow into the car. Hastily, realizing she had made some gaffe, broken one of the interminable patterns, she scrambled into the soft leather-smelling shadows. Remedios followed her. Once again, for such a trivial contact, Emily saw her dark eyes brilliant with excitement. A soft smile lit her face as the driver edged the Buick cautiously through the muttering crowd in the red-walled square beyond the cathedral. Touch one of these lads even with a wing, and he would have a riot on his hands.

"I do not know," said Don Rafael sadly, from the front seat beside the driver, "how much longer we can continue going to Mass. Now it is only words. Soon it will be sticks or stones or anything else they can lay their hands on. In the end they will have arms, like all the rest."

"Jesus Maria," breathed his wife. "Can we not have Mass said in the house?"

"And have them stone the house? And the priest as he comes and goes? No," said Don Rafael gravely, "we will have to wait for God, like everything else, until the trouble is over."

Doña Serafina blessed herself and gave a small unwilling sob.

"*Dios mediante*," she said.

Emily could not help speaking as she and Remedios climbed the stairs from the outer patio. The brilliant sun bathed them in green gentle light through the high glass roof.

"Will your cousin really come?" she asked, and Remedios looked at her, surprised.

"But of course," she said. "It is required."

Emily didn't understand her, but at her gesture stayed with her on the gallery at the top of the stairs, where they could look down on the green swimming gloom of the patio, and the small donkey boy taking the dust of the short journey from the Buick with a cloth; peeling off their white gloves from sticky hands, and unpinning the small mantillas that they wore for Mass. Remedios was bubbling with excitement, but Emily was unable to match her, shaken with nervousness at the unexpected ordeal of seeing Alejandro again. Being in the same room with him; watching the turn of his head and the slow brilliant smile.

Knowing it was all for Remedios.

When she saw the long blue length of the Bugatti slide through the open doors from the bright street, Remedios gave a little skip and a whoop, and raced for the bedroom round the gallery, to slam the ends back into the dark cap of her hair and shake excitedly at the flounces of her dress; teasing out the puffs of her sleeves and beaming at herself in the mirror in happy conspiracy with her reflection.

As she turned to run from the room she caught Emily suddenly in her arms and hugged her, wild to share her happiness. With chill, leaden misery Emily tried to smile back warmly at her, but at the same time she was wondering if her mother would let her come home at once if she should ask her. She could exaggerate the trouble in the town, and say that she was frightened.

Anything to get away. It was more than she could do, she thought, to watch the formal, ordered courtship of Alejandro and Remedios. Would he, as Remedios had often hinted to her, take other women once the marriage was settled down? Have his mistresses while she had her children? Was that perhaps how he saw her, Emily, at the moment? A foreign girl, not worthy of the respect that he would give a Spaniard. Putting her mentally away in his mind until his marriage was established, and he was free to roam.

Anger took her, and her red head was high in the air, round chin jutting, as she went into the salon after Remedios.

Across the room, Alejandro saw her anger. He didn't understand it, but excitement tingled in him, although he didn't move or lift his heavy eyelids. Spirit. The first essential. In a horse or a woman. He stayed where he was and made no attempt to talk to her, until the correct moment came for him to say good-bye.

"Remedios. Emilia. You will forgive me, I have not had time to talk to you."

Remedios nodded, her eyes like stars, and appeared completely satisfied.

But Emily was puzzled by his coolness both that day and through the glittering days leading up to Advent, when he seemed to materialize everywhere.

They would walk in the Alameda in the dusk of a Sunday evening, the lamplit paseo as formally divided as at an evening party; girls down one side with shining hair and bright soft sweaters, never appearing to glance, yet aware of every aspect of the boys beyond the barrier of mothers and duennas. Alejandro always appeared, only apparently to pay his respects to Doña Serafina, and to walk with her as a member of the family; no more than a few small politenesses to both of the girls, and if Emily thought that his eyes rested on her a moment longer than on Remedios, it only served to confuse her more.

He was invited to the huge family lunches. Doña Serafina had been married at sixteen, and Luis, the eldest, was almost forty; down through Paco and Rafaelito to José Maria, who was not yet married, and drew torrents of reproach and exhortation from his mother over what she called his irregular life. He was thin, with glasses and a self-absorbed expression, and listened to his mother patiently and kissed her lovingly and went his way. Emily liked him best of all the brothers. There were three sisters with their husbands, and all the tribe of racing, shrieking, beautifully handsome children. Odd cousins like Alejandro, and in-laws and widowed aunts and ancient uncles, filling the huge old house with their vitality and noise.

At first, finding herself next to Alejandro, by accident or design, Emily had tried to talk to him quietly, below the general level of uproar, some forty people all talking at the same time. But she had found Doña Serafina's watchful eye on her down the length of the long white table and knew she was doing something wrong. For the rest of the meal she shrieked with all the rest. God forbid that Doña Serafina should think she was trying to steal him from Remedios. But she could not help the deep trembling elation at his nearness; the long beautiful hands to which she might slide her eyes while eating. When he turned to speak to her, the whites of his eyes were almost blue, so clear against his olive skin.

Fiercely she applied herself to the claws of her lobster and thought with cold wretched sadness that there was nothing for her to do but go home. She would write to her mother tonight. Even as she thought it, she knew she wouldn't. Shamed by her lack of strength, she accepted that as long as she could meet him and talk to him, however briefly, she would stay. If they let her. Until he was formally pledged to Remedios. Then she must go or break her heart.

When they went riding with their friends out in the hills behind Limonar on Saturday mornings, he was there by permission of Doña Serafina. Always riding with José in the little posse of brothers and servants who found it necessary to go now to guard the girls along the mountain tracks, rifles across the bows of their high saddles. But apart from the courtesies of helping them to mount, and his polite farewell when the ride was over, before he roared off down the dusty road in the glittering pale blue car, he appeared to pay them small attention.

Emily was sick and silent with constant disappointment, yet Remedios glowed with happiness, her radiant face beginning to show all the promise of its beauty. She talked of nothing else but Alejandro. His fine body; his eyes; his beautiful silky hair, his horsemanship; his excellent character. And always in the end the speculation on his possibilities as a lover; in terms so frank as to make Emily blush, coming too close to the secret thoughts of her own wakeful, longing nights.

She began to fear for the blithe contentment of her friend.

"But Remedios," she said to her at last, after wondering for a long time if she should speak at all, aware that she probably faced some complex Spanish attitude that she wouldn't understand. In a pool of golden lamplight that only touched one half of their huge shadowed bedroom, Remedios brushed the fine silky hair that would never stay in place. English hair, she called it, unlike the heavy faultless fall of proper Spanish hair.

Remedios had been speaking dreamily of her wedding gown.

"But Remedios, are you sure about all this?" She hesitated to be unkind. "I have hardly ever seen him speak to you except to say hello and good-bye."

Remedios merely laid down her silver brush and smiled serenely. Emily watched her face in the circle of lamplight.

"Oh, yes," she said, and clearly thought it something in his favor. "He is very correct."

"What do you mean?" Emily asked, not certain of her own motives. Was she really concerned for Remedios, or was she trying hopelessly still to tell her sad heart that he might possibly be hers.

"At home," she went on carefully, telling herself that she loved her friend enough to try and guard her against hurt, "you'd need a bit more encouragement from a fellow than hello and good-bye, before you started planning your wedding dress."

She was thinking of her sisters, and the giggles behind the palms in the greenhouse and the holding hands under the dining table with the mother pretending not to notice; the kisses she'd seen in the dark garden from her bedroom window. And they'd gone out together in the lads' cars to dances, and to Salthill, to the sea, and all over the place. She had thought it all soppy at the time, but now she knew better; knew her own secret aching longing to be racing off into the mountains in the blue car, with the moonlight white along the sea below them.

Remedios shook her head and the black hair lifted in a cloud.

"That is not our way. Alejandro is being very proper. Very Spanish. Were he not of the family, he could not come to the house at all. For a few months he will call on my mother. Always my mother. It would be most incorrect to talk alone to me."

Emily recalled Doña Serafina's cold eye on her at the dinner table. How much worse to be in intimate conversation with someone who was not even Remedios.

"Then," went on Remedios, and her voice was full of satisfaction, seeing no obstacles. "Then all the parents will talk together and speak of settlements, and we shall become *novios*."

She stopped and smiled, looking past Emily into her entirely satisfactory future, with wide soft eyes.

Emily tried not to hate her, and wondered bleakly about the war, ashamed of the faint hope that it might take Alejandro away before all this happened, forgetting that it would take her away also. Would Alejandro go away to fight? And whom would he fight for? Her ignorance took definition from her dreams.

Remedios turned her eyes back to her friend.

"When we are *novios*, he will be able to come and call on me. We can be alone and talk together. Ride together. *Madre de Dios* but he will take me out in the blue motor. And everyone will give fiestas for us and know that we are going to marry.''

Something in Emily's face halted her, and she moved over to put an arm around her friend's waist.

"Querida, do not look so lonely. No matter even when we are married you will be my best amiga. And you shall attend me at the wedding.''

"And when will that be?''

Remedios shrugged.

"As soon as I leave school. June is possible.''

Once more Emily thought about the war, her friend's untidy head resting on her shoulder. She knew a moment of bitter shame to admit the hope that Alejandro should go away to war, rather than that Remedios should have him. What had happened to her?

As if to emphasize her thoughts, rifles cracked somewhere suddenly out toward the hills, and they could hear shouting on the cool wind. They looked at each other, and their apprehension filled the shadowed room and Alejandro was forgotten.

In late November the school was closed down for some petty infringement of the anticlerical laws.

"Some poor nun has said too many prayers,'' said Remedios scathingly.

"Well, then, I shall take you up for a couple of weeks to Carratraca,'' said her mother comfortably, not unduly distressed. Her priorities in education for young girls were pretty manners and good housewifery and a proper acquiescence in marriage, and she could encourage all these as well up in the mountains. "My rheumatism,'' she said, "could benefit with a course from the waters.''

Against the tide of her light voice, rambling on about her arrangements and dredging up anecdotes of other visits and other spas, the two girls tried not to look crestfallen.

Normally they would have reacted with delight to the idea of Carratraca. There was adventure in the long drive through the wild valleys into the mountains, with the car boiling at the top of the steep hills, to the little white spa perched at the end of the long beautiful valley reaching back all the lion-colored miles to the sea. Once it had been a place of legend and scandal, with fine houses and casinos. The empress Josephine and half the great of Europe used to come to the tiny mountain town with bags of gold to gamble, and all the aches and pains of their dubious lives to be soaked away in the healing waters.

But it was still fun. More freedom than at home, in the cool echoing hotel that would by now have great roaring fires against the autumn chill, and games and gossip to pass the evening in the familiar gloomy salon.

He will be waiting when I come back, thought Remedios.

Maybe he will drive up in the blue car when he is free at the weekends, thought Emily.

But it was Don Rafael who lifted his head sharply from his plate of coquinas, pushing aside the empty shells.

"No," he said firmly. "I am sorry, *queridas*, but no."

Doña Serafina halted her torrent of talk long enough to look at him in surprise. It was known to the good God that in a long marriage he had taken little notice of her, like any other Spanish husband. But he had always been discreet with his mistresses, which was more than many of them were, and it was most unusual for him to stop her doing anything she wanted.

"*Por qué*, Rafael?"

Her husband wiped his gray moustache tiredly with his white napkin, and the candles flickered in the autumn wind, rising in the darkness. *Por Dios* but it was a responsibility. The older girls had husbands to make their decisions for them, although in any crisis the whole family would operate as one. But these three were so helplessly in his hands, and he knew better than most, with heavy heart, what was to come. He would have liked to pack all three of them off to Ireland, but he knew his wife would never go, nor allow it to Remedios. For her no world existed outside Spain. Darkness began at the Pyrenees, and she would as soon have consigned her daughter to the flames of hell as send her through it. He would keep the little *Irlandesa* as long as possible, since Remedios, the child of his heart, would be desolated without her.

But Carratraca. No. His mind wandered. It would inevitably be fierce fighting country. A handful of men could hold those passes against an army. When he was long dead, Emily would come driving those mountain roads again, with her own children, to stop to look at the white crosses on the high passes, marking some of the bloodiest battles of the Civil War.

"*Por qué*," said his wife again sharply. Rafael was always going off into a dream.

He leaned back to let the serving girl take his plate, and he watched her go from the room.

"There are bands of Republicans roaming those hills," he said. "Anarchists. Communists. Organizing themselves as much as they can ever agree to."

Getting ready, he thought, to march down on this city when the time came.

"It would be dangerous," he said. "Impossible."

They looked at him and each other, and Doña Serafina took a breath to begin talking again as the girl laid down the roast pork and peppers before her. The wind howled out over the sea and rattled the dark shutters, and in the moment of silence the war moved a step closer in the lamplit room.

The next day, Doña Serafina had a note on thick white crested paper from the grandmother of the other Irish girl, Anna Kilpatrick. She was, she said, arranging a tutor for her granddaughter while the school was closed, and felt it would all march better if she had some company. Would the daughter of the Doña Serafina and her Irish friend care to join the Lady Anna Kilpatrick—Doña Serafina made a small excited sound—in lessons until the school should open again.

Doña Serafina called for José and reached for her pen at her high old-fashioned desk. The old lady was a marquesa and the young one an Irish milady. Of course Remedios and Emily might go.

For a month they spent their days in the tall yellow house on the slope below Gibralfaro, lost in the huge rooms full of dark paintings and fine furniture, and they were little at home. Alejandro seemed preoccupied with his own affairs and did not come riding on the Saturdays, and only once to the huge Sunday lunch. Remedios sighed and pretended to pout and pine and made all the right soft noises for a girl in love, but after that one day, Emily was more concerned with Alejandro himself, sensing some change in him. Some increased seriousness and preoccupation.

It would be the war. Always the war. In these months she understood that ministries had been falling like packs of cards, and it was hard to know who ruled the country from one day to the next. There were stories of atrocities in the big cities and dreadful violence against priests and nuns. No one could escape it, and for all of them, their rich and splendid youth was fading away like the candles in the draft.

Yet, a fortnight before Christmas—the house shuttered for the winter, huge fires roaring in all the fireplaces, and the Levante screaming in from the east to thrash the palm trees of the Alameda—Alejandro's parents came to stay as guests of the house for four days.

Remedios was beside herself, wild with excitement and desperate to impress.

"They will be here to talk settlements, and make all the arrangements," she cried. "Oh, Emilia, querida, I am so happy. I am going to have the most handsome husband in all the province."

No, thought Emily sickly, brushing her red-gold curls a little indifferently to go downstairs to the salon. Not handsome. But marvelously different. And interesting. And the one I am in love with myself. And it has never happened to me before.

She felt sad and chilly, watching Remedios's happiness; her blithe self-confidence, although the young man himself had never said a word. He might be the biggest monster in Andalusia and yet Remedios would be in love with him, because at this stage it was correct for her to be so. All this waiting, thought Emily shrewdly, hitting at the core of the whole performance, made them want each other no matter what. She laid down her brush and followed Remedios along the drafty gallery, pausing to look out one of the windows down into the patio where, in the lamplight, she could see the gleam of the blue car, its black top up against the weather.

During the visit she felt it correct to be quiet and self-effacing, a little surprised by the attention paid to her by Alejandro's strong-faced mother; finding herself often the object of the gaze of his heavy and amiable father, whose slightly protuberant eyes shone with intelligence and good humor.

And as a torture of pain and pleasure that could not be distinguished one from the other, Alejandro was at the dinner table every night.

When they were gone, they held the huge, cheerful, family-only dinner for the Vigil of Christmas, but there was no Midnight Mass to follow it; only their own anxious prayers, kneeling round the chairs in the salon, to welcome the Holy Baby into their troubled world. On New Year's Eve they could not know, watching from the balconies, whether it was fireworks or gunfire that crackled round the barrios, lighting flashes on the dark hills.

They welcomed the New Year almost in silence, looking at each other over their glasses, asking themselves wordlessly what it would bring.

Finally they gathered again for the children's Feast of the Three Kings, and the big house echoed with screams of excitement, and the old floors were covered with torn paper and new toys. For the big, uproarious family lunch with food to feed an army, Alejandro was there, having been with his parents for Christmas. He was charming and polite to everyone, and laden with presents for the children.

No word had been said to Remedios, whose smile was growing a little strained.

"He should have spoken by now," she sighed, going urgently through all the lovely clothes in the dark press for something to impress him. "It is probably that they are arguing about the settlements. If they don't hurry up we'll have this war first, and I'll be marrying a soldier."

"A soldier?"

Emily could barely breathe the word, and turned to peer into the mirror lest Remedios see her shock.

"Of course. Alejandro has always said that he will join the Army as soon as there is trouble."

Not to me, thought Emily. Not to me. But why would he talk to me, who is nothing to him.

But she knew that the Cortes, the parliament of Spain, had fallen and that the danger was growing real. It would be any day.

At the end of January, when the almond blossom was opening tenderly to the first sun, there were two letters from Ireland. One was for the Señor Don Rafael. The other one for Emily herself. She tore it open eagerly. It had been a long time since she had heard from home.

Don Rafael, her mother wrote, a little amused, had been immensely proper and careful in writing to her in great detail about this young Spaniard who wished to become engaged to Emily. He seemed to be all that could be desired in a husband for her, "although in my heart, darling, I had always hoped you would marry an Irishman."

Her mother had written assuming Emily knew all about it, and was party to it all.

But, she went on, it was Emily's heart that mattered, and if this young Spaniard had taken it, then it was for Emily to say yes

or no. She was longing to hear from her directly, but Don
Rafael had been so correct that nothing must be said until the
consent of all parents had been given. "So Spanish, darling,"
wrote her mother. "Try and bring him to see us soon, won't you.
We are all longing to meet him. Is he handsome? I expect he is.
They all are. In any case, you must get married here, my darling.

"Don Rafael is reassuring about the situation in Málaga, but I
do beg you, dearest, if there is any anxiety, to come home at
once. You can always get married when it is all over.

"My dear daughter, all the family joins me in loving wishes
for your happiness—and give all our good wishes to your young
man, I am writing to him. D. Rafael tells me he speaks English,
isn't that a mercy. You are very young, but I know that is usual
in Spain, and no doubt it will be some time before you actually
marry. Please write soon and tell us what you think about it all.
We all hope so much for you.

"God bless you and make it all as you want it.

All our love,

Mummy"

Slowly, stunned and bewildered, Emily read the letter again.
Then she folded it carefully and put it back into the envelope.

Somewhere deep inside her was a sudden leaping joy. In the
distance down below her in the house, she could hear Remedios
singing.

*THREE*

To her complete amazement, Remedios showed no sign of being
upset.

She came running along the dusky gallery where Emily had
gone after reading her letter, feeling the need to be alone, to
accept the whole bewildering business and persuade herself that it
was true.

She heard Remedios calling her, searching, before she reached
her, and stood silent, a little shamefacedly, unwilling to have her

amazing moment darkened by the other girl's unhappiness. But Remedios saw her and came on, running, all around the horse-shoe of the galleries, to fling her arms around her. Emily smelled the perfume of Doña Serafina, and thought with sick guilt that her friend had been crying in her mother's arms. But Remedios was beaming.

"Querida," she cried, and kissed her on both cheeks. "Mama has told me. I am so happy for.you."

Emily knew she gaped at her, embarrassed, running a hand up through her hair.

"But Remedios! I thought you were so much in love with him."

Remedios shrugged extravagantly, throwing out her hands. What, her gesture said, was Alejandro. In the shadows of the paneled gallery Emily searched her face, unable to understand, but Remedios's guileless eyes seemed completely clear of sadness or disappointment, full of affection and the selfless happiness she claimed. Emily didn't know what to say, unwilling to release her own breathless and astonished delight. She couldn't believe the other girl really did not care. Her mind raced back over the weeks that had held little but the name of Alejandro.

"There will be another one for me," Remedios said then, with apparent contentment. "*Mi madre* says he will be far finer than Alejandro."

She looked at Emily with shrewd kindness in her big brown eyes, and a trace of pity.

"There may not be another one for you, *cariña*," she said, "if you have in the English way to find him for yourself. We do not want you turning into one of these miserable old English Tias who never find a husband."

Emily stared at her and then turned abruptly away, feeling the blood rising in her face with the boil of her Irish pride and temper. At the end of the gallery she laid her forehead against the long window, seeing nothing, trying to control herself, raging with the onslaught of shame and disappointment. She was being given Alejandro as a poor relation might be given the family's cast-off clothes. There was something better for Remedios. Bitterly she turned her head.

"So it was all a game," she said, her voice thick with held-back tears of confusion and resentment. What had been real about it all? Any of it? Was she no more than a sort of purchase to Alejandro, who had looked over what was available and taken what he fancied most? A *rubia*, just to be different. Down in the patio she could hear the young boy fiercely abusing the donkey, who did not want to leave his warm place under the stairs and go out into the cold wind. Suddenly she hated Spain and everything to do with it.

"All a game," she said to Remedios. "You were never in love with him at all."

A game they all learned, as young as they learned the steps of the Sevillana.

"You were never in love with him," she repeated.

Once again Remedios shrugged, the deep Spanish shrug, palms out and upturned. She looked alarmed and distressed, not understanding the anger she had aroused in her friend. Above the white collar of her dress her face looked pale and sallow in the shadows, her huge eyes placating.

"One is in love with all of them," she said simply. "That way it is easier."

Emily felt her anger seep away, and pity take its place. For one second she had caught the dead resignation in the eyes of Remedios, who was indeed playing a game, but only as she had been taught to.

Of course she must be in love with all of them, lest she might fail to be in love with the one her parents chose. How could it be possible to know if her love for Alejandro had been real? Or would have been real, if it had ever had the chance.

But what of the other way around?

"What about the young men?" she said, and felt the cold wind along the gallery as though it had just started blowing. "What of the young men? Do they pretend to be in love with all the girls until they find one suitable? Is it a game with them, too? Without love? Really love?"

Remedios stammered and almost backed away, aware of where the conversation was leading. Her querida Emilia, she so adored her, but she was so very difficult with these ideas that everybody had to be in love before they got married. If God was good, then sometimes that came after marriage. Otherwise you had your home and your children, and your safe position in life, and if you were clever, perhaps even a lover. Hopeless at defending customs she took for granted, she looked at Emily with great anxious eyes, and blundered.

"But querida Emilia. Alejandro must be in love with you. Really in love."

"Why?"

"Because . . ." Remedios wished desperately for her mother. "Because you are *not* suitable, so he must be in love with you."

"Not suitable?"

Emily could hear the cold edge to her own voice, and Remedios made a wry anxious grimace, wishing the good God would get her out of this.

"Emilia, we all love you dearly, but you are not Spanish. Alejandro has much courage."

The Judas gate slammed behind the donkey and the boy and his stick, but his shrill cries of abuse still drifted up from the street outside. Obstinate, thought Emily about the donkey. Obstinate. As I shall be until I am sure. She felt a moment of sadness. How much easier to go along with it all, and rush downstairs into the torrent of kisses and congratulations and flowers and fiestas for days to come. How much easier.

Her soft mouth tightened.

"I haven't yet said if I will have him," she said firmly.

Remedios drew away from her as if she had been burned, everything else forgotten.

"Not have Alejandro?" she cried. "But he is so suitable. So rich. He has—*Mis padres*—"

She couldn't speak for shock.

"I don't care," said Emily, and thought again of the donkey fighting the boy and his stick along every meter of the street. It would be easier for the donkey, also, if it just did what it was told. "I don't care," she said again, "if he has all the gold in Spain. He has to ask me himself, and I'll not marry him unless I am sure he loves me."

"Ah, love," said Remedios, and dismissed it, having played at it so vigorously for weeks back. The winter evening was closing in, the high glass roof taking on the purple of the dusk. No one had yet put on the gallery lights, and in the half darkness Emily looked at the pale oval of her friend's troubled face. Remedios knew she had blundered, and Emily lifted a hand and touched her affectionately on the cheek.

"Querida, it is nothing. Do not molest yourself."

She could see the other girl's eyes brighten.

"Then all will be well?"

"We'll have to wait and see."

Were it not for Remedios, she would have rushed headlong into Alejandro's arms. Now she knew she must find out. Alejandro might be one of those Spaniards who just thought it distinguished to have a foreign wife. She must find out if she, too, was being offered as an interesting and prestigious wife, if not entirely suitable. Without love. Facing the day when the babies came. And the mistresses.

Sorrow squeezed her heart. Had Remedios not spoken, would she not have been glad to have taken him on any terms, sure her love would be enough for both of them.

They would all consider her as mad as only a foreigner could be.

"You will go and tell them for me, Remedios," she said.

It was the hour of *merienda*. More than she could do to face all these loving, smiling faces waiting to congratulate her. It upset her to realize that only the women of the family would be there, at that moment; warm and sweet and curious, already segregating her into their birdlike, chattering world. It touched her with fear. She did not want to marry Alejandro to know him only at the evening meal if he chose to come to it, or in bed begetting children, or across some crowded room among the men.

A few incautious blurted words by Remedios had put all these doubts into her head.

She was not really suitable, since she was a foreigner. Would he be really suitable, since he was a foreigner to her? And would she have the strength to say so, if she thought so. Or would she be lost, like Remedios, to all the things like the grace of his body, and the way his hair curled black down the back of his neck. The startling sweetness of his smile.

Would he take the trouble to come to her? Or would he have no use at once for a foreigner who didn't understand the rules. Dear God, what had she done?

Longing for her mother, she sat in darkness with her sore heart beside the bedroom fire, hastily flinging on a fresh log when it showed signs of dying down, as if it were the cherished life of a friend.

She heard them all leaving, down in the patio, the car doors slamming; chattering no doubt of her foreignness and her strangeness and her lack of knowledge of how to behave. She was still there, staring at the glowing logs and convincing herself of her rightness, when Remedios hesitantly opened the door.

"Ah, Emilia. Querida Emilia, there you are."

She switched on the light and looked curiously at her friend's unhappy face. How difficult these foreigners made things for themselves.

"Emilia. *Mi padre* would like to speak to you in his study."

In his study. The place for men and conferences and the secret meetings late into the night, plotting God knew what frightening things for the sake of Spain. The study was not for Don Rafael, the loving family man. Not for kindness and understanding. She would be told there, without a doubt, that she had insulted Alejandro and his rich and influential parents. And that she must go.

Defiantly she opened her drawer and dabbed on some of her secret store of Soir de Paris face powder, to give herself courage.

Remedios watched her and didn't know what to say. The sisters had all gone, gabbling like the geese in the courtyard in Alhaurín, and the mother was down in the kitchen in a fine rage, canceling all the orders she had raced down to give for an evening of celebration. Alejandro should have come, welcomed for the first time into the family as Emilia's *novio. Por Dios,* what else did the *niña* want? Everyone approved.

That I should approve myself, Emily could have told her.

She smiled at Remedios then, and put an arm around her as they went out the door. Poor Remedios. Was it possible she had really taken Alejandro from her, only to make a fool of herself in everyone's eyes in the end? It was as well that Don Rafael was going to end it all.

Don Rafael was not at his vast leather-topped desk, with the dark globe of the world on the floor beside it. He was sitting relaxed in a high-backed chair beside a fire crackling with fresh, sweet-smelling logs of olive. Shelves of old books touched with gold gleamed behind his gray head, and in his hand a tall glass of fino caught the light.

"Emilia."

He stood up with immediate grave courtesy as she came in. Anxiously she searched his face and found no more than the usual austere kindness. At least he was not obviously furious.

"Emilia. Will you do me the honor to come and sit with me a moment. Can I give you a small *copa*?"

She nodded.

"If you please, Don Rafael."

It would give her something to do with her hands instead of tying them in knots in her lap, and it might help her trembling stomach in its struggle for steadiness. She was very sorry before this kind and gentle man. She knew she had upset all their patterns, but she would not agree, *copa* or no *copa*, to marry any young man she had barely spoken to. Not even Alejandro.

When Don Rafael had poured the pale gold sherry from its beautiful decanter, he eased himself back into the chair opposite her across the fire, forced unwillingly into one of the rare occasions when he felt compelled to interfere among the women of his house. Serafina raging around the kitchens in thwarted bewilderment, shouting at the servants and talking like a machine gun, could see no more than that this pale, frightened-looking child across the fire from him would not do as she was told. Like any Spanish girl.

She forgot that Emilia was not a Spanish girl. Nor could the situation be left as it was, insulting to both Alejandro and his parents. He, Don Rafael, had promised Emilia's mother that while she was in his house he would be as a father to her. In this he had failed. Like everyone else, he had given it all too little thought, leaving it to the women, who, no matter what the world might think, were the arrangers of all these things. It must be put right.

"Emilia. *Salud.*"

He lifted his glass in the formal salutation without which they couldn't start to drink. The big green-shaded lamp on the desk threw only a circle of light, and without the glow of firelight she would have been hardly able to see his face.

"Emilia. *Chica.* We owe you an apology."

Over the tall engraved glass, Emily tried not to gape at him.

"Sí, Señor?"

She was astonished and cautious.

"We have upset you. We have completely overlooked the customs of your own country, and thrust you, without consulting you, into ours. We must put that right."

He was very formal, using long, careful words, but it was exactly what they had done. He was right. No one had said a word to her. Yet it was obvious from her mother's letter that she thought Emily knew all about it and had accepted Alejandro for herself. Doña Serafina had swept along, no doubt, as she always did, and this kind, tired-faced man in the other chair had had too many terrifying preoccupations to give it proper thought.

She could find nothing to say. How could she reproach him, the habit of deserved respect gone far too deep. She took another sip of her sherry, hope racing through her like the warmth of the wine. Put it right. He did say that. Put it right.

"I have been speaking with Alejandro on the telephone, and I have talked with Doña Serafina."

He did not say that the furious duenna had told him to take the ignorant little foreigner and do with her what he wished. She loved Emilia and would cool down when everything was arranged.

Emily was barely breathing, her sherry warming in a hand grown hot and damp.

"We have decided it is reasonable to allow you and Alejandro to have some time together, as you would in your own home, before you become *novios*. It is your custom, and he is quite happy to agree to it. He has been a year in England."

"They will be the scandal of all Andalusia," Doña Serafina had wailed, wringing her fine white hands, and asking the Virgin to witness that it was as she had forever known. She was being very Spanish. Foreigners always turned out to be foreigners, no matter how you might love them.

"*Claro*," said her husband dryly. "It is correct." And went his way.

"*Por Dios*," Alejandro had said when he reached him on the telephone. Earlier, when the letter had come, Don Rafael had simply bidden him for the evening to celebrate. They had both been waiting with different degrees of patience to hear from Emily's mother. "*Por Dios*, but what a splendid spirit the *chica* has. I will be completely willing to march the Irish way if that is what she wishes. You will tell me what you think I should do."

It should not take much more than one evening to set it all straight, unless he was completely mistaken about the look in Emilia's eyes each time he talked to her. He was well familiar in marching in the English way. The blue Bugatti had raced many of the green winding roads of England, blond or red hair blowing in the wind beside him. Dinner at some roadhouse, what was that place outside London? The Ace of Spades. Dinner at the Ace of Spades or at some crowded riverside hotel like Skindles on summer evenings and as far afterwards as his charm would take him. Far enough, quite often; so used to their cold, boring monosyllabic men that it was never difficult.

When he raced the car at Brooklands, he could brush them off like flies.

"*Sí*, Don Rafael," he was saying then. "*Sí*. It will all be as it should be."

He hung the telephone back on its hook in the gloomy cavern underneath the stairs. It would be something, he thought, to get it all arranged and have an establishment of his own, even for a while, with this strong-willed little *rubia* to adorn it. He was sick of the ancient shadows of his cousins' house, smelling of antiquity and polish. Some good three-piece suits and a cocktail bar and a fine gramophone in one of these new cabinets. In England they had some excellent ones. With a dog listening, in all the advertisements.

His mind went back to Emily and the suggestions of Don Rafael, who had sounded embarrassed, God knew, with all this women's business.

He must go carefully. The correct approach had been too formal for her, but he wanted her for his wife, and nothing else, and must remember she was not like the others who had occupied the red passenger seat in the Bugatti. She would want such correctness as her own world demanded: no girl to be gained by dinner at a roadhouse, and a windblown drive through the lanes under a chilly English moon. But he wanted her, unable to get her from his thoughts since the day he had first seen her sitting on the edge of the fountain at Alhaurín in her blue dress, beside his flighty little cousin Remedios.

Firmly he went up the dark-tiled staircase, happily stirred with excitement, and told his elderly cousin with grave regret that he would not be in for the evening meal, as he had some business to attend to. Carefully he changed from his business suit into a pair of immaculately creased gray flannels, his navy blue English blazer with the brass buttons, a striped tie under his V-necked pullover of fine pale blue wool. Brown and white shoes. They had a joke about these shoes in England, saying they were only for a man going visiting his mistress.

Well pleased with his appearance, he vigorously flattened the curls that so pleased Emily, brushing them fiercely back from a high parting. Exhilaration touched his face as he peered into the antique flyblown mirror with its gilded frame, which had hung in the same place in this chilly bedroom for some hundred years.

He knew he must go carefully, but he did not think that it would take him long.

With tact from Don Rafael and irritated confusion from Doña Serafina, who no longer knew what was correct, Emily was allowed to wait for him alone in the salon, an edge-to-edge coat of blue velvet open over her apricot dress, small velvet flowers of the same blue pinned by a breathless Remedios in her hair.

The electric lights were off and she didn't think to put them on, and in the firelight and the soft amber glow of the oil lamps in the corners of the room, she looked young and vulnerable and very fierce, glaring at the door and trembling from head to foot with fright. It was, she thought a little hysterically, like beseeching Father Christmas as a child for something beyond your wildest dreams, then waking up at dawn on Christmas morning to find it at the bottom of your bed. Alejandro.

Alejandro knew her panic the moment he came into the room, ushered by a hovering, wildly curious José, who would be torn to pieces down in the kitchen for any news he might bring. He was enchanted by the way she nevertheless kept her red head in the air and offered her hand, gracious and determined as his mother presiding in her vast drawing room in Madrid. He hid his irrepressible smile by bowing low and very formally over the proffered hand, which shook like the leaves of the olives in a winter wind.

"Emilia, Doña Serafina has given me permission to take you out to dinner. If you would care to," he added cautiously. No formality must be left out lest he offend again.

Doña Serafina had nothing to do with it, thought Emily, but she nodded and smiled, unable yet to find anything to say. Nor did they speak as they went together down the lamplit stairs, the only sound the rich rustling of her taffeta skirt. Below them in the patio the blue Bugatti waited in shadows, the spokes of its wheels glittering in the light from the kitchens; warm, splendid reality of dreams, smelling of fine leather and hot oil and the rich cigars from Cuba that Alejandro sometimes smoked. The long gleaming hood seemed to stretch for yards in front of her as she got in, and she was aware of faces peering from the shadows under the stairs, and hushed whispering voices. She felt a little ashamed of the restless donkey, feeling sure that the town house of Alejandro's parents would not have a donkey making smells in the Patio of the Motors. She reassured herself that it was not her house. José materialized from nowhere, his walnut-colored face benign, dragging open the huge doors to let out the car.

I am, she thought, the scandal of the household. But could not care. It was not José, or Lourdes, the cook, who was going to get married. Or not get married. It had to be right for her. Please God, give her the strength to go on saying so, even if she lost him.

As he settled her in, laying a fur rug across her knees, Alejandro smiled at her, his full warm slow smile implicit with the promise that there was nothing he and she could not resolve together. She knew that were she standing up, her knees would have buckled.

But he must ask me, she thought obstinately, her pride struggling desperately to stay alive. He must ask me. I am not something to be exchanged between the parents as if I were a horse.

The night was cold and very dark, gas lamps pale below the palm trees of the Alameda, a few lights glowing high from the decks of ships against the quays as the long car thrummed below the arching trees along the harbor wall.

"I thought," he said to her then, "that we would go to Antonio Martin's. If that pleases you," he added.

"That would be lovely," she said, sick with disappointment. There was nothing wrong with Antonio Martin's. Just that it was so close, only past the end of the Alameda. They were almost there. She was still coming to terms with the first simple pleasure of being beside him, closed in the intimacy of the warm car. Only half his attention on her, so that she could accept the numbing excitement of his nearness. Understand that she, and not Remedios, was beside him in the most glamorous car in Málaga state. Nerja would have been better, or Motril or even Granada, with the dark night slipping past for hours on the high winding roads before they got there.

But the red circle of the bullring lay before them, and they turned out of the Alameda and toward the sea, and her lack of confidence rose again like a chill wind under the fur rug. Probably he was going so close at hand because he was just doing her the courtesy of taking her out alone, as she seemed to expect. To tell her he had changed his mind. Could not marry any girl who had behaved so savagely.

The car slid to a stop and he roared the engine and let it die, the lights of the restaurant glowing against the dark void of the sea. Far out a few vessels passed remotely, and closer in moved the glowworm lights of fishing boats, out from San Pedro or Rincón.

"My favorite restaurant," said Alejandro as he opened the door and gave her his hand to help her out. She felt a sensation far from fear at the touch of his warm hand. Why could it not have all gone right. "You have been here before?" he asked.

"Oh, yes. With the family."

"It suits you?"

"I love it," she answered truthfully. Especially perhaps on a winter's night like this one, when a fire burned in the open hearth and from their table by the window above the shore, they could see only darkness, navigation lights suspended like colored stars against the formless dark.

He would not be hurried, calmly master of himself and his situation, taking all the amiable time in the world to discuss with the benign and bland headwaiter what they should eat and drink; consulting her courteously at every suggestion in a way she realized no Spanish man would usually do. His woman ate what he had chosen, and if she did not care for it, he would never notice. She refused to take a part in it, knowing that until everything was settled, her anxious stomach would react in exactly the same way to Russian caviar or *langostinos* from the shore or a plate of good plain Irish stew.

"Champagne" was all she breathed as the dark bottle arrived beside the table in its bucket of broken ice.

His smile enveloped her then, unequivocal statement of his intentions, his charmed eyes running over the delicate coloring of the apricot dress against the red-gold hair. The nervous courage of the dark-lashed eyes. *Madre de Dios*, but he had come tonight determined to overcome her, and it was he himself who was being overcome, forgetting all the careful things he had planned to say. As nervous as when he took his first girl at fourteen in the back room of a gypsy cantina, on a night out in the Guadaljarras. This was different.

"I am hoping," he said gravely, "we shall have something to celebrate."

With a conviction born of his own enchantment, Alejandro set himself out to beguile her and to kill her doubts, unable to take his eyes from the delicate beauty he might have lost by his clumsiness. Clumsiness and thoughtlessness and ignorance, and he began by apologizing for them all. In the end she was rushing to reassure him, unable to listen to him so denigrate himself, telling him no, that it was she who was clinging too closely to what she was used to.

They had the consent of both parents, he thought with a deep thrill of unexpected delight. There was nothing to delay for. With careful humility and persuasiveness, he had brought the celebration to full flower by the time the waiter laid down two immense bombes glacées. Neither then nor later could Emily ever remember what she had eaten first.

"Mind you," she said in a last proud effort at defense, even though she knew the battle long lost. "Mind you." The bubbles of the champagne were rising in her nose. "I have only agreed to get engaged to you. I don't know you well enough yet to say that I will marry you."

"*Claro*," said Alejandro gravely. "It is agreed"—trying to keep the amusement from his eyes, loving her for the fierce independence she struggled so hard for.

He would handle all that, he thought, when they must come to it! There was not much place for independence in the life of a Spanish wife. *Por Dios*, he would promise her anything to get her, and who knew, they might make a life a little different from the rule.

Fear and sorrow touched him then, looking at her across the candles on the table, the bright room clattering with carefree chatter. The moment of truth for Spain was almost on them, touching with cold apprehension every celebration at this time, when everybody asked "How long." They must marry soon. He couldn't think of giving her all the time her independence asked for. There might be no time for anything at all.

"Do not fight your heart, *cariña*," he said gently. "We need all the time we can get. It is such a waste of time that may be short."

She looked at him, knowing the tragic truth of what he said. Tears crept into the great gray eyes, and he longed to reach over and kiss them away.

"I am stupid," she said. "Stupid, am I not?"

"*Claro*," he said again gravely, and they both began to laugh, doubts and griefs and sorrows consigned to the dark night beyond the misted windows. For them at the moment was a world of light that would go on forever, no matter what the threats. Hands locked across the table, coffee cooling in their cups. Candlelight on both their faces like a gentle blessing. Leaping from past to future and then back again in their eager talking; as though these first precious moments could span all life and hold it for them; what had gone before and what was yet to come. In the end the headwaiter coughed smilingly at Alejandro's shoulder and they came back from the first breathless exploration of each other's hearts into the ordinary world, and realized that they were alone in the restaurant. All the table lights were extinguished except their own.

They laughed and apologized and paid the bill. And looked at each other, knowing they would remember still, when they were old, the night they had the lights put out all around them in Antonio Martin's.

Arms around each other, they raced through the chill wind for the car, aware with fresh rueful laughter that they would have once more offended the proprieties of Doña Serafina, by being out so late.

Alejandro did not have to blow the horn. As the car purred up to the doors, the Judas gate opened narrowly, throwing a thin bar of light across the dark street, outlining the waiting figure of José. Making it clear it was too late for visitors. In the windy little canyon of a street, the dust and rubbish of the day blowing round their ankles, they clung to each other's hands, the house dark and silent as a cliff above them, their relationship even so soon edged with sudden threat and sorrow. As though even this first parting might prove to be their last. Reluctantly he let her go, turning away when the small gate shut behind her and José's courteous *buenas noches*.

In the huge darkness of the patio only one light shone thinly over by the kitchens, and José escorted her up the curved staircase, sent by Doña Serafina to see that the señorita got with safety and propriety to her bedroom.

But his black twinkling eyes were full of kindness, looking at her shrewdly as he lit a candle for her on the dark gallery. Their shadows flared to vague monstrous size on the white walls.

"All is well with the señorita?" he asked her, but it was more an assurance than a question. It must be all over my silly face, thought Emily, that all was suddenly very well with the señorita.

But she was touched by the settled kindness of his look, in the small light wavering in the winter draft.

"All is well, José," she said.

"God is good," he said formally. "*Enhorabuena, Señorita Emilia. Larga vida y muchos niños.*" Long life and many children.

"*Gracias, José, muchas gracias.*"

She hoped Remedios would be asleep, wanting to be alone to go word for word and glance for glance back through the enchanted evening. But not with Remedios. Not with anyone. Not yet. She felt sure the immediacy of their impact on each other had taken Alejandro as much by surprise as it had taken her.

"*Buenas noches, Señorita.*"

"*Buenas noches, José.*"

He turned and went back down the stairs, and the smile had left his face.

May the good God have pity on them both in what was coming, for there was no avoiding it. Nor was it any time for love.

Painfully they knew themselves that this was true. The tide of excitement surrounding their engagement, the fiestas and the gifts and the household treasures that they looked at and talked of buying and of using; the cocktail bar and the gramophone in the handsome walnut cabinet; the ecstatic plans by Remedios and her mother about the actual wedding, which Emily had no heart to discourage. Who would leave Spain for a wedding in Ireland now? None of this could obliterate the other rising tide that threatened Spain. Not one hour of their new astonished love was not touched by apprehension and terror that it might all end when it had barely started. Emily could write no more to her mother than "I do not know. We must wait and see." Who could know what plans to make.

There were no more lessons with Anna Kilpatrick. Neither Alejandro nor Don Rafael would allow any longer even the quiet journey up the Alameda and along the bright spring sea to Gibralfaro. The inner streets of the city were alive with disorganized bands of marching men, sullen-faced and touchy as a keg of powder, the flat black hats of the Guardia and the increasing khaki of the Army never far away. Clashes were quick and fierce, and day and night sporadic rifle-fire cracked across the apprehensive city.

In early February there had been elections. Don Rafael did not go to his office and told all the family to keep off the streets. All day he sat with his ear glued to the crackle of the wireless, men racing in and out with news. Men in uniform came openly now, gold braid heavy on their sleeves, marking their importance; often followed in the narrow streets by jeering youths.

Doña Serafina listened to it all and crossed herself. Gradually she was growing silent, sick with fright for her beloved family, the sons and daughters and their wives and husbands, and all the pretty chattering children, shut fearfully now in their own homes; the great living house grown silent. She lost her tide of talk, the happy recitation of contentments and contrived small problems that had carried her through her ordered and tranquil life. Who knew how much farther they would carry her in this new fearful world?

The government had swung sharply to the left. Overnight the practice of the laws against the Church grew fierce and bitter. The prisons were thrown open to all political prisoners, letting them loose to roam grimly through the cities, making trouble where they would: organizing the leaderless, holding screaming meetings to fan the flames of anarchy already roaring up to engulf the land.

Neither of the girls was allowed now in the streets, and the exhilaration of Emily's hard-won freedom with her *novio* was sadly cramped by fear and caution, and the endless fretting of Doña Serafina, who saw her now, hopelessly mixed in with her excitement over the engagement, as a responsibility almost too much to be borne.

"Señora," Alejandro would say when she did not want to let Emily out at all. "Señora. She is my responsibility now."

"You are not yet married."

"No," agreed Alejandro, and his fine young face was thoughtful. "No, Señora. Not yet."

It had never occupied her mind almost to the exclusion of all else, as with Remedios, but Emily had speculated often, with a mixture of cynicism and romantic longing, on the business of being in love. She had watched her sisters change overnight, to her mind, from ordinary sensible girls to vague, dreamy single-minded idiots who seemed to have lost contact with the real world. Yet there was something in their faces that had stirred her to a restless envy.

None of her thinking or dreaming prepared her for the reality.

Her whole world now, it seemed, was ringed with light; known familiar beauty became almost unbearable; emotions sharpened to the point of pain; a poignant awareness of every detail of the life she had taken for granted up till now. And at the heart of it all the reality of Alejandro. She knew that, like her sisters, she had a foolish and bewildered smile pinned to her face, and found difficulty in wiping it away before the fear and anxiety all around her.

There were deep, half-frightening and yet triumphant stirrings of her body, new to her. The desire always to be touching Alejandro. A hand on his arm for the pleasure of feeling the muscled strength of his body through his sleeve. The surprising solidity and hardness if she was close to him, so different from all the soft female bodies of her childhood.

I am in love, she thought, a little awed. I am in love at last, and Alejandro is my man and nothing will ever be the same again. No matter what may happen, nothing will ever be the same again. Do I live forever. And I know, she thought, even in my ignorance, that it is only the beginning. There will be more, much more. Of which only her instincts could yet tell her.

They followed their difficult courtship through restrictions and anxiety and uncertainty and sudden frantic alarms, grasping every moment that they could together; never speaking of it, but wondering always what tomorrow would bring; closer in every feverish hour in the certainty of themselves, and of their love.

He kissed her for the first time out on a rocky headland on the road to Nerja, the sea below them soundless on the rocks, flat and oily under a gibbous moon; the lights of town and harbor lying behind them pale and harmless, as if no world had ever thought of war.

Yet they had been talking of it, walking on the sandy level of the small cliff, sadly facing the realities of their situation, which in a storybook would lead to peace and love and happily ever after.

Alejandro was not anxious to talk of it at all, painfully aware of much she did not know, wanting only to thrust it all away in the few hours they could have together; pretending they would never end.

Emily wanted it cut and dried.

"I won't have to go home, now I am your *novia*, will I? Will I?"

Her fingers were locked in his, both of them in the chill night wrapped in his heavy hunting coat with its cape, and collar of red fox. They walked as one, locked together under the folds of the coat. His body was warm against hers, and never had there been anything more beautiful to her than the damp-and-hazy-looking moon.

*Por Dios*, thought Alejandro, and held her closer, his heart sick with all the things he could not tell her; all the fearful obstacles rising against their future. In her happiness she had almost forgotten about Spain, and who, he thought, could blame her, for it would bring her little but sorrow. The sand and stones scrunched under their feet, and she looked up at him for an answer through the long fur of the fox, wondering at his silence.

"*Chica*," he said miserably. "You would be safer in your own country."

"But Alejandro, when I am married to you, Spain will be my country."

"*Claro*." What could he say to her? "*Querida*, I may not be here if there is war."

In the darkness she shrugged, and tightened her fingers around his.

"I would wait for you," she said.

In violence and death, he thought sickly, and atrocities beyond belief that were already in the other cities. There was no reason to think that in the end they would not be in Málaga. His gentle *rubia*. His little Emilia. Cold and sickness and loneliness gripped him for the parting she did not yet understand. She had no idea of where it would all end. Which of them had? She seemed to think he would come home from it each evening, as he did from the office of Don Rafael.

He had spoken to Don Rafael of what he intended to do, and sadly the mild man had agreed that she should go home. There was no question of going to Alejandro's parents in Madrid. Already the big cities were impossible.

"Alejandro."

In the folds of the big green coat she had begun to cry. Even now unsure of him and the unbelievable magic fact of his love. Haunted by the terror of its ending. It was less than a month, every day counted like the beads on a rosary of happiness, but she knew herself already vastly changed from the girl who had gone, so blithely full of principles, to confront Alejandro and insist that he ask her to marry him for himself.

She had found these new depths of feeling never before suspected; found the selfless delight of wanting to live only for someone else. Found out much about Alejandro that made him more than the handsome embodiment of dreams. He was quick-witted and very funny, loving to reduce her to helpless giggles at unsuitable moments; laughter, and delight in each other's laughter a great portion of their time together. He was charming and infinitely patient, yet with a strong inflexibility that told her clearly that too much un-Spanish independence would be no part of her life in his house. Flashes of sudden verbal cruelty could hit her like a blow across the face, gone as fast as they had come.

None of it dismayed her.

*Sol y sombra*, she thought. The two faces of Spain. There cannot be one without the other.

It was all Alejandro, and there could never be anyone else on earth for her.

He saw her tears and took her in his arms, protesting bitterly that there should be so much to grieve her. The heavy green coat slipped to the ground, and the hard splendor of his young body was unbearable against the talk of parting and of death.

"Oh, Alejandro," she cried desperately, overwhelmed with sorrow yet to come. "Oh, Alejandro, I do so love you."

He kissed her then, forgetting for a few wild endless moments who she was, in the eager, astonishing response of her soft lips. Abruptly letting her go, he wheeled off some paces into the pallid darkness, leaving her staring after him, her hand to her lips as if to keep his kisses there, trembling with a new astonishment, her face pale as the watery moon.

Alejandro stopped and stared into the darkness at the idle sea. He, too, was shaking.

Jesus Maria. The innocence. The innocence and the will to give. The eagerness to love. What treasure had he here?

Temptation shook him like a storm, for who could say they would ever have a future. Who could say but that this might be their last hour together. Her very innocence would keep her from refusing. Before God, there would be something for both of them to remember.

But it was Emilia. Emilia.

His blood cooled and tenderness rose sadly to take the place of passion. Turning, he came back to her where she stood staring after him, not moving. He picked up the heavy coat and put it around her shoulders, framing her anxious face in the red fur of the fox.

"Alejandro?" Her voice was diffident. "Have I offended you? Have I done something wrong?"

He took her in his arms again, the folds of the coat and all, and kissed her softly, and kissed her eyelids where he could taste the salt tears. She felt laughter welling in him and leaned back and smiled.

"What, Alejandro?"

"You did no wrong, *mi querida rubia. Mi alma.* My little Emilia. But I nearly did."

She moved through her days in a haze of happiness, surrounded by anxious and even frightened faces that did their best to smile for her while their own world fell apart around them. Remedios the sweetest and most loving of them all. Guilt over her touched Emily but could not interfere with her floating content. This was threatened only by the dark sad knowledge that it was day to day until she must go home. Alejandro was implacable.

"*Mi vida.* My life. I would rather have you alive in your wet Ireland than living only as a memory in Spain."

And you, she thought, fear eating at her happiness like a sickness. When it is all over, will you be no more than a memory for me?

Restlessly wandering the house when she couldn't see him— for even the most thin pretenses of planning for a wedding had been dropped—she speculated with Remedios about Anna Kilpatrick. When would she go? Had she gone already? Even her determined old grandmother would have to admit that the situation had gone beyond a passing storm. They were not allowed out, and had always been prohibited the tall ancient telephone in Don Rafael's study, so there was no way of finding out.

One brilliant day in March, when everyone was flinging open doors and windows to the spring heat of the sun, and all the wild land in the country was sheeted with little yellow flowers, the nuns were driven from the convent.

The Republicans, who grew daily stronger in the city, had roared up in a fleet of lorries, rocking on their thin wheels, stacked high with arms. The frightened women had been given one curt hour to leave and start to make their way back to their families, or wherever they might wish to go, to live again in the world as ordinary women. The convent was to be made use of as an arms store.

Many of the nuns had no families to go back to, grown old in the service of God, their family in Christ almost the only one they could remember. They emerged reluctantly into the bright day in their ill-fitting clothes, the small bundles of earthly belongings that the Rule allowed them gathered in their trembling hands. Reverend Mother had divided between them all the money that the convent held, and told the ones with homes and families to make for them at once. The old ones who had been too long enclosed even to recall their dealings with the world, she commended in God to the young ones, and bade them care for them as best they could. The ones without homes she gave into the hands of God also, and instructed them to search for friends, but not to stay more than two together, since they might attract attention. She reminded them that they could now bring harm on any house that sheltered them, so they must seek out only those whose strength in God they felt to be as strong as was their own.

They slipped unnoticed out a small back gate into a lane that the Republicans were unaware of, into a world they had forgotten, and that for many had changed so much they could neither recognize nor handle it. Tenderly the young ones did as they were told, and took the old in God's name, many of them to the shelter of their own homes.

A detachment of the Army had arrived before the front gates, and fierce and violent argument developed, but they did not open fire. Not for Málaga the privilege of beginning the Civil War, and the Republicans seized the convent.

In the late afternoon Don Rafael came home. He went little to his office now, dividing his time between meetings in his house and in the gray offices of the governor along the Alameda.

Every day they looked up at him in silence when he came in, waiting for fresh news, and he had to turn away from the controlled fear in their faces. At the hour of *merienda* there was no one in the salon but Doña Serafina and Remedios and Emily. And the fading echoes of all the happy young noise that had once filled it.

His news that day was for Emily. He turned to her as soon as he had kissed his wife and daughter, carefully keeping his face calm and unperturbed.

"Emilia, *lo siento mucho*. I am very sorry. But it is time for you to leave. It is, querida," he said gently, "like parting with a daughter. I have telegraphed your mother. Two evenings from now there is a boat leaving for Genoa. Rafaelito will go that far with you, and stay with you until your brother gets there. It is no longer safe for you to be here."

Rafaelito, was the only thought that came inconsequently to her mind as she gazed at him in sick unwillingness to accept what he had said. Whatever life might bring now, she wanted it at Alejandro's side. But Rafaelito. One of the married ones. Why not José Maria, who had no one to look after?

But all she said was "Alejandro." Her eyes wide and empty as if he had not spoken.

Remedios came over and put her arms around her, and in her straight-backed chair Doña Serafina began to cry; but the same random corner of her mind told Emily she was weeping not for Emily but for her family, and for Spain. Emily's going was only symbolic of all the greater, terrifying griefs that were overtaking her.

"I am sorry," Don Rafael said, "about Alejandro. But I have talked to him. He would prefer you safe. It is a great responsibility, Emilia."

We cannot now, he said in effect, get you out of the country fast enough.

The sun lay slatted through the blinds in bars, as through the long summers of happiness, and the small food of *merienda*, still brought patiently by José's mother, lay untouched on the polished table; the poured chocolate wrinkling in the porcelain cups; no children to squabble for the little cakes.

Into the sad silence came José, urgently knocking and walking at the same time into the room, lacking all his usual quiet dignity, his eyes wide with alarm.

"*Perdón*," he said, aware at once of the atmosphere in the room. "*Perdón*, Señora. There are two"—he hesitated—"two ladies, downstairs in the patio. One old and one very young. They wish to speak to the señora, and will not come upstairs."

He knew very well who they were. Word of the commandeering of the convent had spread in minutes, but it was not for him to put it into words. And not for his mistress, if she had any sense, to have anything to do with them.

A long deliberating look passed between husband and wife, and slowly Doña Serafina got up from her chair, her tears halted, still wet upon her cheeks, a new look of pity and purpose on her face.

"Serafina, be careful," her husband said. He laid a hand on her arm, and a bar of sunlight was bright across both their faces. Emily and Remedios watched almost without breathing. She paused a moment and looked at him, and in that look was the acknowledgment of all their long life together, and the acceptance of a danger that could destroy the end of it. He shook his head, accepting also, and his face was tender for her.

"It is our place with God to do it," she said, and no more.

They followed her down the long stairs in appalled silence, knowing what they would find, and here the sun was gone, the blue beautiful shadows of the spring dusk washing over the patio. Around in the back where there was almost darkness, keeping well in below the stairs, stood Reverend Mother, her ancient face drawn and gray with shock, yet still holding her impeccable dignity; drawing on the lifelong teaching of strength within herself, which could encompass everything. Riven with humility and grief that she must come like a beggar to the door. José had brought her a chair, and beside her, with a hand on its back in a protective attitude, stood one of the youngest of the nuns. Little more than a child like Emily and Remedios. Not long from the world and still capable of handling it.

With difficulty Reverend Mother got up, a hand on the girl's arm, and they stood together in their shapeless dresses, mute, trained against unnecessary conversation. All Málaga by now would know their need.

"Did anyone see you come in?" Doña Serafina asked, and Emily was astonished at her briskness and lack of hesitation. There was no law yet against harboring these poor souls, but no one could know what tomorrow might bring.

The young one shook her head. Her hair was growing again, and black worldly curls escaped from the scarf around her head.

"José!"

José materialized from the shadows where he had been listening, as he had listened all his life to the business of the house.

"Señora."

"The two small rooms past the pantries. Get furniture from the storeroom and arrange them at once. As simply as possible. The ladies will wait in the small salon. Bring them some food."

"It is only," the young one said, all worldly eagerness and fear not yet trained out of her, "only for Mother here. When I know she is safe, then I can go to my family. And we have some money you can have. She would not be a burden. But you can see, Señora, that she is not fit to travel. God will reward you," said the young one, "Doña Serafina, God will reward you."

Doña Serafina looked gentle but brisk. God might reward her, but the Republicans might also reward anyone who came in and saw them. She bent her head to the old nun, and signed to José, who led them away at once, his face creased with a mixture of loyalty and doubt.

The girl's dark eyes were desperate. Longing to lay down her burden. Reverend Mother laid a skeletal hand on her arm. Too many words.

The small salon was beside the patio doors, one of the many small identical rooms so common in big Spanish homes; used here for unfamiliar callers to wait while José found whether they should be transferred to a similar room upstairs. And then to the family.

The old nun was too weary to do more than make for them the sign of the cross, but at the door she turned and looked back at Doña Serafina and the two girls, standing with Don Rafael still at the bottom of the stairs.

"Inasmuch as you shall do," she said with sudden, astonishing clarity, "to the least of My brethren, so have you done unto Me."

Hand in hand in silence, the girls went up and Don Rafael took his wife's arm. She seemed suddenly grown older, and her fear was clear in her face, but her step up the stairs was strong and steady.

"But, Mama." Remedios only spoke when they were back in the salon. Her mother had the look of someone who had taken even herself by surprise. "Mama, that was Reverend Mother. You cannot put her in a room beside the kitchens. She should be upstairs with honor."

Her mother looked at her, her face still quiet with her new strength, and Don Rafael looked at her in turn, as if he had never before seen her.

"Remedios, *hija*," said her mother. "Daughter. If she is to live at all after what has happened to her, the small room is exactly where she must be. Alone. To regather her mind and her soul in surroundings as close to the convent as possible. They will understand down there. They are good people. She will not, *niña*, be in any mind for chattering in salons."

Which is all I have ever known you to do, thought Emily in amazement, and Remedios was silent.

"Serafina," said Don Rafael again, "you understand the risk." His wife shrugged.

"So be it. She taught me when I was small before I went to Madrid. She has taught my daughters all their lives. Could I leave her to die in the streets? The poor old soul will probably die anyway."

Don Rafael kept his face gentle, but privately he was hoping the old nun might indeed die before she brought disaster on them all. Perhaps when she was a little stronger they might get her out to Alhaurín.

"The young one will be all right," his wife said, as if she read his thoughts. "Immediately in the morning we will send her to her family."

The unexpected visit that long silent evening was not yet over.

Just after José had kindled the crackling fire against the chill and opened the shutters to the luminous dusk, he came back up again.

This time it was Don Rafael he sought, still sitting with them in the salon, as though unable to leave Doña Serafina.

"There is a gentleman," he said, "Señor. His name is Lor' Keene!"

He had the Spanish difficulty with English consonants, and for a moment they all looked at him and did not understand. Emily laid down the wool she was winding for Doña Serafina's crochet, and stared at him a moment.

"Ah," she said. "Don Rafael, it is Lord Keene. The Earl of Keene. That will be Anna Kilpatrick's father. I expect he has come to take her home."

There was silence in which all the faces except Emily's relaxed with relief, but she sat very still, stricken by inescapable reality come so close. Remedios came over and stood beside her, laying a hand on her shoulder.

"Bring him up, José," said Don Rafael quietly. "We will see him here."

He was a tall man with thick graying hair and a high-boned Irish face, his daughter very like him. He had the same air of courteous reserve, with beautiful, slow good manners, exchanging all the courtesies with timeless quietness before he spoke of the sad decision hanging in the air before them all.

He had come, he said, to take Anna home, and had telephoned Emily's mother to say that he would bring her also. There should by now have been a telegram. Had they not received it? He apologized, looking at Emily's face, if his news had been a shock to them.

Don Rafael shrugged.

"It will not be long, I think, Señor, before we are missing more than telegrams. I had already arranged to send Emilia home, but what you are kind enough to propose will be much more suitable."

Breaking her heart, thought Emily wildly, with polite and measured words.

They arranged to combine their plans and travel together on the cargo boat leaving two evenings later.

"That will be excellent," Lord Keene said, "A most immense relief. I am very grateful. The train journey down was not easy, and not suitable for the girls."

"Safe" was what he meant, and they all knew it. Or perhaps at any moment no longer possible. In all their anxious minds was the thought that even two evenings later might be difficult. As Emily's brother had feared, the situation had worsened rapidly. Despite Don Rafael's assurances to him, it showed every sign of going up in flames.

Lord Keene did not stay long. He was anxious to get back to his mother and to Anna. Emily said good-bye to him, trying to see him as part of a life she would be glad to see again, but unable to find him little better than a messenger of death. She waited feverishly for Alejandro, desperate now for every moment she could spend with him, knowing there was no appeal. He would agree with Don Rafael and Anna's father.

Alejandro was late.

By nine thirty Emily was ashen-faced, chewing fiercely at her nails, and Don Rafael was carefully keeping the difficult conversation to other things. The blue Bugatti would be dangerously conspicuous as a rich man's toy if the city should get out of hand. He had opened one of the upper windows, and listened, reassured by the ordinary night noises of the town.

Just before ten Alejandro came into the circle of their worried faces, and with him José Maria, who lived with one of his elder brothers out along the road to Fuengirola. Doña Serafina got up to kiss him in surprise and pleasure, comforted to have even one more child in the empty house. Emily clung to Alejandro's hand until her own fingers hurt, pretending everything was normal, but aware at once, from some sad reservation in his eyes, that there was news, and she would not find it good.

Her own news was bad enough.

"Alejandro. I am to go home in two days."

She spoke under the cover of Doña Serafina's happy flood of talk to José Maria.

"*Cariña*, that is good," Alejandro said. "I am as heartbroken as you, but that is good. It is the only thing to do."

He looked down at her, and his dark eyes were full of sorrow and a curious burning excitement.

"We have news for you also," he said. "José Maria and I."

José Maria looked over then, his thin studious face blazing with something suppressed.

"May I tell them?"

Alejandro nodded, and put his arm around Emily, as if to protect her, and her heart contracted with fear. What was coming now?

Beside his mother, José Maria took a deep breath; half pride, and half preparation for the storm to come. He laid a hand on his mother's shoulder.

"Today, Alejandro and I have signed on for the Army."

Doña Serafina screamed, and burst at once into hopeless tears; no sign now of the brave, calm woman who had accepted the danger of harboring the nun. She could accept anything for herself, but for her children, nothing but the peace and safety in which she had reared them. Don Rafael bent and put an arm around her in her high-backed chair, but there was no concealing the pride and something like relief that glowed in his eyes. Remedios got up and kissed them both. There were tears in her lovely eyes, but she did not cry.

"*Está en las manos de Dios*," she said. "It is in the hands of God."

Emily could not speak, her eyes locked on Alejandro's, answering his silent plea to understand that it had to be.

"You will be killed," gasped Doña Serafina, and her husband

silently gave her the clean white handkerchief from his breast pocket. "You will be killed. Oh, *hijo mio*. Oh, my son."

There was no sound for a few minutes, other than her weeping, quiet now and heavy with despair. The logs hissed and spat in the big hearth, and the room was bright with lamplight, the sky indigo beyond the window; promise of the fine soft nights to come. Picture of security and happiness that might never be again.

"Mama," said José Maria patiently, when her weeping had died down a little. He stood before the fire, regarding her with pain on his thin face, as if he kept his distance and protected himself in some way from her grief. "Mother. It is the Army that will save Spain." Don Rafael nodded. "We cannot leave it to everybody else."

His mother grew slowly quiet, unable to put into words that it was not only his joining the Army that had so upset her, but that for her this was the moment of total truth. The moment—even beyond the encounter with the fleeing nuns, and her house empty of her children—when she faced the understanding that her gracious life as she had known it was at an end. The blue and gold flag folded probably for her lifetime, if not forever. The future offering nothing but grief and fear.

She gathered herself together.

"You will eat some food," she said. Don Rafael patted her shoulder and went back to his seat. That was normal. Food to Doña Serafina was the comforter and stay in all threatening situations.

"I should be glad, Mama," said José Maria.

"If you will excuse us, I will take Emily out," said Alejandro. "We have three days to settle our affairs, and then we will be off to Morocco for our training."

Morocco. Doña Serafina blanched again. It was outside Spain and therefore beyond the known world.

But the three men looked at each other as though Morocco had some special meaning.

"I want to ask Emilia something," Alejandro said. "We will come back and talk to you about it afterwards. Are you ready, *querida*?"

She fled to get her coat and gloves.

"We'll go up to Gibralfaro," he said when he had edged the

blue car from the narrow street. "It may be some time before we can go out again, so it must be special."

The absolute calm of his voice, and the steady smile he turned on her, said as clear as words that he expected no fuss from her. What was to be, must be accepted. But when he smiled at her, she felt so sick with sorrow she did not know how she would withstand the evening. Everything conspired to make it in the nature of a farewell; sitting in their high window, making small haphazard talk while they waited for the food, looking down on all the twinkling lights of Málaga and the port beneath them; choking back all sad speculations as to what would have happened before they could sit there again.

They released their locked fingers when the food came, and firmly Alejandro filled the unhappy silence with tender conversation while they ate, thrusting away fear and shadows until for a while it was like any other happy evening of their love. The restaurant, in an old castillo of the Moors high on the hills above Málaga, was crowded; all the others doing as they did, deliberately setting aside disaster for what time they could.

With the coffee, Alejandro's face grew firm and serious. He lit one of his Black Russian cigarettes, and automatically offered her the other side of the case, where all the little gold-tipped cigarettes lay in colors like bright sweets. She shook her head, a little surprised that he should forget she didn't smoke.

"Emilia."

"Sí"

"Emilia. Today I did something more than join the Army."

She waited, her eyes on his face. What else more desperate and final could he have done? Across the table, he reached out and took her hand, the smoke of his neglected cigarette rising in a thin column up between them.

There was a little silence, and she sensed him gathering himself to speak.

"Sí, Alejandro?"

"I went, querida," he said then deliberately, "today, to see all the proper authorities, and then to the good Padre Eduardo in the cathedral. By tomorrow, everything will be in order, and if you will do me the honor, we can be married on the morning after. There is only one Mass allowed now, at half past six. Would that be too early for you? I would like to leave you as my wife. We have your mother's consent."

He got it all out, slowly and formally, but she knew him well enough by now to know the emotion that made him so deliberate. And his longing for her to agree.

"I am hurrying you, *mi alma*," he said sadly.

It was the one foolish detail that undid her. The question, as though he had organized a picnic to the mountains, that it might be too early for her. It was impossible for her to speak, and the slow tears began to slide down her cheeks. I am like Doña Serafina, she thought. Tears for everything.

"Do not cry, querida. Ay, *mi alma*, do not cry. Weddings are supposed to be happy things."

Not ours, she thought desolately. Not ours. It will still be dark and that will represent it all.

But she smiled at him with tears still bright in the lamplight on her lashes; in such radiant temporary happiness that he was able to reassure himself that not only his own selfishness had prompted him, in the need to tie her and feel sure of her. She loved him too. *Gracias a Dios* but she loved him too, and in God's good time all would be well.

"Will you," he asked, for she had not yet spoken. "Will you be my wife?" He grinned. "Do you know me well enough now?"

"Oh, Alejandro, yes," she whispered. "It will not be so lonely if I know you are really mine." How could she tell him it was the one thing she had dreamed of night and day and thought impossible. She tried to tease him.

"Then," she said, "you won't be free to capture the hearts of all the señoritas in your grand uniform."

With all his heart, Alejandro wished it might be as lighthearted as that. He answered her in the same way.

"And I will know you can't go off on a horse with some Irish fellow who goes chasing foxes in the *campo*."

They laughed then, and sorrow receded and they planned and talked of the future they might have to wait for, but that would surely come. When they had eaten, they went out, arms around each other, into the starlit glittering night, and climbed into the blue car; swooping down the winding hill in blissful happiness, as though their wedding would be no different from any other. To tell the family they had left behind them. Family to neither of them, and yet at that moment, all they had.

Two mornings later, it was still full darkness when they all

waited for him in the stone-cold chill of the cathedral, the side
altar for the Mass a small island of pale candlelight in the great
dark vault. All of the family had gathered, every one of them,
despite the risks; slipping in through a side door to avoid attention,
knowing themselves conspicuously different from the curious
little group of black-shawled women who crept in every morning
to beg the good God for patience, and even occasionally for
happiness, and for the safety of those they loved.

Alejandro was late. He and José Maria had spent the night in a
hotel lest he disturb the old cousins creeping out in the morning
dark. He wanted to tell his parents for himself.

Emily gratefully took the family kisses, which held as much
compassion as congratulation, and wondered if any of the shadowy figures beyond the light would spare her one of their prayers.

With loving care, Remedios had helped her dress in what she
thought of as her best dress. A little longer than her others; pale
creamy silk falling almost to her ankles. Around her neck Doña
Serafina had clasped a beautiful necklet of old Toledo gold.

"*Dios mediante*, querida Emilia," she said, and her amber
eyes were full of love and pity. "You will wear it again for
Alejandro in happier times."

A small hat of the same cream color as her dress tilted over her
red-gold curls, and Remedios with her skillful hands had fash-
ioned her a small bouquet from the first freesias, in from the
greenhouses at Alhaurín.

Emily trembled with nerves and cold and shaken happiness,
the sweet perfume of the flowers creeping round her in the soft
light, reaching forever into her heart and memory. Doña Serafina
wept openly now, tiredly, as if she were growing accustomed to
sadness and would soon have no tears left. Emily looked at her
affectionately, and thought of the wedding she had dreamed of,
in the bare workaday chapel of the village at home that had
known all her childhood prayers. She thought of her mother with
painful longing; still asleep and knowing nothing of it all. Their
wire would not have reached her yet.

Then she thought of Alejandro, and nerves and sorrow left
her. No matter the chill and loneliness and the sad hour of dawn.
It was their wedding day. Within half an hour, she would be
married to him, and although she had to leave Spain, it would be
as his wife.

She saw Don Rafael pull out his thin gold watch and look at it, and began to listen more anxiously for the thump of the heavy door, and his footsteps on the flags.

They waited an hour beyond the appointed time, and Alejandro did not come. Nor José Maria, who was to stand with him; nor any message. In the end, Don Rafael whispered to the sons, and they took their wives and went quietly away.

He took Emily's arm.

"Come, *hija mia*," he said gently. "My daughter. It is better to go home."

Clear, beautiful spring morning lit the streets when they came out, and the sun was flooding the sea with gold; pouring in the long windows of the dining room when they got home, on to the heartbreaking flower-decked table of their wedding breakfast.

In the late afternoon, Don Rafael came with news. All day in numb silence, Emily, with Remedios, had packed her suitcases and got ready for the journey that night; waiting through the hours to hear of his death.

It was, however, only as Don Rafael had feared. Alejandro and José Maria had reported to their barracks according to their orders on the previous morning, expecting two more days of freedom. Such was the urgency of the situation that they had not been allowed to leave again; had been feverishly outfitted, and were even now on their way to Morocco. No chance had been given them to get a message out to anyone.

Doña Serafina was past weeping for her son, and Emily, blank-faced and silent, could find no tears yet for Alejandro.

Left tactfully to herself by Anna and her father, she cried at last that night as the boat slid from the harbor of Málaga, the sad family fading into formless shadows on the quay; slow, difficult tears, filled with pain and disappointment and all the sorrow of the future, understanding the old unheeded saying that her heart might break.

Through half-blind eyes she saw the lighthouse cut the familiar white swaths across the water, and the lights of Málaga twinkled below the shadows of the encircling hills, even as she had seen them that last evening with Alejandro up at Gibralfaro. She looked up at the glowing lights of the restaurant among the pine trees, but out toward Churriana fires were burning, smoke pouring scarlet into the dark sky, and the sharp clatter of machine guns started up, to remind her of why she was going.

## FOUR

The family always said that Mums had eyes like a gimlet, even if she seemed to be looking the other way, and as she folded her daughter into a warm thankful hug, Emily knew she had already noticed her lack of a wedding ring.

It seemed a thousand years and another life away from Spain, a soft blustery Irish day with high clouds racing the pale sky, and the grass so green it almost hurt to look at it. The old house was grayer and darker than she remembered, the horse chestnuts of the short, straight avenue coming up to swelling bud. Her mother must have heard the car, because she was standing waiting, smiling on the top of the curved steps, the door open and the fire glowing in the hall behind her, the forgotten smell of turf lying on the wind.

As Emily climbed out she grinned to see the curtains stirring at the dining room windows. Old Aggie would be in there, peering discreetly, allowing nothing of the life of the house to escape her scrutiny.

"Mums!"

Such heaven to see her, always in her soft Donegal tweeds and silk shirts. The colors of Ireland itself.

"Em, my pet!"

Mrs. McRoss's quick blue eyes roamed her daughter's face for a few moments as they drew apart, holding each other's hands, full of questions and surprise. But Lord Keene and Anna were getting out of the car to say good-bye, and she must greet them, and thank them for bringing Emily home, and all the questions must wait.

Thank you, they said, they wouldn't come in. They'd hit a cattle market in Roscommon and it had held them up. It had been a long journey and Anna's mother would be waiting.

Affable and easy, as though he had brought Emily from Cranmore rather than across half of Europe, Lord Keene gestured to the car.

"I'll be glad to see the end of this thing too," he said. "Believe it or not we hired it in Dublin from an undertaker. It was all we could get. I wouldn't think it's familiar with going more than twenty miles an hour!"

They knew now that they were neighbors, he said, and would see more of each other. Mrs. McRoss must come to Castle Keene and meet his wife.

Emily and Anna didn't kiss each other or even shake hands to say good-bye, the warm Spanish habits fading already under colder skies. But they looked at each other with affection. On the long journey back they had grown very close, each appreciating some subtle reticence in the other. Reacting with a degree of relieved privacy to their life in Andalusia, where every thought and emotion was bandied among the household women as easily as the price of olives.

"You are on the telephone?" Anna asked. The golden cap of her hair had grown a little longer while traveling. Emily thought her incredibly beautiful and was pleased to see her mother's eyes resting on her approvingly.

"Sixty-nine," she said. "Clonfrack 69."

"I'll give you a tinkle," Anna said. "Have to see how the court is at Keene. You do play?"

"I used to," Emily said ruefully. "Before I went to Málaga."

Leaping around a tennis court and showing her legs would not be an activity Doña Serafina would have thought suitable. Perhaps even Clonfrack would still look sideways at a pair of shorts like those they had seen all the girls wearing in Germany on the way home. Anyway, their own tennis court at the back of the garden could well be gone to hay long since. Would she, she wondered, have played tennis and done more modern things with Alejandro? In every question he still rose to dominate her thoughts.

She jerked herself back to say thank you and good-bye, and they waved from the steps as the old black Austin turned laboriously, and drove away.

Her mother slipped an arm around Emily, and without even turning her head she raised her voice. The light Irish accent broadened.

"I can see you there, Willie," she said, "peering round the house minding other people's business. Come on out now and take Miss Emily's cases."

Redheaded Willie ambled out beaming and touching his shapeless cap, as much an inevitable part of the household as the ancient aunts mumbling in the corners in their black dresses back in Spain. Slightly simple, and taken over in a measure of charity from some orphanage or broken-down cottage in the village packed with more children than could be fed. Undertaking every odd task in the household from cleaning the boots and the windows to getting the jackdaws' nests down out of the chimneys before the winter fires.

"Ye're welcome home, M'semily," he said.

"Thank you, Willie."

The quiet of the house struck her at once as she walked with her arm through her mother's, into the square hall with its black and white floor and the fire red behind the gleaming bars of the grate. Absolute quiet, except for the noise of the rooks scrapping in the elms below the garden. Surely it had not always been like that.

In spite of the immense size of the Spanish house, there was always something to be heard when you opened the Judas gate. Shrieks of battle or the clash of pans from over in the kitchen patio; the small boy yelling at the donkey; the children upstairs racing down the galleries, chanting their singing games; snatches of song or the plucked notes of a guitar from some idling servant. Even Doña Serafina's relentless talking, remorseless as the sea. Always noise and the sense of thrumming life.

Aggie came then, her apron spotless and her rosy old face brimming with excitement, to welcome her. Aggie belonged even to the old days, when there had been a father, and they had lived in London. She had raced from the dining room to the back of the house and then come out again decorously into the hall, to pretend she wouldn't do anything so beneath herself as to be peering from the windows in order to take a look at the earl. Although, God knew, it was far from every day there was an earl delivering Miss Emily to the door. And a fine setup of a man he was too.

"Ah, Miss Emily," she said. "God sent you back to us. The welcome of your home to you."

Aggie's splendid and unquestioning faith saw the hand of God in everything, but Emily looked at her bleakly for a moment, knowing it was the Republicans had sent her back. God had nothing to do with it.

"And the fine husband to come later," Aggie went on, filled

with wicked pride for which she would be saying penance on Sunday, not only about the earl on the doorstep, but the rumors of the fine aristocratic young man Miss Emily was after catching for herself out there in Spain; although there was little she herself knew about it, and it that far away. Onions and bulls, and the women always with a lot of grease on their hair and a flower in it. Fandangos they did, whatever fandangos would be. Or was it flamingos.

But wasn't it a queer marriage sent the girl home the second it was over, and a face on her like a ghost. But what else would you expect. Aggie's opinions of foreign countries were little different from Doña Serafina's. She had been born and reared in a sod-roofed farm with two acres of land, five Irish miles of hard walking from beyond the town; come to Clonfrack House as a little skivvy in the days of Madam's mother-in-law, and there ever since except the years in London, and wasn't that very much the same, in God's truth, since she never left the family. Almost convinced by now that they and the house were her own. Gaunt and dictatorial and ready to die for any single one of them were it asked of her.

"Give me your coat and hat now, Miss Emily, and go you in to the fire with your mother and I'll bring the tea."

Another fire was piled in the drawing room in the beautiful Adam grate. By now in Andalusia the sun would be warming the rooms, and the huge fireplace filled with plants. How hot would it be in Morocco? Emily's mind simply would not cease to set one place against the other. It had been the same from the moment they had first landed in the turf reek of Dun Laoghaire.

She paused then and smiled, feeling the special welcoming quality of this room, almost as if she had never seen it before. Beautiful and tranquil. The big bowed windows looking down the slope of the garden to the elms and the park beyond them. An elegant and charming room, yet carrying the subtle patina of contented use. It had seen a family grow up in it. The flowered covers of the deep chairs were a little faded; some ornament placed carefully here and there to hide a mark on the glowing mahogany furniture; a finger gone from one of the Belleek cherubs on the mantel; a rug to hide the spot on the carpet where Joe had once dropped a bottle of India ink. Warm. Rich looking. Heavy carpet and beautiful rugs; long dark green velvet curtains on the windows. Flowers everywhere, that her mother reared herself with such love in the greenhouses opening from the dining room. And books. She had missed the books in Spain. The house here was coming down with them.

Home.

The journey had anesthetized her, the constant change of scenery and company preventing her from thinking. Anna and her father had talked of everything except her situation, Lord Keene so well informed on all they saw that she could not help but turn her back on the cold misery crouching and waiting like a hostile animal, to take her in its teeth every moment that she was alone.

Lord Keene had had business in Germany, and so they had come up through Europe to Berlin. It was the one part of the journey Emily had hated, touched there by the same sense of threat and disaster that had haunted Málaga. She found it impossible not to be charmed by the lovely wooded roads of Charlottenburg, with their fine houses, where they had stayed; their gardens studded with dark tree-hung lakes. She had seen little as impressive as the grandeur of the Unter den Linden, and the pretty crowded walks of the Tiergarten. The cafés delighted her, and the brilliant shops; full of a sophistication that would be a long time yet in reaching Málaga. In spite of all that, the streets, like those she had left behind her, were full of marching men. On all sides they were holding meetings, yelling at gathered crowds; singing and parading and saluting with outstretched arms; brown-shirted, their black and scarlet flags whipping in the wind.

They were building the Olympic Village for the Games to be held there in the summer.

"They seem," said Emily, thinking of Málaga, "to be getting ready for a war, rather than for an Olympic Games."

They were held up as a horde of Brown Shirts went marching singing through the Brandenburger Tor, the sun on the peaks of their caps.

Anna's father turned from the wheel and looked at her somberly, as though wondering whether he should depress her with the truth. She felt the chill of his eyes.

"They are," he said. "They are. A couple of years. No more. Anyone who thinks otherwise is a fool."

"Ah, no," whispered Emily. "Not two. Not two at once."

Then she thought, how foolish, the Spanish one will be over long before then.

"My brother," said Anna, "is in the RAF."

And they all fell silent, thinking of him and all the others like him, if what the father said was true. And of Alejandro and José Maria and all the others like them, left behind in Spain.

"But why no ring, my darling?"

Her mother came out with the question that had been burning on her lips just as soon as Aggie had closed the drawing room door and they were alone. She sat down on the long sofa beside the fire and drew Emily down beside her among the cushions, picking up and looking at the thin hands that held no more than the small gold signet ring her Granny had given her long ago.

"What happened, Em? Are you not married after all? We thought so much about you when we got your wire, although it was all over by the time it came here. What went wrong?"

Emily shook her head. In the leisure of their slow journey there had been time to write, certainly to send a wire. But she had wanted to tell her mother to her face. Now she sat and looked at her, the excitement of the journey ebbing into nothing, and all the pain and loneliness and disappointment of that chilly morning rising to choke her words. The anger began to blaze in her mother's eyes, and so she laughed unsteadily instead of crying.

"Oh, no, Mums," she said. "You don't have to go after him with a hatchet. It's not like that."

"It's as well," said her mother dryly. "What did happen?"

Emily drew a long breath and started on the story she had waited weeks to tell, nor did she stop even when Aggie came in with the big silver tray and what she contemptuously called the English tea her mistress liked. A few sweet biscuits and a bit of cake and maybe a slice or two of barmbrack, when wouldn't the world know at the moment Miss Emily would be the better for a good few hot potato cakes and a plate of ham, and an egg or two after traveling near half the very globe.

She made the most of her time setting out the silver tea service and the old Coalport cups, and as much food as she had dare mass around them. Her apple face as she left the room was a mixture of fury and pity, and the bright unbridled delight of going to be the one to hit Clonfrack with the best bit of news since the day young Maggie Cadogan was delivered of an eight-pound boy on the floor of her mother's kitchen, and never a word known about it until the moment it happened.

"And Miss Emily's not married at all, the poor creature," she told her gaping old sister, who was settled, as was her custom of an afternoon, with her feet on the hot hob burning the soles off her boots, and a mug of tea in her hand stronger and browner than anything Emily or her mother would ever see. Or want.

"Not married at all in the heel of the hunt. And the postboy tired out with coming in and out all the way with all the wires and letters with their foreign stamps."

"Ah, musha," she said, "willy listen to that. And what will have happened to the young man in it all? Did he leave her at the altar like any scoundrel?"

Pride in her family reared up, and Aggie tossed her head and nearly took the old sister's tea away from her.

"Drink that up now and get going," she said severely. "Would you think Miss Emily would be getting herself involved with the kind of cut of a young man would leave her at the altar. Wasn't he snatched away to be a soldier!"

A soldier! The flowered cup hung in midair and the sister tried to wipe the skepticism from her face. Wasn't that the oldest tale since the army of Brian Boru. A soldier indeed! "Wasn't that a strange thing," she said innocently. "Why now would that happen?"

Aggie furiously had no answer other than to hound the old woman from the kitchen and the house.

"Haven't they a war there!" she cried after her into the dusk, from the kitchen doorstep.

But the damage was done, so that by the time Emily's brother Joe came home from his solicitor's office at half past six, he had heard on the way that his poor sister, God help her, had been left at the foot of the altar by some unprincipled Spaniard and not as much as a bit of a ring to show for it, and no more to explain it than that the fellow concerned went off, with her at the altar and all the neighborhood gathered for the wedding, to be a soldier. Did any man with his head on right go off at that tearaway to be a soldier? There was more in it, the village had already decided, than met the eye, and even an eye as blind as Declan Murphy's that was covered, God save the mark, with a milky film since the day he was born.

"To sum it all up, Em, my love," said Joe, "they have you jilted and abandoned, and the whole place is by the heels with it."

"I could drown the lot of them," said Emily's mother furiously, but Joe only grinned when he had kissed his sister, his narrow lively face warm with the pleasure of seeing her again, but his eyes resting a gentle moment on her strained face.

"You'll be needing me professionally, Emmie," he said then, his eyes warm with fun. "I've hit about six strong cases of slander between here and the office. The ones that can count up to nine are at it already. We should collect on the lot of them."

"Joe!"

"Yes, Mama?" he said dutifully, but his grin was wicked. "Can I get you a glass of sherry?"

"Don't try to sidetrack me like that. You're not to talk like that about your sister, even in a joke."

"No, Mama."

Above his mother's head he pulled a long rueful face at Emily, and she felt her sadness lift. It was having to put it all into words for her mother that had so depressed her. It would be easier if she had to speak of it to no one. Talking only of other things. Until Alejandro should come back.

But no one ever could be miserable with Joe around. Dusk was outside, the elms fragile on the purple sky; lamplight and firelight warm, and her mother's little spaniel, Beau, asleep across the hearth. At least she was at home.

Her mother drew the green velvet curtains against the coming dark; Joe dropped down on the sofa beside her.

"And what did the little caballero actually do to you?" he asked her, his eyes warm and loving lest the answer give her pain.

"He's not little!"

"I thought they were all little dark fellows down there. Arabs with boots on, someone said."

She thought of the handsome, well-bred Alejandro, with his fine handmade boots, pale beautiful leather below his short riding *traje*. She began to laugh.

And telling Joe was suddenly no tragedy. All her mind was on Alejandro himself and the happiness they had held together. She got back the reality the journey had blurred, and the first moments of optimism touched her; of real and actual hope that it was not all forever gone. No matter how it might seem now, he was not a dream. He was real, and no matter how long it took, one day they would be together again. She looked down at her

bare hands. If only she had even the smallest ring to show these
gossips. Alejandro's mother had written the kindest of letters and
told her that there was much she wished to give Emily. But it
must all wait until it was safe to travel again in Spain.

"He probably has the wedding ring in his pocket in Morocco,"
she said to Joe.

"We'll get you a good wide metal one," he said, determined
not to let her grieve, "and have 'I AM AN HONEST WOMAN'
engraved on the outside, to show the lot of them."

"Ah, Joe," she said, and laid her head on his shoulder. Not
Alejandro, but love and comfort she would remember all her life.

Her eldest brother, John, and his wife, Patricia, came racing
out of Galway late for dinner, the chill breath of the night on
their clothes even in the short run from the car. Both of them
were doctors practicing in the city, although it had been a hard
road for Patricia. "The Lady Doctor" they still called her and
wouldn't give her a name. But the women were beginning to
bring their children to her now, and lately even themselves. And
although they poured their astonishment from the housetops when
she cured them, and preferred to credit it to some favorite saint or
a circuit of the Holy Well in their bare feet, they came again.

"They're at last beginning to believe I'm a doctor," she would
say, and add bitterly that there were many who just came in for a
bottle of medicine and to have a look at the freak. "For they
think that God made men to be doctors and they make that
clear."

She was small and pretty and black-haired, with dark blue
eyes, long-lashed, and a high color, everything the English thought
an Irish girl should look like.

"There's nothing like an invasion," she would say, "for
changing the whole aspect of a population. I'm nothing more
than a Viking. One of the ones Boru didn't manage to get rid
of."

She kissed Emily warmly when they came in, the shrewd blue
eyes running over this pretty sister-in-law who had been little
more than a child when she had gone away. Just after her own
wedding. Now here she was back, poor love, with her own
tangled tale of love and sorrow, and the damnable business of a
war thrown in into the bargain to mess it up even more. She
herself had lost her father, and seen her mother made a broken-

hearted widow, in what the jokers now called the last little spot of bother, here at home.

After he had been on his rather panic-stricken rush to Spain last summer, John had told her that the little sister, Em, was growing into a raving beauty. And b'God but he was right. Lovely delicate beauty, but the straight assessing gaze of the gray eyes showed that she was no one's fool; nor would she wish to be rushed with too much sentiment or sympathy.

Nevertheless Emily had to go painfully again through it all for them, answering all the astonished questions. She realized with gratitude that her mother had telephoned Pat and John and told them to take it easy. They had been rushing over for celebrations. There were no celebrations.

Joe watched her.

"She's trying to put the best face on it," he said in the end, stirring the fire to a happy blaze, "but the truth of the matter is that this what-d'you-call-him, Allyhandro, went off with one of these veiled bundles from Morocco. Isn't he the lucky lad. I understand there's great surprises inside those parcels."

John looked at her with dark unsmiling eyes, ignoring Joe. Already Emily had changed beyond belief from the clear-eyed child who had begged to be allowed to stay in Spain last summer. Would it have been better to have dragged her home, or had she found something important and inescapable, sorrow and all included. But surely too young and too soon, poor pet. He felt responsible.

At thirty-two, fourteen years older than Emily, he was the nearest to a father she ever remembered having.

"And was he nice, love?" he asked her gently, still ignoring Joe. Joe would say he spent half of his life being ignored by John. "Did you love him?"

God help her, she was only just eighteen, and such things came hard. You never believed they could happen again. And again. And again.

Emily looked around at them all in the warm lamplight, with wide outraged eyes, as if they had not even begun to try and understand anything.

"Was he nice?" she cried. "And did I love him? Yes, he's nice. And I do love him. He's not dead!"

Not yet, whispered her frightened heart in the moment of silence, and then suddenly she began to weep.

John's round calm face creased up, and he cursed himself for a thousand kinds of a fool. He gave her to her mother and Pat to comfort, and went racing to the kitchen.

"Aggie, have you champagne in the house. If you have none, get Willie racing to the hotel as fast as his legs can carry him."

"I have it in the icehouse, Doctor John," she said calmly. "I didn't take it out when I heard it had all gone wrong, with the feeling we'd need it somehow, one way or the other."

John gave her a big grateful kiss.

"We'd be lost without you, Aggie."

"That could be the truth indeed, Doctor John."

"We got it all wrong, pet," he said when Aggie came in triumphantly with the Waterford glittering on the silver tray. Aggie's expression indicated clearly that it was not the first time she had thought the entire lot of them were mad. The poor child crying her eyes out on the sofa, and the doctor yelling for champagne like it was the wedding itself. You'd think he'd have more sense.

But his mother looked at John with an expression of deep gratitude as he poured the bubbling drinks. John always knew what was best to do, and just the moment for doing it.

"We got it all wrong, stupid lot of eejits that we are."

He handed round the beautiful goblets, and she remembered the crystal glass that Don Rafael had handed to her by the fire, the first evening she went out with Alejandro.

"On your feet, the lot of you," said John. "We're here to celebrate Em's engagement, which we all seem to have forgotten. What if the wedding got delayed?" He grinned at his wife. "I began to think I'd never get Pat there to the altar. *Slainthe*, little Em. The man of your choice to you. And forever happiness!"

"*Slainthe*," they all cried, and kissed her. "*Slainthe!* Emily and Alejandro!"

"I haven't had champagne," she said—and now the radiant happiness she had forgotten was shining on her tear-damp face—"since the night Alejandro asked me to marry him."

Joe gave her his big white handkerchief.

"Have a mop," he said.

She began in a rush to talk about him, then, as he really was and not as some failure or tragedy, and they all egged her on and plied her with questions. The only one silent was Mrs. McRoss, proud and touched at the kindness and perception of her sons.

She should have had the sense to handle it this way herself, but she wasn't really to be blamed. She had heard nothing except that Em was to be married on the very day she got the telegram, and it came as a bit of a shock to see her fingers bare of rings. Even though she had known enough to look at the right hand.

"No worry, Mum," John said to her afterwards. "You were taken by surprise. Pat and I had a little time to think, and after poor Joe had walked through the village, I think he thought he was coming home to the Scarlet Woman of Clonfrack."

Aggie came into the middle of all the talking with a pained face to tell them the dinner was apt to be destroyed did they not come through at once, and all they did was ask her for another bottle on the table, which, in spite of her long face, glittered like a banquet with their mother's famous Carrickmacross cloth and the best Waterford; and below Emily's place a little bunch of the first violets from the garden, in a crystal bowl, still damp and fresh from the night outside.

"God love her," said Emily, "she must have gone gathering them with a candle."

They held to the bright mood of celebration that grew upon itself.

"All these knives and forks," said Emily in awe.

"What do you mean, Em?"

"Mums, you will know. You'll remember in even a really good-class house like Don Rafael's, you get only one knife and fork, and you wipe it between the courses on your bread."

"Arabs, with boots on," said Joe. "Didn't I say so."

They kept her talking, reliving all her happy Spanish days, especially the brilliant sunlit one in Alhaurín when she had met Alejandro. For that lovely talkative evening, he became real among them, and she pushed away distance and sorrow; feeling him close. So close that she even glanced at the door, expecting that it might open, and the lamplight shine unbelievably on black close-cut curls.

Her fiancé, they called him, and her mother and Pat were making happy plans for the wedding, her mother unashamedly delighted that it would after all take place at home, however far the day. It would be in the parish church, with a marquee down on the lower lawn like the other girls had had.

"Em, dear," said her mother, "you must have it in the summer. For the flowers."

Its fuchsia hedges were the pride of Clonfrack House.

"Where on earth," said Pat, "will we put all the Spaniards. They're bound to come in flocks. Down to the last fifth cousin."

"Well, not Reagan's, that's for sure." Joe said, and they all laughed at the idea of the elegant Spanish guests in there among the smell of bacon and cabbage and cats, and the threadbare carpets and gray tablecloths of the Commercial Hotel.

"I'll hear no word against Reagan's," said Joe. "They have the best-stocked bar from Galway to Dun Laoghaire and back by Cork City."

"Well, that'd suit you all right," said John, "but we'll want a bit more for Em."

"Boys!" said Mrs. McRoss, as she had been saying to John and Joe since the days of catapults.

You would imagine, Emily thought, that it would be tomorrow. They were just as bad as Remedios and her mother. Yet she listened with bright excited eyes, looking at them all over the little bunch of violets, held up close to her face for the perfume.

Dreaming.

Alejandro. Her fiancé. Her bridegroom. They were right. She had allowed herself to become shut up inside her own loneliness and grief. It was only a delay. All real, it would all happen.

Alejandro.

But in the morning she woke early to soft cool Irish dawn, unable to sleep anymore, and got up to go over to her window. She looked out across the misty parkland shaking off the dark webs of night, the horses wakening as she had done to the first light, moving a little stiffly like ghosts, under the shadows that were trees.

The bubbles in the champagne were dead, and she was alone in Ireland. Alejandro in Morocco, and between them, endless, lay the coming war.

Slowly and determinedly she began to gather up the threads of her life in the house and the village. The same loved life to which she had come racing home, bright with happiness and anticipation, for every holiday from school in England.

"It'll be very quiet for you here, pet," her mother said, always trying to be a step ahead in anticipating the troubles that might beset her children, even though most of them now were long flown from her.

Looking with a certain element of despair at the new mature and quiet Emily, she thought to herself that however hard you tried, they were always able to surprise you. How in God's name could she have anticipated this one? Three years of "finishing" with Serafina's child, and what came of it was a Spanish lover and almost a marriage, which as far as Emily was concerned would still take place as soon as possible. And she thinking all the time that her daughter and the child Remedios were still safely closed inside the schoolroom. And along with it all, the country falling into civil war.

She shivered.

Thank God, she had been out of Ireland for the worst of what happened there, but no one could overlook the terrible results that still maimed the country. There were families would never be the same again for generations. Brother against brother. Father against son. Blood against blood. God help the child.

Emily looked at her, knowing her mind would be racing behind the few simple words about being quiet. Always elegant, even in the old cord breeches she used around the stables, but never without the fine beautiful boots her husband had had made for her in Peales. Long, long ago. Well suited this pale spring day by her Donegal tweed skirt of misty purple. Gleaming against her pale lilac twin set were the pearls that had rarely left her neck since Gran had clasped them there the night before her wedding. Poor Mums, she had little but memories.

"Mums," she said, looking at the pearls. "I have something to show you."

She ran upstairs to her jewel box, still unopened in the bedroom, and came back down slowly, spilling between her fingers the necklace of Toledo gold.

"Your pearls made me think of it," she said. "You've so often told us of Gran giving them to you the night before you married Daddy. Doña Serafina did the same for me. Only it was morning. It was dark," she added inconsequently, and thrust away a stab of the grief that had come with the lovely dawn that morning.

"Beautiful," breathed her mother. "Beautiful. And costly. How good of Serafina. How kind."

She looked at Emily then, a considering compassionate look, eyes like Emily's own, the necklace in her hand glowing like life itself from a random shaft of sun.

"It was real, then, Em."

There was silence between them for a long moment, and without words Emily's status changed. Up till then she had been no more than a child who had been far from home and got herself into a bit of a mess; almost certainly to be resolved by time and circumstance. She was young, very young. If necessary, she would forget him.

But in that silent moment, her mother admitted her to the real world of loss and sorrow that she herself knew well; to be shared as one woman with another.

"I have horses down there eating their heads off for exercise," was all she said, briskly. "Will you come riding with me?"

Emily nodded, and could not speak.

She went determinedly out into the little town one day, picking her way along the manure-spattered streets between the gray-faced houses, deliberately going through the vegetable garden and out a stony alley to avoid the two cottages on each side of the gates, where the women recorded the comings and goings of the family as faithfully as a pair of time clocks.

Sharp eyes surveyed her ringless hands as she handed her money over for her mother's orders, through the small spaces left between the piled merchandise; curiosity coming tangible as a breeze through the tallow candles and gaudy tins of pineapple; a child at her side shrilling for a twist of sugar and the mama would be in to pay for it within the day itself; and women's corsets hanging from a line of string above her head. Over all, the smell of meat and strong porter and heavily salted bacon, and the rich slab of butter on the counter, large as a tombstone.

She accepted the urbane smiles and greetings of the shawled women in the streets, and watched curtains twitch to her passing, knowing they would all be dissecting her like a child would a dead fly, the very second she was past them.

"Have you a spare wedding ring, Mums?" she said one morning desperately. "I could wear it on my right hand, and that'd fox them. I'm fed up with it."

"As you will, darling," her mother said comfortingly but absently, looking up from her writing desk by the wide window.

The sun caught her hair, red-gold like Emily's, barely changed by the gray that touched it, but straight, drawn back and coiled on her neck. Nicer than mine, thought Emily. None of these ghastly curls.

"Just be a little patient, pet," she said. "They have nothing else in the world to think of but other people's business, the creatures. One day soon some farmer will have a five-legged calf or some child will see the Virgin out at the Holy Well, and you'll be forgotten like last week's dinner."

Emily picked up her basket to take the orders out to Aggie, and laughed.

"You're so right," she said. "Maybe I could dress up as the Virgin and waft about the Holy Well a bit, to give them a start."

Her mother *was* right, she knew. It had been the same in the kitchens in Málaga. Go in for a *tapa* and they would all be in a scurrying frenzy with some piece of gossip. Ask them about it in three days' time and they'd have forgotten it for something new.

As always, she went away from her mother comforted.

Her young brother, Ted, came home from Downside for the Easter holidays, filling the quiet house with noise. Charging from one end of it to the other, as she had once done, in the simple delight and excitement of being home. She was glad of his company, lanky and hilarious, with much of Joe's laconic manner. Growing madly out of all his clothes, wrists and ankles hanging out like the scarecrows in the spring fields. While Willie was working in his own haphazard fashion to restore their neglected court, they played strange uncontrollable tennis on a patch of hummocky grass with a tattered net held across it on a piece of rope. "Clonfrack Tennis Club" said the legend outside it in faded paint, but it was rarely played on now, and the way into it had been taken over as his undisputed territory by a long-necked hissing gander; chosen grazing ground for his waddling wives, who picked for seeds among the rank grass along the walls.

When the furious owner caught Ted one day, fencing off the attacking gander with his tennis racket and loud cries of *"En garde, Monsieur,"* he closed the lane with a tangle of barbed wire, leaving them to scale a five-foot wall from one of the small stony streets of the village.

"No trouble at all," cried the long-legged Ted, up and over in a couple leaps and a scramble, scattering the top of the wall back down on his sister. He shouted back at her yell.

"Isn't that why they're loose," he cried. "It's easier!"

Carefully Emily looked up and down the little road and hitched up her dress.

"I'll throw my racket over first," she called to Ted. "I'll need two hands."

She lobbed it over into the thistles.

When the parish priest came gravely down the street a few moments later, from a teatime visit, she was astride the wall, rocking on the loose stones, terrified to move either way for fear of bringing down the wall. No tennis racket in sight; no obvious respectable reason for her being there at all, her skirt gathered irretrievably around her waist. Ted chose that moment to fall into a masterly silence, searching out a leaf of docken to spit on it and apply it solicitously to his nettle stings.

Carefully Father Conlan averted his eyes and appeared to give all his attention to Mrs. Morrisey's cow on the bit of grass behind the opposite wall, but Emily knew furiously that he had not missed one item of what he would no doubt call her shameless posture.

He lifted his hat of thick black velour, and she resisted the temptation to launch into the attack by telling him she thought it far too elegant for a priest. She saw he lifted it carefully to avoid finger marks on the fine pile and longed to tell him not to trouble.

"Good day to you, Miss McRoss," he said, and it might have been the cow he was speaking to.

"Good afternoon, Father," she said, scarlet with embarrassment and rage, and managed to hurl herself over, landing, stones and all, at Ted's feet. He was hooting with laughter, having seen the velour hat bobbing along above the wall, and heard his sister's tart greeting.

"He'll be expecting me to Confession before six o'clock Mass tomorrow morning," she said furiously, scrubbing at the moss stains on her white dress.

Ted hooted again in his unstable voice.

"And why not?" he said, exactly as Joe would.

"Get on down there and play tennis," she said, and went on from sheer temper to beat the hell out of him, humps and tussocks and lost white lines and dandelions and all.

"Mums," she said, still bursting with it when she got home, flinging herself into one chair in the hall and her racket into the other. "Mums, it was awful. He was certain I was going over there to meet some boy. Miserable little bad-minded man. I'm the loosest girl in the parish now, as well as being stood up by some immoral Spaniard. It's far worse than Spain. Far worse!''

Her mother did her best to keep her face straight and sympathetic, with absolutely no success, and when she gave in and laughed, Emily laughed with her, and when Joe came in they told him and he laughed so much he could hardly stand up.

"You'll be a great asset to me, Em," he said. "I'll be the most popular fellow in Galway once the news gets round I have a sex maniac for a sister. We'll have every man in the county hammering on the door. And I hope," he added, "that they bring their sisters.''

She looked at him and felt the opening of some door in her mind; closed so long in a world of narrow propriety, where if such a thing should happen to Remedios, it would be a scandal but never a joke. Or if it was deliberate, it would be hissed about triumphantly in secret for months to come. She realized how dearly she loved Joe and what he had done for her at that moment; understanding for the first time since she came back that she was still young and life was fun; knew the first sudden easing of the cloud of sorrow that had blanketed her since she came home.

"Oh, Joe," she said. "You are a fool."

"Thank God," said Joe piously. "I do my best."

"Put away your rackets," said Mrs. McRoss automatically, and looked at Emily with relief. The child was coming alive again, thank God.

But on no day would anything persuade Emily to leave the house until after ten o'clock in the morning, when she came down to watch for the coming of old Mick Gargan, the postman. All the way up the straight drive from the gates she watched him, counting each stiff, deliberate push of the pedals of his high ancient bicycle; squeezing her hands at her sides to keep herself from racing out the hall door and tearing his bag from his shoulder.

Praying.

And her mother carefully not seeing her there at the hall window.

There had been no chance with Alejandro for high farewells and promises. Never a word of patriotism or heroism, or all the thoughts and ideals that had driven him to do what he did.

No chance to make a last careful picture of him in her mind,

fine in his gray-green uniform with the little patches of gold and
scarlet at his collar.

She was conscious of the turning days as if she saw them in
Spain and not in Ireland, thinking of the flowers thick as stars in
the fresh grass along the roadside to Alhaurín. The illimitable
bull pastures where she and Remedios had gone to visit, drifts to
the horizon at this time of year of white and lilac and soft rose
and sharp yellow, the black bulls up to their hocks in the pale
flowers. The incomparable blue of the spring sea.

And the sun.

Not until the first day of May did anything come. And that
only a letter from Remedios that had taken a month to reach her.
Right at the start she told Emily with her customary thoughtful-
ness that they had been constantly in touch with Alejandro's
parents in Madrid, who had had no word of him except one
printed Army card to say that he was well.

It was better than nothing.

Like a quick brush of his hand. A word in passing.

Alejandro.

Even the name seemed strange in this soft cool land, where
they would turn it into Alexander. Sandy. She smiled. The name
of Alejandro did not belong here in this tender spring, hawthorn
foaming down the hedges at the sides of the drive, filling the
house with its gentle perfume, reminding her of the heavy fra-
grances of the heat. Jasmine; and the *dama de la noche* haunting
the hot nights.

Alejandro.

It was all very horrible in the city now, Remedios went on, in
her thin spidery writing. A great deal of brawling and uproar, and
no ordinary life possible anymore. Her parents, she said, were
talking of sending her away to the *ganadero* near Cádiz. In that
part of the country it was much safer for people like them. But,
she said, she would be too lonely. Mama would not leave Papa,
and Papa could not leave Málaga. Her brothers came to the
house, but most of the wives and sisters had already gone away
with the children to a safer part of the country. They had heard
from José Maria only what Alejandro's parents had heard of him.

Life, she wrote, was very sad and dull and often frightening,
and she thought often of all the happy days they had had together.

She would let her know immediately if they had any news of
Alejandro.

She sent her love to Anna.

But, thought Emily miserably, ''immediately'' this time had been a month. He could be dead before she even knew he was alive. She shook herself. There was no official war yet, and the Army would not be involved until there was.

The next day on the wireless they heard of massive Communist processions in all the big towns in Spain, and of clashes and fighting between the Communists and Anarchists in the streets of Málaga. Spain clearly tottering on the brink of chaos. She could not imagine it as the same country as the one of the heat in the white streets, and the bulls and the flowers.

Surprisingly she had not heard from Anna. During the slow journey they had come to this pleased and cautious affection, respecting each other's reserve, and she had not been left with the impression that Anna would be a person of idle promises.

''Why don't you ring her up yourself?'' her mother asked her. Any diversion would be good for the child. Her heart ached for Emily and her young love, and the patience and dignity of her loneliness. And God knew there was little enough diversion for her here with all of them gone but Joe, and he going mad about some girl down in Attymon, and more there than here.

Emily shook her head about the telephoning. She didn't know the structure and life of the great imposing house, and something stopped her from intruding, until Anna had made the first move.

*FIVE*

Through the blue evenings of early summer she went out with Joe and his friends, including the girl from Attymon. The young men gazed at her in theatrical astonishment, and asked Joe where in all that was holy he had been keeping her.

''Up me sleeve,'' was Joe's terse answer. ''And not for the likes of you.''

Unlike the women of the village, they took her easily, incurious about the stories of some strange adventure with a Spaniard.

It was another world, most of them having never been outside Ireland, and what happened there of small importance.

She enjoyed all the prodigious compliments and all their bright intelligence and the quick wit and endless talk. The same lively world that she had seen flowing through her home all through her childhood, before she went to Spain.

Then she had been too young to join in, but the girls who were here now were the same ones she had played with when she was small, through the rock-bound meadows and along the peaty streams; and in the attics of their houses and hers on the interminable wet days; the attics always thought to be the proper place for putting children and lumber.

Now the girls welcomed her back, grown pretty themselves; several of them in college in the city, full of wit and self-assurance. But she looked at them and listened to their bright chatter and found them young, young, young. As she herself had once been, long ago it seemed. Before Alejandro. Before the chilly morning at the empty altar in the cathedral. And Málaga fading away into the dark sea to the chatter of machine guns.

She felt married, even if she was not, and long gone from the carefree world of these girls, envying them their thoughtless youngness.

They whirled out in the clouded soft evenings, ignoring the gentle, remorseless rain. In a couple of ancient battered cars, with the ones in the rumble seat of the Morris huddled underneath an old tarpaulin. Or in state in Mrs. McRoss's big black Buick, if Joe could persuade her to lend it to him.

Out past the distant glimpse of Anna's home, and the white cottages of Oranmore, where the long finger of the sea lay silver in the gray evenings. Past the tumbledown thatched hovels of the Claddagh, and the rain drumming on the harbor, and a hundred swans like ghosts in the rain. Through Salthill and Spiddal, out into the rocky country on the bleak edges of Connemara to have a drink in a run-down old pub that had become the fashion with the Gaelic-speakers, and the ones that felt themselves the forward thinkers of the intellectuals in the new Ireland.

They drank their black porter among the tall brown men of the hills, who had to scrape hard to afford their dram, and who stared at the smart, talkative young ones as if they saw them in a zoo. Would this fella Marx they were always on about give any more money for the hauling of kelp? And Independence was a fine word, but divil a bit of difference it had made to them, in spite of the fathers and the sons beneath the sod for it.

In the clearing evenings, what they liked to call "The Gang" would sit outside on the dark rocks and watch the sun go down behind the hills of Clare; in a last blaze of gold and scarlet, brushed with the lingering purple of the rain.

They talked and talked, with all the energy and intensity of their youth, and tore the world apart as the chill came up from the darkening water. Politics and farming and sex and religion and their own savage civil war, and the endless tale of man's inhumanity to man. Evening after evening, in the short summer.

When they got to know her better and were tired of chewing over the wrongs of Ireland, they turned all their bright faces toward her and asked her about Spain. Nor did they give a tinker's damn if she had been left at the altar. It was Spain they wanted to know about, and she was surprised and humiliated at how little she could tell them.

Spain for her had been the tight, contented world of the casa of Don Rafael.

To her amazement, they were mostly on the side of the Republicans.

"Why not?" they cried to her stammered objections. "Why not? Aren't the people there rising against tyrants. Wasn't the government of Spain the tyranny of the Few," they cried at her.

"And the mass of the people starving," one of the girls chimed in. "And the rich having all the land and living in splendor. Weren't they all tyrants? Aren't the Republicans right to be destroying them?"

"And never a child at school!" cried another.

They even quoted figures of the percentage of children that never went to school, and she stared at them. She had lived there and never known these things.

Tyrants? Figures? Percentages?

She felt herself woefully ignorant, and fumbled for an answer, wishing she had a proper one, for how did she even know if they were right. Figures could mean anything. She looked at Joe, who was forever saying this, and found him silent, watching her, waiting to see how she would handle it, one eye drooping in the faintest touch of a wink.

The fierce answer that came in the end was born of loyalty to the people she had learned to love. To Alejandro. To Don Rafael and all he stood for.

"I never knew such poverty in Spain," she said tightly, "as to drive half or more of the population to emigrate, as they did from Ireland."

"For the love of God," cried a short, dark-haired young man, aptly named Curly, from out the bog road to Loughrea. "For the love of God," cried Curly, who could have been a Spaniard himself, "isn't that what it's all about. Weren't we in those days starving, under the heel of the British tyrants ourselves. Isn't that the whole story. Tyranny!"

I am ignorant, she thought. Ignorant. What do I know of it. What do I know of Estremadura? Or the slums of Barcelona or Madrid?

She felt suddenly she had spent her three years in a cloister, while a faster world went racing on without her. Where she had thought herself older, now she felt suddenly young and foolish.

She listened to them for a long time, railing against the tyranny of the monarchy and aristocracy in Spain. While the peasants starved.

Slowly in the end she lifted her head and looked all around them.

"I am no one to ask," she said, thinking of Doña Serafina and her folded flag. "I am no one to ask. I have only lived among the tyrants. And would fight for them myself," she added bravely into a stunned silence, "were I a man."

Like Alejandro. And die for them.

Joe came over abruptly and sat down beside her, and after a moment someone changed the conversation and they went racing on to something else, their young voices clear over the dark sea, the light gone now save for one bright strip the yellow of a primrose up above the black hills. The lamps were lit in the bar behind them, and the rocks were growing cold.

"C'mon, c'mon," said someone. "The mother's away to Dublin. We'll go to my house and have a bit of a dance. We have a new record just for you, Emily. Lady of Spain!"

They laughed, and one of the boys took her arm, arguments forgotten, and they went back across the sandy road to the cars.

Always they moved in a crowd, proud of its size and closeness. The Gang. Indeed, the first question any mother asked of a girl going out was how many others were going. A sort of chaperonage,

Emily realized, almost as careful and formal as the old aunts and
the duennas, in Spain. If the girl said no one else was going, then
she would be made to stay at home. Only when a couple declared
themselves serious—and it took all hell to break it up after that,
as many a boy who moved prematurely had found out—were
they allowed to go out alone.

Like herself and Alejandro.

But this crowd was older. Much older, especially the men.
Even her dear Joe, in Andalusia, would have well-grown children
by now. She and Alejandro had been little more than children
themselves. Yet so much older.

She rode a great deal with her mother over the green soggy
countryside of early summer, still heavy with the winter's rains.
They talked a lot about getting the horses into condition for next
winter's hunting.

"I've been lazy these last months of the winter," her mother
said. "Letting Tom Tracy the vet ride them, the poor things,
having to carry his weight. Joe's been too busy to come out with
me. But he has an assistant now, young Paddy Quinlan, and next
winter'll be better for him. We'll have some great days together
again."

Great days together.

Emily looked at her mother, groomed and smart in a sweater
and breeches and boots. Doña Serafina would have a stroke if she
saw her. But what had made her lose all her appetite for the great
days just because Emily hadn't been there? There were plenty of
people would go a day's hunting with her.

Sadly, she realized her mother had been lonely.

But winter, she thought. By next winter it could all be over!
How could that rabble of Republicans resist the Army? It would
all be over by winter and she back in Spain. With Alejandro.
Married.

She turned to her mother and smiled.

"We'll do that," she said. "Great days."

Her mother ran an appraising eye over her. The child had
grown unbelievably in Spain.

"We'll have to get you some new riding clothes," she said,
looking at the thin ankles sticking out from below the too-tight
jodhpurs. "We'll go up to Dublin in the summer and see to it."

Bleakness swept Emily. Despite the kindness and understanding when she first came home, now that she had got her back,

her mother had completely forgotten Alejandro. If indeed he had ever been real to her. She had also forgotten the green-frogged Andalusian jacket with the yellow velvet facings; hanging in the press upstairs; waiting for the return of different great days, in the high Spanish saddle with the heavy metal stirrups. The sun hot on your head and the prickly pears catching at your skirt along the side of the narrow paths.

She kicked her heels suddenly into her horse's flanks, making him jump, and then sending him off at a gallop around the flank of a long bare hill.

"Watch out for rocks, Em!" her mother called after her.

Anna telephoned. Full of apologies for not having done so before. They had been in England, she said. Her brother Dermot, the one in the RAF, had had leave, and instead of coming to Keene they had gone to England to join him. Her father, she said, had a house in Shropshire, and added that there was a girl there at Ironbridge that her brother was keen on, so he liked to spend his leaves there.

"You must come to Ash," Anna said, "in the winter with us. For the hunting. Lovely country. You'd like it, Emily."

Another one, thought Emily, who was sure she would be here in the winter.

She agreed amiably, and there began for her a quiet, pleasant time of friendship with Anna and her family. Going over to Castle Keene to play tennis on the smooth perfect tennis court beyond the orchard, the long gray pillared house sleeping in the soft sun. At some of these tennis parties she met occasionally Joe's friends, and wondered if they preached Karl Marx to the Earl of Keene. They were smoother here and less ebullient, but their compliments no less outrageous.

At other times she would go to dinner, and to stay the night with Anna afterwards, a little surprised to discover that the family lived in one corner of a wing of the great house. Taken on its own, it would be no more than the size of Emily's own home. She remembered being afraid to telephone because the place was so big that she was doubtful about ever reaching Anna.

The big double front door behind the pillars was closed and locked, and the lovely rose marble staircase led up to nothing but shadows.

"I'd steeled myself," said Emily, "to walking half a mile along dark passages with a candle, to get to my bedroom."

Anna smiled, the fitful lights of the Shannon Scheme electricity gleaming in the smooth pale gold of her hair.

"If you slept in the main house, you'd have to," she said. "We only have the Scheme in this wing."

And what of the rest of it, Emily wondered. So beautiful a house. Left to the damp and the cobwebs and even the rats, like so many similar Irish houses of this time.

She loved it there; the quiet atmosphere of the household fitting her own waiting mood. Life here seemed almost suspended, as it was with her. The family was highly cultured and interesting, kindly with the ease and calm of its position. Warmly affectionate as they got to know her better. As Don Rafael and Doña Serafina had been. But the Kilpatricks were broadminded and more amusing, and more sophisticated, and there was a great deal of laughter. Paul, the eldest son who lived at home and helped his father run the estate, was steady and charming and more than a little attentive.

"B'God, Em," her mother said one day when he had brought her home after a weekend. "You could get yourself an earl there if you tried. They're a fine handsome lot."

"Anna says her brother Dermot in the RAF is the handsomest of all," said Emily. "And he's a lord, of course. That should please you, Mums."

But she didn't want an earl. Or a lord. Or to try and get one. She wanted Alejandro, and fended off Paul's attention as she fended off gracefully all the compliments and propositions of Joe's friends.

In Anna's home, at least, she could talk of Spain. They were very anxious themselves, for news of the grandmother, from whom they had not heard for weeks, dug in obstinately in her old house below Gibralfaro. Nor at Castle Keene was there any talk of tyrants.

So she carefully passed the hours. And through them the days. And the weeks. And months. Still waiting every morning for the postman, and listening desperately to the whistling wireless set that no one could get to work properly; grasping for every word concerning what was happening in Spain. Her mother always got the English papers, as the Irish ones, she said, God help them, did tend to think that the death of Tommy Murphy's pig was more important than the death of any king. Or country.

Every night when the papers came on the mail train, the news from Spain would be of violence and disorder; with endless talk of the generals rising, which never seemed to come. Emily would lay the paper down with little heart for what she had read, and go back to Joe and his friends in the little morning room that had always seemed to belong to him; or settle in the lamplight with her mother, to summon her patience to wait for the postman in the morning.

In June Remedios wrote, confusing her with a Bristol postmark and an English stamp; sending her heart thudding for one lunatic moment with the hope that for some wild reason Alejandro was in England. To see her, maybe. Soldiers did have leave. Anna's brother did. Not even the papers or the wireless had yet made her understand the bloody crisis that was overtaking Spain, when no man capable of holding a gun would be spared long enough even to write a letter.

She recognized Remedios's spidery writing and opened it a little less quickly. Still, she might have news of him. Even to see his name written down would help to dispel the gathering mists of unreality. Remedios did mention his name, but only to say they had not heard from him. His mother, she said, had written to Emily directly. Had she not got the letter, as there had been no answer?

"No," said Emily to nobody, standing alone in the cool hall. "I never got it."

And were there more that she had never got, she wondered, from Alejandro himself?

The letter from Remedios was to tell her that she was no longer in Málaga. Her father had had warning that all private traveling was to be forbidden, and before that happened, he had packed off all the women of the family who were still in Málaga, putting them into the cars with their servants who wished to go, and sent them all off to the bull ranch in the wide safe open spaces between Jerez and Cádiz; on the windswept edges of the salt marshes, where, even when the trouble came, there should be an almost bloodless Nationalist victory in that land of rich and ancient privilege and loyal servants.

The tyrants again, thought Emily.

But what of Doña Serafina?

Doña Serafina had refused to leave her husband or her house, even though most of it had been closed up and she and Don

Rafael were living in a few small salons on the opposite side of the patio from the kitchen.

Málaga, Remedios said, was heartbreaking. All normal life finished, and Republican Guards patrolling the streets and standing with machine guns before all the public buildings. Fear and expectancy and sporadic violence held the streets, and any kind of respectability had become an offense. Men had been shot for wearing a tie.

The letter went on. It would come from England, Remedios said, or even Galway, as she had an arrangement to give her letters to friends in the bodegas in Jerez. They would then send them to England or Ireland, on ships going from Sanlúcar or Puerto Santa Maria.

Emily read the message of love that finished the letter, and came back to her surroundings with difficulty, looking rather vaguely around the hall that was her favorite room in the house. Perfectly square, the floor of beautiful black and white marble tiles, on which her mother would allow no rug. White woodwork and dark green walls patched with pictures and photographs, and the stairs going up along one side of it, the carpet the exact green of the walls. Three wide comfortable armchairs stood around the Adam grate where the turf fire glowed through summer as well as winter, for the hall never got the sun. Always on the chests and tables, her mother's exquisite flowers.

She tried to imagine it closed and dark and under threat, her mother living in the little room that Aggie had beside the kitchen.

The telephone rang on the table beside the window.

"Emily?"

"Yes."

It was an effort to bring back her mind.

"Cieran here, Em. What about the flicks tonight?"

"Ah, yes, it's Thursday. Yes, Cieran, I'd love it. Joe's going, I know, and so's Sarah."

"I'll gather you up at half past ten, then."

Spanish hours. The cinema began at eleven.

"Do that. And thanks."

"Good-bye now."

Cieran. One of Joe's friends. Assistant to the local vet. She saw him quite often at Anna's. Dublin, and typical of it. Small and dark and affectionate with a hilarious wit like a razor. And very keen on her.

Nothing wrong with him. Nothing wrong with any of them, indeed, she thought wearily, except that they weren't Alejandro. And she loved the pictures. Forms were dragged from an empty barn and you sat with your feet in the mud on a hard bench for sixpence, for in the sunless dark, the floor was rarely dry, the roof that held out sun having little to offer against rain. The film broke regularly, and the audience screamed and yelled and wept through every inch of it. There was a lot of shrieking and bottom pinching and general fumbling along the benches, and up in the rafters at the back, there were more Occasions of Sin than the parish priest had ever thought of.

Emily sighed and smiled. Which was her world? Would she always miss one for the other?

Alejandro was her world. Where he was, then there she would belong. But she wept with laughter, lying against Cieran's shoulder, at Eddie Cantor and his disintegrating chariot in *Roman Scandals*, and out in the front the fifteen-stone vet Tom Tracy laughed so much he went down through his deck chair and it took five people to haul him out of the frame. The night was clear and soft and bright with stars when it was over, and they all took a turn down to the river before they went home, hanging over the bridge to watch the starlight trembling in the glassy curtain of the waterfall above the mill, and reliving the film, laughing still.

In the kitchen when they got home, they made tea, and she told Joe about the letter from Remedios. He looked at her, his face creased as though the reading had hurt him, and shook his head, and she knew that he was thinking just as she was thinking. That the days of the two parents were almost surely numbered; hiding in the bottom of their house in loneliness with brave courage. Waiting for the rising that never seemed to come, and that would not necessarily bring deliverance for them. In Republican Málaga.

"God help them all," said Joe compassionately. "Would you like a drop of the craythur?"

He waved the whiskey bottle at her, having put a good dollop in his own tea.

"I would that," she said, having never tasted it before, but feeling the need of some comfort even Joe couldn't give her.

"What would Mums say?" she asked as he tipped the gold-labeled bottle almost savagely over her tea.

"She's asleep," he said practically.

She didn't really care for the taste of the whiskey, but by the time she had finished it, she knew she was smiling, although she was not quite sure at what, and Aggie's copper pans seemed to be flashing more gleaming lights than usual on the opposite wall.

"C'mon now," said Joe. Carefully he put the dishes out for Aggie in the scullery, not from tidiness, but because he knew he could carry his head to work in the morning if he didn't, and turned down to a glimmer the hanging oil lamp, which was never allowed to go out, above the kitchen table.

His lively face was sharp with pity and anger. Couldn't the bloody Spanish have got on with their own mess without involving his harmless little sister? He steered her up the stairs and into her bedroom, and exactly as he had planned, although she went to sleep still in sad muddled thoughts of Spain, she woke more tranquilly in the morning after a deep sleep, to all the sounds of Ireland.

Her mother was clattering off down the drive between the hedges in the cool morning for a ride before breakfast. Emily wished she had been with her.

The rosy-cheeked girl who helped Aggie in the house came from one of the cottages beside the gates; sauntering up the avenue in the long grass underneath the trees, in what looked like her brother's boots. Cusheen, everybody called her, and if she had a real name, no one knew it. Her meeting with her mistress did nothing to hurry her steps.

"Good day, ma'am," Emily heard her call. "A good soft day for the horse!"

She heard the big boots crunching on the gravel around the house and felt sympathy with her in the bright morning. Who would want to go to work on such a day, closeted in Aggie's scullery and scrubbing the kitchen floor. A few moments later, as she went along the landing to the bathroom, she heard Cusheen in full high argument with Willie down in the hall, about some fish that Aggie did mean for his supper last night.

Emily closed the bathroom door and smiled. It could all have been coming from the Patio of the Motors in the house in Málaga.

It was bright weather, but with the soft rainclouds of July massing away over to the west, when Emily and her mother came walking back easily from a morning ride some week or two later.

They came up towards the back of the house from the open country, across the stony pastures with their hawthorn hedges and through the line of elms between them and the garden. As they came under the elms, moving from gold morning to bands of deep shadow underneath the trees, she saw Joe up on the terrace.

Without a word spoken she knew he was not there for the morning air. So did her mother.

"Go over the garden, love," she said, and held out her hands for Emily's reins. Emily slid off Cuchulain and raced up the sloping lawn. How often she had heard it said that in dreams your feet were heavy with foreboding. She could barely lift them from the grass. Joe met her at the sundial, set in its circle of fuchsias and lobelia, pinks and lilacs and bright brilliant blue, vivid with the strength of color of the early day.

"Alejandro?"

"No, pet, no. Not Alejandro. But there is news that the rising of the Army has taken place in Spain."

"Where?"

"Chiefly in Morocco. And Andalusia. Two generals called Mola and Franco."

She laid her hand a moment on the sundial, as if the cold stone could steady her. Newsprint swam into her mind. Spanish text. And a photograph.

Franco. The little fat one.

"All over Andalusia, it seems. Algeciras, Seville, Jerez, Cádiz, Córdoba. All initially successful."

She sorted the names from his Irish pronunciation.

"Málaga?" she said sharply.

No word of Málaga.

She looked up in silence at Joe's concerned face, and then along the length of the gentle gray house with its balustraded terrace and spotless paint. Her mother was coming quickly over from the stables. There were a couple of blackbirds going off their heads down in the elms, and she could hear a cock crowing somewhere in the village.

*Arriba España.*

Spain was at war. And so was Alejandro.

Life went on. There were still the outings and the dances and the lunatic cinema, and now all the political talk was of Spain. She listened to it, and was clearly thought a strange and disinterested girl not to be holding any opinions. There was only one question in her mind, and she could not get beyond it.

The summer fields clacked with reapers and binders, racing against the rain, and across the stubble the corncrake complained harshly of the intrusion on his peace.

At the end of July the Galway races gathered in every living soul, from earl to gypsy, that could be drawn from the four corners of Connaught and much of the rest of Ireland as well.

Emily would not go.

"Better you do, little sport, little sport," said Joe, but she shook her head. Too many happy people.

"Darling," her mother said, "it could go on for years. You can't stay at home forever."

Emily looked at her, eyes dark with shock.

For years? A few months, Don Rafael had said.

And for all that happened in the end, on that patchy, wind-swept day of sun and sudden showers, she might as well have gone.

If he is dead, her mother wanted to say to her bluntly, a little irritated, then there is nothing any of us can do about it, and a few hours here or there will make no difference. If he is wounded, then it is almost the same. No one can go to Spain now, except to fight. No one can go rushing to his side.

But she held her patience and was gentle with Emily, managing in the end to persuade her to come up to Dublin with her the following week for the Horse Show; and to buy some new clothes. A good distraction for the child, she thought.

"I never dreamt," she said, "that you would grow so much. We'll have an orgy in Switzers."

She didn't want to tell her either, that privately she thought her Spanish clothes old-fashioned and rather prim, and rather to her surprise Emily found herself totally unable to resist the brilliant atmosphere of Ballsbridge, in the Horse Show Week, bright star of the Irish social year.

How Alejandro would have loved it. And matched it, she thought. The splendid horses, the air of grandeur and excitement; fine men and lovely brilliant women, and for all that the whole thing still like a village marketplace, with everybody knowing everybody else, and the whole lot going mad over Danny Corry, who could have jumped the Customs House itself.

There was inevitably talk of the war in Spain, but rather more as if Spain, poor creature, had fallen to the same disease from which Ireland was only just past its convalescence. There were also compliments and invitations to go dancing, and a splendid new dance dress of pale blue billowing net, sewn with silver threads and a bodice without any top that would have given Doña Serafina the vapors for a week.

And the new young Master of the Fingal Harriers to escort her; friend of her eldest brother.

"Your jacket!" she cried to him, staring, when he came to the Shelbourne to collect her. The dark old paneled rooms were glittering with vitality and wit, the men in their Hunt jackets as gaudy peacocks as any of the women, and knowing it well.

"What's the matter with my jacket?" Fergus cried. "Do I have egg on it?"

He looked down alarmed at his short green jacket with the yellow facings, and smoothed it at his waist, knowing there was no egg, and exactly how fine he looked in it.

"It's the same as mine," she said, and over her sherry told him of her Andalusian habit in the dark green, with the facings of yellow velvet.

"B'God," he said, his eyes running over the sudden charming vitality that so changed her face. She must be dead keen on Spain. "B'God, we must take the field together. We'd make a fine matched pair!

"Spain," he said then. "They're at each other's throats there, the fools."

And that for the rest of the week was the end of Spain; and sorrow and loneliness and even the cold gnawing fear that had come with the news that the Army had gone to war. All drowned in a tide of endless fun and charm.

On the last night, after the last ball, they walked slowly along the quays in an opal-colored dawn, the mist lifting in pale swaths from the line of colored houses over across a river lying like dark glass below them.

Slowly and sedately a Guinness barge steamed past, a few disturbed sea gulls round her mast, and her wake drawn black behind her down the river. Fergus stopped.

"Willya look at that now," he said, leaning over the stone parapet to watch the barge, and there was deep respect in his voice. "Willya look at that now." Emily waved to the man at the wheel, who waved back and shouted something to them, grinning.

"All that bounty," said Fergus reverently, "for the world. Aren't they great benefactors of mankind, the Guinnesses."

They watched it on under the bridge, and then he turned to her and smiled. God but she was beautiful.

"Em," he said. "Em. We've had some great times."

Great times. Like her mother. But they had.

"Oh, Fergus, yes." she said, and meant it. "I've so enjoyed myself!"

More than I believed possible, she thought, and in the gratitude of the moment smiled at him with a warmth he was glad immediately to take advantage of. He leaned over and put an arm around her, moving in for the kiss he thought would be welcome.

Quickly she turned her head.

"No, Fergus, please."

Ah, God, thought Fergus, here comes the Catholic Church, and at the fleeting distaste on his face she felt guilty and unkind. He had done nothing to deserve unkindness.

"What's the matter with me, then?" he asked her. "Am I so repulsive?"

She smiled at him again, easier, and his arm tightened around her in a gesture of responsive affection. Repulsive. She looked at his very Irish face, with the high cheekbones and the crinkling green eyes, hair curling thick and lightly red across a broad forehead. Had she never seen Alejandro, she might well have been bowled over. He waited patiently for her answer, and she didn't know what to say. How sloppy to say her kisses were kept for someone else, even though so far and hopelessly away. But it was the truth.

She didn't have to say it.

"There's someone else," he said, and sighed.

She nodded.

"In Spain?"

"Yes."

He brightened immediately.

"Ah, that's a good splendid distance away, and they're all killing each other anyway. You'll come hunting in the winter, and then it's every man for himself."

Privately he hoped the fella would get a bullet through him, and as fast as possible. But he didn't try to kiss her again, taking her arm and twining his fingers through hers; sauntering on along the quays past the blank windows of Jury's Hotel, where those who had even managed to reach their beds were still asleep, and would be for a long time yet. Beyond O'Connell Bridge toward the sea, the red sun had turned the Liffey to a sheet of fire.

"Bad cess to him," said Fergus, still thinking of the Spaniard.

He saw her off at Westland Row the next day when they were going back.

"Don't forget now," he said to her as the train moved out, reluctantly relinquishing her hands. "The next time bring the green habit and we'll stun County Wicklow."

"Tell me," he shouted suddenly as the train moved. "Did we really see a Guinness barge? Was it there?"

Leaning out the window, she laughed and nodded, delighted. That dawn for her, too, had held the quality of an iridescent dream.

She flopped back into her seat, looking with vague eyes out the window as the mail train clacked out through the suburbs of Dublin; bright gardens of gray houses showered with roses reaching down to the line; then out along the banks of the still canal that held the color of the sky, fringed with ragged marguerites, where small boys fished and screeched and bathed, treasuring their holidays.

Her eyes were bright and her new gray Glen Urquhart suit became her, and her mother thought she had never seen her looking prettier.

She felt her eyes on her and smiled.

"I haven't forgotten, Mums," she said.

"No, my pet. Just a bit for a little while. Which was exactly what I wanted. You did enjoy it."

Emily nodded, and the light was still in her eyes.


There was a letter waiting when they reached home, still lighthearted and touched with the happiness of their holiday.

"I didn't telephone you," said Joe, "as it only came by the evening post, and you'd be here anyway. It must have been lying down there since the morning."

Only local letters came by the evening mail, and the postmark on this one was Plymouth.

Remedios was brief and factual, using no more than a few of the simplest words, as though war had taught her already the uselessness of looking for pity. Or that she dare not be gentle with herself lest she could not write at all.

"The poor child is still in shock," Mrs. McRoss breathed, as she read it after Emily, who had handed it to her wordlessly.

José, wrote Remedios, had come to them at the *ganadero* after a journey full of terror from both sides, for who was he to be wandering free without a gun in his hands, neither killing nor being killed himself. He came on foot. Half-starved, hiding by night, and cadging lifts on slow-moving carts whenever he dared.

With him he carried his broken heart, and the difficult tired words with which to tell them what had happened when they all rushed out to him in the patio of the big white colonnaded house, which looked as if it had never heard of war.

The rising of the Nationalists and the Army had not been successful in Málaga. Against the threat of bombardment from the sea, the civil governor had not dared to act, so that the strength and violence of the Republicans was intensified; enraged by the failed uprising. Don Rafael and many like him were no more than hiding in their own houses, their lives at peril in the streets.

In the nature of the twisted jealousies loosed by civil war, hatreds and antagonisms never before acknowledged had boiled to the surface in the population, like the must on the fermenting wine.

A score of them, José said, and here he began to weep slow sad tears, carving runnels down the dust on his face. A score of them, young savages who would once have been glad of a peseta for blacking the *dueño*'s boots, had come crashing into the Patio of the Motors. It was the old nun, he said. Someone had told them. Or reminded them. They went around kicking open every door until they found her, as if it were worth it, poor old skeleton that she was.

"It must have been someone," said José bleakly, "who belonged in the casa. And had told them where to look."

Foolishly the Doña Serafina had come running, screeching at them for the rubbish that they were; trying to take the old woman from their hands.

In the dreadful silence in the patio, with the sun brilliant and the small birds chittering in the bougainvillaea, they all looked at him and could see her in that moment; in the shadowed ruin of what had been her home; loosing on them in one last outburst all the anguish of her loneliness and sorrow.

"Have her then," yelled one of them, and in a shaft of

sunlight José knew him for the brother of the donkey boy.
Pascalito. His father a good man. "And you go with her!"

He threw her into Doña Serafina's arms, so that the one hail of
his bullets killed them both.

"And you, too, Señor," another of them said with infinite
courtesy and then a cackle of laughter. "We would not wish you
to be left behind."

They came back the next day and threw the servants into the
streets and took the house, telling them they were lucky to be left
with their lives after serving the Nationalist capitalist scum.
During the long grieving night, when they did not even dare to try
and bury the dead, it had been agreed that José should try to
make his way to Cádiz to tell the women. The brothers Ramon
and Javier were already in the Army, and they did not know
where the other one might be.

All this Remedios had reduced to a few painful stilted sentences,
finally begging Emily for her prayers for all of them. She remembered to add that she would pray for Alejandro.

Emily read it where Joe had given it to her; read it with the
same cool sick sorrow with which Remedios had written it, and
the lovely Dublin week faded away to shadows, and the dancing
and the laughing and the Andalusian habit in the mud of County
Wicklow.

Mrs. McRoss was truly grieved for Serafina, for whom she
had cared deeply, but there was nothing any of them could do
except to write to Remedios with all the platitudes familiar in the
face of death, the most inevitable platitude of all. She went
slowly upstairs, thinking to herself, and not for the first time, that
for the sake of her dear Emily she would gladly have no sorrow
to see Alejandro and Spain and the whole gillivrang at the bottom
of some deep blue sea.

As if to defy her, Alejandro wrote himself at the end of
August; a letter as full of love and promise and sorrow for all the
long silence as any lonely heart could wish for.

"Oh, Mums," Emily cried, and in her ecstatic happiness
threw her arms around her mother's neck. Mrs. McRoss smiled
and kissed her and tried to share her pleasure.

Nothing, Alejandro wrote, had changed. His writing was black
and strong and handsome, like himself.

"*Querida mia*, it is as it has always been. My heart was

broken that I did not reach the cathedral on our wedding day, but I have nonetheless ever since felt you to be my wife.''

And you my husband, thought Emily.

''Emilia *mi alma*, it will not take long. We are at the beginning of the end, and the animals that killed Remedios's parents will go back where they belong. The world will be ours again. Wait, my loved one, wait. All will be well. . . .''

The postmark was actually Galway. He had, he said, been in Seville, and was now in Jerez, one of the first fairly small number of regular soldiers of the Army to come over from Morocco.

He saw Remedios, the good God pity her, fairly often, as the *ganadero* lay between Cádiz and Jerez, and was not far away. And in Jerez the rising had been easy, the rabble only holding out a couple of days against the Army.

''But enough of war, *cielo*,'' he wrote. ''It will not last long and then we will be able to take up all our plans. My love for you is unchanged, querida Emilia. All my life is yours.

''Above my heart I still carry the ring I bought to marry you that morning.''

There was more of his undying love and of all their unchanged plans for their life together in a new and better country.

At the end he said, ''. . . but you must spare me awhile, querida, to be a proud soldier of the new Spain.

''Remedios sends you her *saludos*. And I my heart.''

Through the blissful happiness that transformed the day, a small troubling snake of doubt squirmed in her mind for notice. Fiercely she crushed it. Why should he not be seeing Remedios? Were they not cousins who had known each other from childhood? And what family in sorrow did not cling together?

She was a different girl, singing around the house and going off exuberantly every day to help stoke the hay that had been so slow in drying. Joe's friends found her doubly enchanting and made double the advances, and with bright warm eyes and laughter she parried them and turned them aside, sliding away like the will-o'-the-wisps that glowed and danced above the pasture pond at night.

''Leave her alone,'' Joe said. ''The girl's in love.''

''And who,'' cried one of them, ''could be in love with a Spaniard, and them tearing each other's throats out. There won't be one of them left to be in love with at the end of it!''

"Like us," Joe answered dryly.

"Us! Wasn't it the English we were after!"

"Not all of us."

"True for you. But for your sister's sake, I'd be mean enough to hope the Spaniard gets a bullet in his gizzard from whatever side he isn't on. If he knows. For I'm damned if I can tell one side from the other."

Joe left it, although his mind was filled with doubts. Em was happy now, but for how long?

It was on August fifteenth that they heard the news of Badajoz, Emily racing in hot and dusty from the fields lest she miss the news at seven o'clock. Her mother was at her desk by the window.

And they listened in stunned silence to the news of the massacre of Badajoz, where the Army had herded two thousand unarmed Republicans into the bullring and shot them.

"Alejandro," she whispered, white-faced. "It said the Army of Africa. Alejandro."

Her mother couldn't stand her face, and there was murder in her own heart.

"Sweetheart, pet. Maybe he wasn't there."

All Emily could find to tell herself was that soldiers were under orders, and no matter what they were told to do, they were compelled to do it. Little knowing she was trying to answer a problem that would all too soon confront a world shattered by atrocities beside which Badajoz was nothing.

"Thank God," said Mrs. McRoss afterwards to Joe. "Thank God we got her back in time. I wish she had never gone to Spain."

"Mama, it's their war, and we know damned little about it or them. It's like Ireland. It's not yesterday's hates will be coming up there now. It'll be hates a hundred years old or more. Half the poor fools fighting here thought they were fighting Cromwell. Can I get you a drink? You look as if you need one."

The letter from Alejandro came quickly, postmarked Bristol. It was almost without a beginning. Almost incoherent.

"I was not at Badajoz, Emilia. Not at Badajoz. Dear God, I have not slept lest you should think I was. It was the Legion. The Foreign Legion. There are few of us regulars here yet, as General

Franco does not have the airplanes and the Republicans hold the sea. It was the Legion. The Legion.''

"That'd never pass a censor if it saw one," Joe remarked dryly as he read it.

"I have my own news," the letter went on, "and before God I must say that had I been in the Plaza de Toros in Badajoz with my rifle in my hand, I would probably have done the same as any other and been glad to do it. There, it is said.

"You will know that there are not many big estates in Catalonia, but my parents have one of them. Had one of them.''

Emily gave a choking cry at the correction.

"They came at night, the Communists from Barcelona, and dragged them from their beds, and made them dig their graves and shot them. My father first so that my mother should have the pleasure of seeing him die. And the old curé with them, because he happened to be in the house.

"They threw the servants out and fired the house and went off laughing. I was told this by people who watched it. So whom, my querida Emilia, will God pardon? Do not judge me ever, *mi vida*, no matter what you hear, for we can only do as we are told. How I would sell all I have, indeed my life, to be within reach of your comfort. But Remedios is very good to me.''

All the terrible tragic implications of the letter for a moment slipped sideways, out of her mind.

*Remedios is very good to me.*


Through all the golden days of autumn, with the first leaves drifting from the elms and the mists beginning to spangle the thistles and the hedgerows in the mornings, the wireless through its fretted face poured out the cool, impartial record of violence and atrocity, success and failure, on both sides, and the growing concern of all the other countries of Europe.

The last barn doors were closed on the summer's reapings, and the great gold harvest moon of September hung like a lantern over the blanched fields, tranquil, bringing the first hint of long nights and the peace of Christmas. Fires were lit in the drawing room and the dining room from a shovelful of hot sods from the kitchen fire, gusting the house with smoke and the sweet haunting smell of the turf, stacked roof-high for the winter beyond the kitchen outhouse.

Lamps were lit now for the dinner, and at the end of it came

the crisp freshly picked apples, and there were basketfuls of them
for Pat and John to take home to Galway, where their house had
no more than a pocket handkerchief of a garden, and a few
chrysanthemums blasted by the salt wind.

"I tell myself," said Pat, "I can't be a horticulturist and a
doctor at the same time."

"And why would you try," said Mrs. McRoss, "when we
have enough and to spare. And who else would we give it to."

Pat smiled at her across the table, loving her. When you
thought of the harridans some people got for mothers-in-law, she
was the luckiest girl in the world.

They were all careful not to talk of Spain now, as they might
skirt round the certain death of some member of the family.
Emily joined the game, although still listening quietly to the chill
impersonal reports that came over every day, of slaughter and
atrocities on both sides; hopelessly endeavoring to relate it to the
Spain that she had known.

I only knew the skin of it, she thought. Only the skin of it.

At the end of September three of the village lads went off to
join the International Brigade. Emily watched with Joe from the
windows of his office as they marched off to a heroes' farewell,
huge grins pinned to their slightly puzzled faces; the town band
before them blowing and heaving at the "Soldiers' Song" and
the "Internationale," or as near as they could get to it. All the
town's children hopped and skipped along beside them in the
dusty gutters, yelling "Down with Franco," with no notion at all
who Franco might be, but their big brothers had told them to give
it all they had. Behind them marched all their weeping relatives,
their faces buried in their shawls and grimy handkerchiefs.

Emily watched in silence as they passed by. All the black-clad
women and the collarless men; tramping along the narrow gray
street. All the shrieking and weeping. It could, she knew, happen
unaltered in some mountain pueblo up at the back of Málaga.

Joe watched in sour anger, slamming his hand on the windowsill.

"Who got hold of those eejits?" he demanded furiously.
"Eddie Gargan there in the middle hasn't the wits to bless
himself since he fell off a haycart when he was seven. And the
other two are little better. They'll go out there and get their heads
blown off and never find out why. Or even who for."

Emily didn't smile or correct him.

"Wouldn't it be enough, though," she said "to tell them that they could go out there and do all the fighting they wanted, and get paid for it too.''

"True enough," said Joe. "True enough."

Even as she spoke she was wondering bleakly if any one of those might hold the gun or throw the bomb that would kill Alejandro.

Through the cold windy days of November she learned to drive the family Buick, with Joe pretending a thousand heart attacks in the seat beside her. As her mother had predicted, they had many great days with the Blazers, and she saw a lot of Anna, ambling home together to one house or the other through lilac evening touched with frost, and the sun sliding down past the edge of the known world in a blaze of green and scarlet, swimming against the deep purple tide of the approaching night. The first stars pricking from the darkening sky, promise of the cold night to come.

Life was pleasant, and beautiful, and serene, and often the greatest fun; all laid on a base of aching loneliness and an inescapable sense of shame. There had been no more letters, so for every fearful thing that happened she had to assume that he was there, and apportion him his share of guilt. What matter if the others did it too.

Alejandro. Had she ever really known him? Or only the skin of him, which was all she'd known of Spain?

The letter from Remedios came in the middle of December when her mother was awash with Christmas cards and colored paper, and toys for all the children, which Joe would insist on playing with.

"Joe. You'll break it."

Joe was racing around the drawing room pushing a hen on a platform fitted with some device to make it flap its wings and let loose the most terrible raucous squawks.

"Do stop, Joe. You'll break it."

"That would be a kindness to the child's parents," Joe said, and looked for something else.

There were rich spicy smells floating in from the kitchen.

"I think I'll go and see what Aggie's doing," he said then. "She might be able to do with a bit of help."

"God help her," said his mother tranquilly, knowing Aggie was well able to look after herself. "Joe, have you no work to go to?"

Joe's long narrow face was outraged.

"Isn't it Saturday," he said. "And amn't I a rich man now with an assistant."

"Well, you can get on away to Higgins's then, and find out what they did with the bran I ordered."

Joe vanished like a wraith through the door to the kitchen, and Emily was left to go and answer the door to the postman.

"Good day to you, Miss Emily. There's one from foreign for you. 'Twill be Spain, no doubt. Aren't they in a terrible mess out there and the Germans and all with them. Would it be your young man?"

"I don't know, Peter, I don't know." Her hands were shaking as she closed the door almost in his face. "If you go round to the kitchen to Aggie, she'll give you a cup of tea."

She made herself sit down in the green velvet chair beside the hall fire before she opened it.

It was from Remedios, come directly, this one, from Cádiz, as though it would not be so terribly important if it had not reached her.

"Querida Emilia," she wrote, "I find it very difficult to write this letter to you."

He is dead, thought Emily, and she had the feeling of the strength ebbing cold also, from her own body. She forced herself to go on.

"I hope, querida, you will forgive us, and not cease to love us, as we will always love you."

She frowned, trying to make sense of it.

"You know that we have always known each other, and in these terrible days for our country, we are of the same mind and heart and so perhaps it is natural that these things happen."

It went on bewilderingly for a long time, while certainty crept like a tide of sickness through Emily's mind.

Remedios, who said she had not cared about Alejandro.

Only at the end did she put it into plain words.

"We drove out and were married secretly and by special permission in the Chapel of the Virgin of Rocio, La Paloma Blanca, in Almonte, in the dawn of yesterday.

"We hope that our white dove will be for peace, and that you will find it in your heart not to think ill of us."

Not to think ill of them. Dear God.

Alejandro. Remedios. Did they marry with the ring he had bought to marry her?

She shook the letter and turned the envelope upside down and shook it.

There was no word from Alejandro.

No one said "I told you so." Or "It's no more than we were afraid of." Or any of the similar things that would have driven her to fury. The thing was discussed and accepted and then left alone, to give her poor bitter heart a chance even to know that it had happened, never mind to heal. Only by an extra tenderness and quietness did they all show her that she was never from their minds or their compassion.

She felt infinitely grateful to them all, even to Aggie, who without comment laid before her every day all the things she liked best to eat.

Tears touched her often; helpless, intolerable pain.

"Mums, you're all so good to me."

"And if we weren't, who would be," her mother would answer briskly and kiss her, wanting nothing so much as to get Alejandro and his Remedios and put them both through the mincer out in the back kitchen. Slowly.

Only Joe spoke out, suggesting that the Spanish Civil War could be best settled by a *mano a mano* between him and the redoubtable Alejandro.

"Only" he added, dourly, "there wouldn't be much civil about it."

Anna rang.

"Did you hear, Anna?" Emily asked her, hoping not to have to put it into words.

"Yes, your mother told me."

"Can you believe it?"

Yes, Anna could believe it. Her family had been intermarried long enough with Spaniards. Unpredictable was the kind word for it. She steered Emily away.

"Em. We're having the Meet here on Boxing Day. Will you come, and stay the night? We're having a bit of a dance after-wards in the evening. It should be fun."

"Yes, I'd love to," Emily said at once, willing to accept any invitation. After the first shock, pride and anger had come to her rescue, and she was moping publicly for no Alejandro.

Christmas Day was of soft benign sunshine, with the house as Mrs. McRoss loved to see it: every room full. Pat and John were in from Galway, arriving late for lunch, thanks to some unfortunate farmer who had seen fit to have a coronary thrombosis out in the middle of the bog beyond Spiddal, well into Connemara. Felicity and Angus came from Edinburgh with their two small girls, and Sam and Grace over from where they bred racehorses in the gentle wilds of Berkshire. Ted arrived late on Christmas Eve in his usual chaos by the wrong train, having been staying with friends since school was out. And to complete it there was a hilarious telephone conversation with Mike on Christmas Day, following his father's footsteps as a surgeon in St. George's Hospital at Hyde Park Corner, unable to be with them because, he said, he had to carve the turkey for the paupers.

"There's a little poem about that," said Joe from the extension in the hall.

"Joe, be quiet! Remember the children."

They all felt lonely when the call was over. Only one missing. Or so they all felt, except their mother, who could never force such a moment past herself without her own long memories of loneliness and loss.

And Emily. A few months' struggle. All over by Christmas, they had said. Oh, Alejandro.

Angus opened the drawing room door and yelled down the passage at Aggie to ask had she given the dinner to the poor or what, and the day slid back to hilarity and dancing firelight, and tall candles spiking the late-lunch table as the day grew darker, the Christmas tree a glitter of stars and lights and tinsel in the wide window, the golden angel blowing his long trumpet on the top of it for as long as any of them could remember.

"We must have it for the children," Mrs. McRoss had said as she was dressing it, blissfully absorbed, a strand of hair falling from the knot at the back of her neck. Singing "See Amid the Winter Snow" to herself, carefully, word for word. The soft green land behind her out the window.

Joe put down his paper and watched her a long moment.

He got up and kissed her.

"Children," he said then. "To hell with the children, Mother dear. If you didn't have it, I'd go somewhere else for Christmas."

So Christmas Day had been all it should be, and after it Boxing Day was gray and dull, with a great silence hiding in the mist, as if to emphasize that the time of noise and fun and merriment was over.

Pat and John were dropping Emily at Castle Keene on their way back into Galway, the aches and pains of the gray city being unwilling to wait another day for them. She was going to have a late breakfast with Anna and her family before the Meet. The others had already started riding in the gray light of early morning; some lucky one would be coming with Mums in the horse box. Aggie and Willie and the two little girls following for their day of wild peripheral entertainment in the pony and trap.

She saw, for the first time, the front door open at Castle Keene, and came up curiously between the pillars of the wide front steps, as apathetic about the hunt today as she had been about Christmas yesterday, although she would die rather than show it; her spirit as gray and colorless as the December day.

Alejandro. Oh, Alejandro.

There were lamps still lit on the tables, and as she came into the hall Anna came out from behind the stairs, immaculate in her black jacket and white breeches; gleaming black boots. Double to Emily herself except for the gleam of light in the pale gold hair.

"Em! Did you have a good Christmas? Lovely to see you. You're just right for breakfast. We're having it in state this morning in the dining room, and we've had to open up some of the bedrooms for people. I only hope we won't find them mildewed when they come down."

Before Emily could say anything, a door slammed somewhere along the wide corridor running from the top of the stairs.

"Jesus Christ," said a voice. Musical and deep. No accent, but just a lilt to it that you would know it was Irish. "I know now what an Eskimo feels like." There was a pause, and the voice rose. "My boots! Where are my boots? Is Milligan dead or something?"

He came down the beautiful marble staircase in his stockings, fully dressed except for his hat, his stock impeccable, the skirts of his coat perfectly tailored over the white buckskin breeches that ended ludicrously above a pair of hand-knitted stockings in the bright yellow of a buttercup.

(Haven't they a wooden horse to sit you on to fit the things, he was to say to Emily long later, to be sure you won't split the backside out of the breeches. I feel the biggest fool in Christendom sitting there, with no head on it.)

He only saw Anna.

"Anna, some fool's taken my boots. Rustle them up, there's a good girl. These floors are cold."

Smashingly good-looking, Emily thought, like all of them, but as Anna said, this was the best-looking of the lot. Taller than Paul, only the cap of hair a little darker. Brown that looked as if in the sun it would have gold lights in it. Completely unperturbed about his yellow stockings.

He stopped and stood a moment as he saw the girl with his sister. Why had he some idea this friend from Spain was small and dumpy? Tall, she was. Perfect in her hunting clothes. Perfect. Strong fierce little face, and yet delicate. And that red-gold hair curling around the brim of her hat.

Emily knew he existed and knew his name, and tried to understand her sense of shock.

"Where are my bloody boots, Anna?"

"Milligan's polishing them. You can wear Cook's slippers while you have your breakfast. Come on now or we'll have the father after us. This is my friend Emily from Spain. And Clonfrack. Em, this is my brother Dermot."

The pause lasted so long that Anna had begun to look from one to the other.

" 'Morning, Emily," said Dermot then.

"Good morning, Dermot."


*SIX*


The next day she said good-bye to him lightly and thought no more of him than anybody else, finding him, like all her world at the present time, vague and insubstantial, as though it lay, inaccessible, beyond some cloudy sheet of glass.

Diligently she set herself to pass all the time before her, barren, to her mind, as the rock hills of Connemara. Seeking occupation of any kind to thrust away the pain that ripped with every thought of Remedios and Alejandro.

In January the girl, Delia, who worked as a receptionist to

Pat and John in Galway, announced her intention of getting married.

Pat rang up Emily one howling winter day, when she had just come in with frozen fingers from helping her mother in the stables.

"Would you like Delia's job, Em?" she asked her. She and John had discussed it, concerned as they all were about this sad quiet Emily who haunted the house like a ghost. They thought it a godsent opportunity.

"Me? Do Delia's job?" she asked, astonished. As the second youngest in the family, with no great ambitions even before Alejandro, the professional worlds of the older ones seemed far above her head. And her reach.

"Why not, she's only a bit of a girl the nuns got for us. You could make rings round her, Em. Come in for a couple of weeks before she leaves and get the hang of it."

"Why not?" Emily echoed her, taken by surprise, and by the first stirrings of interest and excitement she had felt for weeks.

Her mother sent Joe out to buy a car for her. Just some old crate that would get her in and out to Galway.

"You can't go on the train. They're miles from the station and there's no bus."

Joe came back with an old blue Singer with a top, surveying it critically with a face of distaste, although to Emily it looked perfection, standing there below the steps. My car, she thought, amazed.

"It's what the mother asked for," he said. "An old crate. But Thomsey Pitt tells me the engine is sound, and he knows if I find he's lying I'll hound him from here to New Zealand."

"You'd be gone a long time," Emily said, but something was coming alive in her as she walked around her car.

Her car!

"Show me how to put the top down, Joe."

"For the love of God," said Joe, peering at her over his overcoat collar. "Wouldn't you leave that till the swallows come."

"I'm here now," said Emily, already fiddling with the catches.

John had to keep his car outside his garage after that, grumbling bitterly, so that the open Singer could stay inside all day when Emily was at work. Room had to be cleared in the garage at home so that there was always space for it, moving half a lifetime's dumped rubbish.

"You'd think," said Joe bitterly, "it was the Queen of England's Daimler."

Emily became known along the Galway road morning and evening, clattering between the gray stone walls of the narrow road, waved to by builders and farmers and the men with sacks on their shoulders, working the ditches with slanes. Only the heaviest of rain drove her to put up the top, wrapped against the cold in her soft creamy teddy-bear coat, striped scarf streaming in the wind. Her feet were snug in a pair of warm sheepskin boots the mother had sent to London for, before the foolish child froze herself to death.

Watching her, she would have sent to London for a diamond necklace or the Crown Jewels themselves, did they contribute to this flare of individuality that should surely take Emily away in the end from grief and disappointment. And her preoccupation with the young Spaniard who had proved no more than the dream they had all feared. Surely she was happier.

Emily herself knew that in these months she was not happy. Happiness seemed something tangible she had once known, but that she watched now in other people with faint sorrow that was not even envy. It was not for her. But she was at least content, waiting for nothing now, expecting nothing; no longer poised on pinnacles of longing for letters or telephone calls, or anything else. At times, listening to the wireless, she shied away from a searing and unbearable sadness that asked her, in a persistent voice, how sure she was now that she would have wanted Alejandro to come back to her with his hands bloodied with the atrocities of Spain, no matter what his orders.

It would not have been the Alejandro she had loved.

The telephone rang at the beginning of July, into the middle of this careful living, and her mother called up to her to be quick, it was a call from London.

From London? Mike? Granny? But they would have spoken to her mother.

She raised her eyebrows questioningly as she picked up the phone.

"Emily here."

"Emily? Hello there. Dermot here."

The telephone hissed and crackled like the breakfast eggs in Aggie's pan, and she was so surprised she allowed a long moment of silence.

''Dermot here,'' he said again. ''You remember. Anna's brother.''

''But of course, Dermot. I'm very sorry. I thought you must be my brother or my grandmother.''

''Do I sound like your grandmother?''

She laughed. As a matter of fact, he did. Faint and far away.

''No,'' she said. ''But they're the only people I know in London.''

''Well, anyway, listen.'' She was listening, overwhelmed with the importance of being talked to on the telephone all the way from London, and had no doubt the Clonfrack Exchange would be overwhelmed too, and have it in every house in the village that the young McRoss girl had been called on the telephone by the Earl of Keene's son, with wild speculations as to how much it cost, and what it was all leading to. ''Listen,'' said Dermot. ''I'll be over for the Race Week, and I wondered would you let me take you to the Plate Day and to the dance in the evening. Sorry I didn't write and all that, to ask you, but I've only just found I can have leave.''

Race Week. She had forgotten, plowing on through her uneventful days. Galway races. And she'd forgotten. Or maybe she hadn't wanted to remember.

''Of course, Dermot,'' she said at once. ''I'd be delighted. It'd be lovely.''

She remembered him as easy, and uncomplicated. No emotional demands she couldn't handle. Anna's brother. Like her own brother. No more.

''Yes,'' she said again. ''I'd love it.''

They chatted a few moments of this and that, and then hung up. Emily looked thoughtfully at the black telephone as she laid it back in its cradle and then went out and through the dining room into the greenhouse, where her mother was tending all her treasures in a smell of loam and green leaves. She stood beside her and touched with an appreciative finger a deep rose-pink cyclamen, flowers tall and fragile over their bed of marbled leaves.

''Mums,'' she said. ''Imagine. It's the races in just over a fortnight and I'd forgotten. Imagine. Forgotten.''

Her mother shot her a sideways sardonic glance, her hands black with soft earth, and a smear of it across her forehead where she had brushed back her hair.

"Well, I'll tell you," she said. "You must be about the only one in County Galway that has. Who was it on the telephone?"

"Dermot Kilpatrick. To ask me to go to the Plate with him and the dance afterwards."

"Mmm," said her mother on a rising note. "All the way from London!"

Emily grinned, better able now to take and make such a joke.

"It doesn't mean, Mother, he's going to marry me."

She knew a faint surprise at herself that she could speak so lightly, even about Dermot Kilpatrick, who was nothing to her.

On the usual windy Irish July day, threatening with gray clouds from above the sea, they made their way in through the middle of the swarming throng pouring into the racecourse at Ballybritt. Tinkers and hucksters and drunks; fine men and beautiful women in their inimitable tweeds; families, and crowds of young people playing truant from work; sidecars and donkey carts, and ponies and traps; farm carts so laden that bodies kept falling off into the mud, to be heaved back on again with great shrieking and yelling. Now and again a carriage, dragged out and polished for the day from the cobwebbed shadows of some old coach-house. Ancient beautiful dogcarts with high wheels, and every possible kind of car that ever ran, from the occasional Rolls-Royce to the five-pound Austin Seven held together with string that asked for nothing more than that with the help of God it should get its owners to Ballybritt. Where with the same help of God they would make their fortunes and push the ruins into the ditch on the way home; to buy a new one.

In among them were all the ranks of the foot soldiers, pouring in on race trains and coaches in their thousands; serious-faced men in elderly trilby hats, already flushed with porter, the racing pages and their race cards clutched in their red hands, and a stub of pencil ready behind the ear. These were the hard-betting men from the stony lands of Galway, out for the high day of their year, which would have to serve for twelve months of talking and remembering, through the bitter labor of working their difficult land.

Dermot had come swooping up for Emily in his black Riley with the glittering silver spokes, easy and relaxed as if they had met yesterday, and she suppressed a jag of bitter memory as she eased herself into the low red-leather seat.

They ate their picnic lunch from the long hood of the car when they finally managed to park between a Guinness lorry and a coach-and-four, buttoning their coats against the salt wind from the sea, glad of the shelter of the high flanks of the lorry.

They plowed their way when it was finished, and the first race due, through the vast crowds to the bookies and the stands. And when the great moment came, they screamed and hugged each other as the winner of the Galway Plate came home like a bird over the sticks with their money on his nose. The wind tore at Emily's hair around the edges of her cap, and in the distance the sea was pale and cool as ice. When they met a despondent Joe bitterly tearing up his betting slips, they clapped him on the back with all the condescending cheerfulness of those who had known better, and took him off to the tent for a drink, finding there some of Joe's own friends and passing the rest of the day in an uproarious crowd.

Emily was never able to recall any real detail of that day. Only the uproar and the excitement, and banging their way through the wild crowd, and the smell of salt from the sea from the top of the open stand with the sun chasing great black cloud shadows over the green land beyond Ballybritt.

And a sense of oneness with Dermot that did not go even as deep as thought; simply to be doing together something that they both so loved. Old in both of them as their oldest memory.

And to think, she thought once, that I forgot about it.

Although she paid small heed to him as a person at the time, she knew afterwards that he had been a great part of it. Unassuming, a little quiet compared to the effervescence of most Irishmen; as effortless with the drunken sod-cutter from the estate who flung his arms round his neck and kissed him warmly when he had given him a winner, as he was with his own friends in their well-cut tweeds and soft hats and highly polished brown brogues; smooth beautifully groomed girls with them, who made Emily feel young and badly dressed, perfectly satisfied until then with her blue silk dress and a soft coat buttoned over it against the cold.

There was the usual stampede home when it was all over, to get a bite to eat and get ready for the dance, although that was made easier since, like the pictures, the dance kept Spanish hours and started at eleven, and that meant midnight or beyond before anything would happen.

It was Emily's first time to the Race Night Dance, for she had been too young before when all the others went. There was a certain thrill like biting into forbidden fruit to be going at last into the huge humid marquee with the lamplight vague as the mist that covered most of Eyre Square.

They joined a party of Dermot's friends as the accordions belted out about the "Ten Pretty Girls in the Village School," accepting a small grin from him about the one little cute redhead, although she had grown sick trying to laugh at all the jokes since the song first came out. The crowd were the same highly polished horsey lot they had met at the races, but now the girls all had beautiful expensive dresses, and smoothly waved hair shining in the lamplight, and she grew rather quiet, envying them their sophistication and their bright easy chatter about things she had never done. They were kind to her, all a little older, never leaving her out of anything, yet combining to make her feel ignorant and unsophisticated; to make her see her beautiful blue dress from Switzers, which God knew had cost enough, for what it was: her first adventure with a ball gown.

Yet Dermot, to her faint surprise, set her clearly and carefully above them all, and she caught a few questioning looks passing between them. He was endlessly attentive, dancing only with her, and slowly kindling in her a strange tentative excitement that she would never have believed possible.

As was the tradition of Race Night, they finished up at some three o'clock of a morning as warm and still as the previous day had been cold and gusty, their wraps in their hands, scratching at the tall door of a dark and shuttered hotel, curtains tight against all the lightless windows.

"There's no one there," said Emily, "it's closed." They didn't even answer her, waiting.

The door opened a crack, and light streamed out.

"Willya get in quick," said a hoarse voice, and they eased themselves inside, to find the entire place so crammed with lights and people that it was a long time before they could even move from their small tight space immediately inside the green front door.

"For God's sake," said one of the men then to Emily's astonished expression, "they couldn't leave the population without a drink on Race Night."

"What about the Garda?"

"Ah, they'll be along."

"I swear to God, and it's the truth," said Dermot, threading his way back gasping from the bar with a whiskey for himself and a sherry for her. "There are people actually drinking in the lavatories. 'Tis the same every year, of course, and every hotel in Galway the same."

In due course and time-honored ritual, they had with everybody else in the place to scurry out through the kitchens and the back door, across the nettles and the broken bottles of the yard.

The Garda beat with unhurried tolerance on the front door, waiting patiently until everyone was gone, and their check of the licensing laws would show the place empty; listening as they waited to all the customers streaming laughing and shrieking out by the back.

"It's like Spain!" said Emily, and knew it was. The same casual contempt for authority, and authority's casual contempt for itself.

"Don't they empty it three times a night," said someone, "and the same people do no more than go out the back and wait until they've gone away, then go in the front again."

"And no more is expected of them," said someone else out of the warm darkness.

Dermot and Emily didn't go back in. It was four o'clock and the daylight pale above the roofs of Galway City, the tired revelers beginning to thin out in the streets.

"Have you had enough now?" Dermot asked her, and she sighed, unwilling to let the day go, aware that as the hours had passed it had grown more precious.

"I have," she said, though. "It's almost time for the first race tomorrow, if you know what I mean."

"Many wouldn't," Dermot answered, but took her arm and steered her back through the people in the square, down to where he had parked the Riley, and they threaded their way back around the outside of the Hangar, where they had to stop for a singing line of some thirty people, arms locked across the road, in a wavering Palais Glide. The line broke to let them through, hammering genially on the windows with instructions as to what not to do on the way home.

On the long flat road past Oranmore it was suddenly clear lovely dawn, rose-pink over the green land and the sea all the colors of an opal. After all the happy rioting and the fun of the long night, it touched Emily so surprisingly and so deeply with its peace and beauty, that she felt foolish tears starting to her eyes.

I'm tired, she told herself. I've seen this road a thousand times before.

But she drew her breath in sharply, and he heard her, glancing at her.

"What's the matter?"

"Nothing. It's just so beautiful."

He reached over and took her hand in his, a strong warm grip, and they didn't speak again in through Renmore and the flat fields past Castle Keene.

Dermot grinned.

"The first of them'll be about getting up in there," he said. "My mother's a terrible early bird."

They smiled at each other then, the whole world to themselves, gloriously out of kilter with everybody else. Isolated in an opal dream that for Emily seemed to tremble a little; touching her with the edges of stupid panic. There was more in this dream than she had estimated.

Yet when they stopped outside her front door in the pale light, and after a few moments of desultory talk he turned to kiss her, she knew the panic and the dream was empty. She had nothing to give back. It was not like with Fergus in that other dawn on the Dublin quays. She did nothing to resist or refuse, accepting the warm strength of his mouth, but without sense of either loss or promise. Nothing. Except the desire to get away. And sorrow. Strange sudden sorrow.

"I'm—I'm sorry Dermot," she whispered as he drew away.

"It's nothing. Not to worry."

He was still calm and affectionate. Not apparently annoyed. Not claiming the reward for the evening out. She looked at him in shame that she should be so inadequate, wordless.

He took her chin gently in his warm fingers and turned her head until the big eyes abrim with threatening tears looked full into his own. Gently he shook his head, and his face was tender and regretful.

"My sleeping princess," he said. "All I've managed to do is prove that I'm no prince.

"One day," he added. "I'll come back with an alarm clock."

But he didn't smile, and she knew it was not meant as a joke.

Briskly he got out then and came around the car to open the door on her side.

When she was out, he kissed her again, exactly as Joe might do. Or John. Briefly she remembered that that was how she had thought of him, confused by a welling sense that it was no longer true.

" 'Bye, Emily," he said. "And thanks for the day."

"Good-bye, Dermot. And thank you too."

And he was gone.

On the gravel below the round steps, her blue dress lifting delicately in the first cool wind of morning, she watched the Riley swirl around at the end of the drive onto the Galway road. She felt deflated, and swept by a chill sense of loss and inadequacy; and of some grievous mistake that she might never have the chance to put right.

For the rest of the week she haunted the house, hoping he might ring up. A thousand times she thought of writing to him and caught herself back. But the week passed in silence and nor did Anna ring, and by the end of it she knew he must be gone.

With him went her hard-won content, replaced by a desperate restlessness that no longer had anything to do with Alejandro. Also this persistent sense of loss that had nothing to do with Alejandro either, but gave unbearable poignancy to all the beauty of the passing days of autumn and the chill excitements of the new hunting season, into which she threw herself with fierce determination, resolved to get pleasure from it. The soft land under the blazing blue sky of a good winter's day, the gorse yellow on the hills, and the turf smoke of small cottages straight as a steeple in the still air.

There were young men in plenty, and she flirted with them, and danced with them, and rode to hounds with them and told herself fiercely that that was all she wanted.

From some great distance she observed the cold hand of war reaching towards England, but however hard she tried, she could not invest it with the same reality as the stuttering machine guns on the dark hills around Málaga.

"I suppose," she said to Joe, trying to explain this, "that I feel it's not our war. If it comes, then we'd be neutral, wouldn't we?"

Nor—but she did not say this aloud—have I anyone close to me involved, to make it real.

Joe slammed down his paper and glared at her, his hair in a cockscomb from the sofa cushions.

"What do you mean, not our war? And *if* there is one! Of course there'll be one. This coming year or soon after. Not our war. So you hope. D'you tell me you think that if the Germans take Northern Ireland, they'll sit up along the Border polishing their jackboots and leave us to our neutrality?"

"But they couldn't invade us, if we were neutral."

Joe was scathing, shaking his paper again.

"Ah, no. They'd put on the polished jackboots and come tiptoeing in with flowers for the women and suckers for the children, and could we please have a base or two down there at the bottom to send submarines against the English. Be your age, Em."

She stared at him, and he pointed a long bony finger at her.

"Just wait until one young man of yours is dead, and then ask yourself if it's your war."

Unbidden to her mind came the calm strong face of Dermot. Up in Scotland now, Anna had told her with a sidelong look, asking no questions.

"Would you go, Joe?" she asked him, a whole fresh attitude and a whole fresh set of fears forming in her mind.

"Me?" said Joe. "I think I'd be too big a coward. But there's many will."

"Will? You're sure of it."

He shook his paper yet again as if she were intolerably stupid.

"Of course," he said. "D'you think these old fools bleating about peace are going to do anything to Hitler except make him laugh so much he'll wet himself? Come on, let's go out to Milligan's for a jar. It's too nice an evening to waste talking about other people's wars."

"But you just said it wasn't other people's."

"It is for the moment. Can we take your car? Mine has a flat tire and Willie's too born-lazy to change it."

And so are you, dear Joe, she thought. And so are you.

At Christmastime Granny was ill in London, and Mrs. McRoss planned to go and see her when the Christmas days were over. But on a still, gray Boxing Day, with the scent lying like a mist along the runs and hounds going mad, she took a tumble in a jostle for a stone wall out near Loughrea, and broke her collarbone.

"It's nothing," she protested to them all. "Nothing but a nuisance. But I can't travel with it. Now what are we going to do about Granny?"

"Hasn't Mike got her in the hospital?" Joe said.

"He has, to be sure, but she'll be lonely, the creature. She's never been in a hospital in her life. I mean, to be sick in."

"I'll go, Mums," Emily said, surprising herself with the sudden realization of a need to get away for a while from this life she could find no fault with. "There's no reason why I shouldn't go. I've been training this girl for John. She can well do a couple of weeks on her own."

As soon as she had said it she realized how desperately she wanted to go. To get away—even to the dull, patient routines of visiting Gran—from this loved world where nothing ever happened. What did she expect to happen? What promise did she try to extract from every gray morning, sliding away unfulfilled each evening with the ball of the scarlet sun. Restless. Longing for something, and she did not know what.

"Could you do it on your own, Em?"

"Mother. I'm coming up to twenty. Old."

Joe snorted, and her mother looked at her as if she were suddenly realizing it.

"I suppose you are, darling."

Almost two years, she thought, since the child had come home from Spain, and no one dare ask her yet outright if she had managed to set aside that Alejandro. Still, evening after evening, she crouched at the wireless and listened without comment to the news of the Civil War still raging in Spain. Mrs. McRoss sighed. Anna's so nice brother had seemed interested for a time, but that seemed to have fizzled out. Maybe it would be good for the child to go away.

"I think," she said aloud, "it would be fine. I'm sure you'd manage everything perfectly, Em."

Emily was astonished at the excitement and relief that stirred her. God knew that staying with the old servant in Sydney Street and visiting Gran wouldn't be exactly hilarious, but it would be different.

They were all so happy here in their unchanging lives. Even Joe was exactly the same as when she came home, and had begun to irritate her, always wild after this girl or that, but seeing to it carefully that none of them came to anything. She couldn't bear to think of him turning into one of these genial Irish bachelors who could never bring themselves to leave their mother's skirts.

All the people of the village, too, just like Joe, doing what they had always done, utterly content in the gray confines of their little streets.

"I'd love to go, Mums," she said. "Besides, it's a long time since I saw Gran. I didn't come with you last time."

Too terrified, she remembered, to miss a letter, or maybe even a telephone call, from Alejandro.

London was cold; cold and gray under a gray sky, only the flaring red of the buses lending cheer and color to the drabness of the winter city. But the noise and speed of it exhilarated her at once; life and movement lifting her spirits after the cozy quiet that had begun to swallow her in Clonfrack.

On the morning after she arrived, she went off to see Gran at the hospital; patient under all the instructions of the cantankerous old Lydia, who had been her mother's nurse when she was small, and now cared for Gran with passionate protectiveness that hardly admitted anybody else. Lydia was convinced she could not possibly manage the journey from Chelsea to Hyde Park Corner alone, and with small encouragement would have come with her to see her across the road and put her on the right bus.

Emily extricated herself patiently, and as soon as she was out of sight, decided to walk to St. George's, where Gran had been settled under Mike's supervision. It was too cold to wait for buses, and she was snug in her teddy-bear coat and a small beaver cap low over one eye, light red curls glowing with color in the dead light.

Gran saddened her. Half the size she had been when she last saw her, the bright indomitable eyes beginning to fade at last; her sharp mind blurring and mixing the generations; calling Mike by his father's name.

"Will she die, Mike?" she asked him when they had left her. Mike was halfway in character between John and Joe, with the same red-gold hair as herself, and John's round face, but with Joe's hilarity and tendency always to say the wrong thing. He looked grave and a little distant this morning in his white coat, and she looked at him curiously. Never before had she actually seen him making like a doctor, knowing him only on holidays, when there was nothing to choose for insanity between him and Joe.

Mike put an arm around her and walked her down a long pale corridor with a dark red shining floor, and a long window at the end of it looking out across the park.

"I'm afraid so, love," he said. "But not today or tomorrow."

"Mums was hoping to get her over to Ireland."

He shook his head.

"Too late."

"What is it exactly, Mike?"

"We'll call it senile decay. Everything in the engine is just wearing out."

"Like my car."

He didn't smile.

"Like your car. But we can't buy spare parts for Gran."

"Poor Gran."

"She's had a terrific life, Em. And a good innings. There's nothing to be sorry for Gran for. I hope I do as well."

"I suppose so. But she lost her only son."

Mike looked at her, and in the clear clinical light his eyes were somber.

"She won't be the only mother to do that," he said, "if things go on as they are."

It was coming from every side, this fresh clutch of threats at the heart.

"Oh, Mike."

Not again, she could have said. I have been through all this once. They forgot that, or didn't realize, any of them, what Spain had been like in the time coming up towards the Civil War. And there, now, all the threats had come true.

"It's got to come. You might as well face it, Em."

"Mike," she said, and said what she had said before to no one. Perhaps she didn't know Mike quite so well, and it was a little like confiding in a stranger. "Mike. I've done that once. I've faced it all already. And it did come. So I'm more likely to believe that than most people. That it'll come, I mean."

"We all forget that, don't we, Em. We all think of you as a child who got into a mess."

"It was more than that, Mike."

"I realize. I'm sorry, Em. Yes, I realize."

"And now here it all is again."

"But there's no one special this time."

She gave a wry grin.

"Only everybody's only son," he said.

He leaned over and planted a quick affectionate kiss on her cheek. A passing nurse looked at the same time thrilled and scandalized.

"She thinks I'm your someone special."

"True for you. But I hope you get someone special, Em. It puts an edge on things. Even wars."

"Would you go, Mike?"

"Into the forces?"

"Yes."

"And who would look after all the bomb casualties? We have it all organized. All ready in case the little rat jumps us. We're off the moment the trumpet blows."

They had reached the inner hall, the dim day waiting for her beyond the glass doors.

She felt suddenly lonely.

"Can you lunch with me, Mike?"

"Not today, love. I'll be lucky to get even a sandwich today. But I'll be round to Sydney Street later and we'll go out somewhere nice for a spot of dinner. Right?"

They separated in the big front reception hall, Mike to go back to work and she to go out into the gray cold that was beginning to thicken into ghostlike fog among the stripped trees over in Hyde Park. For a moment she stood on the steps, huddling into her soft coat collar against the raw cold, barely her nose showing between it and her fur cap; trying to decide what to do, and if she wanted a bus, where should she get it. Behind her the swing door banged as someone else came out.

She threw a glance at the tall man in RAF uniform who almost passed her by, and was ashamed afterwards that he must have heard her merely gasp, instead of some more composed and proper greeting.

"Emily!"

"Dermot."

More correctly handsome than ever in his uniform, three stripes, which meant nothing to her at that time, around the sleeve of his greatcoat. Genuinely delighted to see her, bounding back up the two steps he had taken when he stopped. Before he shook hands, he saluted her, and she found that curious and charming. It made her feel very special.

"Dermot! What are you doing here?"

"I may well ask you. I had to go and see a man at the Air Ministry, hence the fancy dress. And there's a friend of mine in here after his Lagonda had a bit of a barney with a bus. What brings you here? Nothing sad, I hope."

She put it all the wrong way around, trying to steady the field full of butterflies that had invaded her stomach.

"My brother's a doctor here. I mean, my grandmother's ill."

"Which?"

What a fool she was making of herself.

She laughed then and felt better, blushing a little at the warm intense pleasure in his eyes resting on her face.

He is pleased to see me, she thought wildly. Really pleased.

"Both," she said then, "both." And told him in a rush about Gran and her mother's collarbone, and Mike being there anyway, and he watched her face and wondered was she out yet from under whatever dream had held her. Some character in Spain, Anna had said.

"Can you lunch with me?" he asked her.

She hesitated only a moment.

"Why not? I must ring Gran's old dragon, that's all."

So she had to tell him also about old Lydia, who would probably set out to try and find her, sure she was coming to some harm, and drag her away home to an inch-square cutlet and one small potato.

"She thinks, you see, that everybody eats like Gran."

"Let's not go there for lunch, then."

He thought he had not heard her talk so much in all the time they had had together before, and she knew herself in the grip of excitement that kept her chattering helplessly.

"What about the Berkeley Buttery? It's only down Piccadilly."

"I don't know. I mean, I've never been there. I've never been anywhere, except Sydney Street and Brown's in Half Moon Street when there were too many of us for Gran. I wasn't old enough before Spain."

Dermot thought of the girls he usually took out, who had always been everywhere. Or said they had.

"Will we go the dangerous way?" he asked her.

Without thought they had walked together around the corner

and faced out over the roaring space of Hyde Park Corner,
Victory driving her chariot away over on the other side, on top of
the arch of Constitution Hill as traffic surged past them in an
endless torrent.

"Or shall we go back," he said, "and cross the road in the
proper place?"

Emily felt suddenly quiet, as if this scene before her was
marked with sudden sharpness. Defined, and the colors almost
unnaturally bright. Marking itself. Shapes of the bare trees over
the winter green of the park; the long brown wall of the gardens
of Buckingham Palace and the phalanxes of bright red buses
churning around to Piccadilly. Straight before them, as if to
remind her of the thoughts that filled her mind, were the dark,
mourning figures of the Artillery Memorial from the last war,
and a column of Life Guards coming like toy soldiers up Constitution Hill, white plumes lifeless in the still air.

She stammered a little, suddenly, and never knew afterwards
why she spoke as she did, other than it seemed terribly important
that he should know.

"My father died there," she said, as if she had never seen the
sharp-etched scene before.

"Your *what*?"

Dermot was completely taken aback.

"My father." She pointed out into the middle of the swirling
traffic. "There. Just there."

Very quiet, he stared at her and waited for her to go on.

"He was a surgeon at the hospital there. Like Mike. A very
good one, I believe."

She paused and spoke slowly, all her chattering forgotten.

"It was my mother's birthday and he was kept late. He went
racing out, he was always in a hurry, right into the middle of the
traffic there, after a taxi. In one hand he had a dozen red roses
and in the other a ruby and diamond clip in a little box. A bus hit
him. He never knew anything about it. Just lay there on top of all
the broken roses with the little box still in his hand. And my
mother waiting with her special dinner ready. . . ."

"Your poor mother," said Dermot, trying to understand why
she had told him, but grasping gladly at this sign of life in her.
This closer bond.

"Yes, I don't think she ever got over it. Hasn't now."

"And you? How old were you?"

"About two."

"But you tell it," he said, astonished, "as if you saw it all."

She still didn't take her eyes from the road, as if she were still seeing it. She could hear her mother crying. That was all she remembered.

"It is a legend," she said. "But at least he died still loving her."

"Ah." He could see the gray eyes full of pain and found it hard to find anything to say, knowing he did not really understand. She was telling him something important, but not directly. He felt a surge of rage against the Spaniard, for it must be him.

"I would think," he said very carefully, "that anything that broke up sooner, was not real love in the first place."

"Like an infatuation, or something like that."

"Yes. Painful, but you get over it in the end. Like measles."

Alejandro. Like measles. He seemed to shift a little in her mind.

Dermot was very careful, wondering what she was up to inside her own mind. Clearing the decks, maybe. He mustn't go blundering in with two big feet. With this astonishing little story on the edge of the pavement of the gray street, she had given him something suddenly of her own secret self. No longer the lovely girl who so much attracted him but left the air between them empty with her pretty chatter. Hiding from life, whatever it had done to her.

This girl who smiled suddenly beside him, her hair a glowing halo in the damp, thrusting it all away, was real.

He smiled back as if the day had just begun, and took her arm and turned her.

"I think," he said, "we'll go around the safe way."

Her gloved hand on his arm, as if it had always rested there, they wandered down Piccadilly, and a pale gleam of sun came out to lift the bitter cold.

Side by side they ambled along, and easy with small talking, peering into shop windows and pressing their noses against the great sheets of plate glass of Jack Barclay's to admire a sleek Rolls-Royce.

"Would you like one, Dermot?"

Question and answer. Finding out about each other. Fact on fact.

"You bet I would."

She looked up at him, disappointed, already surprised that he would like anything so mundane.

"Then I'd sell it," he said, "at once, for something more interesting."

Every simple joke seemed the peak of humor; every small comparison in the shops an utterance of uttermost importance: the rich cars gliding to a halt outside the Ritz like the chariots of the Gods; the gray jumbled façade of Piccadilly stretching on past Burlington House to the god of Love himself in the center of the Circus, a rich, magic pathway never walked before.

He raced her over to buy her a bunch of violets from an old flower lady sitting on her kitchen chair outside the Ritz, wrapped in her voluminous colored shawls, the flowers on her black bonnet stirring in a small rising wind.

"There y'are sir," she said. "The very best I got. And you remember to buy them for her still when she's an old lady, and you're an air vice-marshal. Be as happy then, dears, as you are now."

She pinned the violets to Emily's lapel, and Emily looked over their delicate fragrance at Dermot and found in his eyes the same surprise that filled her own.

They had not realized they were so happy that, in one short hour, it showed.

"It's only Piccadilly," either of them would have said. "Only Piccadilly. We have been here before."

Emily never remembered what she ate that day, but Dermot would tell her afterwards. A good Dover sole and a bottle of Liebfraumilch—for no one was saying yet it was unpatriotic to drink wines from Germany—and a couple of superb ices. After sitting long over coffee on the green velvet banquette, talking of things of eternal importance, they wandered down St. James's Street past the brown palace like a toy castle, and through the park to stare at the ducks as if they had never seen a duck before.

The lake water was leaden and the dark winter day closing in from the corners of the park, the ducks huddled along the edges of the island.

"I'd better take you home," Dermot kept saying, but she paid no heed to him, leaning on the rustic bridge across the lake, the weeping willows gray with the death of winter, and in the other direction the first warm lights of the evening springing in the windows of the palace.

Remember it, something was saying inside her. Remember it all. And the yellow lamps beginning to glimmer along the Mall.

"Come to tea," said Emily.

"In your grandmother's house? But she isn't there."

"Old Lydia is, and she's dragon enough for anyone. She probably won't let you in. I promise you it'll be very proper."

"I should be promising you that."

They smiled at each other a long moment, and he took her arm again, making toward Chelsea along the darkening walk at the water's edge. Emily marched along with brave self-confidence, quaking in her boots as to how Lydia was going to take it. Little Miss Emily, who had always been told to come here and go there, walking in the shadow of her brilliant family, coming home now with a man, to the empty house, and ordering tea.

"Mike will be in later," she said defensively to Lydia and to herself and to Dermot at her side.

"Who's Mike?" he asked at once sharply, and the edge in his voice pleased her.

"My eldest brother. The one who's at St. George's."

"Ah, yes, you told me. Look, it's getting cold. We'll take a taxi."

Nowhere more thrillingly intimate than the inside of a London taxi. Smell of leather and petrol and the close largeness of Dermot beside her; misted lights of dusk sliding past; buses like red cliffs drawing alongside. Fog tangible around the lamps.

When she got out and put her key into the black fanlighted door of Sydney Street, Lydia appeared with all the promptitude of the little old woman who popped out of the house when the sun was going to shine.

"Lydia, this is Squadron Leader"—what exactly was a Squadron Leader?—"Kilpatrick," she said bravely. "We'll have tea now, please, and Doctor Mike will be in around six for drinks."

That'll shut her up, she thought, which it did, and Lydia took their coats in grim silence, the smell of fog on them from the night outside, and did no more than nod her gray top-knotted head at Dermot, as if to say he was no better than she expected, brought in off the streets like this, ignoring Emily altogether.

"Old harpy," Emily hissed as her flat feet clopped down the basement stairs. "She thinks no one exists except Gran. I wonder if we'll get any tea."

"But she didn't even ask how your grandmother was."

"D'you think she'd trust me? She phones Mike every morning and evening."

Nevertheless a beautiful tea of scones and cream and strawberry jam and the first watercress sandwiches came up in no time to the table before the fire. Gentle pink and green patterns of Coalport china and the best silver tea service.

"You've obviously made an impression," Emily said reverently, and hoped she could live up to it all, and not pour the tea into the saucers or something equally awful.

They were on their favorite films and music by then; step by step probing each other's tastes and ideas, charmed to find themselves so much in harmony.

"You mean you've never been to the pictures in Clonfrack?" cried Emily. "Dermot, you've never lived. Of course, you'd be Quality. You'd have to have a deck chair. That's a shilling."

She found herself barely able to see him, although he sat beside her in the armchair, overwhelmed by the sense of his thereness. For lonely hours that she now foresaw, with sudden vision, when he was gone, would be the detail she could not see now. Perfect good looks redeemed from platitude by the slightly overwide strong mouth and the square set of the jaw. Deep-set hazel eyes that seemed to begin to laugh a long way down in them before the smile ever reached his face. All this to be taken out and studied, like souvenirs, after he was gone.

When Mike came in, rubbing his hands and grumbling about the cold, Dermot was standing up, touching with an appreciative finger the row of porcelain soldiers on the mantelpiece, their gilded uniforms glowing in the lamplight.

"You like them?" Mike asked him when the introductions were done.

He showed nothing more than pleasure at Emily's surprise visitor, nodding at the soldiers and holding out his cold hands to the fire.

"Absolutely top hole," said Dermot. "Beautiful. I was just trying to see how many I knew. He's a Polish lancer, isn't he. Look at his frogged jacket. And that's a dragoon."

He moved over to the Wellington in the corner, the drop front open to hold the silver writing set.

"He belongs to Franz Josef of Austria," he said, lightly touching a fine gentleman in a cocked hat and a white jacket, a yellow swordsash and orange trousers buttoning under his Wellington boots.

"Uniforms were uniforms in those days," he said.

"You seem to know a lot about it," Mike said.

"I've always been interested in military history." Dermot turned back to the room. "Probably comes of having Wellington rammed down our throats from the cradle up."

Mike looked mystified.

"One of Dermot's ancestors fought with Wellington," Emily said. "They have land in Spain and the family's a bit Spanish. That's how I met his sister, Anna."

"Anyway," Dermot said. "I prefer to fly airplanes."

Mike grunted and went over to the sideboard to pour them all drinks.

"We'll all be making military history any day now. That fool has every intention of marching into Austria."

They all knew that "that fool" meant Hitler, and silence settled on the warm room. Emily had the feeling of familiar pain. Just as she had seen the sad writing on the wall for the house in Málaga, so she felt the drear threat to all she cared for now. She looked at the handsome young men. Dear God, was it their turn now to stand up and be counted? This room she had known all her life. She had been born in this house, lived here until her father died; come here again and again to visit Gran, who had returned to live in it when they went to Ireland, her mother racing blindly from her memories. Always she had loved the bright colors of the soldiers, crying to be lifted up to lay a finger on them when she was small. God knew, the room was empty without Gran, upright in her wing chair beside the fire, but it was familiar and loved. Great-grandmother on the wall as a young girl with soft hair and reflective eyes, her apron full of daisies, the light falling softly through the curious lamp of glowing fruits and green glass leaves. The top of the piano and every other space crowded with photographs of Great Uncle This in his uniform and Great Aunt That in her Court feathers.

Bombs, this time. There had been a lot of bombs in Spain. Bombs at once, on London. What would bombs do to all this? The warm loved house, and God knew how many more, turned overnight into smoking ruins. So many of the ties of her life lay in London that she felt if the war came it would be almost treachery to be safe in the neutrality of Ireland. Untouched by threat.

Mike and Dermot had already forgotten the war and were fiercely arguing International Rugby, and she smiled, knowing herself forgotten, like any well-brought-up girl around Rugby players.

She shifted them firmly in the end, not willing to allow Lydia to cook for them, because they simply wouldn't get enough to eat. And she would feel Put Upon.

They took a taxi in a night grown clear and cold, the stars brilliant even up above the streetlamps. And as though the conversation had led them, they went to Stone's Chop House, known to all the Rugby clubs of London; gathering place of all the strong young men and their adoring girls; after hard-fought matches in muddy suburban fields; after the screaming excitement of an International at Twickenham.

Mike unwound the long striped scarf that was his only concession to the cold, and Dermot hung up his overcoat by the door. The long room was warm and steamy, alight with talk and laughter, the rumble of young men's voices and the higher chatter of their girls.

Over their huge mutton chops—the small potboys in the striped aprons buzzing like bees between the tables with tankards of beer—over their chops they spoke no more of war or Hitler, but got to know each other as young people since the world began; laying out their lives, their jokes, their loves, to seek a common ground.

Nor in that bright lamplit place, so full of youth and strength, did any presentiment touch Emily as it had touched her in the house. Although in time she and Dermot would stand in Panton Street over the dark bomb crater that had been Stone's, full of the fluttering pink of what they called the bomb flowers; speaking of their first night there together. And of Mike, long dead.

Mike went back to the hospital and Dermot took her home.

He took the key in Sydney Street and opened the front door, gold light flooding out into the street, and onto Emily's face where she stood below him, waiting.

She smiled at him when he turned back from the open door.

"Thank you, Dermot, for a lovely day," she said.

He didn't speak, looking down at her.

"You know about the nightingale that sang in Berkeley Square," he said.

She nodded. Who didn't?

"Well, that bird has shifted," he said. "It's here, in Sydney Street."

He came down the two steps and took her hand. "Emily—"

At that moment Lydia appeared at the back of the hall like an avenging angel, her hair in curlers. She was being Kept Up.

"Hell," said Dermot, and Emily gave him a great mischievous grin, as if to say that it wasn't her fault this time.

With great civility, Dermot said good night to Lydia, and looked at Emily with a shrug.

"Good night, Em. Been a wizard day."

" 'Night, Dermot."

And she had to let him go, watching the swing of his greatcoat as he turned away; the slight correct angle of his cap. At the corner of the street he stopped and raised a hand, as though he knew she would be watching.

She came in and closed the door and knew she was grinning like an ape. Indifferent to Lydia, she capered the length of the hall like the scarecrow in *The Wizard of Oz*.

"Good night, Lydia," she sang out. "I'll put out the lights upstairs."

Old dragon, she thought, but she didn't stop smiling.

Three days later was her birthday. They had been talking about it in Stone's, saying what a shame it would be to be away from home.

Lydia was out, doing the meager marketing that she would allow herself, ever sourly and unnecessarily careful of Gran's purse. Emily had had a telephone call from her mother and, by the morning post, a daft card from Joe. She was getting ready to go and see Gran, and afterwards to have a birthday lunch with Mike. The doorbell rang.

Half in and half out of her coat she answered it, and on the doorstep stood a cherub-faced district messenger, his pillbox hat tipped so far forward it almost rested on his nose; all his brass buttons glittering in the sun. In his white-gloved hands he held a great bunch of roses that almost obscured him.

"Miss Hemily McRoss."

So young it was still a reedy pipe.

"Yes."

"For you, Miss. And a 'appy Birfday or whatever it is."

"Thank you."

She took them from him and scrabbled in her purse on the hall table to give him sixpence. He went off whistling on his bicycle, barely able to reach the pedals, and she stood for a moment in the dark hall, enchanted, her face buried in the fragrance of the roses.

Never for a moment did she question who had sent them, but not until she got down into the light in the kitchen did she find the card. Hand-done. A quick strong picture in black ink that seemed to have been colored in children's crayons. An ebullient small brown bird, perched on a London street sign that said Sydney Street.

Singing his head off.

No signature, no message. Only the nightingale belting out his song, and she understood all the platitudes about your insides gone to jelly. Carefully she put the roses in a tall jug as her mother had taught her, up to their necks in water to have a long drink before she arranged them later.

Her mother came shortly to take over the watch with Gran, and after a visit to Ted at school, Emily was back in Clonfrack by the end of January, two of the red roses in her suitcase, carefully pressed between sheets of blotting paper. At Clonfrack, the ivy underneath the elm trees was awash with snowdrops, and primroses were already opened along the sheltered banks below the hawthorn hedges. Soft weather, the locals said, with mild breezes promising of the spring to come.

Nothing to do, she told herself firmly, but settle down. She would telephone John and say she was ready to go back to work. No point in endless chewing of her nails and waiting for phone calls that might never come. Nothing would happen today or tomorrow. If it ever did.

She had come on the morning mail train, just time to get herself organized before lunch. Aggie, bless her, had been ridiculously glad to see her, so different from that ghastly old Lydia, and the good smells of special cooking floated from the back of the house.

Finished with unpacking, she came gratefully down to the drawing room fire, idly hearing the doorbell ring somewhere below her in the house. Before she could even sit down, the door burst open behind her and Aggie was in the room, her face ashen with potential tragedy.

"Ah, God ha' mercy on us, Miss Emily. A wire!"

Her expression held all the mixture of fright and self-importance of those who bring bad news. To Aggie, a wire could mean nothing else.

Emily turned from the fire. The room seemed to have faded into dark and cold.

Her grandmother was dying. Her mother was in London alone, and yet she never thought of anyone for one single moment except Dermot. As though his uniform gave him some priority in death.

Dear God, so soon. Spinning down out of the sky to a shambles somewhere in the fields. So soon.

Aggie confirmed all her terrors, thrusting the green flimsy envelope into her suddenly cold hands. Nor did she ask herself why anyone should send her a telegram about Dermot.

"Ah, poor Miss Emily, may God have pity on you, 'tis for you."

Flinging her apron over her head with the first howl of ritual grief, she blundered from the room, and with shaking fingers Emily tore open the wire, clumsily, the penciled address showing it was indeed for her.

It was in Spanish, sent from Cádiz by José Maria.

"Grieved to tell you," it said, "Alejandro died wounds received at Tarragona January 14."

It took her a long time to see it and understand it.

The dark smooth skin and brilliant smile, the wit and gentleness and sudden flashes of cruelty like Spain itself. Tenderness and all the empty easy promises mixed confusedly in her mind with the turn of olive leaves against the sun; church bells and the smell of stifling streets, heat heavy against your face. Sharp stutter of flamenco.

All these things had been Alejandro.

Slowly she walked over to the window, shamed by the sick relief that dominated everything else. Every other thought.

A thin gray rain had begun to fall, blotting out the garden, and against it she strove to see Alejandro's face.

Without success. It would come back, but for the moment she could not bring to mind his face.

In mid-March, Austria was invaded by Hitler.

## SEVEN

The tensions of 1938 were no longer secondhand to Emily now
that letters from Dermot were being handed over regularly by the
beaming postman. Nor did she listen any more avidly to the news
of Spain, aware only that the Civil War was drawing, dragging,
toward its bloody close in the northeast corner of the country.

Alejandro had survived almost to the end, and sometimes guilt
touched her that she could find so little personal grief for him. To
have been once so much in love with him, and now able to feel
so little. His treachery with Remedios seemed to have removed
the core of him that she had loved, leaving only the fine handsome shell that could mean little more than all the other young
men who were dying with him. Everybody's only sons, as Mike
had said. And anyone would grieve over them.

And which lasts longest? she wondered. Remembered sorrow
or remembered love? Pain was still sharp when she did recall the
griefs of her relationship with him, because it was the worst
suffering she had known. But the recollections of brief young
love were overlaid now with the warm exciting present; and her
anxieties were not over the political war of Spain, but over
Austria and the Sudetenland, Czechoslovakia, and all the small
protesting lands being swallowed and threatened by the tramping
jackboots Joe had spoken of so derisively.

Dermot. And another war. Dear God, another war, and for her
another hostage in it. The someone special.

Yet she was radiantly happy, and they all watched her with
delight. A new Emily they had not known since she came home
from Spain, racing to intercept the postman with beaming face;
spending long hours on the telephone to Anna lest she had heard
one word more of him than had Emily herself.

Long letters from him. Now at the No.7 Flying Training
School at Little Rissington in Gloucestershire. "Churning out the
cannon fodder," he said, "for Hitler's war. Teaching babies to
fly in the vain hope that they will live when it begins."

He was an old man, he said, at twenty-three, his job now to see that there were plenty more to come after him.

She chided him for his gloomy attitude, knowing the hopelessness of acknowledging fear, since now all that she feared would be so much worse than last time.

"You won't necessarily be killed," she wrote to him. "Think how many people didn't die in the last war."

"Ah, yes," he wrote back, "but Em, my darling, think of how many did. Anyway, it is better to expect to die. We speak of it a lot. Then what a grand surprise it'll be to be alive in the heel of the hunt."

For the second time, helplessly, she knew her lover to be hand in hand with death.

For lover he was now, and made no bones about it since the time he had met her in London. He wrote almost weekly, in quick difficult writing, his mind always racing ahead of his words. But his words were definite. She had attracted him from the first moment he had seen her in the hall at Castle Keene with Anna. But had felt some impossible barrier between them. Something? Someone?

Since he saw her in London, he said, he had felt that barrier gone.

"And I hope, Em dearest," he wrote, "in this dangerous world where time may be short, that there will be nothing more to waste time by coming between us."

"Nothing, Dermot," she wrote. "Nothing."

And nobody.


Dermot asked her to marry him in the high hot days of August, when Europe was boiling toward the Munich crisis, surprised and delighted to get his leave, but regarding it as a dangerous thing.

"They tend to give it to you and then follow it up by something nasty these days."

"Such as what?"

"Posting you abroad."

"Oh, no, Dermot."

She hadn't thought of that one. In trying to make as brave a picture as possible of the coming war, she had seen it as death or nothing. There were other, slower sorrows.

They had taken a picnic and Emily's car, open to the sultry sun, and gone rambling over Connemara, lost and dwarfed in the wastes of the stony hills; coming at lunchtime into Killary for a drink in the dark comfortable hotel at Leenane, which earned Dermot's undying respect by having thirty-seven different kinds of whiskey.

"They ought to forget Croagh Patrick and Lough Derg," he said, "and have a pilgrimage here."

"Joe would lead it with you! And on his knees."

The water of the narrow fiord was indigo dark against the pale stony shores, and they rambled out after their drinks to stand awhile on the old quay, looking down at the myriad jellyfish floating like rose-colored flowers in the dark water. Afterwards, they took their lunch basket and walked up a small steep promontory, looking back down at the hotel and the narrow dark blue sea. The day was perfect, blue sky no more than touched by high white clouds, towing grape-blue shadows lazily over the bare hills. The turf was short and dry, tiny blue harebells clinging with papery grip to the white soil.

They talked little while they ate, contented to be part of the great empty silence of the hills, larks shrilling up all around them from invisible nests, and occasionally the plaintive bleat of a sheep.

Dermot sighed happily when he was finished, and lay back with his hands behind his head. He had taken off his tweed jacket, and his long legs stretched out before him in gray flannels. His eyes were smiling up at her where she sat above the basket of food. He had come back looking fit and tanned, as though he had been out in the air a lot.

She said so.

"Beastly little training planes," he said. "With no roofs. My legs are white."

"You should hang them over the side," she said.

He watched her a long time in silence, and she wondered what he was thinking.

"Em," he said suddenly, flat on his back there among the harebells and the larks and the bits and pieces of the picnic. But he might have been chairing a business meeting, so cool and careful was his voice.

"Em, are you willing to take a calculated risk?"

"With what? Amn't I always a gambler?"

She paused with an apple halfway to her mouth, but he didn't smile.

"With me," he said soberly. "I could easily die in the next couple of years. Or months. Leave you with children maybe. Who knows. All sorts of troubles. I'm no great catch. I'm only the second son. No glamour, old girl, and not much money. You might hardly even have me. Would you risk it, Em? Would you marry me?"

Emily put down the apple.

"Lord yes," she said grinning, trembling a little. "Lord yes, I was wondering if you were ever going to ask me."

"Oh, Em."

He rolled across the gap between them and firmly set aside the picnic. Down in the hotel two chambermaids in a bathroom looked out the window and went racing for their friends to come and watch the two young toffs having a bit of a batter up there plain as you like on the hill. And they grand enough to have their dinner in one of those special baskets with the plates and all.

"Yet aren't they very much like ourselves after all," said one of them with awe, thinking of Patsy Ryan and the bit of grass out there behind the woodshed.

Emily drew away from Dermot's kisses, and took his face between her hands.

"Dermot."

"My love?"

"Don't let's talk about it too much."

He looked astonished, his eyebrows rising. He caught her hands and held them.

"Our engagement? But darling, I want to tell everyone. I want to put a trailer on my airplane. I want it blazoned in every newspaper from the Antarctic News to the North Pole Star."

She laughed and shook his head a little.

"No, stupid. So do I. Not that."

She looked round at the vast bare curves of the hills and the sun and the purple sea and all the bright world, and turned back to him abruptly. The brown face so close to her own; the strange eyes that were neither brown nor green under the gilded hair. The vitality and strength. The life.

"About your dying," she said.

Dermot was silent. They all talked about it a lot, frivolously. To make it real and acceptable.

"You see," she said, "there was someone else before, and it was all just the same, and he died."

"I understand perfectly," Dermot said gravely. "You make it absolutely clear."

Then in the crook of his arm, the remains of the lunch forgotten, she told him for the first time of Alejandro.

"The bounder deserved it," was all he said, when she came to his death. "I'd have killed him myself."

So that, he thought, was what had closed her mind and numbed her, as if she had eaten the poisoned apple like Snow White. Little Spanish rotter, he thought, forgetting the Spanish in himself.

"All I'm trying to say," she went on, "is that everything is different in wars."

"You can say that again."

She persisted against his loving grin.

"You just don't know what is going to happen tomorrow. So let's just take all the time we have, and not think about it too much. Or about the future."

"Poor Em," he said then. "Little rotter. You have more experience than I have, my darling, of war."

"He wasn't little," Emily cried, but this time she laughed, and it was the last time she protested Alejandro's height. Finally letting him go at last. Remembering only, without ever thinking of them as such, the lessons she had learned of love and war.

When all the kissing and congratulating was done at Castle Keene, Dermot's mother insisted on telephoning Mrs. McRoss and Joe, and asking them over for dinner.

By some miracle of organization she got the dining room open, all the long windows flung wide to the hot August night, and the candles in their silver holders above the flowers, circled by life-weary moths from the night outside.

Dinner was all that Emily had once expected from Castle Keene, even the old butler fully dressed in his starched shirt and waistcoat and obviously reveling in it all; bringing Dermot all the good wishes of the kitchen, tears touching his soft old eyes. If this was what Dermot was used to, she thought almost in panic, would she ever be able to keep it up? Although loyalty said fiercely at once that there was nothing wrong with her own home. But the tablecloth was of some priceless foreign lace and the china and linen marked with crests; the late roses massed in a silver bowl the size of a baby's bath. All Dermot's ancestors, Spanish and Irish, and the odd Englishman, looming from the shadows in gold frames.

But all the faces above this grandeur were smiling at her with warm pleasure, their glasses lifted to her and Dermot, and the gentle loving words of Lord Keene's toast brought tears to touch her lashes.

Her mother was smiling from ear to ear.

"I can't help it, darling," she said to Emily on the way home in the old Buick, she and her mother in the back like royalty, and Joe singing at the wheel. "I am so pleased."

"Well," Emily teased her. She felt light-headed with excitement and the weariness of the long splendid day. "You always wanted me to have a lord."

"I wanted you," said her mother bluntly, "to have an Irishman."

Emily thought at once of Alejandro, looking back already with amazement on what seemed almost a child's love.

She was aware of touching far deeper depths of knowledge and understanding, and of longing, with Dermot. Alejandro almost indistinguishable at this moment from the flowers and light and everything else she had loved in Spain.

Then she grinned in the warm darkness, thinking of Remedios's face if she could tell her she had caught a lord.


The next day Dermot was recalled from leave.

No chance for anything other than a frantic telephone call and a dash into Galway to see him for five desperate minutes before he caught the train.

"That beastly Hitler," he said. "It's the Czechs now, and God knows where next. He has to be stopped."

Her fingers twined in his where they stood beside the waiting train, as if by that frail link she could hold him. Smiling fiercely. No sad farewells.

"I wish you didn't have to stop him," she said.

"My darling. Old sport. I am the one you can see. There are others, actually."

"Is it really war, Dermot?"

"Who knows, my love. It's like love, old thing. It comes suddenly and when you least expect it."

He smiled at her deeply, warmly; with all he wanted her to remember in his eyes.

Away at the front the engine was beginning to belch and hiss, piling steam to cloud the glass roof of the gray station. Along the platform whistles blew, and doors were banging their counter-point to partings.

"Look after that girl Emily," he said gravely. "I love her."

One quick, desperate clinging kiss and he was gone, the train moving as he jumped in, sliding away from her along the platform; people coming between them; an old countrywoman in a shawl sobbing her heart out into a red handkerchief beside her. Only a hand then, and the sun on his hair that did indeed have gold lights in it. The curve of the line and he was gone.

They had both come alone, their families tacitly leaving them to say good-bye. Emily's mother was slamming around the stables between the startled horses, furious with the fate that had made it happen to the child again. Like Joe, she had no doubts as to what was to come. Small hopes for Emily, other than some brief happiness in this so suitable of marriages, before she was a widow; or even worse, nursing some war-shattered wreck for the rest of long days.

She was worried at the same time about Gran, who refused to be shipped out of London.

She shoved a horse out of her way with such unnatural rough-ness that it rolled a wide reproachful eye to look at her.

"Get on out of that," she said, "and don't mind me. 'Tis not you that's the trouble."

Emily was driving the Singer slowly through the bright morning to Castle Keene. Dermot had said his mother had sent a message that she wanted her especially to go home that way. The sun fell over the same green-gold countryside, the blue hills of Clare, the small cottages against the shining water at Oranmore. She looked at it all with some terrible care, lest these things she had seen with him might be all now that she had left.

They surrounded her with such love and kindness at Castle Keene that it brought her closer to weeping than the actual parting.

But Lady Keene had something special to say, tilting her head of cloudy hair at Emily in a characteristic gesture.

"Dermot asked me, my dear," she said, "if since he had no time, I could give you a ring until he came back."

"Doesn't trust you, Em," Lord Keene said, twinkling at her. "Wants a langle on you."

But Emily knew that it was more than that. On the short turf above Killary she had told him, among all the other things, of all her humiliating days with the women of the village after she had come back with no ring after Alejandro.

"Come upstairs, my dear," Lady Keene said. "I have a few you can choose from."

No castle grandeur here. A bedroom that could have been her mother's: pale, slightly faded chintzes, and gleaming furniture. Flowers everywhere and the green park in the distance beyond the windows. Paul on a horse riding slowly across it.

Withdrawing a bunch of keys, Lady Keene unlocked a deep drawer and out of a tray inside it, laid before Emily four rings.

"I don't feel anything too grand and glittering would suit you, Em, dear," she said. "Any of these will."

There was an opal all the glowing colors of the dawn; an amethyst so clear and pale that it was almost pink; a sapphire over which she paused for a moment but only a moment. Almost without hesitation she chose a square golden topaz, surrounded by small diamonds.

"This," she said. "This one is beautiful. And I think Dermot would like me to have this one. Beautiful."

"How strange that you should choose that one. But you are right, it suits you perfectly. And how nice for you to have it."

"Why strange?" Emily asked. "It is a little big."

"That's no matter. They'll fix that for you in Galway. But, my dear, it's a Spanish ring. It belonged to the mother of the old lady in Gibralfaro. Dermot's great-grandmother. She gave it to me when we got married. We went on our honeymoon to Spain."

Emily turned the ring on her finger. It was right for her, and so beautiful, and she could not bear to part with it. Yet a Spanish ring on her engagement finger was a symbol of tragedy from which she reared away.

She was being stupid. Everything was not necessarily the same twice.

"It's beautiful," she said. "Beautiful. May I really have it until Dermot gets me one?"

Lady Keene bent her gray head and kissed her.

"My dear. Dermot will get you one of his own, I'm sure. But you don't have to give that one back. It's the first gift of our pleasure at having you in the family."

Emily drove home, weaving a bit, unable to keep her eyes from straying to the topaz gleaming gold in its nest of diamonds on her left hand.

"I'll show them," she said aloud, thinking of showing her hand belligerently across every shop counter in Clonfrack.

This time it was real. Dermot would have leave again soon, even if there was a war, he said. Everybody had to have leave. They would arrange their marriage. Everything would be fine this time. War and death seemed very far away.

She listened now to the news of England as she had once listened to the news of Spain, almost forgetting that that fearful war was dragging itself to its end.

The polished jackboots thundered on, and the manic thousands screamed for Hitler under the fluttering banners of the symbol of evil in Berlin.

They listened to it all in silence in Clonfrack, and could not find themselves neutral, as their country intended to be: as close to the rising tension as if they were in the restless and apprehensive streets of London itself.

"Digging trenches in the park," Emily said, and stared at Joe, appalled. Against bombs.

"Time for them," Joe answered. "Time for them to do something. They've left it all a little late."

"But the park!"

How could she explain to him that Hyde Park was to her sacrosanct and must be kept forever without change. The green, fogbound space over which she had looked when she stood on the steps of St. George's on the first day with Dermot.

Mrs. McRoss was almost daily on the telephone, trying to persuade Gran, who was back in Sydney Street, to come to Ireland.

"I'd go and get her," she said to them distractedly. "Or Joe could go over. You'd go, wouldn't you, Joe? She likes you. She might listen to you."

"She won't come. You're distressing yourself for nothing."

Mike said the same thing when she rang him, crackling and frying on a bad connection.

"Leave her alone, Mother. She's too old to move. And too frail. Leave her in her own house. She has Lydia."

Anna had told Emily exactly the same thing about the old lady in Málaga, whom no persuasion would shift, and in the end they had left her to do as she wished and she had come to no harm.

Joe took the telephone from his mother.

"Are you ready for hostilities, Mike?"

"Just waiting for the off. And no doubt that will come the moment the first bugles blow. You wouldn't know us. Sand-bagged in so we've forgotten what the light of day looks like. Tell Mums to leave Gran alone."

"She wants to go over to her if Gran won't come here."

Mike was rough.

"Tell her to do no such thing, Joe. Better be sure one of them stays alive."

Through the pale autumn days, when the leaves of the elms drifted to the ground on the still air, Emily fretted about Dermot as her mother fretted about Gran. He had left training the cannon fodder, he said, and was now learning something himself. How to fly a Blenheim. A practical step, he remarked, toward being cannon fodder himself, as they moved so slowly that any smart Hun in a fighter could make them into pepper pots.

Emily could not find it funny.

Joe watched them both with a dry compassion.

"I haven't seen a smile in this house for weeks," he told them. "Listen. When it comes, it comes. Going on like a pair of hens won't help either of them."


"And there you are now," he said triumphantly when it all built up to the breathless crisis of Munich, from which Neville Chamberlain returned beaming, after his meeting with Hitler and Mussolini; brandishing his frail flower of Peace in Our Time, and promising England it was safe from war.

On the wireless they could hear the cheering of the crowds at Northolt, and looked at each other across the drawing room, gold and gentle in the light of the setting sun.

A respite. No more. Who but Chamberlain would listen to the word of Hitler. Poor England might for the moment, under the fall of the knife.

"There now," Joe said to them. "Are you happy now? Isn't that the end of it, like the good man said?"

"Oh, Joe," said his mother. "You can't be that big a fool."

Joe got up and moved over to the sideboard to pour himself a drink. He looked at his mother when he turned, and the smile was gone from his face.

"I'm not," he said. "But it seems he is. But it's time," he added. "Time. For all of us to think again and be a bit ready."

Both Emily and her mother were aware in a moment of sharp understanding, aside from the flower of peace and all the cheering, that Joe had said, ''time for *us* to think again.''

His mother looked at him. He had been only a child when they came back to Ireland after his father's death; reared there; spoke with an Irish accent. But she must never forget that his father had been an Englishman; and his schooling was English. Who knew what Joe would do? Oh, dear God, who would have sons? The Flowers of the Forest had bent before the scythe, but at the last moment this time it had been snatched away. They could not hope to be spared again.

After Munich, Dermot wrote more often, as though time might be getting short. He had hoped to have leave for Christmas, but in the end they wouldn't let him go.

All three of them went over to Castle Keene for the uneasy festival, joined by Pat and John, and gathered again for the New Year, hopefully and bravely toasting a future that seemed to hold little but uncertainty and fear. Emily, with her champagne to her lips, could not but remember the *Año Nuevo* she had spent in Málaga, when they had looked at each other over their glasses with the same sad apprehension.

No change came in life with 1939.

She drove in and out to Galway in the Singer and worked for John and Pat and toyed with the idea of doing medicine herself, but what was the use, for she would be marrying Dermot, and they both wanted as many children as God sent them; and at once.

Over in Europe, the swastika reached out to engulf it; snaring small territories that previously had no claim to fame other than their independence. Bohemia. Moravia. Memel.

Mike wrote to say that the air of preparation in London was almost demented. As if every tomorrow might bring the end of the respite. The ordinary running of his hospital was now subordinate to the arrangements for air-raid casualties that might come in at any time. The park he said, was dreadful. Crisscrossed with the scars of trenches.

Poor London.

The cool soft days lengthened into spring, and the rain came gray from the west, so fine it seemed almost suspended in the air. After that the mud, plowing the horses to their fetlocks. Then the flowers and all the birds singing, as if it might never be spring again.

On April first the Spanish Civil War came at last to an end, the Republican forces finally surrendering in the northeast.

Joe turned from the wireless.

"Didn't they pick the perfect day to end it," he said. "Only fools would have started it in the first place. War is never the answer. There's no future to it."

"Even this time?" Emily asked him. "What do England and France do? Give everything to Hitler?"

Joe snorted.

"Give it to him? Isn't he taking it anyway? And he'll go on. That bucko wants the world."

"So England must fight in the end, or be taken herself."

"Indeed. But the questions left at the end of it will be even bigger than the ones now. How long will it take Spain to recover under that little onion-seller?"

Emily looked at him sadly, knowing him right. The little onion-seller, as he called him, had led Spain to victory for everything she had personally known there. And what in her small world had it achieved? Death and sorrow and the breakup forever of a small, contented harmless living. Who now, she wondered, would gather the scattered family back together, giving it the focal center so necessary to every family in Spain. Rafaelito, probably, if he was still alive.

Sorrow, sorrow, sorrow, she thought. All war an endless permutation of human sorrow. And it was all going to start again.

And Mike was right. Dear God, but Mike was right, thinking that someone special put an edge to it. She had felt old over her parting from Alejandro and her almost marriage, putting her on some pinnacle of experience above girls older than herself. Now she felt she had known nothing about it; Spain no more than a romantic image, until the blood she loved had begun to flow.

She could not stand even Joe's loved familiar face and charged out into the gentle evening full of fluting birds, tramping the fresh fields with her hands dug deep in her pockets as the sun went down behind the hills of Clare. Trying to understand it all; to understand what was worth the loss and sorrow.

"But darling," her mother said to her when she tried to talk of all this some days later. "Many wars have been fought for ideals. Indeed, I should think that the Germans would say they are doing

all they do, for their own ideals. But now, Em, you must see it.
It's us or them, and make no mistake, if England falls, neutrality
will get us nowhere."

So Joe had said.

"Survival only, this one," her mother added.

Us or them.

In rising tension they passed the early summer in an Ireland
that looked on both sides with the apparent dispassion of a
neutral, and in secret gave all its support to the beloved enemy.

"Who's a closer friend?" said Joe when they were discussing
this one limpid evening in early June, all the windows open to
the soft dusk and the moths swinging to the lamps. "Who's a
better friend than the fellow you've been fighting with since
kingdom come? Like Ireland and England. Neutral and all, wouldn't
you think they'd favor the old enemy rather than the fellow who
comes in from the outside to attack him? Ireland'll be neutral
only on paper."

"They weren't of that mind in the last war," said Mrs.
McRoss. "Ireland took advantage then of England's troubles."

"She hadn't got her own freedom then," Joe said shrewdly.
"She had no say in the Great War at all except for the thousands
of Irishmen who died in it."

"Joe, you're a philosopher," said Emily.

"I'm all that," said Joe, "and an intelligent man into the
bargain. Will you come down with me now this fine evening and
get the papers, and we'll see where they're all going to land us
next."

The telephone rang over on the mother's desk by the window,
and Emily moved to answer it.

"If that's Bridie Kilmarnock," said Joe, "tell her I'm away at
the North Pole."

Emily smiled.

"Clonfrack 69," she said politely, intending to let Bridie
Kilmarnock down lightly. The girl was mad about Joe.

The line crackled and spat.

"Dermot!"

She made wide excited eyes at Joe.

"Yes, yes, darling. Oh, Dermot, how lovely. Yes, I can hear
you. It's not good, but I can hear you. Yes?"

Joe watched her face change and grow still.

Ah, Jesus Christ, he thought, here we go again.

Intently she listened and reached for a piece of paper and a pencil.

"Yes, yes, my love. I have that. There's no need to ask my mother. I know it'll be all right. It'll be all right. I'll cross tomorrow night and be with you the next morning. Oh, Dermot. Oh, my love. So soon."

Joe gave a deep furious sigh and left the room, leaving them the rest of the conversation to themselves.

She came down to him in the hall a few moments later, her face white.

"Embarkation leave," she said. A new word then, to grow as common as the name of war itself. "He got no notice. He's going straight down to London and I'm going to join him there. It won't be for long."

"Do you know where he's going?"

"Singapore."

No passionate security yet, which later would not allow a soldier to cross the road and say where he was going.

"Ah." Joe tried to give her some of his relief. "He'll be safe there. Nothing happening there."

"I'll go and find Mums," she said. "She'll be in the stables. Tell her."

London tore at their hearts when she reached him. Bringing to Emily, at least, the sharp sudden taste of the probable war. It was so much the same as their one idyllic day. Gray vistas and scarlet buses, but the trees were green above the rough brown stripes of the trenches in the parks, and many of the shops were already sandbagged, or boarded up save for one small square of glass with paper strips. There were uniforms in the streets, and they stopped to watch workmen carrying benches down a steep flight of stairs under a building in Regent Street. They peered after them.

"Air-raid shelters," Dermot said.

He had a lot to do in London. People to go and see in the Air Ministry; last-minute frantic fittings at Gieves for a uniform they were rushing through for him. Half-made boots at Peales.

"I told the poor beggars there was no hurry," he said. "Now I'm asking miracles. And all my tropical kit, too."

"But Dermot," she said, echoing Joe and her mother. "At least you'll be safe there."

He was silent so long that she looked at him.

They were having coffee in the Old Vienna in Coventry Street Corner House. Slowly he opened his cigarette case and eased a cigarette from under the elastic.

"Em, love," he said slowly. "I didn't join the Air Force to be safe. And if all the real war is here in Europe, then I have no use for skulking over there. I don't honestly know why they're sending me, and I'm browned off."

She felt small and rebuked.

"I'm sorry, darling," she said. "Sorry. If I had my way I'd put you in a cardboard box and tie a string round it."

He laughed then and took her hand, both of them unwilling to let even the smallest cloud mar the few days till their parting.

"I'm browned off too," he said, "that we haven't got married. I thought there was time for it. That I'd be somewhere here, whatever happened. I thought they'd want everyone here. God knows we have few enough pilots. But I'm having no race," he added, "for a special license and a wedding somewhere in between my fittings for my boots. Or at six o'clock in the morning in some little London church we have never seen before. That's not for you, my darling."

For a moment she got the smell of freesias, and felt the cold flags of the cathedral underneath her feet. Málaga still dark beyond the doors.

It was once, she thought. And had it all happened as it should, she would have been quite satisfied.

"You'll wait for me?" he asked her urgently. "You won't go off with some smart character with gold braid all up his naval sleeves?"

She laid her hand on his, all the parallels almost unbearable.

Alejandro had told her she would go off with some Irishman who rode horses all over the *campo*. And here she was, sitting with him on red velvet chairs, with the three-piece orchestra sawing away at lilting waltzes from Vienna, and the sun pouring in from Leicester Square, where the hammering of barricades proclaimed the onset of another war.

"I'll wait for you, darling," she said gravely. "Darling Dermot." She looked at him with such a tide of love and sorrow washing over her face that the swarthy violinist with long black greasy hair came over to them to smile with his gold-capped teeth, and give them the happy lilt of "Morgenblatter" to cheer them up. Practicing unknowingly for the dark years when so many sad young couples would carry his music away with them; treasure in their bright memories.

Gran was back in Sydney Street, deathly frail, but indomitable, and the room looked right again with her bolt upright in her wing chair beside the pretty fireplace, where her tired bones needed the warmth of the fire even on the warm days.

She and Dermot surveyed each other gravely and questioningly for a long moment, as wrestlers might circle, and then she smiled at him and he at her. He treated her with a gallantry and deference that was old-fashioned enough to charm her, and bring a soft flush to the parchment cheeks.

She talked to him of her husband, who had been a soldier, and of the Boer War and the relief of Ladysmith and the great dreadful battles of the Great War, which her son had miraculously survived. All more real to her than the shrieking threats of some hysterical fellow over there in Germany.

Through their few precious days they came and went, having tea with her; and one of Lydia's painfully meager meals, for which Gran still made her slow and regal progress down the narrow stairs into the dining room, her black lace shawl around her shoulders. At the end of the meal she pushed the cheese at them.

"Make up on that, my darlings," she said. "The simpleton will never understand that I am not the only person in the world."

"And when will you be married, children?" she asked them then, having forgotten that Dermot was going away.

Carefully they explained to her again that he was going to the other side of the world and had only a day or two. There was no time to be married.

"Like my Julian," she said, off again into the Boer War. "Only we were married. We had time together first."

The faded eyes looked at them across the perfectly set table, suddenly deep with compassion and understanding.

Dermot came to say good-bye to her on his last night. They had been to a farewell dinner at Stone's, where all the young men and their girls still gathered, but now several of them were in uniform. If they felt an air of uncertainty and rather desperate happiness on the faces around them, it could have been no more than a reflection of their own feelings.

Dermot kissed Gran good-bye, and she stood up slowly to go to bed, abruptly dismissing Lydia, who was hovering at the door.

"Mr. Kilpatrick will see me to my room," she said. "You can come up in ten minutes."

Waiting until Lydia had huffed her way downstairs, she laid a skeletal hand on Dermot's arm. The old eyes were clear and bright and unequivocal, but gentle, resting on them both.

"That woman," she said to them, "has ears like a bat." Then she paused and looked into both their faces, her compassion clear for the bleak impossible anguish of their parting, which despite all their smiles and laughter, they could not keep out of their eyes. Anguish familiar to her from long-gone days.

"She has, I said, ears like a bat." The old eyes glowed with something close to mischief. "So be very careful, Dermot, in the morning," she said with great deliberation. "She is up at dawn. I sleep like a top and hear nothing. Good night, Emily, dear. Dermot, I will say good-bye now and God speed you, for I'm not at my best in the mornings. Will you see me to my room, please."

Emily stood where they had left her, absently fiddling with the braid on the edge of the sofa, almost mindless with the surge of happiness, a little touched by fear.

Oh, good old Gran. How could she ever, without being a forward hussy, have put it to Dermot that she was twice as torn apart to be left for the second time with nothing to remember? And he was far too much of a gentleman to have suggested it to her.

Tears touched her for the understanding and kindness of the old lady, and she was shaken, too, by facing, even with such delight, what she had thought of as being long in the future.

But she would be quite unable, she knew, to say no. Already she was trembling.

Coming back along the landing, Dermot did a small, silent war dance. Oh, God bless the old lady. It was the one thing he had wanted, but hadn't dared ask Em, who was far too gently reared to make a proposition like that. But now Gran had done it for him. Given permission. Oh, hallelujah.

They didn't speak of it very much, both of them taken on sight of each other with a sort of tender shyness. Gran had opened the door, but they must go through it.

Nor did they have time for words.

"Will you, my Em?" was all he had said. "Will you?"

Unable to speak, she had simply nodded, swept by a roar of

emotions that she hoped would take her past all the things like guilt and the Catholic Church, and it was all right for Gran but what would Mums say; and there was her total inexperience, and suppose she made a fool of herself and disappointed Dermot so that he had nothing to remember. Because, God knew, she had only the haziest notions of what it was all about.

When it came to it, they didn't do very well. Emily, at least, was held by the last breaking shreds of guilt and doubt. Hurling themselves together in a sense of fearful urgency as though at any moment Singapore would be at once, or Lydia would be hammering on the door and all the one precious night be over in that moment.

Desperately they tried too hard, and in the end Dermot went crashing from Emily's narrow bed. In the faint light through the curtains from the streetlights, she leaned over and looked at him sprawled there on the rug without a stitch on him, and both of them thinking of nothing except whether Lydia had heard the bump.

Downstairs in her bedroom, beside the drawing room, Gran, sleepless as every other night, heard it and in the darkness smiled, remembering.

Upstairs, Emily began suddenly, helplessly to laugh, stifling it in the sheets, and Dermot, climbing from the floor, began to laugh himself, but out loud, letting go all the tension and disappointment.

"Get on over there," he said, "and give me a bit of room. Or d'you not want me. Pushing me out of the bed!"

"Oh, Dermot, be quiet. Lydia will hear you."

"To hell with Lydia," Dermot said, and there was no more talk and after that everything was suddenly much better. Emily lay when he was asleep, his arms locked around her to keep himself in bed, and knew she need have no concern about his memories. As for Lydia, the ever-present Lydia, she and all the memories of her would be the sort of stuff for weaving lonely laughter when he was gone.

He had made her promise not to wake when he left in the morning, stealing out before the dawn bird Lydia should be awake. He wanted no other good-byes. But she heard him go, padding quietly along the passage to his own room, but she kept her eyes closed and buried her face deep in the pillow; feeling the slow hot tears soak it in strangled silence as he came and stood beside her, and she felt he knew she was awake. A light touch on her hair, and her name said once, and he was gone. Into the pale morning and another world.

She shot from the bed when the door closed, to see him as far as the corner along the street; nor could she believe at this moment, watching him, that he was going away from her. As with any desperate wound, the pain would come later.

Inconsequently she wondered how on earth she was going to explain it to Mums, when she didn't go to Confession.

No tight-mouthed parish priest nor any other priest, nor indeed the Pope of Rome himself, was going to get her to go and say to them that she had done wrong with Dermot last night. Carnal knowledge, they would call it. She hugged herself and grinned. And she should say that she was sorry.

Sorry. She continued to hug herself, as if to gather it all together, as the first sun gilded the tall narrow houses across the road. A milkman chirruped to his horse, and as the tears crept hot and slowly down her cheeks, she began in that bright morning all the counting of dreams and memories that was going to have to last till God knew when.


For a long time she heard from him quite regularly, chafing always at being so far away from all reality and telling of a protocol and formality in service life that had left England twenty years before.

War came to England on September third. The prime minister, Neville Chamberlain, announced at last the death of his frail flower of peace, putting an end to all the waiting, a premature air-raid siren wailing behind his tired and defeated voice.

Hitler was now raging over Poland, happily strengthened in both troops, for other theaters, and in his convictions by his pact with Mussolini.

Astonishingly, war came next to Galway itself, with sharp and sudden impact. Off the coast of Donegal the *Athenia* was sunk, packed with women and children making as refugees to Canada. The first submarine victim of the war. Emily saw it all with shocked, horrified eyes, down on the quays in Galway with Pat and John, helping them with the survivors brought ashore there, already relating every casualty of war to Dermot. He was flying over the sea. Would he look so, some day, shocked and bedraggled, but, please God, brought to safety as these people were. Picked up by other ships and brought back almost to where they had started.

Would he look so, one day, hauled from the cold sea in his yellow life jacket with the funny name. Mae West. After the bosomy actress who wanted everyone to come up and see her sometime. Or not hauled out. Floating sightless until the fishes ate him.

She shook herself, knowing that she must not think like that, and gave her attention to John, who was barking at her a little, wanting two survivors driven to the hospital. Dermot was quite safe where he was, and whatever he might want himself, she uttered a small disloyal constant prayer that he might stay there all the war.

That winter of 1939 was one of bitter cold. The fields were white with frost even in the soft country of Galway, and in London, she read, they were skating on the Thames. Oh, to have done that with Dermot, hands linked in the bright cold air. All wars forgotten. Everything was Dermot, but all in memory and longing, and avid listening to those who said that England's little bit of bother would be over by Christmas.

"That's what they said the last time," her mother said tartly, listening to some of this.

"You think it will be longer?" Emily asked her, and her mother shot her a look in which compassion and impatience were mixed.

"Will you look at Hitler," she said. "Who's going to turn him around before Christmas?"

"What about the Maginot Line?"

"Ach," said her mother, and went off to feed the horses.

Dermot still wrote regularly, surprised like everybody else by the state of inaction in Europe. The Phony War, they were beginning to call it. He had written to Emily earlier, telling her on no account to come to London, certain like everybody else that it would be attacked in the very moment of the declaration of war; unable to understand the long pause.

"But don't come, anyway," he wrote. "Please, Em. You cannot know what will happen from day to day. The strange peace could not last forever. I have never been so glad," he added, "of Irish neutrality. At least you are safe where you are."

And you, she thought. You are safe where you are.

In the circumstances, she thought, they were fortunate. As fortunate as possible.

The bitter winter gave way to a beautiful early spring, and with the easing of the weather, like animals wakened from hibernation, the *Wehrmacht* swarmed across the countries of Europe: Holland; Belgium; Luxembourg; Denmark; too small even to resist them; nations falling like sand castles before the bombs and the guns and the relentless thump of the jackboots.

In May came the invasion of France, and all through the gentle sunny days from the fourth of June, they listened breathless, unbelieving, to the story of Dunkirk and the little ships. The last British soldier fit to be moved was off the beaches, and France and all Europe belonged now to Hitler and his armies.

Toward the end of June, Lady Keene rang up one evening.

"Emily?"

Emily's hand tightened on the receiver. What could happen to him, in all sense? But you never knew.

"Yes? Lady Keene?"

"Yes. Are you well my dear? Not fretting too much. And have you heard lately?"

A great deep sigh of relief, and she felt her future mother-in-law must have heard the change in her voice.

"I'm grand, thank you. And I had a letter just today. He's fine but rather bored, and sends his love. He'd rather be in Europe."

"I am sure he would," said Lady Keene. "Dermot was never one for being a spectator. Well, my dear, we would like you all to come over to dinner tomorrow night, if possible. Would you speak to your mother?"

There was a pause, and then she said, a little too calmly, "To say good-bye to Paul."

"To Paul?"

Rooted on the estate. Unimaginable any way else. Emily felt cold.

"He's going into the Irish Guards. A friend of his father's has arranged it."

"But—but—Paul is—"

"His father's heir." Lady Keene said it for her. "Yes, I know, dear, but he thinks it's a good idea to help try and keep something to inherit. He says he doesn't think much of German methods of agriculture."

She listened to the gentle determined joke. Both their sons. She remembered what Joe had said about the Germans getting as far as Northern Ireland, and refusing to sit there polishing their jackboots. And that the first young man she knew to die would make the war her own.

Paul went.

And a few of Joe's friends, for the gas of it, they said. They'd be back in no time at all and Hitler's head on a plate. A few young men here and there around the county went too, for traditions of patriotism older than the Treaty of 1922. But many of them said it was England's war and let the bloody tyrants get on with it, never stopping to ask what would happen if England lost. Reveling in the unrestricted food and the prospect of England's sufferings.

Joe rattled his paper when the news came over the air that Italy had declared war.

"God help us all," he said. "We're done now. They're very fierce fellows."

Emily laughed at him, and he grinned back.

"I would reckon," he said, "it's the first bit of good news that poor fellow has had to read since the day they marched into Poland."

"What about Dunkirk?"

"Ah, come away with you, Em. No window dressing will make that anything other than it was. Defeat. Total defeat and lucky to get away with it as they did."

In early July came a bitter memory, trailing from her other war.

The only survivor came back to the village from Spain. No town band or cheering children to welcome him home as they had seen him off. Only a poor dull creature walking between his anguished parents, while the appalled village peered through its lace curtains; a great raw scar across his head and no memory of what he had gone to fight for, and no thanks from anyone. Given from then on to blind, terrible rages, his life destroyed.

Emily saw him pass, torn with sadness, for how many more were like him. She added him to her list of personal sorrows from her first war, and knew a deep clutch of cold dread as to what the second one could bring.

\*     \*     \*

They clung to the wireless all through the Battle of Britain, and Emily felt closer to it than ever before, even though they were not flying the same aircraft. These boys were flying new small airplanes called Spitfires and Hurricanes. Dermot was in Blenheims. Or had been when he had gone abroad. Not that she really knew the difference.

The long-expected raids came heavily over London, in the wake of Hitler's first defeat in the Battle of Britain, turning night into scarlet day through all the autumn. Mrs. McRoss agonized for Gran, who would not move.

"I am too old, my darlings," she wrote to them in her thin spidery old writing that conjured up at once for Emily a picture of Sydney Street. "Too old to be very fussy about how I die. It will happen soon one way or the other. So just let me stay where I belong."

Joe left them all in such peace as they had, until Christmas was over, and then one dark and stormy evening beside the fire, with the wind howling in the chimneys and clashing the bare branches of the elms, abruptly he told them he was off.

"I feel guilty," he said. "Guilty. I can't sit here on my backside, with all the butter I want, and let the other fellows get on with it. I suppose it's the English half of me floating to the top. I have to go off with the half that's in trouble at the moment."

Bleakly they looked at each other, and Mrs. McRoss seemed to shrink into herself. Then they looked back at Joe, both of them knowing better than to try and offer one word to stop him. Sick with loss already. How they would miss him. The dry satire and the hilarious good humor. The kindness. All that was Joe. His motives would be far deeper than he would ever let them know.

"What will you do?" his mother asked carefully, her face immobile.

Victor Sylvester was tinkling on the wireless, relayed from London, and Emily saw it all in her mind's eye: all the sandbags and the sticky tape, and now a blackout and these terrible raids; bomb craters she had never seen; Mike beside himself with work. All waiting for Joe, who seemed to belong nowhere else but in Clonfrack and in the green Irish country, all his life and friends about him.

"I'll go and consult Mike," he answered his mother. "He should know how to go about it. If I can't do any better, I'll go into some recruiting office and sign on for the King's shilling. I have the business all organized with young Quinlan.''

All organized. Before he had said a word. He looked at his mother's desperate attempts to keep her feelings from her face. Her look of strained polite interest, as if she were asking him if he was going to the pictures tonight.

''For God's sake, Mother,'' he exploded. ''Isn't even young Ted drilling with the cadets at school? D'you think he'll come home when he's done? The very second he's old enough, he'll be off like a bullet.''

He realized the unfortunate word, and grinned.

''Bad cess to me, I always put my foot in it.''

He began to laugh then, and so did they, and after that it was easier.

But inside three days Joe was gone, Aggie weeping in the kitchen with her apron over her head, and Emily and her mother brightly not weeping in the drawing room upstairs as his car turned away at the end of the avenue. He would not allow them to come with him to the station.

Alone together, Emily and her mother lived through the quiet determined days of 1941, marked as if with festivals by letters from Dermot or Paul or Joe. There were visits from Pat and John, and much interchange with Castle Keene, and a bright determination that they were still families.

Joe had managed to wangle himself into the 3rd King's Royal Rifles.

''Ah, God love him,'' cried his mother. ''He's gone to be a Green Jacket. I had a great boyfriend once, was a Green Jacket.''

He was at last in OCTU training to be an officer, and regaled them in his dour way with hilarious stories of his new life.

At the end of the summer term Ted did exactly what Joe said he would do and, with a long apologetic letter home, went straight from Downside into the Army.

His mother held the letter in her hand, and looked out above it at the gentle garden, her face sharp with pain. She looked up then at Emily. She could not take it even as calmly as she had taken Joe's. Her Benjamin; her baby. Almost six feet tall, but still her baby.

''He doesn't know what he is doing, Em,'' she said heavily.

"I cannot stop him. But he thinks it is still a time for heroes. He thinks he is in the last war."

Emily thought of Dermot training cannon fodder. Training babies to be killed. All the shining boys who had gone into the Battle of Britain, and not come out.

"They are all heroes, Mother," she said. "Every one of them."

Her mother sighed and slowly folded the letter, as if she might need to keep it a long time.

"You could be right. Thank God they won't let Angus go. He has to stay and design factories or something. He's a bit old anyway. Oh, dear God, my little Ted."

They were silent. No longer mother and child. Two women staring into the same shadows; afraid of what they might see.

Through 1941 there was no lightening of the shadows, the war lurching desperately from disaster to disaster.

Greece and Yugoslavia were overrun, and Greece abandoned by the British. Tobruk fell, and the splendid carrier *Hood* went down off Gibraltar, taking with her almost every man jack aboard. Husbands and sons and lovers. Grief, grief, grief.

Crete fell to the jackboots, and it was after its fall that they got the first telegram of their war. Joe was listed missing, believed killed.

"He can hardly have been there a day," his mother said, and Emily desperately tried to ease the black pain from her eyes.

"Only missing, Mums," she said. "Only missing. You know Joe. He's not one to go under. He'll be holed up somewhere with some Cretan girl waiting on him hand and foot, adoring him. Joe'll be all right."

But it took almost two months of anguish for the card to come from the *stalag* in Germany where Joe was indeed holed up for the rest of the war, waited on by nobody.

Only then did his mother cry.

"You know," she said to Emily, tears of relief streaming down her face. "You know what Queen Alexandra said when she saw Edward VII dead?"

"What," said Emily gently. She had never admired her mother more.

"She said, 'Well, at least I know where he is.' "

Emily kissed her and laughed too, light-headed with relief.

"Unless he makes a bolt for it," she said. "Put nothing past Joe. I'll go and tell Anna."

Germany was now well into Russia, fit, she thought for anything, swollen with the pride and blood of all her victories.

With sad faces they listened to it all and felt helpless, nothing they could do about anything, other than go about their lives and pray as best as they knew how, and watch for the postman every day.

Paul and Ted were both somewhere in England, and indeed at that stage of the war there was little place else they could be, other than North Africa, itself under siege and pressure, trembling on the edge of being the next place to go.

The winter came cold and cheerless, and they exchanged visits often, to comfort each other, with the family at Castle Keene, Emily's friendship with Anna having stretched now into a close bond between the two houses. Helping Emily remember that in her empty world the topaz gleaming on her finger did really have a meaning. She and Anna discussed often the possibility of going off to join the WRNS. Anything rather than sitting helpless, and better off than most, on the sidelines. And the uniform was so spiffing. Those little hats. Frustrated, they both agreed that they had no choice but to stay at home and give what comfort they could to the parents; getting on patiently with what already made their lives.

On a dark, cold evening on December seventh, when it seemed that even the bright small light of Christmas would never come, they were all together in Clonfrack, the dinner over and Aggie laying down the coffee reverently on the table before the fire, having never really recovered from having to lay it down before an earl.

"But we mustn't make too much of it," she said to her sister, never willing to have her know she was impressed. " 'Tis no more than Miss Emily deserves, and now the young man away to foreign parts, poor creature."

The sister sniffed, thinking it odd, God knew, that it had happened again.

The green velvet curtains in the drawing room were drawn on this dark evening against the misty chill, the turf glowing and hissing in the grate, the smell of her mother's hyacinths heavy in the warmth. Emily was watching the time for the nine o'clock

news and moved over to switch it on. All of them were now
geared to the long, endless chronicle of disasters, wondering
when hope would ever come.

But they were none of them prepared for what the announcer
read out in his soft Dublin accent.

At dawn that morning, even as the Japanese were smiling and
speaking peace in Washington, their fighter-bombers had attacked the vast American naval base at Pearl Harbor in Hawaii,
racing away again unchallenged into the pale dawn, leaving
behind them a shambles of dead and dying, and of great ships
smashed like toys around the harbor.

America was in the war.

Pale with shock, all the women looked over at Lord Keene, as
though he alone might be able to put this fresh terrible disaster
into some kind of focus.

Slowly he took out and lit a cigarette, the black and white de
Reske box printing itself with the moment on Emily's mind.
Never again would she see a de Reske cigarette without thinking
of the shock of Pearl Harbor.

"I'm afraid," he said slowly, "Dermot has had his holiday. It
will be his war now."

His war.

Emily switched off the knob of the wireless and came over to
stand in front of him, trembling, her face tight with shock. He
would allow no extravagant reactions of any kind.

"Have you an atlas, Emily?" he asked, so calmly that it
steadied her, and after a few minutes of digging in the bookshelves,
she came back with her own old Phillips from school, blue-
covered, marked with the innumerable stains of childhood.

They took the coffee away and spread the atlas open on the
low table between them, poring over the far part of the world that
had meant little to any of them until Dermot had gone to Singapore.

"In my opinion," he said slowly, and paused, his eyes on the
map.

Anna swept the loose ends of her hair back behind her ears to
see more clearly. Her fair head bent over the atlas beside Emily's
red one.

"In my opinion," Lord Keene went on, "they won't be
content in going east at America. They'll come in the other
direction too. They'll want India through Thailand and Burma.
And they'll want the Philippines and Malaya and Sumatra for

jumping-off grounds. No mistaking it, I'm afraid. Dermot's war is beginning.''

Good-byes were subdued and anxious, and when the door had closed behind the other family, Emily looked at her mother in mute distress. So far away. Such a feeling of total helplessness, that he could be in danger, or dying or even dead, and God knew how long it would be before she ever knew.

''We'll just add him to the prayers now, darling,'' said her mother quietly. ''Come on to bed.''

Lord Keene might have been laying Japan's plans for them.

The very next day they landed in Malaya, striking south toward Singapore.

Three days later they sank the carriers *Repulse* and *Prince of Wales*, the pride of the Far East fleet, and the news said it was thought there would be few survivors. Emily stood with her hand on top of the wireless, as if it might give her some frail contact with it all, her eyes dark with strain. Could he have been on a carrier? How woefully ignorant she was that she didn't know what kind of airplanes a carrier would have on it. Or even what he was flying now. But probably he wouldn't be allowed to tell her that. It was the not knowing that was so ghastly.

Anna rang up.

''You've heard the news?''

''Yes.''

''Hang on, Em,'' Anna said. Never one for fuss or excess.

''Yes,'' said Emily. What else could she do? Hang on, and see what happened.

The Philippines were invaded, the Japanese armies flooding over the Far East as the Germans had flooded over Europe. The whole known world seemed lost.

On Christmas Day, Hong Kong surrendered.

They saw in the New Year all together, with Pat and John; and drank to it with all the hope and bravery they could summon, but in all their hearts was the sad certainty that they were only waiting for what must inevitably happen. And after that, God knew.

The waiting did not last long.

On February fifteenth, when the fields at Clonfrack were soft with rain, and the first violets showing in the ditches, the Crown Colony of Singapore surrendered, in the interests of the civil population, to the Japanese.

## EIGHT

It was far worse than over Alejandro.

She looked back now on that grief and loss as she might look back on the weeping of a child. There was pain, physical pain, as though sorrow invaded her like a disease; slowing her; clouding her eyes; making her feel old and useless.

Her mother watched her helplessly. This time she did not even have anger to sustain her. There was nothing wrong with Dermot. Nothing. He had been perfect for Emily.

They comforted each other with speculation, as they had with Joe, making each other laugh rather desperately with pictures of Dermot learning to live like Tarzan in the jungle. Hoping against hope, against all the reports of the carnage and destruction at Singapore, that he would in the end prove to be alive and safe, and a prisoner of war.

Thinking then, both of them, that a Japanese prisoner-of-war camp would be like the German *stalag* where Joe was bored, always hungry, and fretting like a caged animal, but basically all right.

"They must be the same, mustn't they, Mums?" Emily said more than once. What did they know about the Japanese, who seemed to have come like a flood out of nowhere. All those hordes out of that nation of islands. But they must be the same, because of the Red Cross and things like that.

"Geneva Convention," said her mother. But already Malaya was sealed off from the world. Who was to check what went on? She thrust all her own doubts and fears away and set herself to keeping a cheerful face for Emily. God damn all wars.

Before Lady Keene, Emily hardly dared express a doubt, so serene and unshakable her calm.

"Darling Emily," she said. "It is a war. We have to give our sons and those we love, and then accept as best we can what happens to them."

"Any news of Paul?"

Lady Keene smiled. One part of her world was good.

"Yes. We had a cable yesterday from Alexandria. All well and cheerful, he said."

Anna, too, had smiles breaking through the anxiety in these dark days of Emily's. She was more beautiful than ever, Emily thought, with her hair hanging in a pageboy bob almost to her shoulders. You often read in books, thought Emily, of people with golden hair, but Anna has it.

"Anna," she said to her one day, "I'm so grateful to you."

Anna looked up in surprise from a piece of sewing. She was doing a lot of sewing lately. Emily hadn't noticed.

"Grateful? To me, Em? But why?"

"Well, it's corny to say you're such a comfort to me, but you are. You never make a fuss, but you're just always *there*."

Anna smiled at her, some unconcealable happiness making her beauty radiant.

"I often think," she said, "I am a very negative person. I can never rush around charming people, like Paul for instance. Or your one and only Joe."

"You don't have to, Anna," Emily said with truth. "You just have to be you."

Anna smiled again, and Emily realized with a shock, and for the first time, that she was more than happy. She was glowing with some secret.

How could she be, thought Emily, touched with sudden amazement and bitterness. With Dermot gone into some void and probably dead. How could she be so happy? What about?

Anna laid down her sewing, and looked a moment out the long window of the sitting room at the bare February garden, soaked by rain, the draggled roses looking as if they would never bloom again for anyone.

When she looked back, the happiness was dimmed in her eyes by pity.

"I'm going to tell you a secret, Em."

Emily waited.

"I'm going to be married. In April, I think."

"Anna."

Emily was swept by more emotions than she could separate, and had to acknowledge that a feeling of betrayal was among the strongest. Anna, who was always there, was going to go away when she needed her most. Anna, who was always so unobtru-

sive that it was easy to forget she would do the same things as
any other girl.

And resentment boiled. Remedios had got married. Now Anna
was going to be married. And the Air Force and the war and the
ghastly Japanese were all stopping her from marrying Dermot.
Why did it always have to be her?

Long afterwards came the surge of sad pleasure brought by her
real love of Anna.

"Oh, Anna, I'm so pleased. But how sudden. And who?
You've kept it very secret."

"Terence O'Dowd," she said, and her answer was typical, as
though she had seen clearly through to Emily's resentment.
"There was always something," she said, "Joe first and now
Dermot, that made it seem a sort of insult to be happy. We were
going to announce it at Christmas, but we were all so miserable."

I was so miserable, thought Emily, sickened with self-reproach.
Why should her grizzling stop Anna being happy? Terence
O'Dowd. With a big training stable in The Curragh. One of the
up-and-coming young men in Irish racing. Sharp and intelligent
and witty. And good-looking in his brown, horsey way. Fine leg
in a boot. Why hadn't she realized, she thought. He'd been here
constantly since the summer. He'd been here for Christmas.

Abrupty Emily got up and went over and kissed Anna.

"Anna dearest," she said. "I am so sorry. I've been so buried
in my own miseries I never even noticed. What a pig I am.
Anna, I'm so pleased for you. Terry's a pet."

A charming lopsided grin and lazy eyes that missed absolutely
nothing. He was more than a pet.

Anna was delighted to talk about it at last, her beautiful face
shining.

"The parents are very pleased," she said happily. "And we've
decided there's no point in hanging around any longer. It might
be months and months before we hear anything about Dermot,
and there's no point."

She leaned over and touched Emily's hand.

"Sorry, Em," she said.

Emily shook her head. This was Anna's moment.

"When, then? When are you going to get engaged?"

"Next week we'll announce it. Terry's coming down. We'll
have a great party and all be happy again for a while."

"And you'll get married?"

"In April. Mother says we should be able to get the chapel clean by then."

"And you'll be going to live in The Curragh?"

Anna beamed.

"I shall absolutely adore it. All those horses. You'll come and stay."

Bleakness swept Emily, aware almost for the first time of how much she had depended on this quiet girl. Of course she would go and stay, watching their happiness with agony. Doing her best. But it would never be the same again. All Anna's life and thoughts would be turned toward Terence. As hers were toward Dermot.

"I wanted you to know first, Em. Wanted to tell you myself. I feel it's awful for you."

"No matter, Anna. I am happy for you."

And deep down beyond the pain, she was.

When April came on a day of blustery unstable weather, when the gray bitter showers were compensated for by sudden brilliant sun and a sky as blue as the Virgin's robe, she watched Anna's lovely wedding in the private chapel of Castle Keene. Still consecrated, but barely used, it was opened up for the wedding, beautiful in its absolute simplicity, fitful sunlight flooding through plain peach-pink glass to fill it with a subtle and gentle glow, gleaming on the great jewel-encrusted sanctuary lamp that must surely have come from Spain: touching the hair of a little Madonna with the clear untroubled face of the child she was, her own blessed baby on her arm. The pews were of some pale, old wood, and the floor of white marble, giving gleaming color to the magnificent carpet inside the sanctuary.

A place of soft light and quietness, and ineffable peace, fit setting for the gentle radiant beauty of Anna, floating down the short aisle in a cloud of old family lace.

Emily was startled when outside the church Lady Keene bent suddenly and kissed her. She looked very beautiful herself, in a dress of green georgette and lace, two cream-colored full-blown roses against the back of her small hat.

"Emily dear," she said. "I had hoped to see you and Dermot in there by now."

Emily stared at her.

In there? Almost she went back to take another look. Ever since Alejandro she had thought of her wedding as belonging in the austere little parish church in Clonfrack: although not, if she could help it, with the austere little parish priest.

But this? To be married in this pomp. And Anna had been married by a bishop. Would Dermot want that? Sadly she realized they had never even got as far as talking about it. Left as she had been left with Alejandro; speculating always on the might-have-been.

Oh, God.

"And Paul of course," added Lady Keene. "He above all."

And Emily reproached herself, not for the first time, that she was not alone with grief.

She answered Lady Keene nicely but evasively, unable even so vaguely to renounce Clonfrack for the second time, and moved on with the chatting crowd making its way along the castle corridors to the big salon for the reception: determined to enjoy her day.

Had Anna not gone away, she might have been able to handle the spring. There had been no word of Dermot, other than all the wireless and newspaper reports of the chaos of the withdrawal from Singapore. Units had been split up, men joining other units or making their way independently to what safety they could find. It was to be emphasized, the reports said, that the normal rules for communications of prisoners of war through the Red Cross must not be counted on, as there was no certainty that the Japanese would observe them.

It could be months. Years, the way the war was going. Or never.

The spring was more than she could bear. Every wallflower that opened velvet petals to scent the mild evenings, every bird that sang its head off in the unfolding blossoms of the orchard, every soft warm wind that blew, heavy with the breath of the awakening country: all these were intolerable. Implicit with so much life and beauty, and he not there to see them. Making pain of every waking hour.

She would never admit the possibility that he could die.

"I would know," she had said to her mother passionately. "I would *know*. Dermot could not be dead and I not know."

Her mother looked at her with pity, knowing how often these words had been said in vain in other wars.

But what is the difference, thought Emily. He might as well be dead. And for how long. How long. All the length of this ghastly, beastly war, that seemed to do nothing but progress from disaster to disaster.

"Oh, *hell,*" said Emily, and watched her mother going quietly about her life, somehow a little smaller than when Joe was at home; bearing the burden of Joe, of Mike in all those dreadful air raids; and Gran; of Dermot; for her.

Poor Mums. She could grieve for her, but she couldn't help what she was going to do. Selfish, but she couldn't help it.

She went out one evening for a walk alone, the wind blowing soft from the west and the rooks quarreling fiercely in the tops of the elms; all the pastures gold with buttercups. Her hands deep in her pockets, she walked steadily over all their land, the late sun red-gold on her bent head. Her decision was taken. All she had to do was find the courage to tell her mother.

Firmly she turned at the far end of the pastures and tramped back, looking already with the pain of another parting at the gray house luminous in the lilac dusk; lamps already lit in the windows of the kitchen, and the small sitting room upstairs that her mother used again a great deal, now that Joe was gone. As if, thought Emily, coming across the darkening garden, she could not bear to see it empty.

Oh, God.

She came in the side door and hung away her coat in the closet off the hall, stuffy with the smell of galoshes and Wellington boots, and went slowly up the stairs trailing her hand on the banister. The small room had rust-red walls, what could be seen of them, and white woodwork, the greater part of the walls covered by white-painted shelves crammed with books; a couple of fine Paul Henrys, which were Joe's passion, capturing all the subtle shifting blues of the west of Ireland. Comfortable furniture, well worn, and an old-fashioned high-barred grate that made the best fire in the house.

Emily sat down on the sofa opposite her mother; loose covers exactly the same color as the walls. She wasn't capable of any preamble that might ease it all, desperate now to have it out and be on with it.

"Mums."

"Yes, dear." Her mother looked at her over her glasses.

Something in her face told Mrs. McRoss it was important, and she laid down her book.

"Mums, I simply cannot stand it here with Dermot gone like this. I'm going over to England to join the WAAF." She spoke with difficulty.

She spread her hands, and her thin strained face begged her mother not to make it hard for her.

"To sort of," she said, "sort of, carry on for him."

Emily knew afterwards that she deliberately blinded herself to her mother's feelings, so desperate was she to escape her own, thrusting away the pity her mother so surely deserved at having to face more loneliness and sorrow.

But her mother did not make it difficult.

For a long moment she sat silent, staring at her daughter, her face full of the pity she would not ask for herself.

"Geraldine," she said, for she was now on Christian names with Lady Keene. "Geraldine and I have been talking of this," she said. "We have both felt you should get away since Anna went. But my darling, the services! Couldn't you find something to do in Dublin?"

Not another one in danger, cried her heart, but she wouldn't say it. Emily was of age and free to go. She must burden her with no emotional blackmail.

"No," said Emily. "Please, Mums, I'm so sorry to abandon you, but I want to be a Waaf."

To be as close as possible, she felt, to the life that had been Dermot's. To wear the same uniform and know the things that he had talked about. To spend the interminable time of waiting in doing as nearly as possible what he did. For no one now had any illusions that it was going to be other than a very long war. And she would not see Dermot again until the end of it.

She tried to say this to her mother, who said, "If ever, my darling. You may never see him again. You must be brave and face the possibility, so there can never be any too terrible a shock. Singapore seems to have been a total disaster. You have to face that he may be dead."

Months, and no word had come. The world gradually finding that the Japanese were going to regard no rules, accept no conventions, about prisoners.

Emily looked at her mother across the warm quiet room, and said what she so deeply felt.

"No, Mums," she said, as if she had never said it before.

"No, I cannot feel it. And Dermot could not be dead and I not know. That's why I'm going. I couldn't endure to sit here till he comes back, and say I have done nothing about this war."

Her mother would not lift a hand to stop her going, knowing the sad and desperate forces that drove her, but in an attempt to keep her close for at least a while, she tried to make her enlist in Northern Ireland.

"I was talking to Peter Cormack," she said, "home on leave, and he was telling me they have a string of recruiting offices all about two feet over the Border and the Southern Irish are pouring over to join in their thousands. He was in charge of one of them for six months."

Emily snorted.

"Well," she said, "it wouldn't be the Northern Irish pouring into them. They're all pouring the other way, down into Dublin to stuff their faces with food and buy clothes without coupons, and get away from the war. No, Mums, I'd not want to spend any time up there—I'll go to London, see Gran and see Mike, and I'll go on from there."

On April thirtieth, soon after the George Cross had been awarded to the battered and beleaguered island of Malta, Emily walked into a bleak recruiting office in the King's Road, and was made a Waaf.

Gran had wept a little, and understood and given her her blessing. Mike had cursed and raved and tried to stop her, knowing it useless all the while, and Lydia had been sure she was going to perdition.

"I knew what I had really done," she wrote to her mother, "when I got as far as Paddington Station to come down to where we are now. Everyone was very kind and polite and we might as well have been going on a coach tour. Then at the station the Sergeant showed us a place marked 'Forces,' and said we could get a cup of tea. Off we went, and I don't know if the rest of them were as simple as I was, but I never thought except about a table and a cup and saucer on it.

"There was a huge wire grid, with thick white cups with no saucers all lined up on it and a gigantic woman in a dirty apron going up and down over these cups with a monstrous teapot that had milk and all in it. What didn't go into the cups went down through the grill, and I felt horribly sure they emptied it out and boiled it up for the next lot.

"If you wanted sugar there was a tin spoon on a piece of string and about thirty people fighting for it.

"That's when I knew I had left home."

But she was far from unhappy. After that first shock everything was so different that there were no parallels in anything that had ever happened to her before. She waded into her new life, doing her best to find common ground with girls she could barely understand. Nor they her.

"Miss la-di-dah!" they called her, without rancor, and amiably mimicked her accent, and she learned quickly to speak only with short and simple words to them. Nor could they understand why she was not willing to rush out into this wonderful world, where in the gigantic NAAFI there were hundreds of men, all waiting for no more than a word of encouragement.

"There's one here," she wrote to Anna, "who was so delighted at how easy it is, that she dated seven different chaps, all to meet her at the main gate at the same time. Then she went down and hid behind the guardroom to watch them all come. They think I'm dreadfully dull and prim; she absolutely killed herself laughing."

But she herself was astonished by their own prim modesty about their persons; writhing in and out of their voluminous issue pajamas with passionate care that not one indecent inch of their bodies be revealed. Washing with fierce speed with towels draped round them. And then lying in bed exchanging in hoarse cackling whispers details of their sexual passages with the airmen, which made Emily blush even in the darkness. Remedios would have loved them.

"I've learned things you certainly never taught me, Mums," she wrote. "And I should be a revelation to Dermot. But kind," she added. "All of them so marvelously kind. Everything from a headache to a hangover, they rally round.

"There's one girl has the most terrible nightmares and wakes up screaming the place down almost every night. There's always someone gets up to go and comfort her. There's another and she coughs so much she wakes everybody else up, but never stirs herself. She gets everybody's shoes."

She did not write about the times she lay awake herself after these disturbances, thinking of her mother and Clonfrack. Only with sorrow for the loneliness she had caused, never with doubt or regret. She would listen to the breathing and the tossing and the mumbling sleep-talk of twenty-nine other girls—she who had never shared a bedroom except with Remedios in Spain—and already in some obscure way she felt better about Dermot. The total diversion of her new life was seeping away the pain; challenging her at every turn to meet something that had never happened to her before, tempered by the sobering realization that no matter how distasteful it became, this time she could not walk out on it and go home.

She felt closer to Dermot, telling him in her mind all the hilarious things that happened to her, knowing he would understand them. It was his world. But, she realized wryly, not entirely. Entering the Air Force as a cadet at Cranwell, he had probably never even touched the depths of living of a common or garden-variety aircraft-woman 2nd class in wartime. The lowest form of life on earth, as their redheaded Drill Sergeant constantly reminded them.

Still, the uniform she put on each day was the color of his own, the badge on her cap the same as in the center of the little pair of blue and gold enamel wings he had given her on his embarkation leave.

She knew his eyes must have rested, as her own did, on a vast parade ground as big as an aerodrome itself, crossed and re-crossed by squads of marching and stamping blue figures. The high white clouds of summer loitered over regulation red-brick buildings exactly the same as those he must have known; the ordered and conventional patches of garden around the Officers' Mess and the commandant's house; all the whitewashed stones around the guardroom and the neat dark rows of wooden huts that were their own quarters, crisscrossed with concrete paths; carefully segregated, airmen to one side of the Station, airwomen to the other.

In a couple of weeks she had almost acquired an affection for the open, windy place.

She had, in fits of laughter with all the other girls, drawn her uniform from two cynical airwomen in a vast and drafty hangar. They had seen more rookies come and go than they could remember having hot dinners, and no longer even cracked a smile at the yelps of dismay that greeted regulation blackout bloomers down to the knees; and stockings apparently made of canvas; shoes so thick that they wouldn't even bend in the hand, never mind on the foot; skirts barely to the knees and four feet wide, or five feet long and a foot around the waist; jackets with one shoulder longer than the other; caps perched on the top of the head or crammed blindlingly over the eyebrows.

Only the severest cases were referred to the camp tailor, and once the fits of hopeless laughter in the hut had subsided a little, it did not take Emily long to realize that it was very like boarding school. As long as the top image was all right, no one cared what went on underneath, and as long as the more terrible examples of underwear were carefully preserved or even borrowed for kit inspections, there was never any need to wear them. Long after the war she was to give her unworn blackout bloomers and her good warm undershirts to a deserving old woman in Clonfrack.

She learned how to put on her stiff new shoes and sit with her feet in a basin of water, wearing the sodden shoes then all day, and thinking of her mother's horror. Yet finding, as the experienced ones said, that they dried to the shape of the feet and were far more comfortable after that. She learned to smooth them off with a hot table knife to reduce the coarseness of the grain, and how to press her new-issue skirts into shape under the biscuits of her bed.

"Biscuits," she had learned to call the three small mattresses that made up her bed, and that her knife, fork, and spoon were called her "irons," and were to be regarded as little less precious than the Crown Jewels themselves. She learned how to make her bed so that neither biscuits nor blankets disintegrated in the night, and how to stack it in the daytime to satisfy the eagle eye of the Corporal in charge of the hut, who was at that time to all of them substantially in the position of God.

Slowly but surely she changed from Emily McRoss into McRoss E.A. No. 2018798. And knew her new identity. McRoss 798. Snapping to attention.

She was perfectly content. She made two friends in the same squad, although they were not in the same hut: Bertha, who had been a secretary and thought the WAAF would be more fun; and Penny, eighteen and straight from school, perpetually in a fluster and, like Emily, there to forget two brothers already gone to war.

"I couldn't stay at home alone," she said, "and do nothing. Or even a job. I simply couldn't. The parents were darlings. They never did a thing to stop me."

They talked with all the freedom of people who knew that after a short while they were unlikely ever to see each other again. Heads together in a quiet corner of the seething NAAFI. And to them she said, as she had said to her mother, "I know Dermot is not dead. He could not be dead and I not know."

In the vast bare room where they had all gone through Intelligence and Trade Selection tests, Bertha as a trained secretary had put herself down for Orderly Room duties.

"Group Captain's Assistant, I'll accept, no less," she giggled, "as long as he's tall, dark, and handsome."

Penny had put down for Clerk SD, although she didn't really understand what it meant.

"I think," she said morosely, "that it means they think I can read and write and not much else. It probably means cleaning the showers. It's worse than school."

"Oh, no." Bertha was all knowledge about this one, shaking her neat dark head. "That's terribly clever. Those are the people who work in the Ops Rooms and put all the plots on the tables. Terribly glam, my dear. You'll catch a pilot in no time at all."

Penny at once went into a flat spin that she wouldn't be able to cope, and had to be reassured by the other two.

"But me, Mums!" Emily wrote home the next day. "You'll never guess what they said to me. The officer just looked at my height and presumably the size of my feet and asked me if I would like to be in the Police. Can you *imagine* it! Me hounding my friends all over the place! Everybody *hates* the Police, great muscular females. Anyway, she realized I took a very poor view of that, and began to look at the results of my tests, you know you have to fit triangles into squares and so on, and know the name of the prime minister. It seems I'd got 100%, so she changed her tune and said how about Code and Cypher. That sounded fine, and then she said there was something rather special coming up, for which she thought I would be very suitable. She wouldn't say any more, but the initial training is for a Clerk SD. That's plotting in Ops Rooms and things. Sounds a great gas, doesn't it. Better than asking people for their passes. I'd be on their side every time.

"I expect to leave here in a few days—"

On the evening before she left, she walked alone around the perimeter of the vast parade ground. Bats were swooping exactly as they did in the dusk at Clonfrack, and the edges of the enormous Station were already lost in the shadows.

She looked all around her at the great open space. The constant traffic of camouflaged vehicles on the road beside her; the endless coming and going of multitudes of airmen and airwomen. This, she thought to herself, was what she had come in to the service for. To be among these people in just such a place. The first stage hadn't been too bad at all, and now she would go somewhere similar to belong. With airplanes, she hoped, then she really would feel close to Dermot's life. Some huge, open place like this, no doubt, but with airplanes. For as long as the war lasted, this would be it.

She turned a corner, all four edges of it bordered with the inevitable whitewashed stones, making her way to where the first lights glowed in the long windows of the NAAFI, blind after blind going down swiftly for the blackout. There was a dance tonight, all the girls madly excited.

With interest, even eagerness, she looked forward to the next stage. There was nothing much wrong with a place like this, until the end of the war. Or rather, she amended, until Dermot came back.

"You'll never believe it, Mums," she was writing a week later, "but I'm living in a workhouse. They condemned it for the paupers years ago, but it seems its quite good enough for us. We have to wash in tin basins set into holes along a bench that is on a gallery wide open to the air at both ends. No running water. What an experience. We have to go across the courtyard to the modern building for a bath!"

This had been a sorting and a sifting, and out of the squad she had trained with there was no one left but herself and Penny and one other, finding themselves arriving in a group of about thirty girls at dusk, on the long bleak station of a Midland town.

Still, she expected to be taken on a bus out into the country to the now familiar windswept Station, and all of them were astonished to arrive at the old gray building in the middle of the town; sensing quickly a new atmosphere; jockeying for the best beds in a long, bleak raftered room where once the paupers grieved and died on their hard truckle beds, under high, barred windows.

Appalled and intrigued, they inspected their washing arrangements and realized they had to go down a flight of iron stairs and along a passage to a loo.

"That'll put an end to jaunts in the night," said someone.

"Oh, my God," said another girl, "just to know it makes me want to go at once."

They found the Orderly Room and reported in, making wide eyes at each other to see Waafs with their hair curling over their collars. By next morning all their own hair had been released from the tightly scraped style of the Initial Training School.

"It's all so *small*, Mums," wrote Emily, "like a family. Of course, I didn't know, but I thought all RAF Stations were gigantic. And we can come and go into the town, which is just outside the door, but we've had a look, and there's not really much to go for. Not even a nice café, and the food's very good here, so I imagine we won't bother much."

They still had no idea what they were there for, nor for how long, but they couldn't care less, reveling in the easier atmosphere and the easing of all the rigors of their initial training, which they had not found rigorous since they had known nothing else; sorting out their talents, the ones clever with the needle tearing apart and altering the more appalling uniforms; washing each other's hair in the draft whistling across the tin basins; happily putting on the nail polish that had been forbidden at ITS. Unwittingly putting together a unit that was to remain virtually unchanged until the day came that Emily left the WAAF. Girls of all styles and characters, the pretty and the plain; the hilarious and the sober, talkative and quiet; almost all of them rushing with eagerness and generosity into their new shared life. A few, the very few, who made it clear, early on, that they must be watched for meanness and a hostile selfishness.

It was not until they had had four days' settling down and relaxing, did they have their first glimpse of the setting of their new life.

In an anonymous red-brick building, a bus ride into the green flat Bedfordshire country, a mock-up of an Operations Room had been built for the training of Clerks Special Duties.

For the first time, Emily saw the huge round tilted table under the bright lights, the map of the southeast of England on it divided into ten-mile squares, each with a large black letter of the alphabet. The ten-mile squares, their new instructor explained, were divided again by ten squares, so that the big letter, with a number from each direction, gave a position of an aircraft to within a square mile.

Several of the slower ones found it difficult to grasp, and
patiently the Sergeant went over it again.

The bright, impatient redhead next to Emily nudged her. Already this girl wore her sharply altered uniform with a style that
belonged to no one else.

"Well, that map tells us something, doesn't it," she whispered.

"What?" asked Emily. Apart from its great size and the
squares, it looked quite ordinary to her, bright under the square,
low-hung lights.

"Tells us where we're going. It's not Scotland, is it."

Emily shrugged. Personally she thought THEM quite capable of
training recruits on a map of Kent and Sussex and then sending
them to the Firth of Forth. Even so soon she had not found logic
to be one of the gifts of Dermot's beloved RAF. There was that
chap she had talked to in the NAAFI at ITS, who was a fully
trained motor mechanic and was going mad having been allo-
cated to the Orderly Room. They had wanted to put her into the
Police.

"Maybe," she said.

She was more interested in the fascination of what they were
being taught. In the huge, bare Ops Room with the large clock
divided into colors, marked, she saw at once, for twenty-four
hours. The tall tote at the top of the table gave her a jolt of
memory, all the aircraft on the table slotted in exactly like the
odds on the racecourse. Hostile or friendly, and height and
number.

They took it in turns around the table, the others watching
from a gallery above; clumsy and awkward to begin with, with
long rods that could reach right across the table, tipped with a
magnet to be released from the handle; slapping down little
colored arrows exactly, or more or less exactly, on the map plots
coming through a headset. Then a little plaque that fumbling
fingers pushed together to say precisely what the arrow meant.
Hostile. A yellow square. Number. 11 + . The little arrow carefully
put down going in the right direction; for which they were all
madly learning the degrees of the compass.

Emily found it fascinating and easy, soon handling her rod
expertly, thinking of Joe and many a long day they had spent
fishing on the riverbanks outside Clonfrack; soon slapping down
her little arrows with ease and accuracy. But many of them
couldn't get the hang of it, blushing and fumbling and clanging

their rods on the metal light shades, the Sergeant Instructor charging around the table tearing her hair, her round face red.

"Don't you realize how important it is," she would cry, grabbing the rods from their hands to show them yet again. "The controller will be watching these plots for all his information about an incoming raid. Deciding what fighters to put up. If he was depending on you lot, you'd all be bombed to extinction before you'd ever managed to pick up an arrow!"

For the first time in months Emily began to know a degree of positive happiness. The new work fascinated her, and the strange air of secrecy that lay over the place where they worked. Red brick; austere. It could have been a school or a hospital. They saw none of it except their own big bright-lit room, the corridors leading to it and the showers off it. Sandwiches were given to them every morning in the cookhouse, and they ate them in the galleries above the table, the big lamps out and sunshine flooding in through skylight windows. Gossiping and speculating, and swapping the details of their lives. Emily found there were several girls like herself with fiancés, or even husbands, already lost to the war.

Word was beginning to seep through from India from survivors of Singapore who had made their way out through Java and Sumatra. News that on one day would bring foolish hope and on another, black despair. One thing was becoming clear. No word could be expected from those taken prisoner. No small dirty note such as had come from Joe on the back of a cigarette packet: "I am a prisoner. I am well."

From those left behind when the Japanese swarmed over Singapore there could be nothing but silence, and years of waiting for those at home.

"But he is not dead," Emily told her newfound friends, exchanging their experiences. "I am quite sure he is not dead. I would know."

To add to her growing content, that year saw the first turnings toward hope in the black course of the war.

While she was still in the Workhouse, the news came of the thousand-bomber raid on Cologne. The first strike back to lift the spirits of the whole beleaguered country.

"I didn't think we *had* a thousand bombers." One of the girls lifted her head from polishing her toenails.

There was always someone who knew.

"My dear! Only just. Held together with string and sticky paper and throwing the bombs over the sides like the last war. My boyfriend's in bombers. He told me something like this was going to happen. Scraped up every kite on the airfields."

"Well, it did make up a thousand."

"Good for morale," said the knowing one loftily.

With the Battle of Midway, the Americans took their first victory in the Pacific and halted for the first time the headlong onrush of the Japanese.

Cautious hope began to break the darkness.

It was the end of June, the weather as benign as the news, when word flashed through the Workhouse that the posting list was up for the end of the course.

Emily clattered down the iron stairs with all the rest, knotting her tie as she went. It was possible to rush about the Workhouse in your shirt sleeves, but going tieless would have been too much.

They gathered in a frantic knot around the board for Daily Routine Orders.

Anglesey or Inverness or London? Right on the doorstep, or half a thousand miles from home and Mum? The more glamorous ones hoping desperately for Fighter Command at Stanmore, where it was rumored that all the best catches were to be made.

RAF Darlowe. All of them except four to RAF Darlowe.

RAF Darlowe.

Nobody had ever even heard of it. In a clamoring body, they besieged the Orderly Room, where the Corporal on Duty knew as little as they.

" 'Baint never heard of it," he echoed them in a thick Somerset accent. "Happen it'll be the end of the earth." Obligingly he thumbed through his papers. "Railway warrants to RAF Darlowe, Sussex. There you be, girls. Sussex."

Sussex. The ones from the South of England were jubilant, the ones from the North morose. Penny, from Eastbourne, danced a jig of delight across the paved courtyard between the Workhouse buildings.

"Come to think of it, I have heard of it," she said. "Only a little tiddly place, all new, somewhere near Worthing."

Only a little tiddly place, thought Emily. Then there must, she thought, be a big air station. Her mind was still set on a large open place. Only there did airplanes and the ghost of Dermot seem to belong. And she would be able to go up on short leaves to London and see Mike and Gran. The bombing wasn't so monstrous now. Nothing would happen. She was a long way from Holyhead and home, but she couldn't have everything.

RAF Darlowe would do.

London to her was the London of just one day, and in the time before she actually joined up, she became reconciled, almost as if they were part of the loss of Dermot, to the terrible scars and craters of Central London. But the journey down to Sussex tore her apart yet again, every one of them silent as they looked out at the small neat rows of suburban houses in South London, gapped like broken teeth, the barrage balloons floating lazily, silver, between them and inner London. Too late for them.

"All those poor little people," said someone. "Poor little people."

It was minutes before they remembered again that they were all young and excited and heading for a new life.

Three Bridges and Hassocks and Haywards Heath, all of them leaning to the coach windows in the bright day, spelling out the journey that was to become so utterly familiar.

Change at Brighton, the Warrant said. There was one girl who had remustered and was an LACW, one rank above their nothingness. They called her Auntie and questioned her every move, and insisted in her carriage on poring over the Warrant for themselves, agreeing that they must change at Brighton. Kitbags to be dragged from the guard's van and shouldered around the echoing station, with the shattered glass roof, to a smaller and dirtier train that would take them along the coast. The LACW counted frantically, having had them on the loose for fifteen minutes, and they didn't help her; in the end taking pity on her and assuring her they were all there. Fresh, excited smiling faces, not one of them that was not thrilled to be beside the sea.

Hove, that was no more than Brighton, and then out into green, green fields, flat as marshes, and the sea shining beyond them. Cyclists and army cars waiting at railway crossings, and the light blazing silver through the narrow windows of a small church up on a hill.

"Lancing College," said Penny, who lived at Eastbourne and was almost at home, passionately proud of her county, and trying to make them all listen while she recited "Sussex by the Sea."

The sea itself swarmed in on them at the great estuary at Shoreham, where they clanked over the wooden bridge and back again into the green flat fields, rich long grass and flowers along the edges of the line.

Two stations after Worthing, Movement Control had said at Brighton.

The LACW was getting anxious, standing up at Worthing, where the more urban ones were glad to see a town of some considerable size, soldiers in numbers in the streets.

"Looks like a bit of talent there," said someone appreciatively.

"Who wants brown jobs! We're in the RAF! I want a pilot."

West Worthing and then Darlowe and they tumbled out dragging their new white kitbags after them.

Frantically the LACW counted and then gave the Travel Warrant to the porter-ticket collector-station master, who received it in silence. He looked in his grimy corduroys as though he had been reluctantly disturbed in Digging for Victory in the allotments beside the line, where cabbages and lettuces bristled and beans dangled on their long poles.

They poured and jostled out through the ticket office, dragging their kitbags behind them, already straightening caps and tucking in hair for the good impression they must give on a big Station.

One by one they halted on the railway station steps.

"There must be a bus," said someone. "It hasn't come yet."

"Must be," said someone else.

A straight new concrete road stretched from the station for about three hundred yards and then ended in a hedge. The joins in the concrete were burst with grass, and dandelions and weeds choked the verges of the road. Beyond the hedge stretched the green Sussex countryside, scattered with ancient trees, spreading soft and tranquil to the rise of the Downs, golden in the declining sun. Below them in the fields a farm cart moved, and clouds of birds were going home to bed. Two fighters raced across the distance.

"I'll go and ask the porter," said the LACW. "He can at least tell us how far it is. There must be transport coming."

He came and stood on the top of the steps among them, his official cap in his hand, scratching his head, with the air of a man about to reduce people to amazement, not for the first time.

"There."

He waved an arm to another parallel concrete road that they could see crossing the railway on a bridge.

"But how do we get there?"

"Be a track at end of the road."

"But where's the actual Station?"

The LACW was a little distraught. She was a conscientious girl with a serious face and bad skin, and knew she should not be asking a civilian for information of this kind. But how else would she find out?

The porter seemed to read her mind.

"All on us knows round here," he said. "Took the country club, they did. There."

They all looked where he pointed, and saw the pointed gable of a white house, buried in tall elm trees no more than a quarter of a mile away.

"Gosh," said a girl. "Is that all?"

He gave her a quick reproachful look as if to say that she should not ask him *that* and went back into the ticket office.

In baffled silence they shouldered their kitbags, and began to walk down the straight white road to nowhere.

*NINE*

The whole place was so new and so secret that they had to scrub it out themselves before it could be used. None of the people who normally did the cleaning were allowed inside it.

At first they could not even see it. Their billets were in a row of small semidetached houses opposite the big one, she and Penny sharing a room with another girl with whom Penny was becoming friendly. Emily looked at the fourth bed and wondered who would come there. It made all the difference to have a real friend, and she hadn't found one yet.

She looked too without success for all the order and the whitewash that she still thought essential to a proper RAF Station. And the airplanes.

A quick race around that first evening had shown them nothing more than the big house with its lawns and towering trees. "Elm Tree House" it was called but had already become "The Elms." And the small red-brick houses facing it; and a little wooden guardroom; and a gate in a barbed-wire fence that wouldn't have kept out a dog. Or an airman, or a Waaf, as Emily was to know well later on, when she wanted to come back to the billet a bit later than her pass allowed, and like everybody else, used the hole in the fence behind the barn.

The barn was a vast shadowy and beautiful structure of Sussex flints, with a stage and a minstrels' gallery, which the country club had used for dances. Promised to them, for a NAAFI, the only instruction for the moment was that soldiers had been in it, and they mustn't use the showers there until they were white-washed.

"Who's going to take a peek?" they asked each other, and the ones brave enough came back out scarlet, and told the others to wait for the whitewash.

The men, they were told, lived upstairs in the big house. Out of bounds to Waaf. But downstairs was the mess for both of them, looking out long windows on to a green lawn with one beautiful weeping willow. Lovely light rooms that gave them at once the feeling of happiness.

"It's all a bit of a mystery, Mums," wrote Emily, "but so beautiful. Such a nice place and the country all round it, and the sea and the Downs. Not that we can get near the sea, apparently it's all tank traps and barbed wire and mines on the beach, but it's nice to be able to look at it. And we have Worthing, which is a big town, quite close by, so it all seems too wizard for words. Except that we simply can't see what we're going to do. There's nothing here."

"Oh, yes, there is," the Corporal of the Orderly Room said when a few of them at last asked him. Gazing a little hopelessly at the sea of paper needed for the establishment of a new Station; but delighted, along with all the men already there, to find himself suddenly in a sea of pretty girls.

"They aren't like ordinary Waafs," he said to the Sergeant of Police, who looked at him sharply.

"They aren't ordinary Waafs," the Sergeant said importantly. "Not for That Place."

But not even Corporal Taylor could tell them what That Place was.

"There's something down there in the fields," he said. "Called a Happidrome. Don't ask me any more because I don't know. We're not allowed down there."

There were a few officers, who seemed to know as little as anybody else, quartered suitably at a distance in some of the bigger houses in the streets across the railway bridge. Only the calm blond handsome man who they learned was their C.O. came and went with any determination, driving his camouflaged car through the big gates and on down into forbidden fields.

They themselves got down there on the third day, having had a day to explore Worthing thoroughly, comparing notes about the pubs and cafés; excited by the presence of so many soldiers. Exhilarated and still a little puzzled by so much freedom. Emily became reconciled to the fact that there were no airplanes and no whitewash. Only a small, small Station, where everyone was still feeling their way and seemed to do more or less what they liked, or thought best. A big lovely country house in beautiful surroundings. How lucky she was, but where was the work?

On that third day they were mustered at nine o'clock, outside the Orderly Room, on the graveled road, all of them with immaculate collars and shining shoes, pressed skirts, and flawlessly short hair, having been told by the gloating Corporal Taylor the evening before that their Boss had arrived, and that was the end of fun and games.

She was tiny, a little dark flight sergeant with curly hair and bright intelligent eyes that assessed the painfully tidy ranks in one sweeping look.

"First thing we'll have to do is get you all some battle dress. You're far too tidy for this job."

They looked at her with open mouths. To a girl, it had been drilled into them in their initial training that there was nothing that they could be too tidy for. Neatness was All.

"It's a matter of being comfortable," she said, and they looked at each other sideways in their immaculate column and wondered what on earth they were going to do. Dig ditches?

She did not tell them then, marching them off down the road into the fields. Their fine precision was already growing rusty, and would grow far worse—watched by a grinning policeman who leaned out of the little wooden hut looking as though they were the funniest thing that he had ever seen, trying to make them laugh.

They got wide eyes and wolf whistles from a couple of airmen coming up the long gentle hill on bicycles; making it clear that a marching column was something hilarious they had not seen since they came to Darlowe. Badges with sparks on their sleeves, Emily noticed.

Right in the middle of the road, the Flight Sergeant suddenly stopped them and ordered them at ease. When the crash of their shoes subsided, there was no sound except the larks and a reaper and binder clacking across the other side of a field. Sounds, to Emily, of home. Farther down a man was slowly leading a horse. They seemed to be in the middle of a farm, but like the one from the railway station, the concrete road they stood on was neglected, weeds in green clumps in the joins, and the ditches full of long soft grass and the yellow flowers of sorrel.

The little Flight Sergeant looked up and down the silent, empty road and seemed satisfied, then she turned to them and her fine eyes blazed with her enthusiasm, and her sense of theater.

"Flight, you call me," she said. "I'm Mary Simpson, but to you I'm Flight. I'm in charge of your training here."

The column, at ease, stirred restless and sighed. More training.

She was alert to their every reaction, and reminded Emily suddenly of a lay teacher at her English convent who had more than half the girls passionately in love with her. This young woman sought also for power, and had much to offer them, to get it.

"I don't mean the kind of training you have had already," she said. "Although you will use some of that."

Theatrically she looked up and down the road again, but there was only the man and the horse, turning in at a gate farther down the weedy road.

"I have stopped you here," said Flight, "so that no one, but no one, can hear what I say to you." Her voice was deep with mystery, and in the bright silence they hung on her words.

"In due course," she said, "you are about to go into one of the most secret places in England. The very first of its kind. You must never never breathe a word of anything you see or do. In due course you will sign the Official Secrets Act and after that it will be a criminal offense if you should talk. Do you understand me?"

Wide-eyed and astonished, they all nodded, standing in the empty road. What had they walked into? As if to underline the reality of their strange new world, two Spitfires raced across the milky sky, so low their shadows fled behind them across the tidy fields.

Flight followed them with her eyes, and when the noise had passed, she spoke, with all the throwaway carelessness of one who knows she will impress.

"From Tangmere," she said with faint disparagement. "We will control night fighters from Ford. Beaufighters."

So there are airplanes, thought Emily with satisfaction. Control? What did she mean, control?

And where? Somewhere called Ford. Not here. Already she was storing up every word, with the certainty that one day she would tell Dermot all about it. Match experience for experience, no longer outside his world. Wasn't that why she had joined?

Several of the girls would have asked questions then, but Flight held up a hand.

"I'll tell you everything else inside the Site," she said.

Inside where? Once more Emily glanced over the fields, full of cabbages and brussels sprouts and potatoes, and could see nothing else.

With a bit of shuffling, as though already they understood that drill was not going to play much of a part in their lives to come, they turned their column and marched on toward the invisible Site. Or Happidrome, as Corporal Taylor had called it. Sounded like a fun fair.

The first things foreign to a normal farm were two aerials, one round and standing still, and a big square one like an upended box that was revolving.

"Ah," said Jenny Spinks in a hoarse whisper behind Emily; the big, bosomy fair girl with a boyfriend in bombers, who always knew it all. "Radar! So that's what it is."

Respectfully they all swiveled their eyes toward the two aerials, sitting peacefully in the middle of a potato field, where a farm laborer dug, among the rills.

Emily barely knew what radar was. Something to do with seeing airplanes at night. How ignorant Dermot would think her, and how far she was from that last war when there was nothing but the stutter of guns in the hot nights, and the sinister Falangistas sweeping through the streets in their black motorcars. She felt a moment of superiority. Sure she was the only girl who had had another war.

It all seemed so far away now. Like a dream. Another war. Another world. Now it was aerials turning in a potato field. They had had enough to frighten them, even at that simpler time.

She tripped over the edge of some camouflage netting and stopped her dreaming. There were wooden huts, nothing unusual, but the camouflage was stretched over a long, blunt, windowless concrete building, itself camouflaged and hidden yet again by the tall green trees left undisturbed about it.

"This is the Happidrome," Flight said dramatically, rolling her great eyes at them, and inside the one door a grinning policeman gave the thumbs-up to a mechanic along the corridor; who in turn went racing down to the secret, smelly world of the mechanics' basement, to spread the glad news that the girls had come.

After all the buildup and the Official Secrets Act, and the air of mystery and the drama, all they did for a week was scrub it, to the ribald delight of the mechanics and the young men installing the telephones.

The new world took shape. More girls arrived and they were divided into three Watches, working around the clock, night work coming up every third night. Emily was B Watch.

The dark, clean-smelling place took on reality. The only bright lights were over the familiar plotting table; all the other small cabins overlooking it, in darkness, lit only by the green clicking traces that went clockwise round and round on the black faces of radar tubes with the same map as downstairs on the big table. The plots they learned to read now were actually real airplanes leaving their small green curves on the tubes as the trace swept over them.

A strange, eerie half-dark silence, with girls murmuring into headsets, drama implicit in their concentration. Spooky, thought Emily. Definitely spooky.

She knew the deep excitement of tracking her first German airplane; saying the word *hostile*. Already imbued with some fierce antagonism for the little green blip on the screen, as though she had been fighting Germans all her life.

They couldn't chase him because they had no airplanes. Their Squadron was not yet arrived at Ford. So they gave him reluctantly to the Spitfires at Tangmere, which Emily learned was their parent Station. Although she was not to set foot in it for three years, no longer having any desire for the whitewash and the open spaces. There was no time at Darlowe for whitewash.

Quickly it became home; waking up in the summer mornings to the sound of the train heaving from the station, and the cocks crowing in back gardens; the vast fresh expanse of sky above the Downs as they went over for breakfast. The smell of the dew-wet grass and great clouds like fans opened above the sea, still faintly touched with the pink of dawn.

She lacked a friend. Among all the other girls who had arrived, none had been put into the empty bed opposite, and Penny and Isobel had struck up a keen friendship. They were the same age, Emily realized; most of them were younger than she was. At twenty-three, she thought herself to be a bit of an Auntie. She got on well with most of the girls, but had no special friend.

It was about a month later that Marianna came. Emily came off Watch at one o'clock, all of them clattering starving up the stairs for their irons.

"Bet you it's mince. Tough as old boots."

"Or dead camel, like we had last week!"

They spent a lot of their small weekly money on eating in the various little cafés and hostels of Worthing, feeling the pangs of their interminable hunger.

Emily raced into the room, and found a girl sitting on the empty bed. Tall, taller than herself, with long legs sticking out, and huge black eyes and her hair falling down, reminding Emily suddenly of Remedios, a ghost from another world. A suitcase and kitbag seemed to have been upended on the floor.

"Hello," said Emily. "You've come to live with us?"

"Hello. I'm Marianna Mason. They told me to come here. Hope you can bear to have me."

Emily smiled, suppressing an instant liking, not wishing to rush in too soon.

Marianna was staring hopelessly at her belongings, a rather larger pile than other people seemed to possess.

"Where do I put all these?"

"Well, we're a bit new, you see, and a bit short on equipment. We don't really have anywhere."

They were to become far less new. But never less short.

"We have no lockers," Emily went on, "so we've all been to the greengrocer and got orange boxes, and then a bit of cloth from home to make a curtain for the front, and Bob's your uncle, there's a locker. They allow them."

"How very ingenious," said Marianna, with clear distaste for all the work involved. "I'll leave them in the suitcase under my bed."

Emily opened her mouth to say that this was not allowed but felt that would have been of little interest to Marianna.

"How old are you?" she asked her.

Marianna looked faintly surprised.

"My dear. Ancient. Twenty-four in September."

"Thank goodness for that," said Emily. "I'm twenty-three. The other two in here are only babies, out of school, and I felt a bit out of it in this room. They're nice, though."

"My dear! I hope they're not too nice. They'll probably disapprove of me. I'm posted here under a Cloud."

Marianna's eyes were enormous, long nervous hands gesticulating, trying to impress Emily with some monstrous disgrace.

A Cloud?

Marianna stood up, stretching slim elegant legs, moving restlessly.

"Where I come from, there's another Happidrome, not finished yet. So we had nothing to do and we used to go swimming in a little river before it reached the beach and the mines. Then there were some empty houses, and one was open so we used it as a sort of beach house. Used to bring beer and food down there. Smashing, it was. But my dear, some sod went and told about it, and They said it was immoral. Immoral! My dear, for God's sake. As if one would want to. I mean they're all married and things, with wives in Wigan!"

Marianna's eyes shone with outrage, and an unassailable innocence that would never leave them all her life. Forever she would find herself struggling in the coils of situations before which anybody else would have seen the DANGER signs in scarlet letters.

"So they split us all up and posted us all off, before we could contaminate each other further. My dear!" She looked at Emily with real concern. "I hope I don't contaminate you."

Emily grinned, suddenly very happy.

"Would you like to put your things away," she said. "And I'll take you over to the mess. It's dinnertime."

Vaguely Marianna looked over the shambles on her bed.

"Ah," she said. "I knew I had some irons somewhere."

From the jumbled pile she extracted a knife, fork, and spoon.

"What about all that lot?" asked Emily.

The days of blankets and biscuits folded and stacked were over, with the whitewashed stones and the big Station of Emily's dreams. But she looked over the other three beds, which were expected at least to be tidily made and empty of litter.

Marianna looked at it distastefully.

"I'll do it all later."

"What if somebody comes?"

"They won't," said Marianna.

Together they walked across the graveled weedy road between the small houses and the big one. Down by the guardroom one policeman was putting his new dog through its paces for another, commands and abuse ripping the air; a corporal mechanic zoomed round them on his bicycle, singing "The White Cliffs of Dover," winking at them appreciatively. The grass of the lawn was very green, and in the weeping willow a thrush was singing its head off.

"Nice," said Marianna approvingly. "Much nicer than where I was. I'm glad I was immoral. Have you got a mug? I seem to have lost mine. Can I share?"

Emily began to see a new pattern in her life.

"I'm really thrilled, Mums," she wrote home. "I think I'm so lucky. I have marvelously interesting and sometimes exacting work, and in a most wizard place. I'm looking forward to seeing some of this country. Lots of stunning little country pubs where they stare at you and sell onion sandwiches. Why did we never have onion sandwiches? Can you send my bicycle or do you think I'd be better to get a secondhand one here? Definitely a must if I am to get anywhere. One of the mechanics has said he'll show me Sussex."

Probably, thought Mrs. McRoss dourly as she read it, be glad to show her a whole lot else as well. But Emily was gone and must look after herself.

"We are so small a Station," Emily went on, "that it's all very family and informal. Except to stagger down on Watch, I haven't marched a step since I came here. And no whitewash, but rather a lot of nice weeds."

That mystified her mother.

"The place," she finished up, "is surrounded by Canadian soldiers. A bit pressing.

"There is a fourth girl in our room now," she added. "Marianna. She seems all right. Fun. Most of the girls on our Watch are very nice which is just as well, as on a Watch we work, eat, and sleep together twenty-four hours of the day. There are a few I find poisonous, but I daresay they find me poisonous too, and it's amazing how civilized we all are about it.''

Mrs. McRoss, in the faraway cool summertime drawing room of Clonfrack, folded up the letter and shook her head. It might as well have come from boarding school. Or Spain. Probably on a small Station, it was not very different. No mortal responsibility except their work. Clothes, food, everything provided. Nothing to do in their off-time except to decide how to enjoy themselves.

She was pleased. Even on paper this Emily was a different one from the strained, sad girl who had waited so desperately for news of Dermot. And that Alejandro before that.

She thought of the Canadian soldiers; the mechanic (mechanic of what?) with the bicycle. What if Emily were to fall in love again? And then Dermot came back? Quickly she got up and got a book to stop herself thinking. These things must resolve themselves. But it was almost impossible for them to resolve themselves in this dreadful war without pain for somebody.

The Squadron came to Ford, the smooth beautiful Beaufighters passing backwards and forwards over Darlowe, where the girls looked up from the fields with a proprietary air.

Emily was quick at the work; fascinated; giving herself totally to the mystique of the small darkened rooms and the air of tension and concentration; the disembodied voice of the pilot on the RT, making it all at last real.

She had become calm now about the plots of yellow hostiles on the table. They were never real. No one could ever believe that they could drop a bomb, until a clutch of white-faced girls came home from Worthing where they were having coffee, telling of the walls of the Assembly Rooms going in and out, and all the chocolate-sipping old ladies diving under the tables. And they with them. Bombs, she realized, were real as well.

They finished their training with the Squadron and became operational, knowing a new tension and terrible excitement in the darkness, eyes glued to the flickering traces; one of the small green blips no longer another friend playing enemy, but a German. A Hun. Intent on killing, if they could not kill him.

The terrible feeling of flatness if he got away.

Blood lust, thought Emily appalled. Real blood lust. We wanted to kill him. And we are all nice girls.

The smokers lit up cigarettes and the Controller rang down for tea, and they all relaxed, watching for the next one.

Would it be the same, she wondered, if they could see the two young men they had been trying to shoot down into the night-black sea? If they saw them as people, with wives and mothers. Had someone in this way shot down Dermot? Months ago now.

It shook her to the depths of her being. She gulped the hot thick tea that an obliging mechanic slapped down before her, and asked the girl next to her for the first cigarette she had ever smoked.

Inexpertly she held it, and breathed in the dry smoke and wondered did she really want it, her eyes on the green trace going round and round in front of her.

She saw something coming off the coast of France. Vague. Definite!

"Bogey!" she said excitedly, and then more soberly gave the Controller the plot.

Unidentified aircraft, moving fast. The other two girls relied on what she told them to get its height and speed. Quickly she stubbed out the cigarette, and bent to her tube. Nor did she ever remember again to have qualms.

The nineteenth of August was a bright clear day. All the day fighters from Tangmere were streaming overhead to support the landing at Dieppe. Babbling with excitement at the idea of even a small force landing again on the shores of France; with overtones of some immense radar secret, they were expected to pretend that none of it was happening, and to take their tests for becoming full-fledged radar operators with the coveted sparks on their sleeves.

Emily wrote to her mother that evening, longing to tell her how cosmic it had all been, all of them waiting in the field outside to take their turn, with the Spitfires screaming overhead, and the whole place crawling with VIPs and trying to teach six weeks work to Marianna in the last ten minutes; everyone in a state bordering on hysterics.

"You'll be pleased to hear," was all she wrote, "that I have got my sparks, and I'm also a Leading Aircraftwoman. No longer the very lowest of the low. We all got through, even Marianna, and that was a miracle. Marianna was an LACW already, I don't quite know in what. She always does everything backwards.

"I'm really enjoying myself here, Mums. It's fun."

* * *

The next day Mike telephoned, getting through with difficulty to the phone box under the stairs in The Elms. Somebody fetched Emily from supper.

"Em! A *man* on the telephone. Sounds gorgeous!"

Emily could not suppress the quick lurch of hope, coming out through the hall and taking the telephone as if it were red hot, her mouth dry. It could not be. It could not possibly be.

It wasn't.

Mike understood the surge of hope, and was gentle with her.

"Sorry it's only me, Em, love," he said. "You all right?"

"I'm fine, Mike. Fine."

If it couldn't be Dermot, then how smashing to hear from Mike.

"What is it, Mike?"

"Sad news, I'm afraid Em. Not bad, but sad. Gran died suddenly this morning."

"Oh! Poor Gran."

Sad indeed, but of all the people she lived in fear for, perhaps Gran could be spared most easily.

"Mums will be upset."

"She is," said Mike. "I've been talking to her. Look, Em, I won't have her coming over. She wants Gran buried beside Grandfather in Clonfrack. I'll see to all that, and go over with the coffin. First, though, we'll have a Requiem in the Oratory. See which you can make, yes?"

He told her the times, and the next day she went to see Corporal Taylor in the Orderly Room. Someone had started hopefully to dig the little garden outside it.

"Grandmothers!" Corporal Taylor said with disdain, sniffing. "Grandmothers' funerals is for office boys. You'll have to do better than that, my dear."

"But it *is* my grandmother."

"It always is. Anyone there to see to the funeral?"

"Oh, yes—"

"Well then. Sorry, ducks, but not grandmothers. No leave for grandmothers."

Every third day she was free for thirty-six hours and free to go as far as thirty-six hours would take her. By good fortune the Requiem in London could be fitted in.

She rang Mike.

" 'No leave for grandmothers,' " she quoted, "but I can be up on Wednesday."

"Good girl," said Mike. "See you then. I hope it's not too noisy. We've had some rough nights lately."

With a race and a scramble she caught the early train, and arrived just in time to fall out of a taxi outside Brompton Oratory, at the same moment as Mike arrived with the blubbering Lydia.

She was astonished at the number of Gran's friends, ranked on both sides of the overcolored church; elderly, most of them, not all; several uniforms. And she was astonished and also appalled that she could find no relationship between the velvet-covered coffin and Gran. Nothing to do with Gran, all this. Gran was love and security and a sort of stern indulgence for as long back as she could remember; always asking a little more than one thought one could do. Rich with her praise for success.

Gran. It was Gran who had given her that last and only night with Dermot. As though yet some other part of him had now been lost.

Sometime she would learn to miss her, but not now, before all these people with the alien coffin. She was glad when it was all done, and the thank-yous said, and all the kind friends gone about their business. There was rain on this unreal day, and all the streets were shining with it, the barrage balloons looking too heavy with wet to stay aloft.

"Can we go to Stone's this evening, Mike?" she asked as they walked home, Lydia snuffling along beside them, no doubt wondering what was going to become of her.

"Where else?" said Mike. "But I have to leave, for the moment."

Stone's. Pilgrimage for lost happiness. For Dermot and for Gran. For lost love. For that, she thought, is surely the grief of death. The love one loses. Do the very old, she wondered, see their allotment of love shrinking, until in the very end they are left, those that live on, with no love at all?

Thinking this, appalled, she spent the day being very kind to Lydia, who took it as no more than her due.

The rain had stopped when they arrived at Stone's that night, and there was a full moon blanching the streets and a fresh smell of wet trees from Leicester Square.

Stone's was no different; even more crowded. Only the young people had changed. All of the men were in uniform now and many of the girls; bright eyes and shining hair over immaculate collars and the square shoulders of their jackets; subtle snobbery implicit in their attitudes that the Wrens came first, and then the WAAF, the Army a poor third. Apart from anything else, it was only the very odd girl who looked becoming in khaki.

They were no longer silent and demure, listening respectfully to all the Rugby talk of their young men. They had their own war now, and above the steaming plates and the clinking beer mugs, they traded experience for experience with their escorts, who watched them for a few short days of leave, with eyes already old from having seen too much.

Emily settled in one of the booths with Mike, and looked all around her, confused with pleasure and the harsh pain of remembering. Mike realized she was being stared at, and felt proud of her. Their little Em had grown into a raving beauty, one of these girls that uniform really suited. Her red-gold hair curled naturally round the edges of her cap, needing neither clips nor to be rolled around a bootlace like Marianna's, and always falling down. The delicate beauty of her face was set off by the formality of her uniform, yet she always wore it with a slightly cynical air of having dressed up in it for fun.

Around her were all the loved familiarities of Stone's, except that the waiters now were all old, the scurrying, aproned potboys younger than ever. The uproar of talk and laughter was still there, and the clattering of knives and forks.

But it was all searingly not as it had been. Or would ever be again.

For the first time in that day of formalities that had failed to touch her, she felt her throat grow thick with tears. Grief suddenly for Gran, and grief and loneliness for Dermot and a sick, unquenchable sorrow for the atmosphere around her. It would be the same everywhere, she thought. Everyone raced to London and grabbed what time they could. It held the noisy bright-lit room, and all the young determined people; made all the lovely eyes more bright and voices just a little loud; sharpened every relationship. Lay in the old-young faces of the men behind their charm and smiles. This poignant unspoken certainty, the unmentionable truth, that young though they were, for any of them there might be no tomorrow.

For Dermot, young as any of them, maybe the tomorrows were already gone.

She shook herself and smiled determinedly at Mike, her business, like all of them, to play the same game. He was very sweet to her, understanding without words. Mike always understood. Dear Mike. The pillar of the family. Mums's prop and stay. Of all of them, Mums said, he was most like their father. What would they all do without him?

"Lamb chops, please, Mike, if they have them. What else?"

"It's a pilgrimage," said Mike, and offered her a Passing Cloud.

She took it.

"You've taken to the weed?"

Emily smiled.

"I took to it the first night I realized that a hostile aircraft actually had young men in it."

No secrets there. Clerk SD talk.

Mike laughed and lit both cigarettes. His fair face was diffident, as if he wondered if he should speak at all.

"Don't hope too much, Em," he said. "It's a long time."

He was sorry at once that he had spoken, seeing her face shrink. He really wanted to tell her to find someone else.

"There are things," she said, brittle but determined. "I told you about the girl at Darlowe whose fiancé is in the Argyll and Sutherland Highlanders. He got back, I'm not quite sure how, through India in the end. But he said that Dermot's Squadron was fighting next to them in armored cars they'd managed to get somewhere. All their airplanes had been shot from under them, but they were still fighting. Mike, he could be anywhere. Armored cars. I wonder where they went then."

Mike was silent.

"In any case, Mike," she said quietly. "I'm not hoping for anything. Just spelling out my life and waiting to see what happens."

Mike's head came up and he stared at her. This bloody war. This exquisite little sister with so much to offer, and all she was doing was spelling out her life. He made a gesture of defeat.

"But you, Mike," she said then curiously. "When will you marry?"

He knew the answer to that one.

"When I'm a Consultant. I want to stay in the hospital, but the hours I work now couldn't be wished on any woman."

"Anyone special?"

Mike grinned.

"Sort of."

Emily asked no more. Mike could close like a clam if he was asked too much.

The air raid when it came was distant, and studiously ignored by everyone in the restaurant. No one telephoned for Mike, who was always on what he called an umbilical cord.

When they had finished their meal, they walked from Stone's around into Piccadilly Circus, where in the warm fine night servicemen and their girls sat around the steps from where Eros had flown. *Arsenic and Old Lace* was just ending up Shaftesbury Avenue, and through the blackout, hopeful Americans raced shouting after the small glimmer of indifferent taxis.

On the corner of the Haymarket, Mike looked at his watch.

"Jerry won't come back now," he said. "Let's make a night of it and go and dance at the Old Queen's."

She saw him off the next morning in the dark smoky chaos of platform 13 at Euston Station, struck with a terrible pang of homesickness as she stood beside the long red train, where already, with the soft accents, it seemed Ireland had begun. That he should be leaving her here, and going to Clonfrack!

They were constrained and silent with each other, both of them painfully aware of Gran in her coffin in the guard's van, and Mums waiting for her at home.

"I wish I could go with you."

He tried to be light.

"Well, you would go away and be a she-soldier."

Whistles blew and doors slammed all along the train, and she thought of seeing Dermot off that last time in Galway. Mike leaned down and gave her a kiss as it moved.

"Be a good girl," he said. His calm loved face slid off into the shadows and, swallowing her tears, she turned away, blind to all the other partings along the moving train.

It was the last she was to see of him. For Mike, too, the tomorrows had been running out. Three weeks later he was called out to an air-raid incident in the narrow streets of Pimlico. There had been far worse air raids, but in between the rickety old tenements the ambulance took a direct hit, blown into fragments and even the fragments buried as the houses came down across the narrow street. They found a few bits of metal and the twisted number plate of the ambulance.

"Nothing, darling, I am afraid we can even bury," said Mrs. McRoss to Emily with dreadful calm. They had given her leave this time. Brothers counted.

She could do nothing to help her mother. She had to go back. For her there would be another careful year of spelling out her life.

Before she met Sam.

## TEN

She had just been on leave and was still torn at leaving her mother alone in Clonfrack, despite all Aggie's stout protests that she was as well as she had ever been with the lot of them under her feet. And weren't Dr. John and Mrs. Pat, and the Lady Geraldine, in almost every day of the week. Aggie had become the Queen of Clonfrack on account of the Lady Geraldine being in every day of the week.

"Isn't it the truth," she said proudly to her sister in the kitchen, "that the real Quality is the least of it, and she no trouble at all."

The old sister nodded sagely, implying long familiarity with the ways of Quality. And that they were the least of it.

Emily had left them all reluctantly, and the good food, and the streets ablaze with lights, and had come back laden with oranges and chocolate for her friends. Collecting herself to go on Watch, she realized she had left all her pens and pencils in the mechanics' basement before she went away. When they discovered that she could draw neatly and accurately, the mechanics made use of her for simple technical drawings, and unless there was a flap on, she had been spending a lot of time with them, given the freedom of their littered and undeniably cozy underground lair. She loved it. And she loved them. Mechanics were a race unto themselves, no officer dare cross them. The entire running of the whole complex site depended on them, and they knew it.

She opened the door in the long windowless corridor, a couple of oranges in her hand, and clattered down the steps preparing to be welcomed back by her friends.

There was only one mechanic there, and she had never set eyes on him before; doing something immensely fiddly at the bench, with a pair of long tweezers and a fine screwdriver, a pair of steel-rimmed glasses on the end of his nose.

He looked at her over the glasses and she was aware of a strong, hostile stare from very dark blue eyes. Under the brilliant unshaded bulb there were fair highlights in crisp curls not unlike her own, but lighter; he might be handsome without the scowl. A corporal.

All this she took in in seconds, disappointed of her welcome, standing at the foot of the steps with her oranges in her hand, not expecting to have to explain herself.

"Bugger off," he said. "You're not allowed in here."

She had been too long on the Station to be intimidated by some bad-tempered corporal. Nobody spoke to her like that.

"Since when?" she flared at him.

He pointed with the screwdriver at the notice on the door. Mouth like a rattrap, thought Emily. Oh, dear, there was always something to disturb the peace.

The notice on the door announced permission for entry to authorized personnel only.

"Out," he said.

It was too close to her leave. Too close to Clonfrack and everybody spoiling her. She had not adjusted yet, and rage boiled.

She glared at him coldly, ready for battle.

"Well, perhaps," she said, "I'd better sign my work."

Seizing a pencil, at the bottom of every technical drawing pinned to the walls, she scrawled "Emily McRoss" in large letters. Where she had drawn on glass, she grabbed a chinagraph, and scrawled in red.

When she turned and slammed the pencils down, he was still watching her, unmoving, with his hard stare from above the glasses.

"I'll come back," she said, "when there's somebody else here."

Picking up her oranges, she stamped off up the steps, and the dark blue eyes watched her go. She could not really understand why she felt so furious. As one of the lowest ranks in the whole

Air Force, you were always being talked to like that by someone. Her mother this time had tried to persuade her to go for a commission, but Emily had stared at her in horror.

"And have to leave Darlowe! And my work! For some piddling commission in Admin counting pairs of knickers! No, Mums, I know when I'm well off. They pay us more, anyway, than the first two ranks of Admin officers, even though we are less than the dust."

But this corporal was too much. Just too much.

"Have you," she asked Marianna in the rest room, when she had simmered down a bit, "crossed this new corporal mechanic?"

She was still seething.

"Darling," said Marianna. "Yes. Crossed is the word. Have you got a chinagraph? I seem to have lost mine."

She dragged her gas mask from its case lest it was in there. A lipstick without a top, and a broken mirror, and a sanitary napkin in a torn paper bag fell out.

"Marianna!"

"Well, one never knows, does one. Be prepared, the Girl Guides say."

She thrust it back into the bag.

"But the men, Marianna."

"My dear." Marianna smiled her lovely, wide, indulgent smile, coping amiably with all the vagaries of the world. "If they don't know about all that by now, they never will. I meant to tell you. They've made us a lovely floor polisher out of them, handle and all. Professional. The only agreement was that we gave them enough of them to make one for themselves."

"Oh, Marianna, you are hopeless."

"But that awful little man. The new mechanic. I think he's on the wrong side."

I wouldn't have said he was little, thought Emily, impressed against her will by the sheer force of personality emanating from a man who had barely moved. Definitely not little in character, anyway. And not so little himself, either. Taller than she was, she would reckon. She was annoyed with herself for thinking so much about him.

"Why?" she asked.

"My dear, he's a total Nazi. Come here. Go there. Do this. Do that. He won't last long like that here. Someone will straighten him out. I think personally he doesn't like girls."

Emily smiled. All her anger gone. He was the same with everyone.

"Do you know his name?"

"Sam Treadwell. Ghastly little man. Have you heard from your brothers and things?"

"Oh yes. All well, Paul's been all the way in the trip along North Africa, and now he's somewhere in Italy. He wrote from Naples. Ted's in Burma. Says that now he's a captain, he's allowed to struggle through the jungle on a donkey, instead of on foot, and that's an improvement. Nothing from Joe."

The whole war had been going well since the breakthrough at Alamein. North Africa was taken and Sicily, and only a few days ago had come the news of Italy's surrender. In the Far East the British troops were clawing back Burma, and holding the Japanese from India. The Russians were advancing on all their fronts, slowly driving the Germans back to where they came from. And in the Pacific, island after island fell back to the Americans.

They were all struggling through the dark tunnel toward the light. It only remained to know how long it would take to get there. Already there was talk of the Second Front in France.

Emily saw Sam Treadwell later on in the morning in the canteen, when in the mad jostle for a cup of tea it was easy to pretend she hadn't seen him, gossiping brightly about her leave with the other mechanics. He didn't speak to anybody, sipping his tea a few moments and then going out and taking it with him.

Rude, infuriating young man. But quite staggeringly handsome without the glasses, in a sort of hard-boned way. She felt curiously deflated: angry for minding that he hadn't spoken to her. He should have apologized. Early, she was learning that Sam Treadwell was no man for apologies. That self-contained character would have to be taken as it was. Or left.

That night in the NAAFI they were showing *Dangerous Moonlight*.

All the Station was waiting for it. All the country had been raving about it. Everybody wanted to see it, and as it was a rainy evening with a cloud base about the top of the elm trees, it was agreed that half the Watch on duty might come up, if nothing seemed to be happening.

They drew lots in the canteen; no moment of the film they would see more breathless and anxious than that one.

"Oh, good show, Marianna. I couldn't have borne not to have

seen it." They could hardly bear to look at the ones who had lost.

"Nor I," said Marianna. "Anton Walbrook just makes my toes open and close with a bang."

Supper was to be afterwards. Every one of the kitchen detail was off to see it too. In the gray heavy evening, the long grass bent with the mist, the whole Station came to a halt. Only the Police remained on duty, pledged to a complex roster of raising anyone who was needed.

When Emily and Marianna raced up from the Site, the whole dim raftered room was full, packed with excited and expectant faces; cigarettes and chocolate rations ready; the two front rows full of officers, as eager as anybody else.

"Nowhere to sit," said Emily at the door.

"Yes, there is."

Marianna was quicker than she was. The shutter was just coming down on the NAAFI counter at the back, and Marianna leaped for two places on the edge of it, the shutter to lean against.

"Best seats in the house," she said as Emily heaved herself up. "Two and threepenny at least, and no spitting, please."

In seconds the counter was full; girls packed the length of it like migrating swallows on a line.

The lights went out and the audience stirred with excitement, and somebody pushed at Emily's knees.

"Shove over." It was a man's voice. Too dark to see him.

"I can't."

"Yes, you can. Both of you."

There was grumbling and muttering and they half missed the credits as a body heaved itself up beside her. She thought afterwards she would never have enjoyed the film so much had she known who it was, but her eyes were glued to the screen.

They suffered and agonized over the torments of Warsaw; and broke their hearts over the poignant notes of the *Warsaw Concerto*. Last Requiem of a dying country. Lost their hearts to Anton Walbrook.

When the lights went up, there wasn't a girl in the packed place who wasn't crying; emotions torn by the romantic and heartbreaking aspects offered to them of the horrors of war. All the ugliness brushed over, reducing it to pure heroism and sacrifice and poignant, intolerable beauty.

Marianna was frankly mopping her face with a large scarlet handkerchief.

"My dear, too much. Absolutely too much."

"What are you crying for?" said Sam Treadwell beside Emily, and she spun around as if she had been shot.

"I'm not," she said at once, blinking and swallowing.

"It's only a film, you know," he said, apparently unmoved.

He did not offer a hand to help her down but let her slide from the high counter by herself, immediately beside him.

She thought of Dermot, and of Mike, and even of Alejandro, dead all these years in a forgotten war, and felt the film had been for all of them. Not this hard-boned, hardhearted—

In the streaming crowd she turned on him, jostled away but coming back, furious once again.

"What d'you mean, only a film! *It happened!* Don't you understand that! Not just like that, but it *happened*. All those people suffered and died. Don't you care about anything?"

She would have gone on, but in the harsh lights above the NAAFI counter she could see the cold blue eyes watching her. As no doubt he had watched the suffering people in the film. As though he looked at a fly on a pin. And she wilted, feeling helpless. Oh, he was frightful. But why did she mind so much? There were lots of other frightful people in the world, but they didn't reduce her to such a mush of fury. What was it about this man?

Around them everyone was humming or singing the *Warsaw Concerto*, still lost in the film. She stood, silent now, a little island of fury, still raw with all the emotions she had so totally identified with, face flushed and her soft hair electric.

"There'll be no supper left," said Sam Treadwell. "I'll walk you over."

A cool night, the rain gone and a hazy moon hanging over the hills. All the grass and the trees smelling of the day's wet, and somewhere the policeman's little dog barking insanely, as if he had just been let out.

Baked beans on toast, and mugs of steaming cocoa, and all of them rolling now in a helpless hilarity that was the reaction to their torn emotions. Never did they feel themselves so witty.

Sam Treadwell was at her side, not talking, he hadn't gone and got her supper for her from the hatch. Just as long as he kept his mouth shut she didn't mind. Over the baked beans she noticed meanly, and was ashamed of herself, that he did not use his knife and fork well.

She also noticed, but didn't want to admit it, that he had beautiful hands; bony, like his face.

When she and Marianna drifted back across the garden to bed, the weeping willow rustled in a rising wind, sounding like the sea, and a few searchlights loitered over the clearing sky away towards Ford and Tangmere. Could be a busy night after all the rain. She yawned. None of her business, thank goodness. Bed, blissful bed, for them.

After the nightly battle to stop Marianna going to bed in her socks, she lay a little while awake between the rough sheets. Isobel was already fast asleep, snoring gently. Penny not yet in. She was having a tender little love affair with the dark-eyed very young airman who helped Corporal Taylor in the Orderly Room, and would be in at the last stroke of midnight. No doubt even now holding hands lingeringly at the gate of the billet.

As she drifted off to sleep, the plangent halftones of the *Warsaw Concerto* still haunting her mind, she tried to work out why it seemed to have been such a smashing day.

After that Sam seemed to crop up everywhere.

"What's your name?" he asked her the very next day, materializing beside her in the corridor of the Happidrome.

She almost refused to tell him. The man put her back up.

"Emily," she said then.

"But they all call you Em."

"Yes," she said, "everybody does."

"Well, I won't. I think it's common."

She gaped at him, furious again immediately. The loved name of childhood; her mother; Joe; everyone. Dermot. And Sam Treadwell thought it common. Why did he always say the wrong thing.

"It's a matter of complete indifference to me *what* you call me," she said. "Complete."

They had come to the little flight of steps leading up to the dark cabins. He stopped and turned to face her.

"You're a very cross girl, aren't you."

"Me! Me! Cross! It's you. It's the things you say to me. You're rude. I think you're very rude!"

Even as she shouted at him she turned away, unable to resist the bold compulsion of the dark blue eyes that told her clearly that Sam Treadwell didn't give a damn what anybody thought of him. And would call her what he liked. Nor in the end, some instinct told her, would she mind, and that made her even more irritated. She didn't like being dominated.

Savagely she went stamping up the steps to her cabin, and with a small smile Sam went on into the Ops Room.

He never called her anything but Emily.

And when he first asked her to go out with him, she found it impossible to refuse.

Excuses came to her lips about going out with Marianna, but she couldn't follow that up. Marianna would not miss her at all. All her spare moments were being spent with a lieutenant of the Royal Engineers whom she had met at a dance in the Assembly Rooms. Marianna wouldn't do.

Nor could she summon a blunt no, as she had done on so many other similar occasions, trying to evade the searching assessment of the blue eyes as she said yes. Dammit, the man gave her the feeling he was able to read her every thought. And her reasons for thinking them.

They were all going out, changing from battle dress; newly washed collars peeled from the windows where they were plastered flat to dry on the glass; newly pressed skirts hauled out from under their biscuits; the dark blankets of their beds littered with cosmetics and discarded clothes.

Marianna was languidly drawing on a fine nonissue stocking, trying to work a hole around so that it wouldn't show.

"Sam Treadwell, Em," she said dubiously. "The man's a fearful bore. He never says a word. Couldn't you do better. Or has he got Hidden Depths?"

"He's handsome in a sort of way," said Isobel, who thought it always her duty to say something nice about everyone. Isobel was not terribly interested in men. God was more important, and tonight she was dragging an unwilling Penny to a prayer meeting over the bridge in Darlowe.

Penny was carefully applying makeup to her round sweet face in the hope that, prayer meeting or not, something would turn up. She compressed her lips to fix her lipstick.

"I think he's a savage," she said then, succinctly.

But they all take notice of him, thought Emily. All of them. None of them hadn't noticed him. That was the thing about Sam. He compelled attention even while he would have nothing of friendship.

"Darlings," said Marianna then, "has anybody got a safety pin? I seem to have only three garters."

"What about the mess?" said Emily, always the most concerned.

"Oh, for God's sake, leave it," said Marianna, struggling with the safety pin. "Anyone who comes at this time deserves what they find."

From that evening on, through the warm golden September days, Sam was never away from her side.

With the first nip of October air, he brought her his gloves, with holes in the fingers.

"Holes in them," he said.

It took Emily a few moments to gather what was needed.

"You want me to darn them?"

Sam looked at her. What else had he wanted? Emily looked back at him. She had never darned a thing in her life. Aggie always did it.

But Sam was waiting for her to say she couldn't, and she was damned if she would do that.

"I'll bring my sewing kit to the NAAFI after Watch," she said. "I've got some wool."

There was hardly anybody else there when she finished her supper and went over to the barn, where Sam was already waiting. Only the woman yawning behind the counter, and a couple of men playing dominoes.

Sam had pulled two chairs up to the fire, and put on soft music from *The Nutcracker Suite* on the gramophone. His collection of records had amazed her. It was one of the few things he had told her about himself. He adored music.

Emily sighed with pleasure. It had been a hard, trying Watch, and she was tired. In the peace and the firelight with the music flowing over her, she thought back to all her ideas of an RAF Station and smiled, thanking God they were not true. So vastly better, this.

Sam had brought her bull's-eyes because he knew she liked them, having access to all sorts of secret goodies from a confectioner friend. He plonked down the little bag on the table.

"Sam, how thoughtful."

She lodged one in her cheek, and he asked her what she was smiling at. Sam himself was not smiling. He had been on forty-eight hours' leave and come back more dour and closed up than ever, his blue eyes hard.

She told him about the big Station of her ideas, and all the huts and millions of marching Waafs.

"Of course," she said. "Initial training was like that. I thought that was it."

Sam looked at her as he often did, as if she knew nothing about anything, and was lucky to have him about.

"Nearly all of them are," he said. "Like that. You don't realize. This place isn't an RAF Station. You might as well be at home. Look at us now."

Outraged, he waved a hand at the warm raftered room with the red curtains drawn across the windows, and the fire dying scarlet in the big fireplace.

What was it in Sam, she wondered, that so resented happiness or comfort, or anything that was easy. It wasn't that he was puritanical. He seemed almost afraid of content of any kind.

She stuck her fingers out through the holes in the glove and wondered how the hell Aggie made those marvelous darns. Over and under, somehow.

"Is it bad then, Sam," she said gently. "To be comfortable and happy like we are."

Sam gave her one look from the dark blue eyes, but the defensive position was not for him.

"I bet," he said, "you've been comfortable and happy all your life."

Poor Sam, so prickly with some secret pain of his own that he couldn't see beyond his nose. As though Castle Keene and being an earl's wife would free Dermot's mother from sorrow and loneliness. For herself, Alejandro and now Dermot.

"Are you very poor, Sam?" she asked bluntly.

"Not particularly."

She knew nothing of him yet. Only that he attracted her to the point where it was silly; touched her with pity for some troubles he would never confess to, and made her determined to find a way beneath his guard to the real Sam. The trouble was that every time they really talked, it inevitably became an argument, and then a quarrel.

Telling him things might be a way to reach him, until he was confident enough to tell her something back.

He got up and went over to change the record, and the two airmen paid for their cocoa and went out.

" 'Night, George. 'Night, Joe.''

They said good night and grinned, and she knew that tomorrow there would be cracks about who was last in the NAAFI last night. This hothouse of a Station! You couldn't move an inch.

The yawning lady said she was in no hurry to go home, and Sam sat down again.

"When I was fifteen, I was sent to Spain," she said.

"Spain!" As if it were the Arctic Circle. "For a holiday?"

"No. For three years." It should have been three years.

"Away from your family. Away from your mum and dad?"

The idea seemed to appall him. It wasn't being rejected by his family that troubled Sam.

"What did you want to do that for?" he demanded.

What indeed, she asked herself now. To be finished, she supposed. A word Sam would not understand. To learn, as a close Spanish home and the nuns could teach them, all the finer points of living and behaving.

And where were they now, all these finer points of living that she had absorbed? Sitting by the fire in an Air Force NAAFI, with a bag of bull's-eyes and a mug of cocoa, darning the gloves of a corporal of unknown origins, whom she realized was falling madly in love with her, obviously against his will.

For herself she did not know. Maybe she still had them all.

"Had a war there, didn't they," said Sam then.

For a sudden moment it was all yesterday. The machine guns somewhere and the stars, and the fires red over in Churriana.

What was all that to do with Sam?

"Yes," was all she said, torn suddenly by old sorrow. Vulnerable in her raw mixed feelings about Sam himself.

"That fellow Franco," he said then. "Mate of Hitler's. Bully."

Back to the tyrants. Perhaps in an impulse of defense for those fading loves, she told him defiantly.

"I almost got married. I got as far as the altar."

"What! In Spain?" He paused. "Rich, was he?" he said.

She told him in the warm dying firelight the story of Alejandro, and he looked at her literally with his mouth open. It confirmed everything he thought about Emily. Untouchable. But never to go

out alone before you got married! Angela's Mum had been a bit
of a tartar but they had managed something here and there.
Enough to catch him, he thought now, bitterly. He still could not
believe it all. Not about those Spaniards.

"All those blokes," he said jealously. "Those Spanish blokes."

"They might as well have been on the moon," said Emily. "I
never got near any of them. Except Alejandro."

But Sam had gone gloomy and hostile, and at the end of the
room the NAAFI lady was putting the lights out.

She gave him his gloves, shamed by the cobbled lumps at the
tops of the fingers.

"We must get out," she said. "Mary wants to go home."

"Take your bull's-eyes," said Sam, and walked in front of her
out into the crisp night.

Never had he said a word about Dermot, all his jealousy for
dead Alejandro. He must know. Everybody here knew everything
about everybody else. And the topaz ring was never off her
finger. He *must* know.

That would be a row, she thought, when they ever spoke of it.

If it had been made of cheap silver and colored glass, she
thought bitterly, Sam would accept the engagement quietly. But
not with a topaz, set in antique gold.

She had not realized how much the Station life could be a
hothouse for an affair. For she was involved now, with Sam, she
admitted that, and could not help it, facing the accusing ghost of
Dermot almost with despair.

It was so easy to be forever in contact, especially with a
mechanic, for a mechanic could go anywhere. Into the Control
cabin at four o'clock in the morning with a mug of tea when
there was a stand-down; fog or low cloud, and no hint of enemy
action, all the others gone thankfully down to the rest room to
sleep. One girl only would be left sitting at the Control telephone,
a tracer clicking at her side, the red alarm-button by her right
hand to get the whole lot of them back in one minute flat,
grunting and cursing and still staggering with sleep, doing up
their buttons as they came. Legend had it they had shot down a
Hun one night before the Controller even got time to put his
trousers on.

But if there was no alarm, then there were uninterrupted hours
in the close warm darkness, no sound but the clicking of the

trace, and the occasional querulous comment over the intercom from the two girls downstairs staffing the table and the tote. The weather on the hour from Tangmere.

Time to talk the world down, and try to resolve some immovable difference that lay between them.

Emily said it was Sam.

"You're prickly," she said. "Prickly. No one can come near you. No one."

He said she was a snob. That it would have been all right if he were an officer, which maddened her.

She had to admit he was endlessly thoughtful. Like remembering on leave that she liked bull's-eyes. If there was a flap on—and Huns pouring across the Channel like the poem about Drake, ship after ship the whole night long, and all of them exhausted and cross-eyed at the tubes—it would be Sam's hand reaching across to put a mug of tea in front of her. He gave it to the Controller too, of course, and to the other two of the crew. But hers came first, and as like as not a sweet, or purloined biscuit tucked in beside it.

She never thought now about killing Germans; gulping her tea and squeezing her hot, tired eyes, and going back for the next one. No longer did she think about the blood on Alejandro's hands for his particular war. It was war and you did what you were told, and if Darlowe did not succeed in killing them, then they went on and killed a great many people with their bombs. She had long ago come to terms with all that, but Sam was another matter.

"We just seem to have no common ground," she said to Marianna. "Everything's fine as long as we don't start talking."

"Well, Em darling, that leaves you plenty of scope."

The winter day was gray and bitterly cold. They had been delayed on Watch, and instead of coming up with the squad they were walking alone up a little pathway running from the Site, around the gardens, to the kitchen yard at The Elms. The dead hedges and tangled briars that lined the pathway were still touched with last night's frost, barren as if spring would never come again, and the Downs were lost in the gray mist. Wound about six times around Marianna's neck was a vast muffler in white and scarlet stripes, for which anybody else would have been long ago hauled up by the Orderly Room. But not Marianna, who in all such things led a charmed life.

"Plenty of scope? Oh, no, Marianna, Sam's not like that."

Marianna dismissed him with one big shrug.

"My dear, in my experience all men are like that."

"Sam has Principles."

"Principles?" Marianna spoke as if they were some dread disease. "How *very* tedious for you. Are you in love with the little man, Em?"

"He's not little," said Emily, and for a moment Alejandro stood beside her. They were walking slowly now, the conversation grown serious. She turned up the collar of her greatcoat against the dripping trees. It was bitterly cold. "We seem to have nothing in common. He has a chip on his shoulder as big as a house. But I think he is in love with me, if he could only bring himself to show it."

"I asked about you," said Marianna.

Emily stared into the mist.

"It's difficult," she said. "He's so awkward. But I tell you, Marianna, that physically he reduces me to a squelch. It's something about those bones. I could jump on him."

Marianna looked at her in amazement.

"My dear, why don't you?"

Emily laughed at her.

"Well, apart from anything else, he wouldn't let me. He has the most monstrous collection of morals and attitudes and prohibitions. I feel sure he would drop me like a stone if he knew I'd even had my one precious night with Dermot. He keeps telling me I'm a lady. And ladies don't do those things."

"What a crashing bore," said Marianna, and meant it, very sorry for her friend. "Animal magnetism, and Principles at the same time. Terrible for you, Em darling. Does he know about Dermot?"

Animal magnetism, thought Emily. That was exactly it. He drove her wild with all his principles and stupid ideas, but one look at the lines of the bones in his face, the movements of the long beautiful fingers, that sudden incredibly sweet smile—and she was all gone to mush like a helpless ninny.

She answered Marianna.

"He must know. He just must do. Nobody has any secrets in this place. And there's my ring."

They came into the white-walled kitchen yard, and the

policeman's black mongrel came bounding up to meet them, jumping to lick their faces.

"Down, Jezzer!"

The lights were on in the kitchen against the dark day, the windows steamed up, and the cooks shouting at each other and banging trays.

Marianna wrinkled her long nose, delighted.

"Irish stew, I do believe. That should suit you, Em."

"We live on it at home," said Emily, pushing open the back door. "Sam said he would keep us a couple of places."

Everything between them was a confrontation and an argument. Often Emily wondered why she went back for more.

On a bright gentle day in December they walked up the long hill behind the Station to the village of High Salvington on the crest of the Downs. And then along the ridge, with all the coast laid out below them in the pale hazy sunlight. No noise; no airplanes. Total peace without a sound or sight of war, smoke rising straight as a spire from village chimneys in the windless air.

Sam, who always thought of such things, had brought his groundsheet, and they spread it to sit on against the railings of a solitary grave on the very top of the Downs, below an oak tree; looking in contented silence down on the small towns spread like a necklace, one running into the other along the edge of the winter sea. From here it was impossible to see the barbed wire and the minefields on the beaches, and it all looked utterly ordinary.

Sam pulled out a packet of cigarettes.

"Have a Woodbine." They were the cheapest cigarettes available.

Oh, God, here we go again, thought Emily. She couldn't stand Woodbines. They'd burn the inside out of a boiler. But that wasn't how Sam would see it.

"Thanks, Sam, but I'll have one of my own, if you don't mind."

She pulled the green packet of Three Castles from her gas-mask case, and Sam's thin mouth went thinner. Amazing, thought Emily, that that same mouth could produce a smile to influence the very angels. Pity it wasn't seen more often.

"Not good enough for you," he said. "Woodbines, I mean. Here, have a light."

"No, Sam. I simply don't *like* them."

Sam blew a long cloud of smoke from his Woodbine, thin between his long fingers.

"Come off it," he said. "You just don't think they are good enough for you. Like everything else."

She was getting angry, and that annoyed her, because she knew it gave malicious pleasure to Sam. He thrived on it.

Sam rolled over on his elbow.

"Well, look at you, you don't look like an ordinary Waaf."

"We're not very ordinary Waafs, thank God. Darlowe isn't an ordinary Station. I've said that before."

"Even so," said Sam, obstinately. "You're all snobs. You're a snob, Emily."

"Because I won't smoke Woodbines?" She tried to be quiet.

"Part of it."

Because I haven't got a Cockney accent, thought Emily furiously, and knew it was more. The uniform under her open greatcoat had been specially tailored for her, out of officer's barathea. At a glance, she looked like an officer. The stockings on the legs stretched out before her were the finest lisle her mother could find in Galway, the thick issue ones kept exclusively for kit inspections. She had had her issue shoes copied at a rush by a bootmaker in Dublin. Perfectly correct, but of soft fine leather. Her walking-out shoes, she called them. Her cap, tossed on the grass beside her, had come from Simpson's of Piccadilly.

"Nearly all of us look like I do."

Sam made a gesture with his hands, and with a flash of memory she knew that had he been a Spaniard, he would have said "*Claro*." Agreed, but not approved.

"But it doesn't *matter*, Sam. I'm me. Just me."

"Of course it matters. To a bloke like me, of course it matters."

To a bloke like him. What sort of a bloke was he?

No matter where he came from, or what he was as a civilian— and he would never tell her—Sam had some indefinable style. Some proud angle of the head when he walked. A calm self-certainty that was something quite apart from his normal taciturnity. His issue uniform always looked right on him and well-fitting, and his unplaced accent only gave a slight broadening to his vowels. Her mother would say, she thought, that you could take Sam anywhere, and then she could have kicked herself for emphasizing the social differences she was trying to deny.

And could Sam take her anywhere? In his world, whatever it was, she would probably cause him more embarrassment than if she took him into hers.

But she would not give up easily.

"You mean, Sam, if somebody gave you the choice between two presents, you'd at once choose the one wrapped in brown paper, simply because it was wrapped in brown paper, and leave the one wrapped in gold with ribbons on it?"

Sam turned to her and smiled the fantastic smile that transformed his whole severe face.

He took her hand in his.

"I'd want to open the parcel and see what was inside," he said. "Then it'd be all right."

They sat in peaceful silence for a while, smoking and talking of this and that, feeling the first faint onset of the evening chill that would eventually drive them away. Emily turned and looked at the grave behind her, carpeted in the summer's dead oak leaves.

"How marvelous," said Emily, "to lie forever like that, and look down on the town you loved."

"How d'you know he loved it?"

"Can't you take *anything* for granted."

"Anyway, he doesn't know anything about it now. He might as well be in the sea."

"But Sam, he knew *before* he died. He knew, even if he didn't know our names, that in three hundred years' time, we would come here and read the tombstone of John Clement Oliver, Miller, of Worthing, buried all alone on a hill where he could see his town. I think it's splendid. I'd like it."

"Slush," said Sam. "They probably wouldn't have him in the cemetery."

"Sam, do you believe in *anything*?"

He really was absolutely impossible. And yet she knew that she was physically attracted to him, monstrously so; just to look at him, so close to her turned her to jelly, and none of his bloody-mindedness could change it. Marianna would say he made her toes open and close with a bang.

She felt at times confused and even frightened. All her loyal heart belonged to Dermot, must belong to Dermot, and he would certainly come back. She knew if Sam pressed her to some closer relationship, she would be almost in a panic. Playing with fire, that's what she was doing. Playing with fire. Sam was fire for her, if ever it burned and smoldered.

"I believe in Sam Treadwell," he said then, and it was an affirmation of all she had been thinking. If Sam Treadwell decided that he wanted something, he would be very difficult to refuse.

They rambled home hand in hand down through the bare trees, with the gray mist creeping up the hillside. The warmth and strength of Sam's hand in hers was like the fire at Christmastime and the angel on the tree. All her body was aware of him, tensed for some marvelous experience. The bitter day bright just because he was there. I'm besotted by him, she thought. Absolutely besotted by him.

Listening to some long tale he was telling about his service in North Africa, but noticing only how the cold brought such a handsome color to his cheeks and how his somber face lit up when he was interested.

Yet that same chill corner of her mind that she would not look at told her that if Sam pressed her, she would want to turn away.

Oh, God, was it perhaps true what he said? Was she indeed a snob? Was that what it was?

As if to emphasize the end of the afternoon, which had seemed stolen from the war, a whole squadron of Spitfires went tearing along the coast from Tangmere. There was a war, and one day it would be over, and what of Sam then?

She was lonely, coming up toward midnight on Christmas Eve; lonely for her family and all the Christmases gone by; lonely for Midnight Mass in the bleak little chapel at Clonfrack with the simple crib at the back beside the font, and all Clonfrack bursting their throats singing "Adeste Fideles." Missing Ireland; missing all of them.

Missing Dermot more than she had for a long time. His absence had left her vulnerable to Sam, and all her muddled feelings over him, to her sense of guilt. How difficult it all was.

Not guilt because of anything, God knew, that she had done with Sam. Sam saw to that, more moral than old Lydia herself, chewing her dentures over everything back there in Gran's house. Guilt lay, she admitted wryly, in her own thoughts about Sam with Dermot's topaz smoldering on her finger, in the certain creeping knowledge that there would be no happiness in it all in the end, and yet she had not the strength to send him away. At the moment she was having her cake and eating it, but it was impossible that this would last forever. Something must crack, one way or the other.

The Germans gave no sentimental Christmas truce to Darlowe, popping out over the French coast in single, seemingly senseless, forays that were little more than an irritation. They kept them well away from the English coast, so that under the Christmas stars outside, the children of Worthing slept on blissfully beside their waiting stockings.

It was after one o'clock before they all flopped back in their chairs, weary with concentration, and nothing more for the moment to do. There was some laughable rule somewhere that said no girl must spend more than an hour on the tubes. If there was a flap on, all night was nothing.

"Happy Christmas," they found time then to say to each other. "Happy Christmas." And before the Controller could call him, their pilot came through on the RT.

"Hello, Highlight. Highlight. Limbo Two Zero. Compliments of the season and all that. Any more trade? Holding course. Out."

"Hello, Limbo Two Zero. No trade at the moment. Happy Christmas to you. Out."

"Roger, Highlight."

Before he switched off, like a special gift to Emily, he gave them in his clear young voice a few lines of "O Come, All Ye Faithful"; probably, like her, thinking of his own family and his own Christmases; not in Latin, but the same carol that was sung through all her childhood—her very essence of Christmas. She thought how his family would like to hear him now, singing away out there in the night, airborne halfway to enemy-occupied France. They all sat in the darkness, their faces green in the eerie electronic lights, and smiled at each other, and Christmas was as warm and present as under any tinseled tree.

Emily no longer felt lonely, and knew suddenly that it was going to be a lovely day.

Sam came in then, into their closed darkness, with a tray of tea. She hadn't seen him since they had come on Watch, as there had been a mechanics' flap on in another cabin. One of those occasions when, they liked to boast, were it not for them, the whole place would erupt in a monstrous sizzle and a great flash of blue light so big it could be seen in Germany.

"Happy Christmas, everybody. Mugs of tea for the serfs and a cup and saucer for the officer as befits his rank."

"Thank you, Sam," said Flying Officer Graham, one of the nicest. "Happy Christmas to you."

"Happy Christmas, Sam. Happy Christmas."

"Bless you, we were dying of thirst. No one remembered us."

"Flap over?" Emily asked him.

"Yes. We won't blow up."

He gave her a faint small special smile.

"Oh, wait," she said. "I've got some sweet biscuits. My mother sent them. I thought we ought to have them tonight."

She was delighted Sam was there to share them.

They could have no lights on, because they were still controlling an airborne fighter and were on alert. But in the close, amiable darkness they began Christmas with thick tea and sweet Bourbon biscuits, and Emily knew the extra warmth and splendor that it was even to have Sam's eyes on her. She would forget all her guilt and just enjoy Christmas. It would be marvelous.

Her eyes had never left her trace. A tiny blip of light showed up just crossing the French coast.

"Trade!" she cried, and the tea mugs were slapped down and they were off again. Sam cast a professional eye over their tubes and then slid out, laying a hand on Emily's shoulder as he went.

The trade proved to be a lone fighter of their own, coming back from God knew what solitary foray over France. Coming back safe for Christmas.

"I'm glad he's made it," said one of the girls. "Ghastly to be killed on Christmas morning."

They saw him down, and after that the Germans stayed at home to sing "Silent Night," and weep sentimental tears for family and Fatherland, and in another hour the crews were allowed to stand down.

At the end of the long corridor leading to the canteen it was clear that the noise there had already reached the decibels of Christmas. Flying Officer Graham grinned and turned into the officers' rest room with something in his face that said he might have preferred to go on and join the noise.

Emily never reached it. At the turn of the passage beside the notice board, Sam beckoned her from the door of the telephone room, his blue eyes very bright with some secret pleasure.

With all its hundreds of wires serving the complex telephones and intercom, it was the second heart of the Happidrome, as the mechanics' basement was the first. The telephone engineer must have been down helping create the noise in the canteen, for Sam stood alone between the racks of colored wires.

"What's up, Sam?"

"Nothing. I just wanted you by yourself. Brownie's gone out to the aerial. Apparently all the chap there can hear is himself wishing himself a Happy Christmas."

Emily giggled.

"These telephones! Yesterday evening all we could get at Fighter Command was the sports store!"

Sam smiled at her as if everything she said were perfect.

"Oh, Sam," she said. "Happy Christmas."

"A little while back," said Sam, "you lectured me."

"*I* lectured *you*? Sam, I wouldn't dare."

"You lectured me about things being wrapped in parcels. That I would always pick the brown-paper one."

Ah, yes. When he had said she was a snob.

Goodness only knew where he had got the gold paper, but the silver bow at the top was aluminum filings.

"What is it, Sam?"

So much trouble. The gold parcel she had accused him of rejecting.

"Look," he said. "You told me it was only the inside of parcels that mattered."

In a small red box, nestling on a bed of mechanics' cleaning waste, was a silver chain holding a crystal heart with the letter *E* embedded in the center of it in gold.

"Oh, Sam!"

"I made it for you. It's plastic."

"You *made* it. Oh, Sam, how smashing!"

The hours of patient work it must have taken, smoothing a lump of plastic into this. The patience; the love that must have gone into its making. And all she had for him was a nice woolly scarf she had got her mother to buy in Galway. Nice, but dear God, not this evidence of devotion.

She wanted to kiss him, desperately, but knew that Sam would not encourage such a liberty. He was watching her face, extracting every ounce of her pleasure, his eyes dark and intense.

"Don't break it," he said suddenly.

"Why should I? I love it."

"It's my heart," he said, and she knew he didn't mean the gift, but she refused to be drawn.

"I think it's beautiful," she said. It was, so clear and fragile. "I'll take great care of it."

Down the passage they were making fine harmonies on "While Shepherds Watched," one girl's exquisite voice soaring above all the others.

"No," said Sam. "You'll probably break it."

He took her hand and touched the topaz on her engagement finger.

"It's nothing like this," he said.

She lifted her eyes then and looked into his, and could not bear it. As if he challenged her, and feared she wouldn't rise to it. Like a sudden chill invading the strange, functional room, she felt the sad premonition of all the arguments that were yet to come.

"We wish you a Merry Christmas," they sang down in the canteen. "We wish you a Merry Christmas. We wish you a Merry Christmas and a Happy New Year."

On Boxing Night, Sam was doing an extra Watch for someone, so she put her name down for an invitation from a Canadian regiment up in the hills somewhere beyond Storrington.

It was months since she had been out without Sam, and she felt a curious mixture of release and regret. A long time too since she had the fun of being squashed with about thirty girls in a transport, singing their heads off as they bashed upward through the winding country roads, leaving the pinpoint lights of tiny villages behind them in the darkness.

They gave all they had to "She'll be Coming Round the Mountain," and "Home on the Range"; "There's a Troopship Just Leaving Bombay"; "The Quartermaster's Stores," and the sad nostalgic songs of Vera Lynn, which almost brought them all to silence.

When they got to the hutted camp in the black folds of the hills, the Winnipeg Rifles, the Black Devils, one of the wildest regiments in Canada, treated them all like eggshells. The food was unbelievable and the floor so highly polished that people kept falling down. When Emily remarked to one of them that she had never met such polite soldiers in all her considerable experience, he answered morosely that the commanding officer had made it clear that were it otherwise, the whole lot of them would be shot the following dawn. Or worse. He seemed to feel unbearably restricted, and Emily felt a terrible disappointment for him.

She danced every dance, and thoroughly enjoyed herself and almost forgot Sam, until late into the night, when they all crowded out into the cold darkness to watch the searchlights and bomb flashes of a considerable raid down on the coast.

Absolute panic took her, standing there among her friends and the soldiers, her mouth dry and her heart racing, staring horrified at the bright explosions. One fire.

Sam! Sam. Oh, Sam, be careful! My love, be careful!

She could have started running, then and there, stupidly, down the black winding roads to get to him, in a passion of anxiety and protectiveness. Sick with fear.

Then she checked herself, appalled at her own shattered feelings. What in God's name, she thought, was she allowing herself to get into?

*ELEVEN*

Nineteen forty-four came in as the year of hope; everyone looking to the Second Front that would ultimately win the war.

For Emily now, the war meant Sam. Since Christmas she had almost let memories of any other life go, giving herself up to the enjoyment of his love and indefatigable attention, as an exhausted swimmer will fall onto a shore and lie there, indifferent for the blessed moment to all the dangers that lie beyond. It had been so long since Dermot. So long. No word came from the Japanese camps, and it took all her faith now to understand that he could be still alive somewhere.

She still believed it, but left him aside in her mind from all that was happening to her now; finding her memories of him growing as dreamlike as those she held of Alejandro. Sam belonged to the war and Dermot to after it, and from the pain and difficulties of that distant transition, she shied away.

Sam belonged to the long dark Watches and all the strains and tensions. To the sorrows of loss when one of their fighters was shot down; to the exultance of victory when they painted another swastika on the Station scoreboard; to the rowdy hilarious canteen, and the jostling mess. To evenings before the NAAFI fire in a group that seemed to have been together forever like a family; trying to sort out Marianna's disasters, which were as natural as her perfect nature and her lovely smile. To the bare brown winter Downs where they rambled on bitter days, coming back down to Worthing under the great arch of the darkening sky to eat fish and chips at the Orange Café, as though they had never had a meal before. Pimm's at the Stanhope, and Sam inevitably drinking bitters and looking down his nose at her snobbish drink. Dancing the night down at the Town Hall in Worthing, and walking home through the blacked-out streets, talking, talking, and quarreling less, content to let their differences lie, as though there might never be a future that would have to be resolved.

Wings for Victory, and Salute the Soldier, and running great parties and concerts in the barn with Marianna, to raise funds. Films and mixed hockey and mixed football, and visiting celebrities and games of squash with Marianna down at Ferring Grange, cycling through the bitter air in five or six sweaters. There were various shocked attempts by various new officers to organize Darlowe, through all of which Darlowe remained obstinately and unshakably itself. A few faces that had been there since the beginning were lost with great sadness through new postings, a few new ones merging in in their stead.

All that was Darlowe. And Sam.

The dark brown fields of winter below the Downs took on the green shine of spring, in what everybody in the war-tired country regarded as the year of hope.

Her mother wrote to her in February to say that she was going over with Dermot's parents to Ash, their house in Shropshire, for a couple of weeks. Anna would be coming over with their baby son, as her husband, Terry, was going to be away.

Could Emily perhaps get a forty-eight-hour leave? It would be so lovely for all of them to see her. And not so far to travel, just to Shrewsbury.

Emily could, and did, get a forty-eight, feeling with astonishment a slight sense of shock and deprivation at leaving Sam's world. She could not remember when Sam had last gone away, even on a thirty-six. He seemed to have no other world but Darlowe. And her.

Ash was an old timbered house, standing in a greening valley among the soft round hills of Shropshire, in rich farmlands where war had never come closer than the distant rumble in the dark nights of German bombers on their way to Liverpool, and in the deep farming country, food had never gone short.

They met her in Shrewsbury, small, safe and provincial, its ancient timbered houses leaning toward each other in the back streets. She thought of South London as she had seen it from the train, torn and shattered, the long streets gapped like broken teeth. London itself between King's Cross and Paddington ravaged beyond bearing.

She let the incredible peace lap over her, and smiled at the loved faces in the car. All of them, she thought with a surge of sorrow, looking a little older and more lined; more touched with the anxiety and grief they could not escape. She held her mother's hand in hers and asked for news.

Ted was well. They had had a letter from him last week from his jungle, swearing the war would be over in no time at all. Telling them to get the drinks organized; it would be a terrible thing did he come home and find the house dry. He would, he said, have a couple of the Japanese bastards dried on his mantelpiece.

Paul was somewhere in a secret headquarters in London where General Montgomery was assembling his staff for the invasion.

"Nothing from Joe," said Mrs. McRoss, and her face looked suddenly thin and small. Thinking of Mike, thought Emily. She felt a sudden reversal of roles, a fierce protectiveness toward her mother. An absolute terror of anything that might bring her more sorrow.

Or disappointment, she thought, and suddenly it seemed that Sam was in the car with them.

"Nothing," said Lord Keene, as if he read her thoughts, easing the ancient Talbot through the village of Ironbridge. The river to their side was partly frozen; a hard winter, up here. "Nothing, of course, from Dermot."

All through the two days she had to live with their loving assumption that there was no one else remotely in her mind; that she was simply spelling out her life waiting for him as she once had done. She longed to talk to her mother, tell her all about Sam, but she couldn't do it. It would worry her, and her mother had enough of that already. Also it was clear to Emily that the one anchor now in her lonely life was her relationship with Dermot's parents. Nothing, nothing, must be allowed to put a strain on that.

Not even to Anna could she talk. Anna, still calm and quiet and affectionate, had gone off into another world, utterly preoccupied with her adored husband and her lovely little baby son, whom they had christened Dermot.

She smiled at Emily over the baby's head, as sure as the rest of them.

"Have to have a Dermot to fill the gap," she said. "Even though it won't last. It must be awful for you, Em."

"No, it won't last," said Emily, and meant it, still deeply secure in her heart that Dermot would come back. And what then? What, then, of Sam?

She listened to Anna, and thought that marriage, if possible, had managed to make her still more beautiful, and told her of Marianna's capers, and all the funny bits of the strange family life that was Darlowe; played with the baby, and carefully rode the frosted fields with Anna on borrowed horses. Lord Keene had not thought it correct to keep his horses there, eating their heads off, with the war on. Ash was now a farm, devoted entirely to producing food, run in the family's absence by a competent manager and an elderly couple in the house.

There was a vast peace about Ash that soothed Emily past her uneasiness; this ancient house nestling in the folds of the hills, looking for hundreds of years over its serene and prosperous acres. Just for the brief holiday they had brought in wood for the vast fireplace, and opened up the dining room.

"Normally, when we are here, we even eat in the small sitting room, but now there are just too many of us. But there's plenty of wood."

With no conveniences like central heating, most of the rambling house was bitter in the grip of frosty cold, the small sitting room and the kitchen like islands of warmth and comfort. Only Anna was allowed the luxury of a fire in her room to keep the baby warm, and even he spent a great deal of his time in the kitchen, doted on by the old couple, who clucked at him where he slept like a puppy in his basket by the range.

Emily looked at them all one day, all of them and young Dermot in the one small room, whose well-worn armchairs reminded her of Clonfrack, the baby penned with cushions at the corner of the sofa. Lord Keene was on his knees before the grate, trying to coax the fire into greater efforts, with the minimum of coal.

"The next time we come," he said, "we should bring a cartload of peat. Give me a newspaper, Geraldine, and I'll try and whistle up a draft."

He held the newspaper before the fire; and in the frosty day it roared at once, scarlet behind the paper, scorching and blackening the center of it.

"Oh, James, be careful," said Mrs. McRoss. "Be careful."

Should anything happen, this old house would go up like tinder. She glanced at the baby, examining his toes, oblivious.

Just in time Lord Keene crushed the smoking remnants of the paper in his hands, smiling indulgently at the frightened faces of the two women as he got up. The fire blazed and crackled cheerfully.

How can Sam say we are so different, thought Emily. How can he? Just so would he go down with a newspaper before his grate and frighten the life out of his wife. Why should he always be labeling her as something different. Something bad. He would be perfectly at home here, if he would let himself. Oh, dear. If only it wasn't so *important* to her what Sam thought. She couldn't get away from him even here.

In the evening, when they made very special efforts for her last meal with them, Sam would not have been so pleased.

In the raftered dining room the great open hearth with the crest above the mantel was piled with logs, bravely attempting to drive the bitter cold into the dark corners of the room. Along the old refectory table, candles in silver holders wavered slightly in the draft no fire could kill.

"We brought piles of them from Ireland." said Lady Keene. "Saves the electricity, and looks special. For you, Em dear."

In the shifting light of fire and candles, the long table glittered with crystal and with silver, the dark red walls faded away around it into the shadows. A quiet air of splendor and ancient custom, long taken for granted, Lord Keene in a favorite old velvet smoking jacket that his grandfather had worn at the selfsame table; handsome and distinguished.

Oh, God, is this what Sam means? Sam would hate this. This is what he means by being a snob; the gold-wrapped parcel he didn't want to open. For a moment she felt deeply shamed that for these two days she had not worn the crystal heart. Nothing to do with being ashamed of it, she told herself fiercely. Nothing. Only that she could not sit with Dermot's parents with another man's heart around her neck. And Anna might have seen it.

The meal was beautiful and special for her, whom they all thought, with certain justification, to live on bully beef and boiled potatoes. The only thing that spoiled that was that she *adored* bully beef, but dare not say so.

But that did not stop her enjoying the Irish ham; and potatoes mashed with cream and butter and onions, and the fruits of the orchards, lovingly and thriftily bottled in the last golden days of the preceding summer. To make it an occasion, Lord Keene had gone down to the cellars that never knew heat or cold, for the best of his wine, and when the meal was over he stood up to make a toast. Candlelight in pinpoints in the dark ruby of his lifted glass.

"The most important toast," he said, "that any of us here can drink."

He looked all around them with tenderness and sorrow on his face and hoped he was not asking too much of their fine control. God in Heaven, but wars were hard on women; even the ones like his Dermot's lovely Emily, who took their sorrows with them in uniform into a man's world.

"To absent friends," he said.

Emily pushed back her chair and stood up with all of them to drink the toast, and had to look away from the bright tears in her mother's eyes lest she crack herself; her own throat thick and her feelings in turmoil.

Two gone; one dead; one prisoner and one missing, believed killed. Loved ghosts beside them in the flickering shadows.

It was a long minute before any of them could speak again, and then Lady Keene asked determinedly where they would like coffee.

"Here," said her husband at once. "Here. We spend enough time huddling together up there. Let us be ourselves tonight."

Ourselves.

Not for a moment had Sam left Emily's mind. She could literally feel him standing there, behind her high-backed chair; in the shadows beyond the candles, smiling with the familiar cynical twist to the thin lips, the blue eyes cold. Telling her he always knew that when it suited her she would leave him for all this. Leave him where she had found him, to go back where she belonged.

She felt sick with treachery to everyone.

The awful thing was that she was afraid in her heart that Sam was right. Someday she would hurt him. Break the crystal heart. But she could not find the courage to end it now. No reason now. Not yet. Nothing need be decided yet.

The old house had deep-cushioned window seats in the thickness of the walls, and when she was alone in her bedroom she sat there for a long time, huddled in her greatcoat against the cold. The long gentle stretch of fields was white with frost, the trees like specters, all the land glittering under a great full moon. On the South Coast, she thought, such a moon would mean extra alertness and that indefinable air of excitement and anticipation. No stand-down tonight. A bombers' moon, if ever there was one, down there. Here, the blanched, still countryside slept in utter peace, and expected nothing more menacing than the coming of the scarlet dawn.

Such peace.

But it brought no solace to her; for no matter how long she brooded could she resolve anything, haunted only by the shaming feeling of treachery. To whom? To Sam? To Dermot? Or was it only to herself?

There came into her mind the distant day when she had first met Alejandro, and how she had watched a similar gigantic moon hanging like a lamp above the olive groves, the soft night full of perfume and cicadas.

Spain, so very long ago.

Dear God, she'd been a *child*, she thought. A child, in that love of Alejandro that she had thought was everything.

When they kissed her good-bye the next morning on the cold, windy platform of Shrewsbury station, her mother gave a small maternal twitch to her tie.

"Darling," she said. "I am *so* pleased you always wear your cap dead straight. So many of them wear them on the sides of their heads and it looks frightful."

That, Mother dear, she thought but did not say, is one of the things that Sam would class as not being like an ordinary Waaf. Wearing one's cap like a Guardsman is what he would call snobbish.

She tilted it rakishly to make them all laugh, and her mother kissed her again.

"Em," she said, "you *will* remember, won't you, to telephone Uncle William and Aunt Agnes. They are only the other side of Sussex, and so anxious to have you come to lunch with them. I know they're quite old, but they're grand people. You'll like them now you're older yourself."

"I'll remember, Mums. I only remember them vaguely."

There were whistles blowing and doors slamming and it was time to climb into the train; to bridge the gap between one world and the other.

It was perhaps the effort to bridge that gap that made her do what she did. She could not herself be sure. To try and show Sam that he *did* belong? Or that he didn't? And that would show her up as the mean snob he said she was. Trying to prove herself superior. Or just the same. Oh, dear God, trying to prove just what?

But she did it.

"Sam," she said, when she had made her telephone call. There was little time now for long uninterrupted talks on Watch. The enemy seemed to be growing edgy in his suspicion of invasion, nagging across the Channel every night in annoying twos and threes, in between nights where the raids went on from dark to dawn. She spoke to him quietly in the crowded noisy canteen with everybody jostling and desperate for tea. He couldn't very well start a row there either.

"Sam, I'm going to go and have lunch with my uncle and aunt over at Forest Row next Saturday. It's a thirty-six. I asked them if I could take a friend. Would you like to come?"

Sam looked at her without moving his head, a long glance, his blue eyes dark with the suspicion that he was being got at in some way. He put down his mug.

"What's wrong with Marianna?"

Emily was patient.

"I aked you, not Marianna."

"Can't go eating all their food," said Sam.

"That's all right. They live in the country and grow a lot of things. Aunt Agnes said there was no worry about that."

There was a long pause, and he didn't look at her.

"Okay," said Sam grudgingly.

Emily looked at his closed face and thought she must be mad to be so held by him. Dour and difficult. She could not tell him here with ears flapping all around, even though they were now accepted generally as a "couple," that one of the easier reasons she asked him was that she simply wanted to have him with her. They had never been on any journey together. She wanted childishly to sit with him in the train and look out the window together, and discuss what they saw. Hold his hand through the tunnels. Silly.

"Don't put yourself out, Sam," she said, and he had the grace to smile his beautiful smile, and at once she forgave him everything. Helpless.

It was still cold on the Saturday morning when, with a ridiculous sense of adventure, they waited for the train at Darlowe station. Even Sam was happy, determined to enjoy their day, the first time they had shared anything except the life of the Station, and what lay around it.

Under her happiness in the simplicity of the outing, Emily was nervous. Sam was capable of anything. It was a bit like taking a bear to a tea party and hoping for the best. Aunt Agnes was her father's eldest sister. So they were quite old. Uncle William had been a High Court judge, but was now retired. Emily had not seen a great deal of them, for they never for some reason came to Ireland, but all her recollections were of great kindness, and gentleness, and Aunt Agnes had sounded lovely on the telephone. Her mother would be absolutely furious if she did anything to upset them. Please, Sam, behave.

At the end of the journey through the dark wet country, Aunt Agnes met them at Forest Row in a pony and trap. It must be Aunt Agnes, they reasoned quickly at the top of the station steps, because there was no one else there.

She was an immensely tall lady, looking up at them from the trap with a smile of welcome already on her long, intelligent face, wrapped in an ancient Burberry and a big woolly scarf, a man's trilby hat clamped well down over her gray hair.

"My dears," she cried as they reached her. "You're so welcome. Emily darling, you haven't changed a bit. All these years and still just as beautiful. Please do forgive me for not getting down. It's the knees, you know, they get a bit stiff. And what is your friend's name, dear?"

"Sam," said Emily.

"Hello, Sam dear. You may call me Aunt Agnes, like Emily. And my husband will enjoy to be Uncle William."

She had an extraordinarily sweet toothy smile, and Sam gave her back, to Emily's surprise, the full blast of his own blue-eyed charm.

"Pleased to meet you, Aunt Agnes," he said. And looked it, and with that, a little astonished.

It was Emily who was astonished then, when he went straight to the head of the old chestnut pony in the shafts, greeting it with the same pleasure as he had greeted Aunt Agnes.

He came back to the trap and looked up at her.

"May I drive him? Please?"

Emily gaped at him. She had been about to exclaim with pleasure at the pony and the shiny brown trap, saying it reminded her of being at home in Clonfrack. Now she was upstaged by Sam.

"My dear," said Aunt Agnes, "certainly, if you can."

"I can."

"Where did you learn to drive a horse, Sam?"

Emily's surprise would not allow her to keep quiet, although she knew the question rude as soon as she had asked it. Why shouldn't Sam be a farmer's son?

He gave her a level blue stare as he started to climb in beside Aunt Agnes.

"My father," he said, "did a milk round. We kept the pony at home."

He took the pony with skill and familiarity down the high-hedged country roads under the dripping trees, until they turned down a narrow lane between high banks, where already in the grass the clumps of primroses were pushing through, and the tall spikes of daffodils, despite the late bitter cold.

In a small whitewashed stable yard Sam helped Aunt Agnes down, while Emily stared at the unnatural courtesy in silence. He then expertly unharnessed and stabled the pony for her, hens clucking around their feet and pecking at the cobbles.

"My dear Sam." Aunt Agnes seemed quite overcome by him. "You are quite the best guest we have had for ages." She beamed at him. "Bring him in, Emily dear, he deserves a drink. I think your Uncle William will still be down at the lake catching lunch, but he won't be long. Take off your coats."

"Fishing?" Sam looked interested, handing her his greatcoat in the dim square hall.

"You fish, Sam?" she asked.

"I have," said Sam. "My dad was mad on it."

"What an *interesting* young man he is, Emily."

I am beginning to think so, thought Emily, a little grimly.

"How d'you manage to feed the pony?" Sam asked. "Isn't it very expensive? And hard to get the fodder."

Aunt Agnes smiled like a conspirator, all teeth and bright eyes.

"Cheaper than petrol, dear. No—there's a farmer up the road there, and his wife does eggs, so I deliver the eggs for her round the village and so on, with the trap and Benny, and in return he gives me fodder. It's all barter, this war, you know. Emily dear, what news of all your soldiers. Do you hear anything?"

Emily told her and she clucked unhappily over Dermot, bringing the scarlet to Emily's face under Sam's eyes when she said, "The poor countess. So awful not to know one way or the other."

Sam's face closed like a trap, but Aunt Agnes was unaware of any undercurrents, fussing with their greatcoats in the boot room off the hall.

"You must never give up hope, Emily dear," she said as she came back. "You will see. We'll be coming to Ireland for your wedding, all in God's time. Now let us see if William is coming and we can all have some sherry. So difficult to get now. We only have it for a treat, and poor William does so miss it."

There was constraint between Sam and Emily as they followed her down the long room and stood beside her at the window. It was a curious room, long and very narrow, with windows on three sides, a great ground-length one at the end opening onto a square wooden-floored veranda that gave Emily the curious feeling of being above the sea. But it was the Ashdown Forest that flowed away on all sides below them, rising to the winter sky beyond the valley. Skeleton trees, above the dead yellow of old bracken and sodden grass, gave the place a strange primeval look. There were no other houses in sight, and down in the steep valley below the garden lay a sullen lake, still and yellow as the bracken, clouded by the mist of the damp day, trees and bushes crowding to its banks.

Emily gave a small involuntary shiver.

"What a Stone Age sort of place," she said. "I expect to see little men running between the trees in skins. Brandishing clubs."

"My dear, I have no doubt that they once did. A great place for charcoal burners, a little later on."

"There'll be birds in summer," said Sam.

"Oh, dear, yes. Are you interested in birds, Sam? You must talk to my husband. He spends forever sitting there on the veranda with the glasses."

"I had nothing like that," Sam said. "But we lived right on the edge of the town, and my dad used to take us into the country. He was mad about birds."

Sam and his dad. Emily felt a surge of something close to jealousy.

All her ideas were being shattered. She had always thought of Sam, with his mechanic's skills, as being the child of industry. From some back-to-back grim house in a smoky dark provincial town.

She had to come here, where even she was a stranger, to learn that he was a milkman's son with the country at his doorstep. Anger was growing in her. Serve him right, if she had got the whole thing wrong. He should have told her for himself. Why couldn't he?

"Ah," said Aunt Agnes. "There's William. I do hope he has caught enough for lunch. I expect he has. The lake is full of them. Trout and perch and roach. All delicious."

They all looked down for a moment at the thickset figure of an elderly man in a tweed hat and Burberry raincoat exactly like his wife's, carrying a rod and fishing basket; plodding up from the yellow lake, where the long steep path rose into the gardens and disappeared into a shrubbery.

"There now! Come and sit by the fire." Aunt Agnes led her brisk way back down the long room, avoiding the small tables and comfortable armchairs with a skill astonishing in a woman of her ample size. "I'll just go and tell old Margaret what to do with it. Everybody now just has one servant, if any, called old so-and-so, but Margaret really is older than ourselves, which gives us a certain pleasure.'' She flashed them her disarming toothy smile, and Emily felt a pang of affection for her, seeing clearly in the elderly woman the probably wayward big girl who had caught the young William's heart.

"Better," said Aunt Agnes to nobody as she went out, "than the poor young things from the village who wash the glasses with the floor cloth. They know no better, bless them."

When she had gone, stiff constraint fell in the comfortable room. Emily flopped down onto the long red sofa by the fire, but Sam prowled among the furniture, looking at the photographs and the pictures and portraits on the walls, not speaking, his mouth in the thin narrow line that had begun to annoy her.

Thinking no doubt, she reflected irritably, that in this house he would be classed with the ones from the village who knew nothing about anything. Oh, *Sam.*

But he was quiet and civil and unintimidated by Uncle William when that formidable old gentleman came in; quiet himself, and exquisitely courteous, but with a pair of penetrating light gray eyes still lit with the blazing intelligence and perception undimmed in the brain behind them.

"Six beautiful trout," he said with satisfaction as he poured their sherry, the ebullience of Aunt Agnes dimmed in his presence to a sort of deference that was almost flattering. "Two each for us, Sam, and one apiece for the ladies."

How sweet, thought Emily, watching them with touched astonishment. How sweet. So old, and she still absolutely adores him. Will that ever be for me? and who with?

The dining room was another strange room, paneled in pale wood, with no doors to it, set at the turn of the right-angled house, its windows looking out at the green wet hill down which they had driven in the trap. Over the fireplace hung a portrait of Uncle William in all the majesty of full-bottomed wig and scarlet robes of his judgeship.

Emily saw Sam's eyes on it, and on the collection of knives and forks beside his plate, and began to feel curiously that the whole thing had been a mistake.

"Soup, Sam?" Aunt Agnes prattled on. "We actually have a few bones in it today. I did a delivery for the butcher yesterday, and he gave me some beautiful beef bones."

Beautiful soup. Emily laid down her spoon. Sam had watched her across the table covertly before picking up his own.

"Aunt Agnes," she said, breaking a roll of hot homemade bread, "I think it's the pony who keeps you in all your comforts."

There was even butter on the table, and Emily hesitated to touch it, lest it was their meager ration. If it was, it must be all of it, sitting there on the silver dish.

"Take butter, my dear, it's quite all right." Aunt Agnes had sensed her hesitation. "Of course it's Benny; gets us everything. We'd be lost without him. Living on whale meat and that dreadful pink stuff."

"Spam," said Sam.

"Yes. Spam. Such a frightful color."

"It's you, my dear, we would all be lost without," said her husband quietly. "It's not Benny who keeps the whale meat from the door."

Aunt Agnes flushed with pleasure, touched by a look of extreme youth that came to her so incongruously.

The six trout came in, swimming in more butter procured by the willing pony; scattered with herbs and parsley fresh from the cold garden. With them came a cheese soufflé, golden and splendid and light as a cloud, and a silver dish of green beans.

"We put the beans in salt in the summer," said Aunt Agnes, as though driven to explain everything that might seem like privilege. "We had such masses of them, we were able to give lots away. That marvelous old Margaret, she is such a cook. Don't worry that you are eating our cheese ration. The farmer's wife, you know, where I get the hay for Benny, makes the occasional cheese."

Sam smiled at her, his face softening. At the head of the table, Uncle William applied himself diligently to his fish.

"And the pony, I suppose," said Sam, "delivers the milk."

Aunt Agnes twinkled back at him.

"Oh, no, dear, only the eggs."

They all knew in the moment's silence, that all these good things that had provided this wonderful meal had been paid for by Aunt Agnes; in long hours behind Benny's plodding brown back, going from house to scattered house around the countryside; frozen in the dark short days of winter; wearied by the heat of summer. A few extra eggs today; some milk tomorrow; a small packet of fresh cheese or butter.

All so that her dear William should not have to live on this dreadful pink Spam and whale meat.

Old William in his turn fished the lake and walked the forest with his shotgun for pigeon and rabbit and, with the help of an ancient from the village, filled to profit every square inch of the vegetable garden he had made from the lawn at the side of the house: tomatoes and cucumbers and vegetable marrows, and grapes from the old vine, in the greenhouse, and logs dragged patiently home from the endless supplies of the forest, and sawn up for the fires. Thus was their wartime life.

Emily listened to them with humility, knowing of the grandeur and elegance and importance that had been their lives, full of admiration for them, and thinking that here was something, surely, that could get behind Sam's closed face.

Something to tell him that people did not have to be condemned out of hand simply because they were as grand as Aunt Agnes and Uncle William had once been. As grand as he thought she was; which was rubbish.

It would all be far worse now that he really knew Dermot was the son of an earl. But why, she asked herself, confused and a little silent over the beautiful fish, was she bothering so much? How could it matter? Everywhere she moved among her family they were making it clear to her that she was doing no more than waiting for Dermot.

She took some more of the delicious tangy sauce from the silver sauceboat and passed it on to Sam, who would not meet her eyes.

Oh, God. She was all in a muddle now as to why she had asked Sam here at all, and in even more of a muddle as to how it was all going, now that she had done it. He was getting on almost better than she was, with all the talk of freshwater fish, and birds; things she had never even heard Sam mention before.

"And where do you come from, Sam?" asked Uncle William, over the apple pie.

"We bottled the apples in the autumn," said Aunt Agnes with her conspiratorial and apologetic look. "And the cream—"

"Comes from the farm where the pony delivers the eggs," said Sam.

"Indeed."

She beamed at him.

He answered Uncle William.

"Hertfordshire, sir," he said. "I live in a town called Letchworth. In the north of Hertfordshire."

"Ah, Hertfordshire. A very underestimated county. People think the only beautiful country around London is to the south."

Sam nodded.

"And what do you do there, my boy. Or did you do, before this dreadful war?"

"I'm a gardener, sir. I'll get my job back when it's all over. If I want it," he added.

Beside him Emily laid her spoon and fork with unnatural quietness on her plate, boiling with fury. Why had he never told her these things? Leaving her to find them out just by listening at her uncle's table. All he had ever done was ask her endlessly about herself, and then close up in silence when she tried to question him in return. Perhaps he had not really been all the time sufficiently interested to tell her anything.

Maybe it didn't matter to him whether she knew anything about him or not. The unhappiness and insecurity of the idea appalled her, and drove home to her the sick knowledge of how much she had taken Sam for granted, certain there was only one heart in danger, and that was Sam's. Instinctively she touched the crystal heart beneath her shirt, and found her hands trembling. Carefully she folded them in her lap, and stared determinedly— for God's sake, there was nothing to cry about—out the long window at the end of the shadowy room, where above the steep green hill the sky was darkening with all the woolly look of snow.

Sam was going on talking evenly to Uncle William.

"No, sir. Not that kind of gardening. Letchworth's a Garden City, you see, sir, and I work for the Council."

"Ah, yes, I recall, the very first one. Go on."

Uncle William's keen gray eyes were fixed on Sam.

He really finds him interesting, thought Emily, not quite sure if she was pleased or furious. She had envisaged the day with Sam being humbly impressed all the way. Not holding his own like this. I'm horrible, she thought. Horrible. Sam is quite right. I am a stupid snob. He's making me feel a fool.

"Yes," said Sam. "So there aren't all that many flowers. But more grass verges and trees than you'd believe. And a lot of shrubs. I work mostly with the shrubs."

Emily was flabbergasted.

"How did you come to be a mechanic, then?" she asked, too abruptly for politeness. Sam turned to her, and in his eyes she could see the row to come.

"Always liked it," he said. "Built my own radios right from cat's whiskers' days. Became a radio mechanic when I was called up."

Uncle William was full of excitement at the head of the table.

"Shrubs, my boy. Shrubs. That's the thing. I've a considerable little shrubbery at the side there. Some nice things in it. When we've had coffee, we'll go out and take a look. Tell me what you think."

"Be glad to, sir. I saw it from the window."

The long pale room was growing dark, Uncle William's stern portrait receding into the shadows above the sinking fire.

"Come, children," said Aunt Agnes. "We'll go into the drawing room for coffee. We don't want to keep up two fires, and we'll soon get cold here."

"And did you grow the coffee, Aunt Agnes?" Sam asked as she handed him the small fragile cup. He had taken the logs from Uncle William's hands and built up the fire for them, and now it spat and flamed and crackled in the wide hearth. All the light they wanted; making for them an island of peace and normality against the gray day outside; and against the war beyond it, whose effects Aunt Agnes seemed to be defeating single-handed.

"Come, Sam," said Uncle William when the coffee was finished, all of them crumbling under the lethargy of the excellent lunch. "Come and see this shrubbery of mine. Be glad of your expert opinion, but it'll be dark if we don't go soon."

He heaved himself out of his deep chair with almost more alacrity than Sam, and with a flurry of greatcoats and rubber boots and scarves, they were gone into the gray day.

Beside the fire Aunt Agnes gratified all her curiosity about both families, Emily's and Dermot's, producing a catechism of kind and loving questions. Fervently Emily thanked her stars, her feet out happily to the crackling logs, that Sam was not there. Both questions and answers would have driven him to whatever fury it was that consumed Sam at any mention of her life and background.

Aunt Agnes even asked about Alejandro, having only heard the outlines of the tale, so for a few improbable minutes, with the dangerous dusk of war falling over the English countryside outside,

Emily brought back the warmth and beauty of that other world.
And the beginning of that other war.

"You poor child." Aunt Agnes's long face was somber with
concern and sympathy. "You were only a child, weren't you."

"Yes," said Emily, and meant it. "I was only a child."

The men came in soon, red with the cold, rubbing their hands
gratefully before the fire.

"Can't think what's happened to the weather," said Uncle
William. "Nothing's growing. Shouldn't be like this at this time
in March. Your young man gave me some excellent tips, Emily,
m'dear. Knows his job."

Emily almost opened her mouth to say to them that Sam was
not her young man. They knew perfectly well that Dermot was
her young man. On her engagement finger the topaz flashed
amber lights from the fire, and she twisted it on her finger as if
she sought reassurance of that fact.

But Aunt Agnes only beamed, seeing nothing in it.

"I am sure he did," she said. "I am quite sure that Sam would
do well at anything he did."

They drew the red velvet curtains against the bleak day, and
Aunt Agnes lit two old oil lamps such as Emily had not seen
since the ones that threw their gentle gold light over the salon in
the house in Málaga.

Aunt Agnes realized it was becoming a joke, and gave a
deprecating giggle, glancing sideways at Sam.

"One must save the electricity," she said. "They want it for
the war."

Sam and Emily sank their differences for a moment to exchange a hilarious look. Their personal piece of the war used
enough electricity to keep a small town going flat out.

Tea was fresh scones and strawberry jam, and wafer-thin
sandwiches of cress as fresh and lovely as spring itself.

"I grow it," said Aunt Agnes as she passed the Crown Derby
plate, the deep blue rim glowing in the lamplight. "I grow it on a
saucer on a piece of flannel, like we used to do when we were
children."

"And the jam is homemade," said Sam, and they grinned at
each other like conspirators.

"Of course," said Aunt Agnes.

"From strawberries grown in the garden."

"Indeed."

Across the fire Uncle William smiled at her with the serene
smile of a man long happy with his lot, and the gray eyes shot
approving glances at Sam from under his heavy brows.

Peace and apparent plenty, and the war belonging in some
other world, were there no train to catch.

But there was.

Before they left, they went out onto the veranda to look at the
weather, pulling the curtains carefully close behind them. The
sky was clearing, an odd adventurous star showing here and there
between the thinning clouds, and below them the lake held the
last of the light, dark like unpolished pewter.

In the trees leaning to its edge, the darkness lay no heavier
than the tension between Sam and Emily, each of them furious
with the other; waiting only, with infinite politeness, to be alone
before they allowed their personal storm to break.

Aunt Agnes wouldn't allow him to drive Benny back to the
station.

"No, dear boy," she said as she lit the two old carriage lamps
on the trap. "These lanes have no lights at all. I know them and
Benny knows them, but you don't. It's not safe."

Uncle William waved them from the stable yard and went back
into the six o'clock news, and they clopped off over the cobbles,
behind Benny, into the pitch-black night.

Aunt Agnes and Sam chatted happily, but for most of the way
Emily said nothing at all, pulling down the flap of her cap over
her ears against the raw cold, and only half listening to them.

Brooding on Sam, and trying to understand for herself why she
had brought him there at all. There was no doubt it had been
Sam's day. They had both adored him, and she knew she felt
sulky and aggrieved, like a spoiled child. But Sam had not been
fair to her. Nor was she used to taking second place. Especially
to Sam.

Aunt Agnes was in a bit of a hurry by the time they reached
the yard below the dim, blacked-out glimmer of the station. She
kissed Emily warmly and shook Sam by the hand, pumping up
and down, full of pleasure with him.

"Made your own gloves, I expect, Aunt Agnes," he said.

She heaved with delighted laughter, reluctant as he was to let
go the joke.

"Dear boy, how did you guess? I have to rush now, I'm
afraid."

"Going to church, Aunt Agnes?" Emily said.

" 'Fraid not, my dear. Not tonight. I'm due on duty."

"*Duty?*" they said together.

"Yes, dears. I work as a telephonist with the Observer Corps. You know, reporting in all the airplanes they spot."

Emily and Sam stood dumb, understanding that any of the plots that came from Group, to be slapped down on the big table under the lights labeled with the sinister yellow of the hostile, might have started here with Aunt Agnes. In this dark countryside. In some open, cold post, in her Burberry and her man's hat.

The indomitable woman clattered away through the yard gates into the pitch-black night, and they stood together in an unyielding silence, full of things they wanted to say about her; full of admiration; full of hilarity. Aunt Agnes and her self-supporting habits could be a joke to last for weeks.

But anger held them both in silence, up the dark steps and onto the murky blackout of the station, where only three other passengers were waiting, huddling in the cold gloom.

Sam began it the very moment they were in the train. There was a soldier half asleep in the opposite corner with the collar of his greatcoat round his ears. They could barely see him in the faint blue light from the ceiling of the carriage; Sam ignored him anyway.

"What were you doing!" he said fiercely, the very moment they sat down. "Trying me for size?"

The jolt of the old train as it started threw him almost into her lap, and that would normally have made them laugh; both of them always alert to the ridiculous.

Not tonight.

"What were *you* doing?" she countered, gray eyes snapping with anger. "Telling them all sorts of things about yourself that you've never told me! *I* was never told you came from Hertfordshire. *I* never knew you were a gardener. Oh, yes, Aunt Agnes, I know all about ponies. And birds, and fishing. And oh, yes, Uncle William, I know all about shrubs. Why was I never told any of these things?"

Cruelly she mimicked him, her face ash-white under the cold blue light, and sharp with anger. Sam's mouth was set in the hair-thin line that led him to be called Rattrap even among those who would say they were his friends.

"I never thought you wanted to know."

"Why shouldn't I have wanted to know!"

"You'd have thought it all beneath you."

Had she looked she would have seen the flare of uncertainty and defensiveness in Sam's eyes. The same uncertainty and defensiveness that had made him conceal everything about himself lest it not be good enough for this lovely girl with the red-gold hair, who was everything his heart could ever dream about, or his mind concoct.

It was fear that had stopped him ever telling her anything. Fear lest she would turn away from him back to her own world, where her young man had given her that great stone set in gold to wear on her finger; while all he could give her was a plastic heart. And she didn't seem to be aware yet that it was his own heart, more vulnerable than he would dare to admit. To do what she wanted with it. For as long as they both should live. There would never be another Emily.

She was raging.

"What d'you mean, thought it all beneath me! D'you realize that was *Sir* William and *Lady* Agnes you were with today? Did they find it all beneath them? You could tell them! Tell them *anything*. But not me!"

There were tears in her eyes of temper and wounded pride and wounded love or something like it, and he longed to explain to her that she had been too precious to risk losing. But blimey, thought Sam, a Sir and Lady, and I told them he was making a pig's mess of his shrubs. Some day you'll learn, Sam Treadwell.

"They seemed just like ordinary people to me," he said stubbornly, and it was one of those moments when she didn't know if she loved or hated him, magnetic blue eyes and fine bones and wonderful smile and all.

"Well, of *course* they're ordinary people!" she shouted at him. "That's what I'm always trying to tell you. I'm an ordinary person. Not anything special."

Not for me, you're not, thought Sam. Not you, my most special love. You are no ordinary person. Nothing in this drab world to match your specialness, nor will ever be again.

For me.

But he yelled back at her, knowing he was going to lose the argument anyway. Getting confused.

"They just seemed to me more easy to talk to! More willing to accept me for what I am!"

"How do I know what you are, when you would never tell me! How am I supposed to accept what I don't know!"

The soldier in the other corner stirred and grumbled in his sleep, and Sam lowered his voice a little, but he was no less angry and resentful.

"You just wanted a chance to be sure," he said, "that I'd try to eat my soup with a fork, and put my boots on the piano. What do they need to show off with all those knives and forks for, anyway?"

Emily was cold with fury now.

"They'd have the same knives and forks, Sam, if they were eating alone in the kitchen, which they often do. *I* eat every day with you with one knife and fork, and I never say to you that I find it strange. I just accept it. Why can't you be as tolerant?"

Sam knew he was losing.

"Well, anyway," he muttered, "they were jolly nice people."

"Sam, that's just what I'm trying to *say* to you. You have to open the package to see what's inside it. The wrapping doesn't matter."

Or, dear God, was he right and in her heart she had been putting him to some sort of test? If she had, he had won hands down.

For the day.

But she could hear Aunt Agnes.

"Such a *nice* young man my niece Emily brought to lunch from that place she's stationed. Knew all about my pony, and William's shrubs. But, of course, she's engaged to the Earl of Keene's son. Missing, you know. So sad."

She felt bewildered. Would it all matter at all were it not that unwillingly, and full of guilt, she had to admit that she was well on the way to being in love with Sam.

In their furious silence the train suddenly jerked and clanged to a halt, and even the one blue light went out. In the pitch-darkness outside, when the hissing of the engine died away, they could hear the distant sirens wailing. Like banshees, thought Emily, remembering all the old tales Aggie used to tell her as a child. Banshees, wailing for the dead. Sad and harsh and disembodied over the black countryside.

The air of their silence changed. This was their common enemy. The night, their battleground.

Sam let up the blind a little, and away over to the east

searchlights probed the dark sky with an air of purpose. He got up and leaned carefully over the sleeping soldier to look out on his side.

Black darkness. Nothing. There might as well have been no world.

"All to the east," he said. "Nothing to do with us."

"As long as we're not late," said Emily. "We could miss the other train."

"We'll get a chit from Movement Control in Brighton. Should think we're somewhere a bit north of there at the moment. I'll open the window. It's safer."

They sat then in a more companionable silence in the bitter cold, the thread of their anger broken, looking out, across country they could not see, at the distant searchlights; hearing very faintly the hoarse uneven throb of German engines.

"Making for London," said Sam. "Poor bastards."

There were voices by then along the train, and in the corridor, and sudden bursts of laughter.

Somewhere up toward the front a girl began to sing "The White Cliffs of Dover." Pure and sweet and sad; disembodied as the sirens in the darkness, silencing everybody else, bringing them so easily to the sick nostalgia that haunted all of them; who thought so constantly of their past, since there was no certainty of any future.

"You must understand, you see, Emily," Sam said suddenly in a very careful, reasonable voice. He didn't want to be blamed for starting the fight again. "You must understand, you have destroyed my life."

"*I* have! Destroyed your life! What d'you mean, Sam, destroyed your life?"

"You heard what I said to your uncle today. I'm a Council gardener. Was. With a small salary and a small house and a small life and never looked a yard beyond it. It was all I wanted. Don't you understand, Emily? I never knew girls like you *existed*. Not just you. The lot of you. I've never been in a house like that today in my life. But I know now it exists. I know *you* exist. How can I ever go back to what I was before? What do I do?"

In the pitch-darkness she could only see the pale oval of his face, but the strain in his voice told her of months of thinking he had not revealed. And she had danced along the surface of his feelings, pretending that tomorrow, and the necessity to give answers, would never come.

Now she knew instinctively that Sam would soon be looking for answers, and she could no longer pretend he was just part of the war, like battle dress and bully beef and the green clicking traces in the dark cabins. Nor did she know what answer she would give, any more than she had known why she asked him to come today.

To help her to decide what?

Guilt and compunction touched her and all the confused love that she felt for him, and she forgot her anger and leaned over to take his hands, taking refuge in what she had said so often before.

"It doesn't *matter*, Sam. It really doesn't matter! All that. It's the people that matter."

He was silent a long moment.

"You really think so, Emily?"

"Of course. Of course."

She was desperate to reassure him. A doubtful and uncertain Sam was so completely out of character, she couldn't bear it.

"Okay," said Sam then suddenly, and that was all. For some reason it bothered her more than all the rest of the conversation.

"Well, I'm glad that's settled, then," hoarsely said the soldier in the corner. The pale face emerged like a tortoise from the shadows of his greatcoat collar. " 'Ow d'you expect me to get a bit o' kip with you trottin' out all your class-conscious life history. Don't have none of this game meself. Me an' my missus is from the same buildings, and that's it. One knife and fork each," he added tersely before vanishing again into the shadows of his collar.

Emily caught the gleam of Sam's teeth, but she couldn't smile herself. The soldier had hit a nail on the head. *Sam had a wife*, and that was the heart of it. She had always known it, but had deliberately blinded herself to it. Just as she felt he blinded himself to the existence of Dermot, glaring at the topaz ring as an intrusion.

It was all too easy to make anything outside the small closed world of Darlowe cease to exist.

But Sam did have a wife, and it was becoming very clear that she was one of the things he did not want to go back to.

Now probably she had made things worse than ever between them. Oh, Lord, what had she done.

Suddenly, acutely, she realized she had let herself get into a mess.

As they walked, peaceably now, down the white straight road from Darlowe railway station, Sam said, "Well, I think your Aunt Agnes is one of the most smashing people I have ever known. No matter what she is."

She squeezed his hand, knowing it was as close to an apology as she would ever get from Sam.

At the Guard Hut they found Marianna, everything from her gas-mask case, except the gas mask, littered on the ledge of the hut before a phlegmatic Corporal of Police. With relief Emily noticed that this time there was no sanitary napkin. Not that Marianna would have minded.

"Darlings!"

She fell on them with wild relief, smelling richly of Evening in Paris.

"Darlings, *do* tell this man who I am!"

"Tell him *what*?"

Who didn't know, and love, Marianna?

"A terrible bother." She peered into the darkness of the Guard Hut, where the policeman's face was little more than a pale shape, like the soldier's in the train.

"Em, it's a *strange man*. He doesn't know me. And I seem to have lost my Form twelve fifty, and he won't let me in because he says he doesn't know that I belong here. *Me!*"

The policeman had kept indifferent silence, and in turn Sam and Emily peered in at him. Indeed a strange man. How could he be? The Police at Darlowe were as familiar as the smell of the cookhouse and the darkness of the Happidrome.

"Stuff it all away, Marianna," said Sam. "Here, Corporal." He got out his own identity card and pushed it into the light. "We all belong here and it's bloody cold, so let's get on with it, shall we? Unless you'd like to get on the blower to the commanding officer to come and identify Marianna."

"He wanted to get poor Corporal Taylor out," said Marianna, aggrieved, ramming her belongings into the spaces round her gas mask. "I've only been to the pictures."

"He'd have suffered if he did that," Sam said. "Open the gate, mate."

Muttering about regulations and only doing his duty, the policeman did so. The girls then gave him a sweet good-night. After all, he would be here to stay.

The gravel crunched under their feet along the road, and somewhere beyond The Elms an owl was hooting. One of the windows in the mess showed a chink of light; late supper for the evening Watch. Peals of girls' laughter came from one of the billets.

"Quoting regulations," said Marianna. "And asking for identity cards. We'll have to teach him better, won't we."

"Probably comes from some big Station," Sam said, and in the darkness Emily smiled.

"I thought he was quite sweet, really," said Marianna. "I want to see him in the daylight. Rather yummy, I thought."

Emily and Sam laughed then as they had not laughed together all day, both of them grateful for the frivolous presence of Marianna, which took the constriction from a good-night that might otherwise have been difficult.

With her there, it was easy just to say "Good night, Sam. Thank you for coming."

"Good night, Emily."

But not easy for Sam to admit he had enjoyed himself.

### TWELVE

No weather in the beautiful spring that came so suddenly, after the bitter winter, was brighter than the hope and optimism lifting all the war-weary hearts. Anzio and Cassino and the Allied armies pushing on for Rome; success after bitterly fought success in Italy and on the Russian front; and in the Far East, so remote a war that sometimes it seemed a separate one, the Americans walked again on the islands so long held by the Japanese who like the Germans were now on the defensive; the Italians long surrendered. The Chindits gaining ground in Burma.

It will be over by Christmas, everyone was saying. Over by

Christmas. Exactly as they had said in the shocked September of 1939, almost five long, dark years ago. With the Second Front coming any day, it will all be over by Christmas.

And they will all be coming home.

From the cold hungry *stalags* of Germany and the swarming unlisted bamboo stockades in Malaya and Burma, where they needed no barbed wire, the green jungle itself sufficient barrier to the escape of the half-starved and the sick and the ill-treated.

Coming home.

Emily listened to all the happy girls chattering in the canteen as if it would be tomorrow, so filled with single-minded longing that it shamed her; unable now even to fix her loyalty between the half-forgotten dream of Dermot that was thinned every day by the live, forceful, and determined presence of Sam, who had never said another word about their quarrel over Aunt Agnes and Uncle William.

Always there, the dark blue eyes watching her as if she might disappear; giving her the uncomfortable feeling nowadays that he was planning something she did not understand; waiting for something. It was not like Sam to give up a point so easily.

Blossom spread itself in pale tender clouds around the farm-houses in the green fields below the Downs, and from the woods below the Happidrome in the warm afternoons, the cuckoos called and called again, making mockery of war and doubt; asking only that the bright spring world be taken as it was, for youth and love.

All very well, you stupid bird, thought Emily, listening to one calling himself hoarse from the dark trees. But it's not as easy as that.

In the warm days, when released for a break from the tubes, they brought blankets out and spread them in the field outside the Happidrome, sprawling gratefully in the sun and fending off the attentions of the farmer's big brown horse, who shared the field with them and seemed to have as little work to do as they did. By day.

The nights were filled with urgency and long desperate hours glued to the tubes, keeping at bay as far as possible an enemy who must be aware of the concentration of troops gradually assembling along the South Coast.

Hostile plots almost nightly, of up to a hundred Huns. Or more.

Tension and urgency and the small tightening of fear that was excitement in itself. Calm thought and terrible concentration on those two little blips of light, mechanics charging in and out with tin hats and scared expressions trying to assess the function of their aerials shaken by blast. Sudden pitch-black darkness, and emergency lighting coming on, and all the gear gone dead, and for all they knew, all the Huns in France converging on them.

Always the laughter that was never far away.

Somebody was looking for Sam, one racketing night.

"He went out to the top aerial," said another of the mechanics. "A packet of incendiaries fell behind him, and he ran so fast he got airborne! He's down on the table plotted as a Hostile!"

Dawn and silence, and exhausted red-eyed girls clamoring in the canteen for tea, all the night fighters home and the tired pause before the patrols going up at first light.

Such was last night.

When they had stood down just before the dawn, Emily had come out for a breath of air before going for tea, standing alone in the gray silence just before the light came, all the long stretch of fields and hills still holding the dark of night; only a strengthening strip of primrose light above the Downs making promise of the coming day. She could just see the two aerials turning steadily, keeping their watch out over the enemy sea, and in the field the dark hole made by the bomb that had shaken them in the night.

Thank goodness it hadn't killed Horse, who came rambling over to say good morning, his soft nose pressed into her palm, hoping for a piece of apple and a carrot.

"Not at this time of the morning, Horse," she said. "Where would I get carrots now?"

Unless Sam knew I wanted them, she thought. Did Sam know she wanted a carrot, he would find one for her, dawn or no.

She sighed, not quite knowing if it exasperated or enchanted her to be so spoiled.

She stood there with Horse and watched the color creep across the fields, and one last solitary Spitfire streaking home to Tangmere, no doubt thanking God for it; black against the brightening lemon yellow skies above the Downs.

So grateful. So grateful that, since she had felt she had to take her share in the war, it was in this lovely place.

"Gorgeous, isn't it, Horse," she said. "Absolutely gorgeous."

Although they had been told nothing about it officially, it must be right about the coming of the Second Front. And not too long away, with all these soldiers pouring onto the coast. She was willing to admit that she was basically very ignorant about the war. They all were, locked in their own part of it, with the only source of information the ancient wireless that crouched like a brown beehive in the corner of the NAAFI. If you could hear it above the noise, or nobody yelled at you to turn it off until Vera Lynn, or to turn it off altogether, then it was the source of all the news. Somebody must listen to it, as most things seemed to get around the Station by grapevine.

But she had never even heard Churchill. Always been on Watch.

"All that history, Horse," she said. "And I've never heard it yet."

Horse had dimensions now, big and brown and solid in the growing light, blinking at her over the fence with his long improbable eyelashes, the fields behind him green and damp with the freshness of the morning.

It had been chance, only chance, that had brought her out here on that marvelous morning when they had rung all the church bells to celebrate the relief of Tobruk. Village church after village church taking up the message all along the rise of the Downs and the flat land between them and the sea. Unearthly, heartbreaking, in the still morning that was barely day. How many dead since they last rang? How many homes listening to them in loneliness and sorrow that no victory could heal.

Emily had been back several times to Clonfrack on leave, climbing the station fence in dawns like this, before even the porter was awake, to get the milk train that would catch the Irish Mail at Euston at nine o'clock. She had there heard the flat tinny clang of the bell of the parish church; the deep gentle boom from the convent on the Galway Road. And the sweet peal of the cathedral in the city.

How much more poignant must it be for all these people who had heard no bell since 1939. Even for her it had been enough to cry for. At the same time a mourning and a promise. Some message that all that was yet to come would still be worth it.

Joe, Mike, Dermot. Bells for Mike, who would never come back. Bells for all the Mikes of the endless war.

Tears streaming down her face, she had stood there quite

alone, and by the time she thought to rush in and tell the others what was happening, they had ended. Nor could she quite believe in them then, in the misty silence. Phantom bells belonging to another world.

Now in this later dawn, when all the promise was being slowly, desperately, fulfilled, someone came out the door behind her, and she turned away from Horse.

"I thought you might be cold," said Sam. "I brought your jacket."

Aware of her, wherever she might go. Always aware of her. He would find her if she went to the bottom of the sea. It was only surprising that he hadn't realized she wanted carrots for Horse.

"Thank you, Sam. I just came out to look at the morning. Isn't it marvelous. I was having a chat with Horse."

The sun was up now, drawing the mists of the night into long ghostly strips of white over the green fields, touching the tops of the Downs with gold.

Sam gave it all a perfunctory look and dismissed it, his eyes coming back to her, full of intensity.

"Doing anything next thirty-six?" he asked her abruptly.

"You don't mean today?"

It had been a long hard night, and she wanted to go to bed. Thirty-six-hour passes always began after night duty, and if it had been a bad night and you rushed straight off, then it was that night again before you got any sleep. They did it all the time, but it had to be worth it. She felt like pottering today, and doing her chores and sitting in the sun with the girls in the back garden of the billet. Nice idle day.

"No, not today," Sam said. "Three days' time."

"That's all right. What's doing, Sam?"

He looked very fierce about something, the blue eyes flinty in the clear light.

"I want to return your invitation," he said. "Want you to come to lunch at my home—only we call it dinner."

She didn't know what to make of it, knowing it rude to hesitate, but there had been nothing gracious in the way the invitation had been given.

More like a threat.

She stared at him doubtfully, and Horse, who did not like to be ignored, stuck his big brown head in between them. She patted his nose absently, trying to fathom what Sam was up to.

"With your wife, Sam?"

Delicate ground, this wife who must never be mentioned, but around whose very existence she sensed trouble as clearly as the onset of thunder on a summer day.

"With my wife." A wintry smile touched the long thin mouth. "I don't have any uncles and aunts," he said.

"But, Sam." She didn't know what to say. "Won't she mind you bringing a girl home?"

"She won't have to, will she."

"That doesn't sound very—happy. She might be furious. Have you told her?"

"That I'm bringing someone to dinner? Yes, I wrote and told her."

Still Emily hesitated, unhappy and doubtful, sensing unpleasantness.

"Well, will you or won't you?" Sam said. "I came when you invited me."

She was being churlish. Sam had indeed come when she invited him.

"Yes, Sam, of course. I'm sorry. I just wasn't quite sure I was wanted."

Sam's marvelous smile spread across his taut face.

"I want you," he said, and the slate blue eyes were very bright.

The day was wakening. The short sturdy figure of the farmer was making his way across the dew-wet field with a bridle in his hand. A day's work for Horse; somewhere cattle lowed for the morning's milking, and the first train rattled into Darlowe station.

Looking into Sam's face, Emily felt suddenly a nervous impulse of retreat. She pulled her jacket around her shoulders and pretended not to see the invitation in his eyes. She found him bewildering; opening some new phase in their relationship that she didn't understand. And Sam-like, he would not explain it.

She turned her head from the kiss she knew was coming, and hated herself for doing it; moving toward the door. One of the other mechanics slammed whistling through it on his way out to the aerials. He only grinned at them, the new sun shining in his glasses, but she knew that soon all the Watch would know that she and Sam had been seen in the dawn in the field. Been there all night, probably, they would say.

A bit of the old platonic, Darlowe called it.

She couldn't smile about it, this morning.

"I *am* cold, Sam," she said. "Let's go in and get some tea."

And indeed it seemed to her that the soft morning breeze had grown inexplicably cold. Chilled by some sadness not yet here.

On the following Friday, not quite understanding why, she dressed with extra care. Her best uniform, buttons and cap badge glittering, her walking-out shoes buffed like mirrors with one of the ubiquitous sanitary napkins.

It had been a long, weary night without much joy, and she would have preferred to do as the other three; rolling thankfully into bed as soon as they had had breakfast, grumbling at her for keeping the curtains open until she was dressed.

With great ostentatious sighing, Marianna rose majestically from her bed and tied a black scarf around her eyes, falling over with terrible oaths as she climbed back in again. Emily only grinned. Anyone going out on a date always had priority of everybody's comfort, time, and clothes, and everything else. When she finally drew the curtains against the lovely day, it was Isobel who lifted her fair head from the pillow, mindful always of the right thing to do or say.

"Have a happy day, Emily."

Emily thanked her, but as she clattered down the bare wooden stairs of the little house, she felt a cold nervous certainty that this was the last thing she was going to have. There was something more behind Sam's inimical invitation than mere hospitality.

They all thought she was clean off her head to go out with Sam anyway.

Sam was waiting at the guardroom, as spruce and shining as she was herself, his cap angled on the crisp hair. Typically he had already walked up the white road to the railway station and bought their tickets, forestalling any argument from Emily, who had long stopped arguing anyway; knowing by now that Sam's pride was as touchy and explosive as a magnetic mine swaying in the dark seas.

On the way up, in a crowded carriage, he was silent and withdrawn, and she began to grow a little edgy. Feeling she could have done better things with her day than sit speechless staring out the window of the crawling train at the bomb damage that had ripped and scarred the outer suburbs of South London. At long last came the jerk of the points leading into Victoria; and the terrible jagged craters there, some of them already old enough to be soft with the rose-pink flowers of willow herb, which she had known in gentler times along the river at Clonfrack.

The bomb flower of the shattered city. They said that around St. Paul's there was little more than a desert, and all of it pink with flowers. At Victoria that day all the glass was gone from the roof, and two of the platforms closed; and one wall gone, wide open to the shored buildings of a toppling street.

Sam didn't apologize that it was difficult to get a taxi. It would never occur to him to take one, so they saw little or nothing of London. Only the damage around Victoria and the same ghastly mess beyond King's Cross.

In between the two stations, the strange, appalling limbo of the Tube.

Emily took Sam's arm.

"I've heard of it," she said, "but never seen it."

All along the platforms of the narrow stations the familiar tiled walls were covered with bunk beds three tiers high, the red trains roaring and rattling along between them into the darkness of the tunnels. In these bunks whole families now had lived a troglodyte life for years, pouring down in the creaking lifts with food and blankets and bored whining children each evening as darkness fell, and the searchlights probed the sky above the city.

Many stayed there all through the days, having nowhere else to go.

"It gives me the creeps, Sam. It smells, doesn't it?"

"They don't notice it," Sam said, but even his severe expression had broken into pity. "I expect it gives them the creeps too, but it's better than being dead."

"No, it doesn't give them the creeps," she said, and knew she was right, and thanked God she never had to make the choice. "I would think that after a while they thoroughly enjoy it. I expect they'll miss it like anything when it's all over. Like a club."

Just as she knew that when the time came, she would miss Marianna and Penny and Isobel, and all the rest of them, and all the forced intimacy of their lives. All the fun. All the shared sorrows.

And Sam?

She looked at him, but he wasn't looking at her, hanging on to his strap and swaying with the noisy movement of the train. His eyes were on the darkness speeding past them, and his mouth was set again in its thin uncompromising line.

He looks, she thought, as if he were going into battle. And if he is, then it seems I am going with him.

Hatfield, Welwyn, Knebworth, the little stations of Hertfordshire; small red towns buried in the new leaves of many trees. Bigger houses awash with apple blossom and the flowers no war could kill. Bomb damage ended now, and the train ran on through flat rich country Emily had never seen before.

Stevenage and Hitchin, where they had to change onto a Cambridge train. Sam began to come alive, as if the past here touched him more than the awkward present.

"That's Ickleford, along there." He pointed down the long straight railway line. "Where my dad used to take me fishing. We went on bicycles. Long way it was, and Mum packed our lunch. On the level crossing we used to put pins on the line when the Flying Scot was coming. Squashed them dead flat. Lovely train. There's an old Roman camp up there too. Me and my sister used to toboggan down the sides on an old tray. Sandy it was, and very slippy. Smashing."

She looked at his face, and hers was gentle.

"You had a happy childhood, Sam."

For a moment he looked at her with clear bright eyes, hiding nothing.

"Yes," he said.

"Where's your sister now, Sam?"

He gave a small shrug.

"Married in Scotland."

"And your parents? Your mum and dad?"

Never had she dared ask these questions before.

"Dead," he said tersely. "My dad got pneumonia. Out in all weathers, you know, and then my mum had a stroke. Couldn't live without him, I reckon."

Small unexpected picture of a happy marriage and a loved child that filled her with tenderness, and the first glimmering of understanding of Sam's fierce defenses.

But those defenses were up again, the dark blue eyes forbidding.

"Train's coming," he said, and she knew she mustn't ask him what happened to him next.

When they got out at Letchworth, she looked in vain to begin

with for the Garden City Sam had described to Uncle William.
Only at the end of a long sloping road full of shops did she begin
to see it; a straight wide road, as far as she could see, lined with
majestic horse chestnuts whose candle flowers were opening to
the sun. On one side a green, tree-scattered park and on the
other, the high hedges and foaming blossom of the gardens Sam
had boasted every house to possess.

"It's *very* pretty, Sam," she said as they crossed the road.

Sam looked down his nose.

"Tatty," he said.

"Well, I expect it's difficult with the war."

She looked back at a sandbagged warden's post they had just
passed, plastered against the brick wall of the corner like a
swallow's nest. Was there really much war here?

Had they ever heard a bomb?

Sam had gone silent, marching a little ahead of her, up a small
rise to where the road opened at a bend, small houses fanning
away along two roads.

She looked at them with a cold certainty that this was where
Sam lived, and reminded herself that she had just said there was
a war on. Men gone and no money to spend. The rows of little
houses were all intact; no broken-toothed gaps or tarpaulins
covering gaping roofs, but they looked as tired of the war as
everybody else; white paint gray around the windows and dark
stain flaking from the front doors.

As Sam boasted, they all had gardens. Long gardens and many
of them given up to vegetables. Here and there an old man leaned
above a spade, looking curiously at the two young people in
uniform, as if from another world. One touched his cap and
spoke to Sam.

"Morning, Bert," said Sam but did not stop, as if he had
something he must get over with.

Most of the gardens were derelict, all the men gone and the
women out at war work, a garden now only for those lucky
enough to have the old ones living with them. There were rusty
corrugated sheds and piles of rubbish and an air of dereliction;
here and there the round hump of an air-raid shelter.

Emily had grown silent, embarrassed. What was Sam trying to
prove?

At his gate there was a huge bush of white hawthorn, filling
the sunny day with sweetness.

She touched the small blossoms.

"How lovely, Sam. We have a lot of hawthorn along the fields at home."

The perfume made her suddenly sick with longing for Clonfrack, but Sam did not want to know about her nostalgias, kicking irritably at the weeds growing over the path of a long narrow garden that must once have been pretty; up a slight slope and terraced with rocks that were still bright with the purple of aubretia and the white of alyssum; the sunshine yellow of the creeping saxifrage. All stronger than the weeds.

A budding lilac stood beside the door.

"Needs pruning," Sam said dourly.

The door was a long time opening. Sam knocked and knocked again, and Emily thought, it's a small house, surely someone must have seen us up all that long path. She saw the curtains stir at the window next door, and knew the bush telegraph would be beating as surely as in Clonfrack. She began to wish she had put on her working uniform.

There was no greeting from the young woman who finally opened the door, lank hair swinging in a pageboy around a narrow face.

"Oh, Samuel," she said. "I didn't expect you so soon."

"I told you" was all Sam said.

"Yes. But I had Things to Do."

Emily was to realize that she spoke all the time as if what she said, no matter how trivial, had capital letters and was of illimitable importance.

Sam stood back and let Emily go in, and she tried not to notice the stale airless smell of the hall. This was Sam's home, and she was prepared to make his day there as happy as she could.

"Hello," she said, and realized she didn't know the girl's name. Sam's wife, and he had never mentioned her name. She was on edge, aware of trouble and that before the day's end she would be drawn into it.

Sam's wife stood away from her and offered no hand; no welcome in the dark hall lit only by a small window of frosted glass beside the door. No kiss for Sam. Only the smell to welcome him, which a good draft would have got rid of.

"I didn't realize, Samuel," she said then, in her flat, portentous voice, as if Emily weren't there, "that your guest was a Young Lady."

''This is Emily McRoss,'' Sam said doggedly.

It saddened Emily desperately to see Sam already reduced to something less than himself. Anger was beginning to grow in her. At him. At the nameless wife and the whole performance; standing in the dark smelly hall where any moment the door was going to shut for the day on the lilacs and the hawthorn and the bright sun, closing her in with problems she didn't want to face.

Marianna and Penny and Isobel would be just crawling out of bed for lunch, and deciding what to do for the lovely day.

''Well, Miss McRoss,'' Sam's wife said. ''You'd better come into the Front Room.''

''Oh, for God's sake, Angela,'' said Sam. ''Can't we just sit in the living room.''

Angela. How, thought Emily, could she have been called anything else? It was going to be a long day, and she must find something to like about her. The thing was, she could be most attractive, as tall as Emily herself, but thin, with some lanky grace she would not cultivate, any more than she would allow her narrow face to smile, setting it in this silly mold of sullen superiority.

Perhaps I'm not being fair, Emily decided. Perhaps I'm jealous of Sam's wife. Something she had not had to reckon with before. Sam had been all hers.

The room was cold with the chill of disuse, in the small grate a fan of pink fluted paper that did not look to have been disturbed for years. The walls were covered with a nondescript wallpaper so dark it was almost brown, and the linoleum floor almost entirely obscured by an imitation leather suite too big for the room, both armchairs and the sofa and the mantelpiece, and two small tables, in their turn, all covered by no-colored pieces of crochet. Must be Angela's hobby, thought Emily. In a corner on a small chest, a brown wireless like a tombstone crouched on its own crochet mat; the window and the lovely day completely obscured by dingy net.

It was the most ghastly room that Emily had ever seen, and she realized that the general smell was lack of air. Years of cooking and never a window open to the sun.

''Do sit down, Miss McRoss,'' said Angela.

''Emily's my name,'' said Em, still determined to do her best, although already almost too angry with Sam to look at him. Angela didn't answer her, and she sat down carefully on one of

the slippery chairs, tensing all her muscles to stop her sliding off.
How long was this day going to last?

"You'd better stay here and entertain Miss McRoss, Samuel,"
Angela said coldly. "I can manage," she added then, implying
at once that whatever Sam did would be wrong. But Sam knew
very clearly that if he stayed with Emily there would be a row,
and without looking at her, he followed his wife out into the
kitchen.

Not a book, not a paper, one picture of "The Light of the
World," by Holman Hunt, above the mantelpiece and a large
Bible beside the wireless in the corner, and one solitary photograph with two brown vases on the mantelpiece. She got up and
looked at it. A fiercely moustachioed man glaring into the camera,
and a gaunt woman in a plain hat who could be Angela grown
old. Hers, without a doubt. This did not look like Sam's Mum
who had packed lunches for an amiable Dad to take Sam fishing,
and presumably provided the pins for squashing under the Flying
Scot.

Irritably she moved to the window. She felt like a prisoner. No
doubt Sam seemed to have here a whole packet of unhappiness
and trouble, but he should have talked to her about it, not
plonked her down into the middle of it. She realized that he was
taking her up on all the times she had said that surroundings
didn't count, it was the *people* that mattered. Obstinately, she
clung to her view. It was Angela that was wrong. Sam didn't
have to have this obviously loveless, cheerless life, even if he
was a gardener. Dear God, it wouldn't take much effort to begin
by opening a window and getting rid of the terrible smell that
was beginning to creep in from the kitchen. Let in the lilacs and
the sun.

She must, thought Emily, be boiling meat in cod-liver oil.

"Whale meat," Angela said without apology when they reached
the big deal table in the living room, which was at least more
cheerful since it had windows at both ends and a back-boiler
grate where a fire popped merrily.

"Whale meat!" Sam said in disgust.

"There is a War On, Samuel, you know."

"I had realized," said Sam, away from his home and his job
now for three and a half years.

"One is lucky to get Whale Meat, of course." Angela assumed an expression of exhaustion. "Had I realized your Guest

was a Young Lady, I would have tried to find the necessary hour to Queue up for a Piece of Cod, although even then one can be Disappointed.''

Emily watched her, mesmerized, as she put out the strange solid dark red meat onto three plates and set beside them a few boiled potatoes and some mushy dried peas. Fortunately, like corned beef, she loved mushy dried peas, but she was thinking, and knew Sam was thinking, of Uncle William and Aunt Agnes and the fish from the lake and the vegetables from the garden and the pony who worked to provide all the other things.

"Surely," exploded Sam, "you could try to grow a few vegetables in the garden."

She lifted languid eyes and Emily wondered if Sam had ever managed to get her angry or had he spent all his married life beating against that torpid indifference. No wonder he was closed up like a clam.

But he shouldn't have thrown her into the middle of it.

"Surely, Samuel," said Angela. "You forget my Bad Back. And I have my War Work to do."

Sam grunted, and devoted himself distastefully to his whale meat, but Emily, embarrassed because she had been taught all her life to be polite, pushed her dark slab to one side and ate the boiled potatoes and the mushy peas; not even for politeness could she face it.

"I'm sorry," she said to Angela's long disapproving face. "I'm sorry, but I just don't like it."

It was like the Ministry of Food's wartime recipes. Always good for a laugh, but nobody in their right mind actually ate them. She was willing to bet that Angela used them faithfully.

It was almost impossible to tell within these shrouded rooms what was happening outside, only the occasional close trill of birdsong reminding them that somewhere there was all the tender beauty of an early summer. Emily was growing restless and irritable. Sam had torn her to pieces by telling her that after knowing her, his life was destroyed and he could never go back to it. She almost snorted. Life down a coal mine would have destroyed him for this.

He and Angela went upstairs together, and hot with embarrassment, Emily could hear them quarreling; Sam's voice raised; Angela's in the flat capitalized tones of rejection that she appeared to offer to all of life.

She tried to go out into the neglected garden, but the long window was locked and she was not going out through the kitchen where the whale smell still hung like a miasma. She knew she would not have been welcome in there anyway.

Sam came down again, rattrap mouth and angry dark eyes, and flung himself into the old armchair by the fire that was draped in the ubiquitous crochet, in multicolored squares.

"There's a train at six twenty," he said. "We'll catch that."

She did no more than agree. No time now to start rowing.

Angela gave them thin tea and sugarless biscuits, and through her flat, uninteresting conversation, Emily sensed some new preoccupation. She kept glancing at the clock.

"Are you waiting for the news?" Emily asked her. For God's sake, something, anything to say, but even as she asked the question she realized that this flat-voiced, flat-fronted boring girl might have her sorrows and anxieties too. Be waiting for news of someone.

"Oh, no, Miss McRoss." She gathered up the teacups more briskly than she had done anything that day. "Oh, no. We shall hear That later on at the Post."

When she came down a little later, she was in navy blue overalls with the patch of an air-raid warden on her shoulder; self-important and self-conscious as a child; placing a gas mask and a tin hat on the table, and a small knapsack.

Emily tried not to look at Sam. If there were desperate air raids here, he had never mentioned it, and she was very conscious of her own tin hat, back under the bed at Darlowe. She found it very useful for keeping her spare makeup in.

"You going to be down there alone all night with that silly little bugger?" Sam said suddenly, and Angela nodded with tight lips and a small air of contempt. Emily felt she had stumbled on a bit more of the row that had been going on upstairs. Sam had no *right* to involve her!

Before she could even speculate on who the little bugger was, there was a rattle at the front door and he came in, middle-aged, less than medium height and very thin with strong glasses that magnified assertive bright brown eyes. Hung about, as Angela was, with all the paraphernalia of an air-raid warden; an enormous torch in his hand, although the declining sun still seemed to be bright beyond the shrouding net curtains.

She thought of the night a couple of months previously, when

German E-boats had been sighted immediately off the coast. They had all been ripped from their beds and allowed no lights; not a torch between them, groping their way over to be mustered in The Elms. All the mechanics at the Site had apparently been trembling with excitement, wondering if they were actually going to be the ones to press the ''Destruct'' buttons on all their priceless gear. Because Emily could draw, she had been asked by the C.O. to do a new copy of the defense map of the Station; and out of all the hilarious girls speculating about blond handsome Germans landing on the beach, and how long they should resist before they gave in, she and she alone knew, with cold apprehension, that should there be any real final threat to this highly secret Station, then the naval guns at Littlehampton were to be turned on it and it was to be demolished.

Irrespective of personnel.

The E-boats had slid away into the darkness, and everyone had gone yawning back to bed.

''Miss McRoss,'' said Angela, ''this is Mr. Peashell.''

A different Angela, pink-cheeked and deferential, fluttering as if Winston Churchill himself had walked into the room, the whole conduct of the war in his large capable hands.

'' 'Evening, Miss McRoss. 'Evening, Corporal Treadwell.''

He gave them one carefully measured glance from the bright brown eyes, putting them precisely in their place in the scheme of things, laying his torch down like the Holy Grail on the living room table. Its light was carefully blacked out to a slit.

''Got your torch, Angela dear?''

''Yes, Stanford.''

''Sandwiches?''

''Even some coffee, Stanford. For a treat.''

''Good. Good.'' The bright brown eyes beamed at her.

Emily gaped. They had not been given coffee after lunch— dinner—today. It had been a long day, full of strains and even shocks, and her balance was fragile, tipped at the moment in the direction of hopeless, helpless laughter. Oh, but Marianna should be here. No one, but *no one* in this world could be called Stanford Peashell. She saw Sam glaring at her and choked it back.

''When do you go on duty?'' she managed to ask politely.

Stanford Peashell breathed in importantly.

''One hour before dusk,'' he said portentously. Emily felt as if she were back at school. "The hours of darkness, as you know, Corporal Treadwell, are the dangerous time. We have to be prepared. Checking everything one hour before. The telephones, the stirrup pump; the buckets of water. It is necessary to be prepared."

He stood like a small puffed-out frog and touched his big torch like a talisman.

"And how many," asked Sam in a dangerous voice, and Emily realized he knew quite well. "How many bombs have you had on Letchworth, Mr. Peashell?"

Peashell was not perturbed.

"None yet, Corporal Treadwell. None. But it is necessary to Be Prepared. There *is* a war on, you know."

"So I understand," said Sam dourly.

"Bloody Boy Scout," he added under his breath, and meant it to be heard.

Open hostilities were stopped by Angela, who came in with a martyred look and a bucket of something called Brickettes for the fire: coal dust pounded together with water into little black balls like potatoes.

Peashell lunged at the bucket.

"Angela *dear*. You should have asked *me* to do that, if no one else would."

Angela simpered like a cherished woman, and Sam's mouth tightened to the rattrap.

"Time for our train, Emily," he said abruptly, and Emily lunged gratefully, quick with relief, for her cap and gas mask off the peg in the smelly narrow hall. The train, she knew, was not due for another hour.

"Ai think," said Angela, "that it Would be Nice if we all walked down together. The Post is on the way to the station."

Bitch. Bitch and bitch and bitch, thought Emily, who did not usually think in such terms, reading the other girl like a book. All the posturing Angela wanted was to have Sam watch her vanish for the night into the warden's post with the ghastly little Peashell. Carefully she kept her eyes away from Sam, not able to bear to look at his thin-lipped face.

Oh, Sam, poor Sam.

"Ready, dear?" said Peashell, proprietorially. "Got your key? I'll lock up for you."

They walked down the steps through the garden where Sam kicked morosely at his weed-choked flowers, and in dead silence down the short hill in the lovely evening with the thrushes shouting in the hawthorns and the lilacs, and all the trees with more leaves than they had had that morning, and Sam's life as he had known it, finally coming to cheap and unkind pieces in his hands.

The warden's post was the one they had passed that morning, and Peashell produced the key with ceremony.

"Another night's work," he said, and Sam and Emily both stood, too sad with all the ugliness to answer him.

"Good-bye, Miss McRoss," said Angela, and then turned a cold flaccid cheek to Sam, but from where Emily was standing she could see the bright triumph in her eyes. She felt sick with sorrow for Sam; for the real old-fashioned heart of gold that lay behind the sharp tongue and the rattrap mouth; which he offered to anyone with so much difficulty. Which he must have offered at some time to this mean, small-minded girl.

Oh, Sam, poor Sam.

She had forgotten, as they walked on up the long hill toward the station, that she had been furious early on; thinking this was some childish getting his own back, for Aunt Agnes and Uncle William; telling her deviously again she was a snob.

This was more. Not even for all his monstrous complexes would Sam have so led her into the barren bitter center of his marriage.

Why then? Why? Why had he done it?

Sam stopped suddenly, and a large pregnant girl had to walk around between him and the greening hedge, looking at him indignantly, her hair swinging. He never even saw her.

"Emily," he said. "Emily." His eyes blazed at her darkly, with God knew what appeal and torment, and she moved at once to take his hand.

"Sam, don't look like that."

The blind gaze still held her.

"Emily. You've seen it all now. Seen everything. Know just what it would be like. Will you marry me, Emily, when I get rid of her?"

Almost choking with difficulty, she knew the answer at once and must give it. All the hazy romantic thinking about Sam resolved in this second in the lambent dusk of a mundane shopping street in Letchworth Garden City. All the talking and the long rambling on the Downs, and the breathless shared excitement of their work; the music in the warm NAAFI on cold starlit nights; the comradeship; the fun; the deep endless kindness that was Sam.

All this, which at times she had been tempted to think more than it was.

She was sick in that second with guilt and shame, knowing that in her own loneliness she had taken all Sam had to offer. More, more, more, dear God, than was ever fair.

"Oh, Sam," she said, and there were tears in the dark gray eyes. "Oh, Sam. I'm sorry, sorry, sorry. So *sorry*. But no, I know it wouldn't do."

Sam's face grew tight and cold. He gestured bitterly back toward his home.

"It's because of all that," he said tartly, "isn't it? Not Uncle William and Aunt Agnes. Not good enough for Miss McRoss."

She could have hit him. All pity fled.

"No, no, no," she shouted at him. "No. Don't you realize that if you were married to me, it wouldn't *be* like that! I wouldn't *let* it! Being a snob has nothing to *do* with it."

"It would be the same. There'd be no money to be different. I'm only a gardener."

"I'm different, Sam! And believe me, oh, Sam dear, believe me, if I thought it right, I'd marry you without a penny. Oh, Sam, I'm sorry!"

All my fault, she thought, and could have cried with shame. He thought to show me the worst, and that I would rise to it, and I haven't.

Without realizing it she was twisting and twisting the topaz on her finger.

Sam nodded at it.

"It's because of him, then," he said.

Gravely she looked at him, quiet.

"Oh, Sam," she said, and echoed the sad question of so many girls of the war. "Oh, Sam, how do I *know*? Once yes, oh, yes, there was no one this side of the moon and stars but him. But now. I have changed. He may have changed. How do we know, Sam. We can't put the clock back. We'll just have to wait and see."

Sam looked at her unblinkingly.

"If he comes back."

"If he comes back."

He stood a moment longer, then he took her arm.

"That's my mate's shop over there," he said. "Come on and I'll get you some bull's-eyes."

J. Beddoe: Confectioner.

Engraved on her mind now, surely, like the day that Alejandro failed to come, and that Dermot was reported missing.


They stood in darkness on the railway platform with the scent of lilacs coming from beyond the wooden fence, and the high bridge against the last soft color of the sky. There were cabbages in the little railed-in beds, where the bright flowers had once been the pride of the Garden City.

Emily could do nothing to break the silence, feeling that through the long day she had been through two separate storms, battered by guilt for adding to the unhappiness of the man who stood beside her.

Oh, poor Sam. And what a *rotten* day!

Somehow they must hammer out a new relationship, but it would take time. Friends they must be; she could not let Sam go like that. But she must never lead him on again to think there might be more.

For the moment she could not think of anything to say.

"Sam," she said then suddenly, beginning to laugh weakly, helplessly. A thrush in the lilacs threw out a few repeated notes into the dark, as if she had disturbed him.

"Sam. If your wife marries that man, she'll be called Angela Peashell. It's not *possible*. Angela Peashell!"

It was not too dark to see Sam's face break into a grim reluctant smile as the train came in.

"What else," he said, "does she deserve?"

He took her hand then, in a grip so fierce it hurt her. Leading her to find a carriage.

Emily, his Emily.

He, too, had had a bloody awful day. Put it all on the line, and it had failed.

Unaccountably, in the middle of her laughing as she was climbing into the train, her bag of bull's-eyes in her hand, she began to cry.

## THIRTEEN

It was said afterwards that the date of D-Day was bandied freely around the bars and streets of Worthing, long before it happened, but if that was so, it never got as far as the dark secret rooms of Darlowe, where there was no more than endless hope and speculation; and the high excitement of knowing that whenever it should happen, they would be inevitably at the heart of it.

Travel was forbidden, both in and out, for more than twenty miles from the Station, and many urgent courtships and meetings took place in towns like Horsham, on the edges of the forbidden circle.

On the Station they were put on to something called "iron rations," and after a few days of it Emily realized that she should not perhaps have been so superior about Angela's whale meat. There were sausages and margarine and cocoa, all made of soya beans, the sausages totally uneatable and the margarine dripping in oily yellow streams around the edges of their plates. More than ever they were all driven out to eat in the cafés and hostels of Worthing and West Worthing.

"Well, what are we to do with it all?" cried the exasperated boys in the cookhouse, watching it all pile up. "What do we do with it when no one will eat it?"

The girls grinned while the men offered their suggestions, the politest being that it would do very nicely for the policemen's pigs, who waxed fat and smelly in a secluded corner at the top of the back lane from the Site, keeping their figures and their value on the cookhouse waste, at no expense to the astute policemen who had invested in them.

Sam shoved away his plate in disgust.

"Not the first time I've had this muck," he said. "When I was in North Africa, I saw a whole wall in a camp built of tins of soya bean sausages that no one would eat."

"How singularly stupid," said Marianna. She tipped up her purse on the table and separated the money from the hair clips and the buttons, to see if they could possibly go out again at the end of Watch for fish and chips in the Orange Café. "How singularly stupid. Men! Any woman would have more sense than to go on buying things that nobody was going to eat."

"Any woman," said someone else tartly, gathering up her unused irons with a clatter, "would have more sense than to start a war in the first place."

Sam smiled his rare sweet smile across the table at Emily.

"I've got one on my hands at the moment," he said, "and I reckon a woman started it."

She shot him a glance, gray eyes level, only the hint of a smile answering his.

"You'll not win it, Sam."

"Stop bickering, you two," said Marianna, "we'll be late for Watch."

"Will you listen to what's talking," cried Emily. Marianna always felt that Watch began at whatever moment she saw fit to ramble in. But she gathered up her things and went, with a last glance at Sam to tell him she meant what she had said.

With great difficulty she had said to him, after the day in Letchworth, that they should see less of each other, as the whole thing was getting out of hand. Depriving herself with pain, of a daily happiness far greater than she had realized until it was over.

Sam had looked at her for a long time, and then shrugged as Sam would, and agreed with her; leaving Emily with the unhappy feeling that his agreement had meant nothing other than his willingness always to do as she wanted. Had she wanted the stars from the sky, he would probably have started to crawl up the beam of a searchlight. Nevertheless she and Sam avoided each other now as much as was possible; speaking only as they would speak to anybody else; sitting together at meals, as they had done today, only when it happened by chance.

No more rambling in the long flowering grasses on the tops of the sun-drenched Downs, leaning against the grave of John Clement Oliver; watching the blue silk sea far away below them, and wondering when they would see it black with the boats of the

Second Front. No more moonlit rambles home after a meal or a dance or the cinema in Worthing; always taking a pilgrimage down to look at the moon-blanched beaches through the tank traps and the coils of barbed wire. Watching the unreachable waves frothing up onto the desolation, and longing for a swim. No more companionable evenings in the NAAFI, drinking cocoa and talking down the world, listening to the sad poignant singing of Vera Lynn. Songs of heartbreak and good-bye and the longing for the end of it all, that spoke for everyone.

No love making to regret and sorrow for, thought Emily wryly, on account of Sam's Principles. Was there ever a stranger courtship? How had the man, she wondered, held her at all? But he had. And did, and she was bitterly lonely.

She tended to remember only the good things about these months of going with Sam; forgetting the tight mouth and the steely blue of the eyes; the dogmatic obstinacy of his views; the contempt for her and everything she was, even while he said he loved her.

She had allowed herself to fall more than halfway in love with Sam; heedlessly; and was filled with guilt that she had ever let him think that she might marry him. Filled with guilt lest she had caused him unnecessary pain.

God, what a mess.

But it wasn't, she told herself furiously, the fear of poverty, and of Sam's life, that made her back off. She would be perfectly, absolutely happy with the right poor man. Perfectly happy to marry him, no matter how little they might have.

Sam would laugh out loud, she knew, if she said that to him, and point out sardonically that she was not very likely to be put to the test. With a withering glance at the topaz on her left hand.

She twisted it on her finger and knew he could be right. But she insisted they separate before she hurt him further.

"Don't think, Emily," he had said, even as he had shrugged and agreed, "that you will get rid of me as easily as that."

"I'm sorry, Sam. I keep saying I'm sorry, but it's no good. It wouldn't work."

So they stood now at opposite ends of the canteen, and ate their meals at different tables, and Sam leaned over her in silence, not touching her, to tune her radar set. Emily thought of the little Virgins that pious ladies brought home to her mother from their pilgrimages to Lourdes, made luminous so that they shone in the dark. She was as conscious of Sam, wherever they were, as if he too were luminous, and could not be closed out from her eyes.

Conscious and guilty.

She joined a pleased Marianna, who had never thought much of Sam, in the high, hectic life of all the unattached girls of the Station at that time. In these days leading up to D-Day the coast was every day more tightly packed with soldiers, all anxious to cram as much pleasure into life as possible, before the bugles blew and summoned them back to a war that was war.

They were almost the only girls along the coast, now that the travel ban was off, and could have gone romping off to three parties a night, did they so wish, the daily notice board overlapping with invitations. Through the soft blue evenings of that beautiful May, there was the touch of drama to it: all of the intensified air raids on the massing landing craft; sirens wailing above the fox-trots, and the crump of bombs; when they came out, searchlights frantically racing the purple summer sky. Through it all they danced as if they, too, might never dance again.

They danced with their own Saskatchewan Light Infantry, coming smart in their kilts from their tents beyond the elm trees to meet them at the gate. With the Regina Rifles and the Tactical Air Force, and the Welsh Regiment with the black ribbons so waiting to be pulled at the back of their collars; with the Winnipeg Rifles down in their walking-out uniforms from the hills; the very gentlemanly Sharpshooters, and the Cherry Pickers in their glamorous red trousers; and the Scottish Borderers and the Highland Light Infantry. Once Emily had a marvelous evening with an Irish medico called Marcus O'Rourke from Galway, who was with the Desert Rats, and had come all the way from El Alamein to Tunis with Paul.

"I'm going to marry his brother," she cried excitedly, and for a moment only Dermot was real. "When he comes back."

"Where is he?"

Cold fell on them like a winter wind.

"I don't know," she said. "He was last seen with an armored car in Singapore. He's in the Air Force," she added.

He gave her a long look.

"Well, we'll be neighbors, then," he said, "when you're married. Will we dance now?"

Clonfrack and Castle Keene and Galway and Dermot and all

her Irish life rose up there to confuse her in the packed ballroom
of the Worthing Assembly Rooms, with the band blaring away at
"Dearly Beloved," and when she passed her friends on the floor,
she looked at them as though she barely knew them.

"We are all far from home," said Marcus O'Rourke gently,
and she loved him for it.

Marianna was having another kind of trouble. Emily found her
doubled up with laughter against a pillar.

"What's happened, Marianna?"

"My dear, I've been stood up."

"Stood up?"

"This little soldier came up and asked me to dance. My dear,
he only came about to my waist."

Emily looked at Marianna's long elegant length and grinned.

"So off we go onto the floor," went on Marianna, "and we
go hippety-hop about three times around. My feet and his were
just never in the same place. In the end he stops in the middle of
the floor, and says to me that he's sorry, I'm just not his kind of
girl! Walked away and left me flat. Never, my dear, such
humiliation. Left me standing in the middle of the floor. I'll
never get over the shame."

Even as they stood there laughing, a tall fair captain of the
Scottish Borderers came up and asked Marianna to dance.

"Can you bear to, Marianna?" Emily asked her. "Think of
the shame!"

"Would you think I'm your kind of girl?" she asked the
mystified young man.

He recovered rapidly.

"We'll discuss it on the floor," he said, and with a swing of
his kilt and a swing of Marianna, he was gone.

Emily went back to Ireland and Marcus O'Rourke.

They made no dates with any of them, for who could know if
there would be a tomorrow. As they piled into transports or
six-deep into taxis to go home, they were always a little silent,
knowing that every night might be the last; the same elated
excitement never to come again.

Marianna, always the most impressionable, heaved herself in
over the back of the transport one night, sniffing hard and
scrubbing at her face with the cuff of her jacket.

"Darling," she grabbed at Emily in the dark lorry. "Darling,
do you have a handkerchief?"

"What's the matter, Marianna?"

Emily groped up her sleeve for a handkerchief and gave it to Marianna, who was now in floods of tears.

"Look!"

Emily bent to see a fistful of paper Marianna held out to her.

"What is it?"

"Clothing coupons," said Marianna, and went into fresh gusts of tears. "Clothing coupons and sweetie coupons. David, his name was. In the Scottish Borderers and oh, my dear, so ravishing in that kilt, tall as a hop pole and such a dancer. He gave me these just now because he said he felt he might not be needing them again. Awful, Em. Awful. I feel as if I've robbed a grave. Two little children, he said he had, and he said he didn't want to go and be a hero, he wanted to go home to them and to his wife. It's not *right*, Em. I can't bear it."

Emily sat close to her in silence while her tears subsided, for what was there to do or say. He was only one of hordes of them, God help them, and there was nothing to do but bear it; all or any of it.

But sitting in the dark rumbling truck as it trundled back to Darlowe, thinking of it all, Emily was surprised and humbled to realize how the gilt and the edge had gone from her own life without Sam. Sam, whom she had taken so much for granted; without glamour or distinction. Sam, whose own feelings she had taken so lightly; so little allowed for. Through all the gaiety and the emotion and all the glamorous young men, she was lonely for Sam with his tight mouth and his bony face, and that sudden ravishing smile that could turn her heart to water.

In these tense nights before the Second Front, the Happidrome took across the Channel many aircraft called Intruders. Lysander aircraft out of Ford, slipping across to France in the moonless nights, with anything from tobacco to small arms for the Resistance workers; with agents going in to work behind the lines of the invasion. To collect agents coming out, their jobs completed, waiting, in disciplined patience crouched in some shelter, for the squat shape of the Lysander with its spread-eagled legs to come dropping from the dark of the sky. Down between a straggly row of smoking lights, in some cramped French field.

Emily often had the task of taking them over, waiting drymouthed in the following dawn for them to come back, lest

some error of hers had taken them in over France in a wrong and
dangerous place; into disaster over the enemy guns.

For an Intruder it was not an ordinary screen, but a glass
tabletop about two feet across, light brilliant under it, and the
same map as the table, with its grid squares, drawn out on the
illuminated glass, the safe path for the Intruder marked thick and
black from Ford to the coast of France. He must keep total
silence on his RT all along that line, lest he betray himself to the
ever-listening enemy, who would organize a welcome party for
him at his landfall.

It was Emily's task to keep him on that line; with a stopwatch,
his position at every minute worked out; her eyes glued to the
revolving trace to see that the little blip of light that was the
airplane came up on every sweep exactly where it should. Not
taken off his course by wind or drift.

Should he leave his black line, it was her business to call a
Controller, who would in turn call the pilot and direct him back
again onto his safe and proper course.

Quiet, concentrated, responsible work, alone in dead silence in
the dark cabin, the brilliant floodlit Ops Room spread out before
her, the Lysander she was tracking shown on the big table by a
green arrow being moved steadily across the middle of the Channel.

Sam came in when she was doing this one evening, when they
had been separated about ten days. Determinedly he sat himself
down on the other side of the glass screen. Ridiculous. But she
was, as always, deeply disturbed by his close presence. It was
not necessary for him to touch her. He was destroying her
concentration. She smiled at him and cursed herself for feeling
stupidly tremulous, and thought how the upward light became his
bony face, and then went on carefully with what she was doing.
Checking. Tracking.

"Emily," said Sam fiercely, without preamble. "It's no good.
For me it's no good."

She no longer felt tremulous. Only furious.

"Sam, be *quiet*."

She relayed the next plot down to the floor and the green arrow
was moved on.

"I can't stand not seeing you, Emily, and I'm not going to
give up so easily."

"Sam, I'm *concentrating*. What happens if I take this kite in
over the French guns."

Sam looked down at the screen, all the strong bones of his face picked out by the light. We look like a couple of fortune tellers crouched over a crystal ball, thought Emily. Ridiculous.

"Go away, Sam."

"He's dead on course. No troubles there. I never see you alone anywhere else."

"Sam, I can't talk and do it properly. Please, Sam."

"Don't talk. Just answer. Will you marry me?"

She gasped and gaped at him, and stared at him for half the sweep of the trace.

"You have no finesse, Sam."

"I don't want finesse. I want you."

"Sam, I said *no*. You're being a nuisance."

Her next plot was so irregular that the girl on the other end of the telephone down on the table glanced up at her as if to ask if there was anything wrong, her face full of righteous reproach.

"*No*, Sam," she said again. "Not then or now or any other time."

How could she have been lonely for him. He was being a pest.

There was no time for gentle speech, held by the sweeping trace and the stopwatch and the thick black line to France.

"He's okay," said Sam again. "But you need a bit more brilliance."

He waited until she had given the next plot and then tuned the set.

"If I promise not to ask you again," he said then, "will you go out with me again? If I promise?"

She was distracted. Afraid of making a mistake; afraid of the Controller coming in to check on the Intruder. One did not chat with one's boyfriend with a Lysander halfway to the enemy coast.

"Sam, go away. Please, go away."

"Well, will you?"

"You're blackmailing me, Sam. You shouldn't be here."

She glanced up from the screen and his smile was broad and sweet in the electronic light; his eyes determined.

"Yes," said Sam.

She must get rid of him. He was distracting her, and for God's sake, however melodramatic you liked to call it, the pilot's life was in their hands.

"All right. But no marriage talk, Sam."

"Cross my heart. See you tomorrow. All platonic."

He waited for the trace to go around once more, darkness around their island of light. Then he touched Emily quickly on the hand and was gone.

She looked down at the floor. The walls of these cabins over the Ops Room were almost all glass, and she and Sam would have been clearly visible in the light from the Skyatron. The girl on the other end of the line would be one of the first to say that she thought Intruders were one of the most responsible jobs, malice added since she was not allowed to do them, and so what was Emily McRoss doing talking to Sam Treadwell with a Lysander on the table.

Bending again over the screen and the straight black line, Emily was furious. Of course she was furious. Sam had jumped her. Nor did she trust his promise to be platonic. Furious. He was a pest. She was just getting used to doing without him. A real pest. But the light from the glass table picked out the warm pleasure kindling in her gray eyes, and the small contented smile creeping about the corners of her mouth.

It was very soon as if they had never been apart.

Avoiding the packed noisy bars and restaurants of Worthing; keeping for themselves a strange false quiet away from the frenetic celebrations of all the massing soldiers who would soon be gone. They went out for drinks, the despised snobbish Pimm's for Emily, and a beer for him, with their onion sandwiches in small pubs on the fringes of the town; or even as far away as Ferring, with soft lilac-scented nights for walking home along the lanes, where sometimes, in spellbound silence, they listened to the nightingale and wondered, each of them, would they ever hear anything so beautiful again. Emily tried to reconcile the peace and loveliness with the reality of the vast army gathering on the coast, and found it difficult at times to understand which of them was truth.

Over Sam she tried to stifle guilt, unable to resist the undeniable happiness, the security, the very warmth of being back with Sam, persuading herself that guilt was no longer involved now that she had made it clear where he stood, and where she stood. And he had accepted it.

As always in moments of doubt, as if it were a talisman, but barely thinking of Dermot, she twisted the topaz on her finger.

Why should they not be friends? Ridiculous, now they understood each other, to be apart. Ripped by some real sadness close to tears, every time some dance orchestra on the wireless drifted into the sad cadences of "In My Solitude." With Sam the other side of the room.

Deliberately she blinded herself to the dark watching of Sam's eyes, which held anything but easy friendship. To the passionate attentiveness that would not allow her to breathe, were it possible for him to do it for her.

"She wrote to me today," he said suddenly when they had been going together again for about a week, watched by the amused eyes of the Station. "Said she wanted a divorce."

She looked at him, startled. They were walking together up the long white road from the Site, where she had stayed on to complete some drawings for the Technical Officer. The Watch had gone on without her, but Sam had waited, and now they ambled up at their own pace, both of them in shirt sleeves in the warm sun.

"Angela?" asked Emily sharply.

"Angela. I believe the Americans call them 'Dear John' letters. Very sorry but I have found someone else. Peashell!" he exploded suddenly. "Jesus Christ, to be ousted by Peashell!"

"But Sam," she said reasonably. "Why do you mind? You don't still want Angela."

How could he, when he had asked *her* to marry him.

"Not on your Nellie," Sam said. "It's my pride, I suppose. I should have had the guts to get rid of her long ago. Peashell is not the first, and all of them old enough to be her father."

Bitterness and the wounded pride smashed down all his usual reticence, his disciplined face vulnerable and awry. She looked at him with pity and a creeping apprehension. It would be more difficult than ever to say no. Unable any longer to shelter behind the existence of Angela.

But she understood. Dear God, how well she understood. As if it had just happened, all the bitterness and smashed pride that had been hers over Remedios and Alejandro flooded back. She moved to tell him and then held back. It was his own sorrow he wanted comfort for, not an old rehash of hers. But Alejandro had taught her that there was no comfort. Only pain and pain and pain that had taken years to die away, and could still rise up to tear her at a moment such as this.

"I'm sorry, Sam" was all she said. "Oh, God, I'm really sorry. Poor Sam, what a mess for you."

She longed to touch him; come close to him and offer to his poor bleak face the small comfort of contact. But they were on the road from the Site, and so still officially on duty. Any passing officer would have taken a dim view of her with her arms around Sam.

In silence, with Sam brooding on the shabby tatters of his life and Emily groping for the answers that might not make him feel unwanted yet again, they marched up side by side on the weedy concrete road. As if they were discussing the bright weather or the Second Front, or the odd interference that had baffled them on the screens during Watch.

Had she married Alejandro, she thought, then it could have come to this with her. For how could he have been different, simply because they were married? Emotionally she had long let Alejandro go. Now, on the sunny road in England, she looked on that blissful Spanish love, and knew a sick relief that it had come to nothing.

Already she was wondering, was the breakup of Sam's marriage due to her? Would Sam ever have taken her to his home, were it not for his feeling that he needed to give a brutal answer to the visit to Uncle William and Aunt Agnes? Was her presence with him just enough to tip that petulant girl?

Oh, dear God, what a blundering mess she was making of it all. Long ago, now, he had told her on a Christmas morning that she would break his heart.

"Not your fault, Emily," he said as if he read her thoughts. "All fell apart long before you." He paused a moment, and she couldn't bear the stoic sorrow of his face.

"Sam."

"Trouble was," he said, "you showed me what it *could* be like."

"Me and Aunt Agnes and Uncle William," she said in a small voice, and Sam did not deny it.

"Does it make any difference?" he said then.

"Does what? To what?"

She understood him perfectly and was backing away.

"Will you be willing to marry me now I'm free?"

Emily stood still. She had just about begun to lose the feeling of being cornered by Sam. She thought he had really given up, and meant it about being friends.

"Sam—no marriage talk. You agreed."

"It's different now."

He stopped too and kicked stubbornly at a clump of dandelions breaking up through the seam of the concrete.

How could she get it through to him, without hurting him even more, that nothing would make it any different. Nothing. That for all his attraction, which had made her almost lose her head, she knew that Sam was not for her.

"Or is it because you're a Catholic. No divorce."

"Sam, it's *nothing* outside ourselves. If I wanted to, I would marry you no matter what. Nothing outside ourselves."

He would not accept that, not even answering, and a guilty voice inside her asked her whether she was sure that was absolutely true. She had condemned Alejandro out of hand, and so had everybody else. But had he, too, realized that however much he loved her, it would have been a mistake? Moving back to Remedios and the world to which he had always belonged. Was Sam right, and she was like that also?

Confusedly she thought of Clonfrack and Castle Keene, and Uncle William and Aunt Agnes.

About Dermot.

Was she really perhaps, as Sam said, refusing him because he didn't belong to that world?

Refusing to marry a poor man?

Sam tramped on dourly with his mouth set in the rattrap. Emily followed more slowly, loving him enough to be sick with sorrow that she couldn't give him any happiness; but in spite of the doubts that clawed her, still firm in her certainty that no good would come of it. If it helped him to accuse her of snobbery or religious bigotry or anything else he wished, then she'd accept it.

The Technical Officer came swooping past on his bicycle, which he always rode as if it were a Typhoon dive-bombing some French railway yard. He looked back at them, and the yards between them, Emily walking behind like a Chinese wife.

"If you don't want her, Treadwell," he yelled at Sam, "I'll have her! Or does she bite?"

Sam had the grace to grin and turn back and wait, but he didn't speak again, nor did he come through to eat lunch with her.

Marianna sat alone in the WAAF section, a congealing plate of nameless food in front of her.

"Em. I've saved you some liver. It's cold, but otherwise there's rabbit and I know how you feel about eating our little furry friends."

Emily slipped in in front of the cold brown mess and tried to look grateful. But Marianna was right, of course. Like most Irish people she regarded rabbits as vermin, and would as soon have eaten a rat.

She pushed her hair from her forehead with a tired gesture.

"Treadwell trouble?" asked Marianna, aware of Sam scowling over his solitary meal in the next room.

Emily nodded.

"He won't take no for an answer. So exhausting."

Marianna shrugged and spread her long fingers.

"My dear. It's my experience that none of them want to take no for an answer, and it's always exhausting. Tell me, Em darling, do you have ideas for getting rid of the smell of fish?"

"Of fish?"

"Well, you see, there was this smashing captain in the Guards Armoured, and you know last thirty-six I went out and stayed the night in the YWCA because I wanted to wear my own clothes."

Emily had been with Sam, otherwise she'd have been in on the jaunt, about a dozen girls going to the dance in Worthing and staying the night in the local hostel, ruled over by a dragon far more fierce than anything they knew in the WAAF. But at least it gave them a chance on these warm summer nights to go dancing in their own clothes.

"Yes," she said.

"Well." Marianna was plaintive. "I wore my lovely gray woollen jacket. You know, the one with the long hair. This chap wasn't here all the time, he had to go up to London the next morning. So I went to see him off. There was only this sort of trolley thing to sit on. Darling, how were we to know it had been used for fish boxes?"

Emily smothered her helpless laughter. Never mind Marianna. Imagine some smart captain going up to town for some conference, stinking of fish and unable to get rid of it.

"Where is it?" she said. "Your jacket."

"My dear, it's been two days and nights in the garden, and I still can't get rid of the smell."

"God," said Emily. "Let's go and have a look at it."

"Emily, dear, you are so kind."

After a couple of days Sam was back, but never a word more was said of love and marriage. He really has given up, thought Emily, and began to relax again with him; to accept the pleasure, of his company that she could not deny.

"Come and have a drink at the Mulberry," he said one evening. "I'll buy you a Pimm's and promise to behave myself."

All the other girls were going to some fabulous dance in the Town Hall, and for a moment she wavered, longing to be with them. Then Sam smiled his irresistible smile, and she gave in. If he was unhappy, then she was at least partly responsible, and she couldn't abandon him.

"Okay, Sam."

They had their drinks, and he behaved himself to the point of never once protesting her Pimm's, and afterwards they rambled down Sea Lane beyond the Mulberry, to stand at the barbed wire and look out at the sea, and the long stretch of golden beach in the declining sun.

"Wonder if they have any idea what's going to hit them over there," Emily said, staring over the quiet summer sea towards the French coast. "Wonder if they are waiting, like us."

Sam snorted.

"They'll be fools if they don't have some idea," he said.

He was doing an extra Watch for someone, and had to get back. They sauntered home through the clear beautiful evening, past little gardens awash with flowers, the great expanse of the Sussex sky turning to violet above them; the last birds singing defiantly, the first star hanging clear above the dark line of the Downs.

Absolute summer peace, giving the lie to all the thronging soldiers and the landing barges they knew were massing in all the harbors farther along the coast. Giving the utter lie to the very existence of violence and war and death.

Peace, astonishingly, even between themselves, so that they walked in companionable silence up over the white arc of Darlowe Bridge across the railway line; past the light antiaircraft gun at the Station end of it, exchanging a few words of sharp chat with the two soldiers who manned it. Past even the shelter from the high concrete walls of the bridge, nothing beside them but a sloping bank of long grass going down into the fields.

The air-raid warning and the Messerschmitt came together; the wailing sirens and the howling sudden scream of engines. One brief glimpse of the black shape hurtling in over the roofs of West Worthing before Sam flung her down in the grass on the side of the road and threw himself on top of her.

Seconds only. Of the terrible scream of the engines and the mad chatter of the antiaircraft gun, and unbelievably the *spat spat spat* of a row of bullets, nicking the tarmac only a few feet from where they lay plastered in the weeds.

One of the soldiers let out a bellow of triumph and the firing stopped. Cautiously, not believing it was all over, they sat up. The Messerschmitt was already over Ferring, black against the clear green and yellow of the sunset; wavering now like a broken toy, trailing a plume of scarlet fire for a few desperate moments before plunging into the distant fields.

One of the soldiers was doing a wild dance of triumph around his gun.

"Got 'im!" he yelled. "Got the bastard. Got the bloody Hun. You all right, mates? Didn't get yer, did 'e?"

Sam and Emily looked dazedly from the soldier to the stitching of bullet marks sputtered along the road beside them.

"Sam." Emily was touched to the quick tears of shock, her eyes filling. "Sam, you lay on top of me."

"Wouldn't have done much good," Sam grunted. "I'm not armor-plated."

"Emily," he said then, and neither of them moved to get up. Emily sat there with her hands covered in dust and the juice of the crushed dandelions smeared across her face. "Emily." He pointed to the bullet chips across the road. "You see, love," he said hoarsely. "You never know how long. Will you marry me, Emily? Will you?"

She could see that he was blinded to everything except his own petrified realization that he might have lost her. To her own surprise she began to laugh, a little light-headed. Helplessly.

"Oh, Sam," she said. "You're like one of those children's toys that you knock over and they lie there for a few moments and they roll round up again exactly the same as before."

"Yes," said Sam, and did not smile. "Exactly the same as before. Will you marry me?"

She sobered then and looked at him gravely, the big gray eyes still dark with shock, the red-gold curls holding their own rich light in the limpid evening.

"I'm sorry, Sam," she said. "No."

He sat a moment looking at her almost as if he might be saying good-bye, and then he kissed her, sitting in the dust and weeds at the roadside, as he had never kissed her before, leaving her gasping and humble at all the promise implicit in his kisses; setting her away from him in the end and looking at her with eyes so full of pain that tears touched her own.

"Why don't you go the 'ole 'og?" yelled the soldier from the gun. "Go on. 'Ave a bash. We don't mind. 'Ave a bash!"

Sam never turned his head or smiled.

"I'll never ask you again, Emily."

She felt cold with a sick sense of unpreventable loss.

"I'm sorry, Sam," she whispered.

They dusted themselves down, and got Emily's cap back from where it had rolled down the steep bank, going on slowly in silence down to the Station. They were besieged by the Police for firsthand news. Emily let Sam do all the talking. All she could think of was the black plane wavering against the sunset with its trail of fire; the plume of black smoke where it had crashed. Nor did she think at all of the fact that she and Sam had missed death by inches.

Only of Dermot, wondering had it been like that for him, in the hot skies of Singapore. And she not knowing. Long, long ago, and she not knowing. Almost forgetting, for an unbelievable time.

Slowly she walked on back to the billet, her cap in her hand, leaving Sam with all the curiosity and excitement. There had been a telephone call to say that the Hun had come down in the fields beyond Ferring, with no damage or casualties. Except to the pilot.

And to herself and Sam, for they were casualties. It was all at an end. She knew he meant what he said this time. Never again. Sorry Sam.

She was sick of the uncertainty of her life, filled with a longing she had not known for a long time, to know definitely one way or the other. At least she had known about Alejandro. Both of his infidelity and of his death.

Facts; to be met face on.

The billet was completely empty, all the others out at the dance, her feet echoing on the wooden stairs. Alone in the deepening dusk with the last light lying over the sea, she lay down on her bed and gave way to the slow hot tears of unbearable sorrow. But she couldn't tell even herself what exactly it was she wept for.

Simply for loss. Loss, loss, loss. Alejandro. Dermot. Sam. Always loss.

"Well, how were we to know," said Marianna after it was all over. "How were we to know it would be the Eve of Waterloo. No one told us."

When they asked permission, no one suggested to them that they should not at that moment give a party, and the air of tension and high excitement and no-tomorrow along the crowded coast seemed to demand it. Everybody else was giving parties, and no one said to them there was a danger that by the time their party came, many of the guests would have gone off on another outing of their own. That they, too, would call a party.

The streets were still thronged with soldiers, and the nightly dances packed to the doors in the Assembly Rooms. Their own Canadians still grinned at them from the tents beyond the elms. The Squadron was intact, and the nights now singularly quiet. The Channel was empty of shipping plots on the big table.

It had, they thought, to be something special, special, special. To match the hour. To match the mood. Something for everyone to remember when these frail days were gone. The party for its time.

It was always the same few of them that organized all these things, and when they had thought and talked, and talked again, and done a great deal of walking around the small streets of Worthing, Emily and Marianna went down the long hill past the Site, to where at the bottom of it lived their friends the Tactical Air Force; in their tents along the shade of a great green hedge. Deep in the summer grass.

"Darlings," said Marianna when they arrived. Marianna was usually left to do the talking in such situations, as she would take on and charm the devil himself for anything she wanted. "Darlings, we need a truck."

The Orderly Room Corporal was called Lofty. For obvious reasons.

He uncoiled his long length from the orange box on which he was sitting outside the Orderly Room tent, and gallantly put aside his cigarette. Beside him the radio was playing softly "Smoke Gets in Your Eyes," and for a sad guilty moment Emily thought of Sam, who was indeed without his love. Keeping his cool distance. His lovely flame had died.

Lofty's dark eyes crinkled down at them.

"For you, girls, anything," he said handsomely. "Anything. A truck. An Air Force truck. Just for the day, or did you wish to keep it?"

"Oh, Lofty dear." Marianna would not have the frivolity. "Just for an hour. An hour would do nicely. And someone to drive it."

"No trouble at all," Lofty said. "None at all. And will you come with flowers to my court-martial? Bring cakes to the glass house?"

"Lofty. Now listen."

They told him why they wanted it. All dead secret. No one must know a thing before the night. For the party they were going to turn the NAAFI into a Victorian public house. For days back they had been going around the antique shops of Worthing begging or borrowing all the Victoriana they could find. Kindly people had ransacked their shops. Stuffed birds, and a great stuffed pike leering from a glass case amid green rigid reeds: bobbled curtains and a vast spread of an aspidistra in a hideous yellow pot. Pictures of Highland stags at dawn and sunset and dinnertime, and little girls romping in pinafores and long fair curls. Four heartrending representations of the "Life of the Prodigal Son." Painted mirrors and framed texts and, to set the theme, two large gilt-framed portraits of Victoria and Albert themselves, for hanging over the bar.

"A dream," said Marianna. "It'll be a dream. People have been so kind. But you see, Lofty, darling, we have to get it all here."

She looked at him with great beseeching eyes, and Emily grinned and kept quiet and let them do their work.

He hummed and hawed and muttered and grumbled that it would cost him his corporal's stripes, but Emily had been right in leaving it all to Marianna, and in the end he not only managed to get them a truck, but even got it legally, with proper permission, and an airman to drive it for the afternoon.

"Provided," said Lofty, "that we're asked to the party."

"But of course," Emily said. "You're family."

Lofty smiled down at her, his long face curiously sad.

"For the moment," he said. "I must say my sisters never looked like you. Not so much of a nuisance either."

"*Dear* Lofty," said Marianna graciously as she sailed away. "*So* kind."

All the little antique shops they had visited were in the narrow back streets of Worthing, so they decided to let the airman park the truck about the middle of them, and go then on foot to collect all their trophies bit by bit.

Which was how they came, all unexpectedly, laden down with the strangest burdens they had ever carried, to see the Desert Rats go marching back to war.

They heard it all before they saw it. Singing and the thump of heavy boots, and the dull rumble of tracked vehicles, thin cheers rising over them. Men singing.

"Em! Something's happening!"

"Yes. Quick. We mustn't miss it."

A tiny dark and overcrowded shop in Park Crescent, presided over by a tiny benevolent old lady, had given them two stuffed birds and the spreading forest of the aspidistra in the yellow pot, a bundle of fringed curtains, and a picture of a heavily muscled racehorse in a fine gold frame.

With it all in their arms they saw that people had begun to run toward the High Street, pulling their children after them, anxious to give them some splendid memory of which they could in time speak to their own children; who would barely listen, uninterested, not believing in their parents' wars.

Laden and slow, Emily and Marianna panted at last into the crowd, their arms full, the curtains trailing and the aspidistra shaken loose in the pot and waving like a jungle tree. Breathless. With some great sense of urgency. Believing tiredly in their own long war, and that these men might be going out at last to end it.

The Desert Rats.

A column of khaki that filled the street as far as they could see. Marching. In trucks and on carriers. Singing with all their hearts down the sunlit English street the song they had stolen from the Germans, and sung all the long, long glorious campaign across the desert from El Alameine to Tunis. Poignant. Nostalgic.

"My lady of the lamplight," they sang.

"My own Lili Marlene, my own Lili Marlene."

Their deep strong voices crashed back from the buildings on either side, and the crowd sang with them and many of the women wept and they all managed to cheer at the same time, holding up their waving children in the sun.

"It's real," Emily said, gripped by something close to awe. "Marianna, it's actually going to happen. They're going."

"Oh, dear," gulped Marianna, a pile of curtains draped around her neck and a stuffed bird in her arms. "I'm afraid, Em, I'm going to cry and I can't do a thing about it. It's all so bloody marvelous."

They laughed in the middle of the cheering crowd, and people banged them on the back simply because they were in uniform. Part of it, even though they might not be marching down the street. Everyone was wildly excited, tears streaming down Marianna's face, and in the end, to the delight of the people around them, Emily put down the picture of the racehorse and mopped Marianna's face with the end of one of the brocaded curtains.

"Ugh," said Marianna. "The smell of dust. Oh, Em, isn't it smashing."

Her cheeks were smeared with black from the ancient curtains, and Emily could do no more than laugh helplessly herself, tremulous in the staggering excitement of the moment.

Then she sobered.

"Has it occurred to you, Marianna," she said, "that that might be all our guests there, marching away down the street?"

"Lord," said Marianna. "I hope not. No, come on, Em, they can't take them all on one day. Or can they? Anyway, that little airman we have in the truck mightn't wait. We'd better go."

They pushed their way out again through people too elated even to notice them, the final victory already in their excited eyes.

It was beginning.

Where could these troops be going other than to Europe.

The end was beginning.

As the two girls went off down the side streets, where people stood smiling in their shop doorways, they could still hear the soldiers singing, more faintly, away behind them.

They had changed their song.

"Wish me luck," they sang now, "as you kiss me good-bye."

The heartbreak message of Vera Lynn.

"Em," Marianna said, and her great eyes gleamed in her smudgy face. "I feel it in my bones that it's going to be a marvelous party. Going to be splendiferous."

Heartbreaking, it would be, thought Emily, and bittersweet and sad. And yet she knew Marianna was right. It would be terrific.

"If there's anybody left to come," she said again, as if to placate the gods.

She wondered if Sam would come, and if he did, would he dance with her?

There were plenty of their guests still left to come.

They packed the barn, the excitement of the great moment of history in their young faces, and drank and sang and danced all evening to the loved tunes of their day. To "Jealousy" and "Dearly Beloved" and "I'll Get By" and "Lili Marlene," to "Night and Day" and "Smoke Gets in Your Eyes" and "A Sleepy Lagoon" and "I'll Be Seeing You." When it all got too much, they sang "Roll Out the Barrel" and "Shine On Harvest Moon" and "Boomps-a-Daisy" and "My Old Man Said Follow the Van." And in the end, for some daft reason, "White Christmas," with the soft wind of June blowing in through the open windows, and that was almost more than anyone could bear.

They vanished in pairs through the brocaded curtains, up into the dimly lit Snuggery, where under a soft lamp and a bowl of roses, Marianna had hung the text that said, "Be Sure Your Sins Will Find You Out." Testing it for truth herself by spending most of the evening on a sofa underneath it. They rambled out onto the terrace of the barn and across the lawns in the pale moonlight and the rising wind. Coming back in to drink again, where Victoria and Albert gazed severely down from above the bar. And to dance. And dance. Young and vigorous and splendid in their uniforms, and many of them already into the last days of their lives.

"Marvelous," said Emily, sprawling exhausted in a chair. "Absolutely marvelous. Best we've ever had, wouldn't you say so, Marianna."

"Divine," said Marianna, groping at her fallen hair. "Quite divine. I adored every minute of it."

"I never saw you dancing at all," Emily said accusingly. "You spent the whole evening upstairs with that sergeant pilot."

Marianna gave up the battle with her hair and grinned wickedly.

"That's what I said, dear. Quite divine."

The last guest was gone. The last laughter drifting distant in the darkness. With the Squadrons had gone the biggest stuffed bird and one of the stags at bay and the aspidistra, and the most harrowing picture of the Prodigal Son and several of the texts.

"I know they'll be welcome," Emily said. "We had to give none of those back. I like to think of them decorating Dispersals. It's the sign of a good party."

The willing, including Sam, who had come but who had not danced with Emily, were already collecting up the forest of dirty glasses and putting back the chairs.

"Better help, I suppose," said Marianna. "Come on, Em."

Emily was near one of the open doors, and when she stood up, she paused to look at the night outside.

"It's got windy," she said, surprised. "Very windy."

It was June third. The night of Saturday, June third.

How were they to know, as Marianna said afterwards, that they had given the ball on the Eve of Waterloo.


The following day they were all tired and idle, lying around on their beds going over and over all the juicy details of the party, and what everyone had been spotted getting up to; not encouraged to go out by the cool wind whistling from the west, piling the sky with low gray clouds. Watch from five to ten was uneventful, and the invasion seemed as far away as ever. All boring and a bit of anticlimax. They were glad to go wearily to bed for a long night's sleep.

The next morning, on Watch, there was a flurry with the overexcited pilot of a French Spitfire, who had called up to say he was orbiting something in the middle of the Channel, but did not have enough English to say exactly what. The Chief Controller sent for Marianna, who had fluent French, to try and get some sense out of him in his own language.

"Stupid little Frog," Marianna said, coming back into the back cabin "He was too conceited to admit that his English wasn't good enough. He refused to speak French. Seems there's some unidentified smoke in the Channel. Anyway, it's a right circus. Two American fighters have arrived, and a Walrus. I would imagine a Flying Fortress is expected at any moment. But girls—"

They looked at her, aware of something in her voice.

There was nothing doing, no Controller there, the three girls idling before their equipment, ready to leap to any alert.

"There's something happening on the table," Marianna said. "Makes one wonder. Convoys, my dears. But not going *along* the Channel. Going *across* it! Makes you think, doesn't it."

"No!" cried Emily, and like bullets she and Margaret, the third girl in the crew, were out and across the passage into the empty Searchlight cabin that overlooked the Ops Room.

"Gosh," said Margaret after a long moment of awed silence. "Em, do you think this is IT?"

"Not enough," said Emily, although she felt herself almost shaking with the excitement of it. "Not enough. But maybe they're minesweepers or something going ahead of the main invasion."

Between Southhampton and the Cherbourg Peninsula, the small ship-signs of convoys faced in a steady line across the Channel.

"Why aren't there floods of Huns going after them?" asked Margaret, and Emily shook her head.

"Why indeed."

But the circus with the Frog and the column of smoke proved to be the only incident of the morning, and even that had proved to be nothing; some jettisoned flare. No more.

Nor was there any comment or report from Group about the convoys. Almost a conspiracy of silence to pretend that they weren't there. Yet they all went back up to lunch with the reluctant feeling that they might just be leaving all the action to the other Watch.

They sat with Sam for lunch because there was nowhere else to sit. It was corned beef hash, which Emily adored.

They asked him what he thought about the convoys.

Sam addressed himself to his food, taciturn.

"We'll know tonight, won't we," was all he said.

"And what," said Marianna, "is everybody doing this afternoon?"

"Washing my hair," said Emily promptly, "and lying in the sun, to wait for this evening."

"Oh, darling. Will you be using your rollers all afternoon, or can I borrow them." Marianna shoved at the inevitable drooping lock. "Mine's filthy."

Emily smiled at her. It was always something. Marianna seemed to lack every single necessity of life. But she gave back so much in love and generosity that no one minded helping her out.

"We can share," she said.

They went back on Watch at half past nine, through a still, bright evening. All touched with a hope and expectation too deep for words. The march down was almost in total silence.

The girls coming off Watch were wild with excitement and unwilling to leave, bitterly jealous of the Watch taking over for the night.

On the table in the Ops Room, the map square V for Victor was black with convoys from top to bottom. The Channel solid with them.

Everyone playing it very cool, trying to pretend they were taking it all in their stride. That it might still be nothing.

"We have," said the Chief Controller with a terrible calm, "been taken in before, by regattas."

But the time came a couple of hours later when the convoy reports were so many that they had to take them all off, and make that part of the Channel a convoy area. A block, a solid block, of shipping. Going across to France.

"Jesus, Mary, and Joseph," said Emily. "Marianna, it's true."

And what difference, she wondered suddenly, would this make to the Far East? To Dermot. Would the Japanese have to be taken on when all this was over? She thought of Aggie at home, who in moments of trial was apt to lift her eyes to the kitchen ceiling, and cry "How long, O Lord, how long!"

The strange thing was that there was not a Hun in sight.

"Stunned, my dear," said Marianna at Emily's elbow. "They're obviously stunned. Standing over there boggling, no doubt."

As there was no work for them, the girls were free to cram themselves into the front cabins looking down on the Ops Room floor; watching the invasion build unbelievably before their eyes, on the table and on the tote. The mechanics were all there too, until the Commanding Officer threw them all out, so they went quickly down and stood along the wall of the Ops Room underneath the cabins, where he couldn't see them but they could still see everything.

"Told you you would know tonight," said Sam as he went, and his eyes like everybody else's were very bright. She knew a moment of sadness not to be sharing this with him, as they had shared so much, but the events of the night were too great even to spare much thought for Sam.

The movements began to go up on the tote. They had never seen it so full. Like the runners, thought Emily, for a full field for the Grand National at Fairyhouse.

Hundreds of them. And hundreds and hundreds. Of heavy bombers. Of transports, tugs, and gliders. The first wave to the beaches before the seaborne troops in the landing craft.

History, thought Emily. I am standing here seeing one of the greatest things that has happened in history. Every moment of boredom and petty restriction and bad food and horrible food is suddenly worth it. I am here seeing history.

Everyone was immensely calm, quiet. Almost oppressed by the magnitude of what was happening. After five years, they were going back again into France.

It was D-Day. June sixth.

There was still nothing to do, so that when the time came for the aircraft to be due over, most of them went outside into the field with Horse, to see the numbers on the tote turn into airplanes.

They came in their masses; a still, lovely night with light cloud and a rising moon, and flying low against the cloud, the number-less aircraft filling the entire sky. There was a defiant hint of victory in that they were all carrying their lights; the sky alive with them over a dark countryside that had known no lights for years. Over the dark country, and on across the sea, to the beaches of France.

Emily felt Sam's hand close on her arm, as though, no matter what principles or promises, he could not bear to be away from her at that moment. She turned and smiled at him and laid her hand over his. But no one spoke much. There was a portent in the moment too big for any of their words.

Apart from one wild false alarm that scrambled the Squadron, there was nothing to do all night. The Squadron landed and went to Dispersal and never a Hun lifted his nose over the French coast. All Darlowe could do on the night as desperately longed for as the first Christmas, was watch the picture on the table and the tote, and thank God, with something like awe, that it was happening.

Emily went out alone again at dawn. Six thirty, which she learned later was the time the assault began over on the beaches. The morning was absolutely still, a strange metallic light hanging between the full moon and the first light, the aerials turning like something in some futuristic dream against the clear sky and the darkness of the trees.

One bird sang.

D-Day. It was happening. Years of defeat and despair were over. I will be able to tell my children, she thought, that I stood here tonight. Dermot's children, she thought fiercely, suddenly, taking herself by surprise. As if the events over there across the Channel were in the nature of some promise of his safety.

Although they had no work to do, there had been a state of alert all night, and exhausted with excitement, they all slept through the next day until six o'clock. All four of them, Emily and Marianna and Penny and Isobel, walked across the bridge into the town, and listened to the King speak on the wireless in an Army canteen full of soldiers, who would themselves be over there in days.

The serious hesitant voice came to the end of its message of hope and promise, and with the wheezy old harmonium of the canteen, they all sang "God Save the King," as they had never heard it sung before.

As though they meant it.

Marianna wept again.

"My dear, all so heroic, and it makes me feel so guilty that we usually only come in here to sing hymns, because they give you a bar of chocolate if you do. And Methodist hymns at that, when you and I are Papists, Em. I'm sure there'll be a judgment on us."

They laughed at her and joined the soldiers in a great meal of fish and chips, and as darkness fell they all grew quiet to listen to the transports and the gliders going out again.

After that, it was all more or less anticlimax.

The work of Darlowe was defensive, and as there was no longer anything to defend against, they were idle. The *Luftwaffe* was far too busy on the defensive itself, on the other side of the Channel.

Even when the first of the grinding, flaring, flying bombs came over on the twelfth of June, it was clear after a few days of fierce flurry trying to intercept them, that they were out of Darlowe's reach. Not even if the Squadron flew the Mosquitoes until the rivets popped, were they able to catch them. They had to be left, infuriatingly, to the Typhoons and the guns that were stationed farther east.

The soldiers along the coast thinned out, more of them disappearing every day, and the frantic social life came to an end. The girls were idle. Sewing or reading in the warm sun of that lovely summer; sitting in the field outside the Happidrome watching the fighter sweeps come and go from France; lifting their heads to the sonorous drone of the Flying Fortresses, going over high, to paste hell out of the Germans in front of the Allied advance.

They folded away their printed addresses from General Eisenhower about the invasion, to keep them for souvenirs in days to come. They listened every day to the news of the steady advances after the nightmare beachheads, which had lost them boyfriends, fiancés, and husbands.

And wondered if they would ever work again.

Emily came back one lunchtime when the invasion was some twelve days old, cycling idly back from the shops in West Worthing, wondering if they were going to face yet another Watch without a stroke of work.

As she propped her bicycle against the front gate of the billet, one of the girls flew out from the downstairs room.

"Em! There's been an officer looking for you!"

"An officer?"

She stared at her dumbly, with impossible hope. She realized she had begun to tremble.

"An Army officer. Staff job. All red tabs and things."

Hope died but not completely, and it made her realize how much she wanted hope to live. Not impossible she told herself, that he had lost his own uniform and was wearing somebody else's.

"Absolutely smashing, Em. Tall and fair and terribly handsome."

Oh, God.

"Where is he now?" she managed to say. "Where? Has he gone?"

"He has to catch a train to London at two ten. Until then, he said he'd wait at West Worthing station. You all right, Em?"

"Yes, thanks, I'm all right. Thanks, Pat."

She barely remembered getting back there, pounding up the
bridge on rubber legs that seemed to get her nowhere, like the
worst of nightmares; mindless; pedaling madly through the streets
oblivious of traffic, so that it was only the grace of God that got
her in the end to the moment when she flung her bicycle down on
the steps of the station. A clucking porter picked it up and
propped it against the wall, but she didn't even give him a
backward glance.

The last flight of steps, and her throat was dry.

He was the only person on the platform, standing not ten yards
away, an Army holdall at his feet. There was a strange rank
smell.

Familiar. Oh, dear God, familiar. But why in Army uniform,
the red band of Staff around his cap? Her dry mouth began to
frame his name.

"Der—"

He heard her footsteps and turned at once.

"Paul!"

She was too sick with disappointment to dissimulate. Too
shattered. Too torn with the shock of possibility.

"Oh, Paul, I thought you might be Dermot."

He thought she was going to cry, and didn't ask her how could
he be, in this uniform, but took her hands in his and kissed her.

"Em, dear. I'm so sorry to disappoint you. What a rotten
second I must be. No news?"

She shook her head, unable yet to speak, and then slowly
pleasure filled her face as she realized that if it could not be
Dermot, there was no one she would rather see than Paul.

"How come you're here?" she asked him. "Paul, what a
lovely surprise."

He had come from Caen, hitching a lift across the Channel on
a destroyer, for a conference of some sort in London.

All Clonfrack arrived with him on the gray, grubby station of
West Worthing; the green hills and the peace and the mountains
and the light on the sea at Oranmore. And the astonishing,
shattering fresh agony of the dulled, almost forgotten, pain for
Dermot.

She had become islanded in the small, obsessed world that was
Darlowe. Preoccupied with Sam, knowing that in that direction,
at least, she had made a mess of things she could never repair.
Broken the crystal hear. It was like a veil between her and the

world outside, that must go on when Darlowe was finished and in the past.

"Oh, Paul," she said. He looked more handsome than ever. A little heavier than Dermot. God knew, he could be skin and bones by now. A little fairer. "Oh, Paul," she said suddenly, and did not know she had even felt it. "Paul, I'd like to go home. I've had enough of this."

"Christmas, Em," he said, like everybody else. "We're going through them like a dose of salts. If it goes on in the same way, Christmas. I want to get home too. I'm not too happy about the estate."

She didn't ask him why not. Christmas, he had said. Christmas. He'd added to her longings the firelight and the tinsel and the angel on the tree, and what they always called her mother's Christmas face. Christmas at Clonfrack. And no war.

"Wouldn't it be smashing," she said wistfully. And then, "Paul, what's that perfectly terrible smell?"

He grinned and looked down at his canvas grip.

"Camembert cheese," he said. "Everyone wanted to send a piece to someone. Personally I think it's past survival now. But it gets me a carriage to myself."

There was no time to ask him about his personal war. His train was already clanking into the station. She saw him and his isolating stink into a carriage, and kissed him good-bye with more sadness than she could understand.

"Won't be long now, Em," he said, understanding.

He was so like Dermot, leaning out of the carriage window as she waved him good-bye. As she had once done long ago in Galway. Long, long ago. To Dermot.

Slowly, when he was out of sight, she went back down the steps and through the tunnel, taking her bicycle under the accusing eyes of the old porter. She rambled into Darlowe late, glad to have her lunch quite by herself; feeling a little strange and alienated from the other girls. Almost as if she had been on leave.

She must write at once and tell her mother. She could imagine her ringing up Paul's parents. And the pleasure. The amount they would make, of that chance meeting of their children in the distant war.

Through the golden days of the late summer, it was victory,

victory all the way. By August twenty-fifth, the Allies had taken a screaming and rejoicing Paris.

Paul could be right, thought Emily. By Christmas it would all be over. In Europe. And what then of the Japanese? She found that with even vague hope of the end, she was thinking more of Dermot. Telling herself not to be foolish; so much time had passed, how could there be hope.

In Darlowe there was nothing to do but pass the long uneventful days as best they could. Those of them who wanted to, and that included Emily, worked in the fields that now produced all the vegetables for Darlowe. Long warm days of utter quiet in which the war had left them; the frenetic days no more than memories; following on the NAAFI radio the daily reports of successful fighting in which they no longer had a part.

Down at the bottom of Sea Lane, below the Mulberry Hotel, the soldiers cleared a strip of beach for them, the threat of invasion no longer to be thought of. Under the paternal and watchful eyes of the Coastguards, they were free to spend their idle days swimming among the gamboling porpoises, and baking on the yellow sands they had stared at through the tangled wire for almost three years.

Apart from the fighter sweeps which were no business of theirs, and the high passing blocks of the American Fortresses, the war had begun to seem very far away. A remembered menace that no longer seemed even a menace, in the cheerful news on the wireless each evening.

Brussels was liberated by September third.

Straight through now to the heart of Germany.

To Berlin and the end of the war.

It was only a matter of time, everybody said.

The beginning of the V-2s on London on the eighth of September was no more than a horrifying reason to make them long even more desperately for the inevitable victory, which must surely be coming soon. Swimming; sunbathing; rambling with Marianna on the Downs, where the flowers of summer were dead in the drying grass; trying not to remember when she had walked in all these places with Sam, who behaved now as though she never had existed. It was another strain.

"Like living with a ghost, Marianna," she said. "He's there but he's not there."

"Maybe he never cared at all," Marianna said.

"Oh, yes," Emily answered her somberly, and knew it to be true. "He cared. He still cares."

"You will forget him as soon as we have bowler hats and can go home."

"I wonder," said Emily. "I wonder."

They passed the first half of a golden September that was filled with hope, and when they first heard of Arnhem on the seventeenth, it seemed to them no more than another step on the road to final victory. Arnhem. A town on the border between Holland and Germany, where the Allied forces had made one of the biggest airborne assaults in history, to take the bridges over the Rhine and clear the pathway straight through to Berlin.

"After Arnhem," said Field Marshal Montgomery, "the war will be ended this year."

They were so conditioned to hearing nothing but news of success; so used to hearing the wireless news as no more than another step always towards the end and home—success in Europe, in Russia, in Burma, with the Americans in the Pacific—that they all found it difficult to believe or understand when the first guarded news began to come through of the tragedy of Arnhem. The total and shattering failure of the operation.

Wide-eyed and appalled, they looked at each other across the ancient crackling wireless in the NAAFI, and found it impossible to accept.

The great airborne landing had been decimated, the bridges remained uncaptured, and the victorious rush through Europe had been halted. The sun seemed dimmed, and the splendid gold faded on the September fields, the inevitable few weeping, shattered girls being comforted by their friends.

"We'd better polish our buttons again," said Marianna resignedly. "It's going to be longer than we thought."

No one, at least, that we know, thought Emily. Thank God for that. But a fortnight later, she got a letter from her mother.

She thought nothing as she opened it, except to be pleased to get it.

"Darling Em," her mother wrote. "So sad a letter to have to write to you. So sad. There seemed no point in shocking you by sending a wire, for what could you do, any more than all the rest of us.

"Darling, Paul was killed at Arnhem."

Emily had to stop there, blinded by a rush of tears, her mind full of the fine handsome young man with his load of stinking cheese; smiling his good-byes as the train drew out of West Worthing station.

Forever now. Forever. Oh, God, she thought desperately, will there be no one left? No one?

"I waited to write to you," her mother went on, "to see if there would be any news beyond the wire. His mother and father came over here at once to tell me. God help them.

"But they had a letter very quickly from his colonel, who knows Geraldine well. It seems he was in General Browning's headquarters on some ridge outside Arnhem and he went off in a jeep to try and locate someone they had lost touch with. The jeep hit a mine and three of them were killed at once. He is buried there.

"So dreadful for them, darling, with Dermot so long missing. Always the best that go. Always the best. My heart bleeds for his father. His mother is being very brave, but I have been bothered about James for some time. He seems worried about something; maybe the estate, without either son at home. I don't know. But this has shattered him completely.

"Dearest Em, I am so sorry to bring you such sad news. Please God this awful war will be over soon, even with this setback. Then you can all come home."

All? thought Emily.

"We have had nothing recently from Joe," added her mother.

She wrote a little more of the general news of Clonfrack, and Emily felt sick, longing to be there. There was a note in her mother's letter of sorrows growing too much to be borne. The sad miseries of the war reaching out even into the gray streets of Clonfrack, where the lights still shone out warm at nights, and the small shops were full of food and clothes and luxuries the war-worn countries had long forgotten.

Painfully she waited until she was alone in the billet, and set herself to the task of writing to Lord and Lady Keene. She would have been the last of all of them to have seen Paul.

With his unfailing instinct for knowing there was something with her, Sam, having avoided her carefully for weeks, came and sat down beside her in the NAAFI that evening, where she and Marianna were having a cup of cocoa before going to bed.

The wireless crackled out the news of the regrouping after

Arnhem, and the preparations for a fresh outthrust into Germany, and news of the American successes farther south.

She could barely bring herself to care.

"Present for you," Sam said, and laid down on the table a bar of nut milk chocolate. All that he could offer.

Except his heart, and she had already broken that.

He blurred and shivered through tears she could not suppress, but she managed to smile at him.

"Thanks, Sam," she said. "From your mate in Station Road?"

"From my mate in Station Road."

And what in the name of God would he say, thought Emily, thinking of it herself for the first time, if he knew that now Dermot would be the next earl? He should at least understand that although Paul had been a viscount, he had died like any other man.

Marianna said good night and went off to bed, and Emily let her go, glad, no matter what she wanted to shout at him about the death that could take the highest and the lowest, to have Sam with her for a while, talking of this and that, and never of Paul; grateful for all the tender comfort he could never manage to put into words.

He walked her <u>back</u> across the garden, and above the elm trees hung the great gold harvest moon, blanching the beauty of their own small peaceful world. There was nothing anymore to be feared in a full moon. Bombers' moons were now for other people.

A month later it was the hunter's moon that waxed like a great yellow lantern above the Downs, and Emily was able to look at it and know that by the time it was full, she would see the pale unearthly beauty of it over the fields beyond Clonfrack.

Three days more, she counted as she woke up. Three days more. She knew that this time she would find it very hard to come back. Darlowe was moribund, and they were all a little edgy with the boredom, feeling there were far better things they could be doing with their lives outside. And she knew it would be difficult to walk away again from these three sad parents who had lost so much.

"Watch it," Marianna had said to her one day when she grumbled. "Watch it, or they'll post you to Burma. They still have a war there."

She had laughed, but on this particular morning she got fed up even with Marianna, because they couldn't get her out of bed. The night before, she had been dancing her feet off somewhere, out on a late pass, and now they couldn't shift her.

It was a bad morning.

Somebody had managed to block the drain of the washbasin, and in the flood of water already all over the floor, Emily had to wash as best she could under the running water in the bath. When she came back, Marianna was still a comfortable hump beneath her blankets, Penny and Isobel already gone to breakfast.

She broke a fingernail on her collar stud and alternately swore at that, and shouted at Marianna, realizing through it all as she looked out their window that autumn had already touched the rough fields between them and the railway line; even a touch of frost, maybe, before the sun came. It only served to increase her irritation. Time was passing and leaving her behind.

Comfort came with the thought that in three days she would be looking out at Ireland, where the grass stayed green all winter. Already she could get the sooty hot smell of platform 13 at Euston, where for her it seemed that Ireland first began.

"Marianna!"

The heap of blankets didn't even stir. Marianna always slept covered to the point of suffocation.

"Marianna! It's almost Watch time."

Marianna only grunted and turned over.

"Darling," she murmured. "There's nothing to do. They'll never miss me."

"There's something called roll call," yelled Emily.

Marianna did not surface.

"You'll manage, Em," she said comfortingly, and drifted off.

By the time Emily went raging from the billet, she was too late for breakfast, the Watch already gathered in its ragged column outside the Orderly Room to march down to its nonexistent duty. They were already getting concerned that if there was a victory parade, not a soul on the Station knew how to march.

"Not fair," Emily fumed at the girl beside her. "Not fair. I'd get into trouble just as much as she would. They could stop my leave."

She went cold with fright at the thought, and it did nothing to improve her temper that she successfully answered Marianna's number as well as her own, and nobody did indeed miss her.

Oh, God, she wanted this leave so much. Nothing here had changed that she had loved so much before. Nothing. The elms were fading gold, and the green rise of the Downs against the milky October sky was serene and gentle. From the small cottages on the lower slopes smoke rose straight in the windless air.

Beautiful. Beautiful. Nothing had changed. It was she who had changed, still ravaged by guilt over Sam, whom she could hardly bear to look at; filled with grief for the hopeless waste that was the death of Paul; no longer sustained with the heady excitement, the sense of being involved with history, of the invasion.

Sometimes now she felt so *old*. So really old. She thought back through all that had happened to her, and looked with disbelief at the girl who had waited to marry Alejandro.

She wanted to go back to Clonfrack and lick her wounds.

Marianna came sailing into the Happidrome half an hour late, munching happily on a bacon sandwich.

It was the last straw.

"Where'd you get that?" demanded Emily, furious.

Marianna made a sheepish face. Poor Em *was* on edge.

"I got no breakfast, thanks to you."

"Oh, poor Em. I am sorry. Have a bit. I got it in the cookhouse and came down on my bicycle. What's doing?"

Emily snorted and wouldn't even look at the sandwich.

"Nothing," she said. "Nothing. I'm going out to help Corporal Robertson plant cabbages."

Marianna let her go, her long lovely face guiltless but compassionate. Em needed to go home. She'd had a packet.

By lunchtime, Emily had been soothed by the quiet morning in the field, sitting astride an empty sack on the broad back of Horse, who had been borrowed for the occasion, while the large, perspiring Corporal Robertson followed behind, steering the harrow. There had been a peaceful half hour sitting under a hedge in the sun, eating the elevenses that the Corporal had been wise enough to bring from the cookhouse; listening to the quiet talk of the simple, happy man, who had no thought but to pass the time until he could get back to his wife.

"Older than me, she is," said Corporal Robertson. "She needs me, see. Won't be long now."

Emily thought of Sam with pain. Nothing to go back to. But there was no question of weakening. It would never work. Why did she know so certainly that it would never work?

She smiled at Corporal Robertson, and thanked him for the bread and cheese, and he gave her a pat on the shoulder with his big hand, as if to comfort her for something. But did not ask for what.

It was a little late when she reached the mess.

"Bar's open, Emily. Let me buy you a beer before lunch."

The small bar at the foot of the stairs in The Elms opened spasmodically, whenever they were lucky enough to get an allotment of beer and Pepsi-Cola. Emily recognized Marianna's offer for the olive branch that it was, especially as she knew she was dead broke, and could ill afford the beer.

She knew better than to refuse.

"Thanks, Marianna," she said. "I've earned it. I only hope we aren't here to eat the cabbages."

"God forbid," said Marianna, and pushed her way into the crowd around the bar.

The telephone box was only just across the hall, but with the uproar in the bar Emily didn't hear it ring, and it was with a fresh surge of irritation that she heard them shouting her name.

"Telephone, Em!"

"Emily! Phone!"

She turned out reluctantly from the crowd. She knew exactly who it would be. Who it had been for most of the week. There was a sergeant pilot from Ford badgering her for a date. Younger than she was, if you please, and certain he was God's gift to all women. She couldn't get him to understand that he wasn't God's gift to her.

When she picked up the telephone in the cramped box under the stairs, she had little patience to offer him.

"Emily McRoss," she said. "Hello."

There was a long pause and no answer. This damned phone. Always hit and miss. She shook it.

"Hello," she said again, louder.

"Em," said a voice then, hoarse and disbelieving. "Oh, God, Em darling, is it you?"

She had to put out a hand to steady herself against the wall, and for seconds she couldn't find her own voice, her lips dry.

"Dermot," she managed then, and could only whisper. "Oh, Dermot, it's not true."

He was recovering, excitement shaking his voice.

"It's true, Em," he said. "Oh, my darling, how are you?"

"Dermot, Dermot, how are *you*?"

All the questions then, both of them falling over themselves to talk. How? Where? After all this time? "In God's name, where have you been?"

"Sumatra," he said. "I'll tell you all about it when I see you. Got picked up in the end by a sub. I sent a cable from India, but obviously it never arrived. Oh, Em, Em, my darling, when shall I see you?"

"I've got leave." She could hardly speak now for the flood of joy. Oh, but God was good. "Leave, Dermot, in three days. Where are you?"

"Sydney Street. I have leave too. We can go to Galway together. Jesus, I thought all the time you were at home there. Glory be to God, a Waaf!"

"Dermot?"

"Yes?"

"They told you about Paul?"

"They did."

For a few moments they were silent, acknowledging sorrow, and then they were off again.

"Look," Dermot said then, "I'll have to stop now or Lydia will have the telephone out of my hand. Irresponsible, she thinks it is. I could have written you a letter."

The disordered world was tumbling back into its old appointed places. Dermot. Lydia. Sydney Street. Clonfrack.

"Eleven thirty-seven, Victoria, on Thursday," she said, and couldn't believe it. Couldn't believe it. "Don't be late."

"I'll be there. You'll know me. I'll be the fella with the sarong and the hibiscus behind his ear."

"Oh, Dermot."

The world was swimming as she came blindly out of the box, the windows on the stairs shifting in bright prisms of blinding light, shot unreasonably with darkness; her shaking legs barely able to get her to the bottom of the stairs, where she flopped down, her head upon her knees.

She heard several speak her name, their voices concerned, and foolishly she couldn't answer them. It was Sam who came and took the red-gold head between his beautiful bony hands and lifted it.

A long moment he looked down into her face, ashen with shock, but the gray eyes blazing with uncontrollable joy.

"He's back," said Sam.

She was coming around. Face still framed by his hands, she nodded.

"Yes, Sam," she whispered. "He's back."

"Darling," said Marianna at his elbow. "Darling Em. In the circumstances, I think you'd better take a gulp of your beer."


## FOURTEEN


They were married early in December in the chapel of Castle Keene, and for the last time Emily put away her ideas of marrying in the cold bleak church at Clonfrack, realizing it was a dream she had created, like the certainty that she would spend her WAAF life on a vast Station, all wind and whitewash.

She had no problem getting a special leave, even though she had had leave in October. Marriage now was a valid reason for leave, as people like Dermot reappeared from strange corners of the world.

He was little changed, she thought, that first leave. Marvelously little changed, although she could not quite say what she would have expected to have happened to him. She saw him before he saw her, with a surge of uncontrollable excitement, waiting for her beyond the ticket barrier, and felt as if her collapsing legs would never make the last few yards.

He was standing peering down the platform, and she realized she would be unfamiliar to him in uniform. He was not in a sarong, but in a uniform that hung loosely on him, and a great incredible smile when he saw her. When he took his cap off to wave to her, his hair was silver.

As she hugged him she could feel his bones.

"Oh, my darling, you're so thin," she said to him when the first hungry kisses were over. She was aware that people were watching them with benevolent smiles, and that she was crying, and she couldn't care less on either count.

"So thin!"

"I was never keen on rice," he said. His eyes were on her

face as if it was the most beautiful thing he had ever seen. "Oh, Em, my darling Em. Listen, love, if all you can do is cry, I'll go back again. I thought you'd be pleased."

That made her laugh, and she sniffed and giggled into his handkerchief until they could bring themselves to stop saying "Oh, Dermot," and "Oh, Emily," and pull themselves together enough to go out and enter the battle for a taxi.

"Look," he said then, "I don't want to face Lydia yet—let's put your bag in the left luggage and we can go back to Sydney Street after lunch to change."

They were both in uniform and had to be in civilian clothes to catch the Irish Mail at Euston at nine o'clock.

"I want to have a walk round the West End with you," he said.

"Oh, my poor Dermot, you won't like it. It's not like you left it. Do you find it all awful, darling?" she added.

"Pretty gruesome. I don't think I'd mind quite so much if I'd been able to do anything to slam them in return. But just to have sat and let it all happen is pretty galling."

"It wasn't your fault, darling."

"Made no difference."

He looked, as she knew she might expect, graver and more serious, with some new terrible patience in his eyes, but every so often his face broke up into the old hilarious smile, teeth startlingly white in his brown face.

She said this.

"Your teeth look so white. Like a Colgate advertisement."

"Amn't I the lucky lad. There's many will be coming back with nothing more than a few black stumps. I wouldn't think the Japs have many dentists. As for it not being like I left it, Em darling, nothing is like I left it. Nothing."

She wanted to say "Not even me?" but something held her from making any such frivolous remarks yet; from mentioning almost anything, lest there be some disastrous answer; lest she touch some terrible experience. His own story must be told in its own time.

He had taken the taxi to Hyde Park Corner, and she smiled to see it. He was retracing the steps of their first day together.

But then, of course, they spoke of Mike.

"I'm sorry about your brother," he said. "It always seems to be the best that get picked off."

"My mother said that about Paul."

They were silent then awhile, touched with grief, until they began to ease into the sheer delight of being together again. Happiness that seeped up slowly because it was so impossible to believe in it. The reality of years of dreams, beginning to take positive shape in the long gray stretch of Piccadilly before them; the scars hidden by distance, looking almost as it did before, the grass of St. James's Park unalterably green over to their right.

"Oh, Em," said Dermot, and the grip of his hand around hers hurt her so much she could have screeched, but she made no sound. "Oh, Em, if you could only understand how much this means. How much. And my time was nothing to that of the poor bastards in the camps in Malaya. Nothing."

He sounded almost guilty, as though he would have preferred to suffer with the rest.

"Well, thank God for that," said Emily firmly. "Thank God you got out." But she would not ask him how. When the moment was right, he would tell her.

They drifted back to happiness and drifted down the sand-bagged length of Piccadilly and across the Circus, where Dermot mourned the lack of Eros, every step recreating some part of the long, lonely gap.

Inevitably, though neither of them mentioned it, they came to what had been Stone's. The hole was neat, square, not going beyond the boundaries of the building, as though, with the bomb that made a direct hit that night, God had said "This I will take, and these with it, and no more." Already the rose bay willow crowded from the corners of the blackened crater; the bomb flower that knew no season; flowering always like a memorial.

They leaned a long time in silence over the iron rail that protected the crater. Thinking of Mike. Thinking of all the bright ones that went that night this hole was made. Thinking of themselves.

"You know," said Dermot then, her hand in his. "I simply threw a fit when I heard you were a Waaf. Thought I'd find you madly and irrevocably in love with a group captain or some such."

Emily let it rest a long moment.

"Why not a corporal," she said then.

"Oh, no, darling. You're officer material."

She felt about an inch high and thick with shame, although she knew Dermot meant it as a compliment. To Sam it had been a bitter fault.

Then she smiled and laid a finger on the rings on Dermot's sleeve.

"I must be," she said. "I waited so long for these."

"Em," said Dermot then, and did not look at her but down into the ragged chasm of the bomb crater, his thin face somber. "If I'd come back and not found you waiting, I don't honestly know what I'd have done. It's all that kept me from going crackers."

She laid her head against his shoulder, and could find nothing to say.

Someday, but this was not the moment, she would tell him that she had had no group captains come her way, but had nearly, nearly, but not quite, fallen in love with a corporal. Not quite. A savage rude corporal by anybody's standards, who seemed to have nothing to recommend him, but for her there had been something. A lot. Enough to make her almost lose her head. Enough to confuse her for a long time, but she had held back in some way she didn't understand at the time.

She understood it now. There had never really been anyone but Dermot. Loneliness had confused her, but deep down there had been no one else.

And she had wrecked Sam on that. Poor Sam.

"We'll have to find somewhere else to eat," was all she said. "Until they rebuild Stone's."

He was silent then, leaning over the iron railing there in Panton Street, above the hole that had been Stone's, where they had eaten and laughed and fallen in love all those long years ago before the world fell apart. He stretched out his gloved hands and clasped them, and Emily cried out.

"Dermot. Your glove is—empty!"

"Not quite," he said, and took it off.

No fingers were missing, but on his left hand three of them were bent almost into his palm.

She took the maimed hand in hers and touched it gently, sick with pain for his lost perfection, and yet knowing in her heart it was nothing compared to what had happened to others. If this was all, thank God.

"Please tell me, darling," she said.

He drew a deep breath.

"As you know, Em, I was with Thirty-four Squadron. Flying Blenheim Ones. Absolute museum pieces, but they were all we'd got. They in due course got shot from under us, or we got shot out of them, so off we go to see how else we can get into the fight. So we find ourselves some armored cars." He smiled as though even yet the recollection was good. "Marmo Harringtons. And off we went to war again."

He paused and sighed.

"Wasn't much more of it for me. I remember some load of Jocks from the Argylls beside us and then something took me out. They told me afterwards that in the middle of this holocaust some pompous stick of a brigadier comes up and tells them to get out of his tanks and get back to our airplanes. They pointed out that there weren't any more airplanes, so he said get back to our airfield, and they couldn't be bothered to point out that there wasn't an airfield either."

Emily thought of the ray of hope that had come to her long ago when she got the roundabout message that 34 Squadron had been seen fighting in armored cars.

"I heard about that," she said.

"You what!"

He shook his head in disbelief when she told him.

"I don't know how long we were on the streets, and God love their hearts, they were dragging me all the time. I had a furrow in my head. Nothing, darling. Only my scalp, and my hair's grown over it, but it had put me out. Then they heard over some jeep radio the order for surrender and every man for himself, so like all the rest of them, they made for the beaches. Me along with them. They saved my life, Em," he added gravely.

"To this day, I don't know how they got it. They just said they took it, but I came to myself in the bottom of a fishing boat, great big sail over my head, laden with blokes so it was almost awash, and going like a bat out of hell before the wind for Sumatra. Singapore burning like Guy Fawkes Night behind us, and ships sinking like ninepins. All hell."

He paused again, staring down into the crater.

"And how was Sumatra," she asked him almost timidly, afraid he would close up.

"Better than a Jap prison camp," he said as he had said before. "We even had a medico. Couple of friends dragged him unconscious into the boat, like me. He was furious when he came around two days later. Wanted to stay with the chaps in the camps. Wanted to go back.

"By the time he'd become fit to function, my fingers had set all wrong. Nothing wrong with him, thank God. Some explosion had just blown his brains right out and in again. But he couldn't do much for any of us. No drugs, nothing; except what he had in a knapsack on his back."

He paused.

"My wounds were nothing," he said. "Nothing. Japs didn't hold Sumatra in any strength," he went on. "I imagine they just felt it was there any time they wanted it. We were virtually unmolested on the west coast. Worst that happened to me was that I shinnied up a tree to hide from a Nippon patrol, and they came and camped under me. I was in agony. Scared rigid I'd pee down on their little heads. Bastards," he added. "Little bastards.

"So," he went on then, "the tide of the war changed, and submarines began to patrol the Malacca Straits earlier this year. In time they got us off."

"How many?" Emily asked.

"Not as many as when we started. I had some obscure fever when I got to India. That's when I sent the cable you never got."

He was silent then, staring down into the crater, and she knew better than to question him. He had told her the bald outline, and his attitude told her that at least for the moment, that was all she was going to know. There were dark places now in Dermot's mind that she would probably never share. All she could do was help him to forget them.

"Darling." She slid her hand into the crook of his elbow. "Shall we move on? They're not serving here today."

He straightened up and looked at her and smiled, and touched her cheek with his good hand.

"You're quite right, Em," he said, and smiled. "It's all over."


It was all so gorgeously exciting when December came.

Marianna had agreed, enchanted, to be a bridesmaid, and they giggled their way up the long, crowded journey to Holyhead. Until Crewe they had to sit on their suitcases in the corridor, but after that they got seats, crammed elbow to elbow in a carriageful of soldiers in crumpled and unaccustomed civilian clothes. Going home, as they were, to Ireland. And full of it. Singing over and over again all the sad, haunting songs of their country, until in the end a despairing voice rose in the darkness in the corner.

"For the love of God, lads, is it leave you're all going on, or a wake? Will you either hold up or give us a bit of cheer."

Mrs. McRoss met them off the boat in the cold bright morning, and Anna with her and the little Dermot. Emily had seen them all only in October, but it seemed now in the clarity of her pure happiness that she was seeing them for the first time in years. Through no haze of loneliness or sorrow.

Nor had the pale sun of a December morning ever seemed more beautiful as they came in, gliding past the hazy cone of the Sugar Loaf and the tall spires of Dun Laoghaire. Never more white the wings of the screaming gulls; never more the very essence of coming home, was the smell of salt sea and fish and turf smoke, that was Dun Laoghaire.

Her mother seemed to be in the same state of mind. Beaming all over her face, she saw them all into the car and gently but firmly dislodged young Dermot from the steering wheel.

"You drive, Anna," she said. "You're better in the city than I am. And I can get to know Marianna. I've heard so much about you, my dear." As she settled in the front with the small boy in her lap, she looked around at them, and Emily saw the brightness of tears in her eyes.

"Mums," she said, but Mrs. McRoss's smile only widened.

"Isn't it marvelous," she said. "Marvelous to have nothing to do but be *happy*. We have three gorgeous days for laying waste to Switzers."

Emily looked at her tenderly. There was only Ted to worry about now, and Ted was one of these strong run-of-the-mill characters who would surely be all right. Not, however much she loved him, one of these bright special ones of grace, like Mike and Paul. Marked, almost, for death, when death was on the rampage. There was Joe, of course, God love him, but that should only be a matter of time as the *stalags* were overrun. Germany was not Japan.

"I hope you've got plenty of money, Mums," she said, and grinned, but this time Mrs. McRoss did not smile back.

"Enough," she said. In her heart almost nothing could be enough to make up for all the years of sorrow that had besieged this child, who had done nothing to deserve any of it.

The shining sands of Killiney glittered in the early morning sun, sparkling in the tidal pools, bait-diggers in a dark frieze along the shallows.

"Look, Marianna," she said. "Killiney. Isn't it lovely?" But Marianna, who loved her sleep, stared at it with drowsy eyes.

"Divine," she murmured. "Quite divine."

Emily, too, had fallen silent. All they had managed on the boat last night was a wooden seat on the upper deck, and not even Marianna, the great sleeper, had managed to sleep on that.

Mrs. McRoss surveyed them as a general might survey exhausted troops.

"You can have a few hours now," she said, "and we'll start in the afternoon. 'Tis no way from Anna's to Switzers."

It was one of Emily's greatest pleasures in the few hectic, exciting days, to see how Anna and Marianna got on together. They did more than get on: they flowed together like two streams that have long been coming down the same mountain. Complementing each other. Anna in her serene quietness and Marianna in her effervescence. Emily watched them. Marianna would curb her floods of speech and listen with rare attention to Anna's quiet voice. Anna in her turn would watch Marianna in the full flood of her extravagances, a small smile on her face, as though she saw something in Marianna that she had long desired in herself.

My friends, Emily told herself. How fortunate at this splendid moment before her marriage to have them there together. Friends for such a time, for she knew, looking at them, that whoever else might come and go, Anna and Marianna would be there as long as life itself.

Such happiness. She wanted desperately for everyone to be as happy as she; to gather all those she loved around her and see them at their best. So she was delighted to see Lord Keene looking better than when she had seen him in October. In spite of the delight and excitement of Dermot's coming back, he had still been gray and silent, the fine edge gone from his handsome presence, the straight, dignified shoulders stooped. The dark hair with its distinguished streaks of gray had become suddenly almost white.

She had been horrified and sad. In her mind he was one of these strong perfect people who could ride unmarked through the sorrows and troubles of the world. She remembered him coming, full of authority, into the salon of the house in Málaga, that first time, taking everything into his firm hands, relieving them of all anxiety and responsibility.

And Remedios and Doña Serafina quite floored by the looks and presence of the "English" milord.

It shocked and grieved her to find him only human.

"Is he ill, Dermot?" she had asked concernedly.

"My mother says no." he said. "But Paul's death was a terrible blow to him. I don't think he'll ever get over it. I'm a very poor substitute. The estate is troubling him too. I don't know what's the matter. He said he wouldn't ram it down my neck the instant I was home. We'll talk after the wedding, he said, whatever it is. I must get it out of him, or he will be ill."

She was pleased, when they arrived down from Dublin after the orgy of shopping, to find him looking better. More color in his thinning cheeks and some resumption of his old authoritative manner.

She kissed him, relieved.

"You look better," she dared to say, although it had been admitted at no time that he was ill.

He smiled at her affectionately and patted her hand.

"Of course I'm better," he said. "How could I be otherwise? I'm about to get a beautiful new daughter, and I'm *very* pleased about that."

And there was Dermot himself, waiting on the steps in Clonfrack when they drove up that evening with the car filled to every crevice with parcels and packages and boxes. Aggie hovered brazenly in the hall behind him, too excited to do her usual trick of hiding behind the curtains and then running out into the kitchen to make an entry.

"Won't the viscount," she had said, lingering on the word, to the old sister, who had been reduced to outclassed silence. "Won't the viscount be needing help to handle all the goods they'll be bringing back from Dublin, and the poor young man with his hand in a straitjacket."

Dermot indeed had his hand now in plaster. Emily touched it at once, inquiringly.

"They're trying to straighten my fingers," he said. "They won't have to pay me so much pension if they are straight as they will if they're crooked."

"Oh, Dermot." She hated to see him even so little maimed.

"Only three days more, Em."

Aggie and Marianna and Mrs. McRoss were unloading the car.
She and Dermot stood in a moment of snatched quiet beside one
of the hall windows. When they had been in Sydney Street in
October, a strange barren Sydney Street, with all the lovely
colored soldiers and the apple chandelier, and all Gran's other
treasures packed in the cellars for safety, he had not come to her
room.

"There's no urgency now, Em, love," he had said, and she
could have wept at the ravaged thinness of his face. "We can
wait, can we not, now that we know it's real and forever," and
she had smiled and agreed and kissed him, preferring it that way
herself.

"Besides," he had said, and grinned his old grin. "I'm petrified of Lydia now that Gran isn't here to protect me."

Now she looked at the deep glow in his hazel eyes as he said
three days more, and knew that for both of them these last few
weeks had been almost longer than the long, long years of
separation.

"I hope we are able to manage it all in three days," she said.
"I hope it won't be absolute chaos in front of all these grand
people on your side of the church."

"Every single thing is ready down here. You know my mother.
And yours. You just have to walk into the middle of it, and say 'I
do.' That bit's important."

He kissed her then, lightly, tenderly.

"Better help with the loot," he said. "Three days, Em. Now
introduce me to your smashing friend with the long legs. You're
lucky I didn't meet her first."

Emily smiled with deep content and called to Marianna, who,
on being introduced, rolled her great eyes at Dermot above her
pile of parcels, balancing on the lowest step up to the front door,
no hand free for formal greeting.

"Darling Em," she said, but the great wide smile was for
Dermot. "I think you've been very clever. *Decidedly* clever.
Hello, Dermot."

There was no time for thought, for emotion, or for anything
else other than the helter-skelter race to be ready. Sorting and
packing the newly bought trousseau; standing patient but fermenting for the small alterations necessary by the local dressmaker to

her dress and Marianna's, the woman so overexcited that she was almost possessed, traces of spit oozing between the pins that she held between her pale lips.

For God's sake, thought Emily, I hope she doesn't sew it up along the bottom like an apple pie bed.

"Darling," said Marianna, "do you think the lady knows quite what she's doing?"

Darkly, Emily answered that they could only pray.

On the last day there was a fever of telephone calls, and enough people for the Galway races, it seemed to Emily, arriving at the Great Southern Hotel in Galway, where they would be doing enough winter trade to bring smiles to their faces.

There was a party in the evening for both the families, and the astonishing sight of Lydia, with an expressionless face, handing around trays of bits and pieces that by her standards would have kept a family for a month.

Aggie's old sister had also been pressed into service, crammed by Aggie with terrible threats into her good black dress and a spotless apron, and her laced boots polished, handing around drinks with her eyeballs popping for the grandeur of the people she was handing them to, and the promises in her excited mind, of years of talking in Clonfrack, indeed until the grave, and never a one to equal her experiences.

Across it all, Dermot's eyes met Emily's and mutely they promised each other that soon, soon would come their part of it all.

Themselves alone. Till death did them part.

Before Emily had realized it, she had reached the point where she was standing before the long swing mirror in her bedroom. She was dressed with the lovely froth of white lace they had found in Switzers, and she looked at herself long and solemnly. An unfamiliar Emily, with wide, excited eyes, that she would never see again beyond this day.

Beside her over a chair lay her grandmother's bridal veil, clouds of it, which Aggie had stayed up half the night to iron; borne across from Sydney Street in its original black tissue paper by old Lydia, with as much care as if it had been the Crown Jewels themselves. Emily could imagine her, bolt upright all night on a seat, refusing to be parted from her suitcase. Mrs. McRoss was giving a last gentle touch to the little spiked circlet of camellias from the hothouses at Castle Keene, that would keep it in place, her own head beautifully crowned with softly moving ostrich feathers.

"Mums," said Emily. "For something old, do you know what I'm going to wear?"

"What, pet?"

Marianna came swanning into the bedroom, in a cloud of pale rose-pink organdy, one full-blown rose, to match it, in her dark hair.

"Marianna! Oh, Marianna, you look fabulous. How I wish Joe were here. They'd make such a marvelous couple, wouldn't they, Mums!"

Marianna twirled happily before the mirror.

"Time for everything, darling," she said. "Time for everything. Today is yours. And you look exquisite, Em."

She asked Mrs. McRoss to make some small adjustment to the back of her dress, and Emily turned to her jewel box. Something old. What older and more beautiful than the necklace of Toledo gold. She was in white from head to foot, and that gleaming at her throat would be magnificent. She would wear it for Doña Serafina, who had wanted to see her wearing it for happier times.

"I'm going to wear Doña Serafina's necklace," she said.

Her mother looked up startled.

"How perfect, Em," she said then. "How beautiful it will look."

This, she realized, would be true, but surely it would be like a ghost at this wedding. She would have liked the child to wear something more marked by happiness.

Emily opened the old mahogany box that Gran had given her long ago, and moved aside a few loose things to reach the red velvet case of the necklace. She lifted it, and stopped.

Beneath it, its silver chain tangled, lay Sam's crystal heart, but the two halves of plastic had split apart, the golden *E* lying loose between them.

A long moment she looked at it. He had said she would do it.

"Sorry Sam," she whispered. "Sorry, sorry, Sam."

It was the last time she apologized to him. She turned, then, the necklace for Alejandro running like a river of gold through her fingers; asking her mother to put it on.

The veil then, and the fragrant coronet of camellias, spiked for good fortune with white myrtle, and Aggie thundering up the stairs, trumpeting that Dr. John was down there in the hall, and shouldn't all the rest of them be gone.

Bursting into floods of tears when she saw Emily.

A cable from Ted, miraculously, as they went out the door. From Rangoon.

"Hoping this finds bride and groom as it leaves me in the pink your loving Ted."

"Idiot," said Emily. "Idiot."

And missed Joe unbearably.


There was a pause for a few moments under the shadowed arches at the back of the small chapel, while Aggie and Marianna settled the voluminous fine folds of her veil.

Someone put a bouquet into her hands, exquisite wax-white camellias to match those in her hair, put together by the head gardener at Castle Keene. She looked down at them, and instead of seeing them saw the pale fragile colors of the freesias from the Finca de los Angeles; felt again the cold dark chill of the vast empty cathedral at dawn; knew one moment of blinding grief for the fine, dazzling presence that had been Alejandro.

Not for one second at that moment did she think of Sam.

Alejandro. And now Dermot.

John touched her gently on the arm.

"Come back," he said. "You're getting married."

She looked up the short aisle, banked with white and gold chrysanthemums, to where Dermot stood fiercely erect in his black morning coat, the plaster looking like a white glove on his left hand, his hair in the candlelight still silver from the faraway sun.

Turning to John, she smiled at him, a serene, enchanted smile through the clouds of her veil.

"I know," she said. "Come on."

The chapel was so small there was little chance to see anyone on the way down the short aisle, the small exquisite organ nearly blowing all its golden pipes in triumphal music.

The beaming families, God love them, in all their finery. Aunt Agnes, all delighted teeth, with a strange edifice of ancient felt drooping around her delighted smile, Uncle William foursquare beside her in an ancient frock coat.

Aggie bawling into a spotless handkerchief, and old Lydia

upright beside her, looking as if she wanted to cry too, but was damned if she would now that Aggie had. And that terrible old sister who haunted the kitchen.

At the back, all the workers and tenants of the estate, crammed into the carved pews in their Sunday clothes, boots and faces shining; all looking at the bride and groom as if they watched a chapter from a fairy tale; the lovely Miss McRoss, and she away all these years doing great things in the war, and the young man himself come home from the dead, when everyone had given him up for lost. The pair of them one day to be the Earl and Countess of Keene themselves, although God save the mark, that wouldn't be for years yet, and the earl no age at all.

There was the family wedding breakfast in the pillared ballroom of the castle, and all the loving toasts that brought Emily close to tears; the kisses and good wishes and telegrams and cards. All going past her like a haze, through which she realized she must grasp it all and remember it. Remember it, for the treasured gold of such a day would never come again.

They all piled into cars then and went racing, with horns blaring, over to Clonfrack for the hooley, where Mrs. McRoss had invited the village.

The only room big enough to hold the crowd—for they knew that no man, woman, or child capable of rising from its bed would stay at home—was the village schoolroom, the folding doors that divided it now parted and the desks banished to the yard. The benches were set about the walls, and above the porter barrels in the corner, the mild and gentle face of Our Lord looked down at them, a long finger pointing to His bleeding heart, lest in the revelry they should overlook His message. The walls had been looped haphazardly with tired and faded bunting left over from some forgotten festivity, among which hung the gay, inconsequential drawings of the children.

In one corner was placed a circle of kitchen chairs for the Quality, and a long trestle table at the end of the room was stacked with more food than most of the visiting Quality had set eyes on since the war began.

From Galway, Mrs. McRoss had hired a ladies' band, three groaning accordions and a shrieking violin, led by a Miss Rosie O'Grady. They wore bright green satin suits and cowboy hats and heavy leather boots, all of them completely indistinguishable one from the other, with their high color and jet-black hair. Any one of them could have been Miss Rosie O'Grady.

The parish priest would race on to duty the very second he got back from the celebrations at Castle Keene, where Emily had been compelled, with great reluctance, to invite him. His place he knew. It was in the circle of chairs reserved for the Quality, for what else was he in the eyes of God or man. Over a glass of yellow lemonade, as at all similar functions, he would hold uneasy court, his small watchful eyes forever darting round in the endless search for the Occasions of Sin in such a place. The young ones pitied him a little, because he would never have the sport he got in the winter when he could make regular sorties out into the darkness to drive back the hot-blooded couples for whom dancing was not enough, searching round the ancient tombs in the churchyard and prodding with his walking stick into the bushes along the river. Legend had it that one winter night, seeing the dancers growing few, he had beaten no less than fifteen couples, fiercely, out of Curran's hay barn, and all his protests to their parents went unheard, for musha, didn't they do the same themselves when they were young, and wasn't half the fun of it escaping from the priest.

The green satin Rosie O'Gradys were in full swing, the porter flowing, and the party already roaring, when the car horns were heard screaming through the village, the wedding party, thanks to Lord Keene's fine champagne, well ready for joining into any-thing that came.

There was a long unsteady speech from the corn merchant, who had been elected to give the wedding toast on account of what was described as his fine turn of the tongue, but few people had the patience to listen to him.

Emily had barely found herself getting up from her kitchen chair with a full glass of malt whiskey in her hand, to bow and smile her thanks beside Dermot, when the accordions belched into business again, and she was swept off to the "Walls of Limerick," the whiskey poured into someone else's glass, God help them, but they could cope better than she could.

With her dress and veil looped on her arm, she raced through the "Walls of Limerick" with some young man she had never seen before, glistening with enthusiasm and sweat, and then she was passed from hand to hand, dizzily footing the jigs and reels with more young fellows whose faces she could barely remember,

other than in various wild escapades of childhood. To a man they
wore bright navy suits and Brylcreemed hair flat on to their
heads, their shoes losing their Sunday shine on the knotty, dusty
floor. All of them maddened by the black porter and the excitement of the hour into the never-to-be-forgotten bravado of asking
Miss McRoss to dance.

With deep hilarious pleasure she caught a glimpse of Marianna
deliberately bewitching the parish priest, and of Aunt Agnes
carefully and deliberately learning the steps of the jig from the
chemist's assistant from the Medical Hall, his red head barely up
to her waist, and her long slender feet making nothing of her
height and weight.

"Look," she was crying to all who would listen to her, a
beatific smile on her face, "I can do it. I can do it."

"Yer great," Emily heard her partner yell. "Yer great. Yer
hoppin' like a fairy."

Aunt Agnes beamed with gratification, and leaped even higher,
while Mrs. McRoss led a stunned Uncle William back to the
kitchen chairs and the malt whiskey to recover his breath.

John and Pat were in their element, both of them fine dancers,
flushed with the happiness of the day and the good drink, leaping
away opposite each other as though there were no one else in the
world.

Ah, God, thought Emily with a sudden intolerable pang of
sadness, wouldn't Joe be in his element today. He'd be going
mad.

Before sorrow had a chance to grip her, the accordions thundered suddenly and the fiddle rose to a high piercing note,
holding it a second before they launched into the throb of
"Jealousy." Almost without time for the customary mutter of
"Willya dance?" she was lurching off around the floor in an
unsteady and distinctly passionate tango with the cowman from
Daly's farm out on the road to Attymon; wrapped in the scents of
hair cream and porter and, she could swear, the last unmistakable
traces of manure.

The fire in the one grate did nothing for the big room, and the
air had assumed something of the character of a cold miasma,
rich with the fumes of the good drink. When she shook herself at
the end from the grip of the cowman, Emily was hot and cold at
the same time, left, as was the custom, to find her own way back
to the kitchen chairs, desperate for a breather. On the way, she

came up against Dermot like a stranger, his hair on end and his expression wild, his plaster stained brown with porter.

"Sweetheart," he cried, as if he hadn't seen her for days, and then, "Let's get the hell out of here."

"Oh, darling! I wanted to suggest it before I fell down or got my dress torn or something. I feel I've lost my pristine radiance as a bride. Let's only get married once, Dermot."

He kissed her quickly.

"You look absolutely perfect to me," he said. "And yes, once will do for me."

"Can we really go now?" she asked him.

"Look at them," he said. "They'll never miss us now. They'll be battering here till dawn."

They missed them enough to swarm after them out of the doors to see them go, crammed on the steep steps calling out blessings and good wishes, and the stronger of them chasing the car almost all the way to Clonfrack House, behind its trailing burden of old boots and rattling tin cans.

John had driven them to the house to change, and when they finally left, with only the families to say good-bye, Dermot took the wheel of the Buick, which Emily's mother had lent them. A couple of miles from the village, on the road to Oranmore, well out of sight of everyone, Dermot stopped abruptly.

"Sorry, darling, you'll have to drive."

He looked at the plaster as if it were an enemy.

"Dermot, of course, your hand! Why didn't you let me drive at once?"

"Showing off," he said. "Just showing off. Couldn't let my bride drive me away. Tell you the truth, it hurt like hell."

"Silly," she said, but she felt a pang of sorrow for lost perfection. They changed seats and she drove on into the pale December afternoon. They were not going far, as their time was so short. A friend of Dermot's had lent them a cottage just around Black Head on the south side of Galway Bay, on the wild shores leading down to the Cliffs of Moher. An hour or so away, no more.

They drove awhile in tired silence, both of them full of all that had happened through the long day. Later they would begin to talk it all out, saying, do you remember this and did you see that. For the moment, Emily skillfully weaved the familiar old car along the narrow winding road between the boggy winter ditches.

"Well, Viscountess," Dermot said at last. "How does it feel?"

For a second she forgot the road and glanced at him in blank amazement.

"Well you are one now, aren't you darling. My Viscountess."

How had she forgotten, and been astonished to be reminded, as though it were the only dubious part of that splendid day. What Marianna would call that fiendish little man had given her a complex. Sam had actually managed to give her a complex. She was furious.

Taking a hand from the wheel, she laid it a moment on Dermot's knee.

"Darling Dermot," she said. "I am happy to be your driveress, your cookess, your floor scrubberess, your viscountess. Any ess you like, just as long as it belongs to you."

He gave the hand a kiss and put it back on the wheel.

"My Em will do," he said.

They came over the mountains between the promontory of Black Head and Slieve Elva, down to the open Atlantic, as the light was going out of the sky. A great panorama of a Christmas sunset spread before them, deep purple down at the sea and old rose faded in above it, with long streaks of green and yellow; melting up into the dark blue sky. Inishmore and Inisheer and Inishmaan suspended dark against a limitless turquoise sea.

"Oh, look at it," cried Emily. "Look at it. Just like all the Christmas cards I painted when I was a child. All it needs is a whopping pointed star, and the Three Wise Men in silhouette."

"They'd get the camels' feet wet. Down there on the left, Em. It's only a track. The cottage is right on the shore. A bit more and we'd be in your Christmas card."

He stopped at the door and opened it before he kissed her.

"Welcome, my darling, to all I can offer for the moment."

They cared little, for those few days, about what they would do, but there had been talk of fishing or even a little sailing, if the weather allowed on the dangerous coast.

In the morning the wind and rain awoke them, the gale hammering and rattling at the doors and windows as if it demanded entry for the sheets of rain.

They found oilskins in a cupboard, and wrapped in them, they staggered along the shore, where the gigantic seas ground and dragged the loose stones up and down the sand with a roar that made talk impossible. The gray fearsome sky hovered above the piling waves, huge threatening cliffs rising black and streaming at either end of their little bay.

"It's like one of those fearful Victorian pictures of a shipwreck," yelled Emily as they clung together, almost blinded, on the little jetty. "All we need is a couple of broken masts sticking up out of the rocks."

"It happens," Dermot yelled back. "Frequently."

They fought their way to the one minute shop in the village that was obviously the living room as well, and were received with a massive benevolence that did little to hide the roaring curiosity behind it.

"At least," Dermot said to her when they came out, "this time you have a wedding ring."

Mostly they piled up the turf to a glowing mountain on the flat hearth, and stayed where they were; almost bewildered by their happiness; talking endlessly and falling companionably silent, and talking again and making love; cooking and eating large confused meals at all sorts of unsuitable hours when the fancy took them. Listening to the rain on the thatch drumming away their time.

For three days.

On the fourth evening they were sitting with one of their confused suppers between them on a small table by the fire. Lamb chops and black puddings because Dermot loved them, and buttermilk and brown bread and salt country butter, and an earthen bowl full of raspberry jelly.

The heavy sudden drumming on the door was in full keeping with the wildness of the streaming night.

Dermot looked at her and raised his eyebrows, already pushing back his chair.

"Maybe you've got your shipwreck after all."

When he opened the front door, without any invitation the wind blew in the little man whose wife ran the post office, like the shop, in the corner of her one room. He stood dripping on the floor, trying to catch his breath, and with difficulty Dermot closed the door behind him.

"What can we do for you, Matt?"

Matt's eyes were wide and bright with importance under his soaked black cap. From the sides of it the water ran down in rivers into his coat collar.

"'Tis for you, sorr," he said. "'Tis the telephone. They said to go out and get you, and they ring it again in fifteen minutes. Fifteen minutes. That'd be time, d'you see, sorr, for me to be here to get you. 'Twas a gentleman, sorr."

Dermot was already reaching for his oilskin.

"I'll come."

Emily got up.

"No," he said gently, as though premonition touched him. "You stay here. Whatever it is can wait that long." He gave her a tender reassuring grin. "Matt says it's fifteen minutes there and back."

He kissed her, and went out with the little man into the black, screaming night.

As soon as he fought his way back in again, what seemed hours afterwards, she started to her feet and ran to him, seeing in his shocked face that the news had not been good.

"Dermot. Darling. What is it?"

His plastered fingers fumbled with the fastenings of the oilskin, and she helped him, fumbling herself, feeling the numbness of his own shock. As she eased the streaming yellow coat from his shoulders, he turned around to face her.

"My father is dead," he said.

"Your father! How can he be—" She almost started on the banal statement of how can he be, he was fine at the wedding.

"Oh, my darling," she said then. "Come and sit down."

Almost blindly he moved over to the fire as she told him; spreading out his cold hands to the turf; staring; trying to absorb it.

"What happened? Can you tell me what happened?"

She poured a glass of whiskey and put it into his hand, and he took it automatically.

"Nothing," he said then. "Nothing happened, that's the thing. Apparently he was out all afternoon riding the fences. When he came back he said he felt rather tired, and that he'd go and lie down for a while. When my mother went up to call him for dinner, he was gone. As if he just fell asleep."

"Your poor mother."

"Your mother is with her. Anna is still there too. And John. It was John rang up."

"We must go back."

"Not tonight. There is nothing I can do now to justify your driving through the mountains on a night like this. That's how to make two tragedies from one. First thing in the morning we'll go."

He took a deep instinctive gulp of his whiskey.

"Sorry about the honeymoon, darling."

She knelt beside him and laid her face against his.

"It was fabulous while it lasted," she said. "Oh, my poor Dermot, I'm so sorry."

They made love that night with an air of grief and finality, as if they expressed in it their sad certainty that nothing for them would ever be quite the same again.

Many of the guests had not yet gone home, and in sad silence the coffin lay before them on the same spot where, only a few days ago, Dermot and Emily had stood to be married.

Dermot telephoned and arranged an extended leave for both of them, but after the muted and unhappy Christmas at Clonfrack, it was necessary for both of them to report back.

"I'll get a compassionate discharge now, Mother," he said. "I'm wounded, and the war's all over but the shouting. Plus this. But I must go back in person for Boards and things. I'll pull all the strings I can to get Emily out too. I understand they're releasing married women with any compassionate reason to go. God knows they can manage without Em where she is."

"There's an awful lot to see to, Dermot," she said, and he looked sharply at the drawn thin face below the cloud of graying hair. She was trying to tell him something. "Your father—" she said.

His face was gentle, and he kissed her.

"You go off up and stay with Anna until I come back. Don't worry. I'll sort everything out."

She was quiet, still subdued with shock, and she did no more than nod, although she looked at him sadly for a long moment. Dermot watched her from the room, and then ran his hands through his hair.

"You're tired," Emily said, watching him. "All these-lawyers."

"All these lawyers, indeed." He lay back in his chair and stared at the fire, and she could see that his mind was not with her. "Things aren't as they should be, Em."

"No? I thought your father's will was very plain and very detailed. No?"

The firelight showed up the wry twist to his handsome face. Emily thought with shock and anger that he looked suddenly much older.

"The thing about a fine detailed will, my darling Em, is that you need the flat cash to carry out all the instructions."

He stood up briskly, and leaned over to kiss her.

"Don't trouble your pretty little head, as old-fashioned husbands used to say. I've only just begun, and I could be quite wrong. D'you realize, Em, that because of this damned war that affects neither of us, we've got to separate in two days. When we do both get out, we'll have to move in here properly."

Emily nodded, not quite believing. She still felt no more than a guest at the castle, quite unable to accept the idea that she would be mistress of it.

"There's a lot to arrange," she agreed. "I'm terrified of making your mother feel unwanted."

"My mother, who is a good and wise lady, has already decided to buy a small house in The Curragh near Anna. Castle Keene will be entirely yours, my darling."

Emily stared at him.

"Blimey," she said, and it might have been Sam speaking.

Dermot kissed her appalled face, and for the first time since the telephone call, they laughed together in the unalterable secret world of their own happiness.

"You'll be marvelous," he said.

The only consolation for being back at Darlowe, and away from Dermot, was in seeing Marianna again.

"Poor Em. So rotten for you. So rotten for both of you. Really spoiled it all, didn't it."

They had talked long enough for the moment of her troubles, Emily thought.

"Is it very boring here now, Marianna?"

They were sitting on their beds in the billet in their overcoats and gloves, the weather gray and bitter and the tiny coal ration able to do little to combat the icy chill of the almost empty house. Penny and Isobel had both been posted, and for the last two weeks Marianna had been alone in the cold room.

Marianna didn't answer her question at once, and for the first time Emily really looked at her, realizing guiltily that her friend's lovely face was radiant, although as always with that slightly offhand look, as though she were laughing at herself.

"Well, you see, Em, darling, there's this chap."

Emily grinned at her affectionately. How many of Marianna's tales had begun like that.

"I knew him when we were children," Marianna went on. "Small children, you know, jelly for tea and all that. Always I knew him. And there I was in the village street at home—my dear, one goes home *every* thirty-six now, there's nothing else to do—when he came up to me. Back from Burma for some shadowy reason. Well, there you are, Em darling, that was it. Just it. We'll be getting engaged on his next leave. Anyway, we'll all be out soon. Honestly, Em, I'm bats about him."

She looked at Emily, almost shy, astonished that such a thing could happen to her. Emily leaned over and kissed her.

"Marianna, I'm *so* pleased. So happy for you. How smashing."

So happy in her own happiness. Delighted to find that now all her hopes and plans would be the same as Marianna's. Their children, she thought, with a great leap into the future, certain of it, would know each other. Grow up together.

"Oh, Marianna, it's lovely. What's his name?"

"Alastair. I mean, imagine, Em. I've danced my shoes off with half the Army and nearly as many of the Air Force, and I have to go and fall head over heels and overnight, for someone I knew with blackberry jam on his face. I must say, he's better-looking now. But imagine, Em."

"Much better that way," said Emily.

Then, as offhand as she could manage it, "How's Sam?"

Marianna looked at her nails.

"Sam's gone."

"Gone?"

Emily stared at her, touched with guilty sorrow, even while she knew it was the best thing that could possibly happen.

"He apparently applied for a posting a couple of months back," said Marianna.

When Dermot came back. Poor Sam.

"Where to?" Emily tried to seem no more than just interested.

"I don't know. He was very uncommunicative. Just packed up and left."

Emily stared out at the winter fields and blew on her cold fingers. A train like a toy ran, slowing, into the station.

"I'd like to have seen him."

"And what would you have said to him—Countess?"

Marianna's voice was not too gentle.

Emily shrugged.

"Good-bye. He's on my conscience."

Marianna stood up abruptly and almost fell over, forgetting her legs were wrapped tight in a blanket.

"Sam's all right," she said. "He's gone off now with all he ever thought and wanted to think about the so-called upper classes confirmed. They are spoiled, selfish, unkind, and treacherous. That certainty will bolster him against a lot."

"You never liked him."

"He had a chip on his shoulder no one could move."

"I wonder," Emily said sadly, and let it go, and then thought the moment right to change the conversation by launching for Marianna into the whole mixed story of the honeymoon and the death and funeral.

"We thought it was a shipwreck," she said, "when the little maneen came hammering at the door."

"My poor Em," said Marianna, when she came to the end of it all. "You really are getting life in a lump at the moment. Like these tablets of concentrated food they give the soldiers. But I'm truly sorry about Dermot's papa. I thought he was a sweetie."

"He was. He was always very kind to me, even when he didn't know me. When we had to leave Spain and I was so miserable over Alejandro."

"Dear God, how the child has *lived*," said Marianna. "And how does it feel now to be a countess?"

"It doesn't," Emily said bluntly. "I can't realize yet I'm Emily Kilpatrick, never mind the countess bit."

"Well, anyway, it'll all be very grand, being the Countess of

Keene. That gorgeous great house. You must have us to stay *frequently*. It'll be lovely for you, Em.''

"I expect so," Emily said. "I expect so. But I honestly haven't had time to think about it very much."

There was about a month with virtually nothing to do except long for Dermot and write to him almost every day; trying to be happy for Marianna, who went racing off with a blissful smile on her face on every thirty-six, to spend it with her young man, now on some unspecified task in the War Office.

The winter was cold, the gray days seeming made for loneliness and frustration; the only warm place in the Station was beside the NAAFI fire.

She was there one evening with Marianna, nursing a mug of cocoa and contemplating the boredom of night duty, when an airman shoved his head around the door. It showed the change in Darlowe that she didn't even know him.

"Kilpatrick," he shouted. "Telephone for Kilpatrick."

With a start Emily realized that that was her. Kilpatrick still seemed to belong only to Clonfrack and Castle Keene; McRoss had belonged to Darlowe.

"How kind of you to come across," she said to the unknown young man as she bolted for the door.

"Comin' anyway," he said. "They said you was here."

"Thanks anyway."

It was pitch-black, but she ran all the way, avoiding the trees by instinct, and crashing at last in through the back door where she was not allowed to go, down the long passage past the men's quarters to the telephone in the hall.

"Dermot."

She had hardly breath to speak.

"How did you know it would be me?"

"Darling. I just knew."

"Where were you?"

"In the NAAFI. Quite a canter. I was terrified you'd have gone away."

"Poor sweet. Listen. Have you got a thirty-six this week? I'm in London."

"Oh, Dermot. Darling what luck. I was coming up anyway tomorrow to see old Lydia. Mums wrote to say she'd been ill."

"She's all right. Tough as old boots, that one. Come and see me instead. I need you much more."

All the gloom of February was gone, the night suddenly as bright as the sun of June. She realized she was grinning like an idiot at the telephone.

"Will you meet me, love?"

"No, I'm sorry. I have an appointment in the morning with my father's London solicitors. I saw them today too. So I'll be in the city. Do you know where the Savoy is?"

"Of course."

"Meet me there at twelve thirty. More or less. Okay?"

"Dermot, how *grand*!"

"We'll make the most of it," he said, and she didn't understand him, too excited to question.

"How are things going? Getting organized?"

"Tell you when I see you."

It was only after she put the receiver back, her face radiant, that the feeling crept into her mind that there had been something strained and muted about his voice. Probably tired, poor darling. Careering endlessly around to all these lawyers couldn't be much fun.

He was quiet too when they met, but Emily was distracted by the opulent thrill of being in the famous dining room of the Savoy, even though the wonderful view of the river was still sandbagged over. A headwaiter as reverential as a bishop took her overcoat and cap.

"I put on my walking-out uniform for the Savoy," she said happily. "What are we celebrating?"

He looked at her a long moment, thin still, his hair darkening. She decided the dark shadow in his eyes must be still his father's death, because he smiled then and took her hand across the table.

"Every hour I am with you is a celebration, darling Em," he said. "But I wanted you to have a very special lunch today. I have something to tell you."

"What, darling? Something nice to go with the lunch?"

"Let's order and get settled."

She had nothing exciting to tell him. No baby yet, that would have got her out of the services at once on a Form 35.

As if he read her mind, he said, "I'll be out in a month. I'm on indefinite leave pending discharge." He looked down at his fingers. A little straighter now, but not much. "A small pension," he added, "for what it's worth."

It was not until they had ordered and were waiting for the soup that he spoke again.

"Have a cigarette, Em."

He passed her the box of thin colored Markovitch he always kept for her, buying them every time he passed through Dublin. Only then did something in his manner catch her attention, and she looked at him over the lighter.

"Am I going to need it?" she asked him with sudden percipience.

He lit his own Three Castles, and carefully put back the lighter.

"I have bad news for you, Em. I'm sorry."

What could be bad news in their world? Her eyes grew big and dark with fear. Had he had some terrible illness in Sumatra? That fever in India. And now he was going to die of it? Oh, Jesus God.

". . . spent practically all of the last two months with solicitors," he was saying. "I'm afraid, darling, I have to tell you my father was not very clever in his affairs, in fact he made a catastrophic mess of them. It appears there has been chaos for many years. Bluntly, my love, by the time the debts and the death duties are paid, we're not going to have a penny. It will be necessary to sell Castle Keene. He was up to his neck in debt."

Money. That was all it was. Money. She stared at him, light-headed with relief.

"Are you telling me we won't have any money? We'll be poor?"

"Yes."

In sheer reaction she hardly managed to keep from laughing in his face. He was all right. In the last minute she had lived his death. No ghastly illness. Thanks be to God. He was all right.

No money. In the heel of the hunt, no money. She felt Sam's relentless class-consciousness, that no matter what he felt about her would never let her forget some so-called superiority simply because her family seemed to have more money than his.

Unable to love her freely for what she was herself; trying always, even when he said he loved her, to compress her into some shape that he insisted on.

Now she and Dermot had, it appeared, no money.

In that moment she shed all her guilt and sorrow about Sam.

Dermot, watching her with anguish, mistook her silence.

"I'll give you a divorce, Em, if you'd like. You have every right. I didn't ask you to marry a cripple and a pauper."

She forgot Sam; forgot everything else, leaning over the table to take his hands in hers, her eyes upon him, full of love.

"My dearest dearest," she said to him. "I married a chap called Dermot Kilpatrick. I never for a moment married Castle Keene. I've never had it, darling, so I won't miss it. I will only be sad for you, who should have had it all."

"No. Paul should. So you see I haven't really lost anything either. I never thought of any of it as mine."

"Soup, madam. Sir."

She released his hands to make room for the waiter.

"You must understand I mean really poor, Em. The estate is hocked to the neck. My father was very keen on his foreign investments. Germany. France. Italy. All gone down the drain, of course. Death duties will put the lid on it. We have to sell."

Emily remembered a bright day in early summer, in all the excitement of the invasion. A dreadful smell of Camembert cheese.

"Paul said something to me," she said, "about being worried about the estate."

"I bet he was. If he had a clue, I bet he was."

They talked all around it through the soup, and through the ragout of mutton that followed it, feeling their way around what seemed to be the ruin of their lives.

"You know my mother is going to give me an allowance," she said. "You can use that. And then there's your pension."

"Your allowance is for you, my darling, and as for my pension, that'll be very useful for feeding the cat if we should have one."

He laid down his knife and fork and looked at her across the table.

"The loss of the estate and everything that goes with it is just something that we have to swallow. Now I come to the part we really have to talk about. To which you can say yes or no."

She waited, her eyes fixed on him.

"Em, love. I'll do pretty well anything in the world for you. But please don't ask me to settle in a little two-by-four terrace house and push a pen somewhere. However poor. I'd go mad."

She thought at once of Ridge Road, Letchworth, and Sam and Angela. Sam hadn't known he was going mad. But Dermot would.

"We can do better than that for both of us," he went on, "if we have a little courage."

He paused and now she could see excitement flaming in his eyes.

"There's a place there's money left," he said. "But we can't get it out. We would have to go to it, if we want it."

"Where?" she asked him.

"Spain. Málaga."

Spain.

Speechless, she stared at him, absorbed, unaware of the waiter who removed the plates. Spain.

Of course. Why had she not thought of it? The old lady in Gibralfaro was Dermot's grandmother too.

"Did you go there?" she asked him.

"Why, yes. Every summer, I should think, until the one you met Anna. I got too interested then in airplanes."

Every summer until she met Anna.

And Alejandro.

What, she wondered briefly, might have happened had she met Dermot first, that year? Who would she have loved?

Nothing would have happened, she thought then. Nothing. She was still too young for Dermot, ready only for the more obvious splendor of Alejandro.

Excitement begin to kindle inside her. Before she had even managed to accept that they were down, he was setting them up again.

"It's been so long," he said then, "with the Civil War and then our own war, since anyone has been able to go there, that we have tended to forget. The old grandmother died eighteen months ago. All we know is that the housekeeper is keeping the whole place intact until someone can come. My father could have gone through Lisbon, but I think even he was seeing the red light by then, and thought the expense too much. He could bring nothing out anyway. The house there is ours now, Em. And any money that there is."

She could find nothing to say.

The tall yellow house on the slope of Gibralfaro; looking back to Málaga and east to the dark blue sea. Beautiful and shadowed with old, high-beamed ceilings and the garden tumbling down the hill perfumed with jasmine and roses; small fountains chattering in tiled patios. Days of happiness with Anna. In love with Alejandro.

"Darling!" she said breathlessly. "It's even got bathrooms."

"It's got everything," he said. "But I couldn't be idle, Em. I'm too young just to take whatever the old lady has left and idle my days away in sun. There is the finca out at Loja. I never had to inquire how much it made, but there is always a market for olives. My father had a man running it, but he was old, and for all I know he's dead and the whole place fallen to pieces. But it was a nice house, and the land is mine and we could get it all going again. A finca in the country, a few horses. All very pleasant. But it will all be a gamble, and mountains of hard work to begin with, at least."

She thought of the Finca de los Angeles, and the leaves of the olives turning silver in the sun; the palm trees in the patio and all the flowers; the voices in the sun of all the people she had loved.

"We would be remaking the world," she said.

"My darling, in Spain there will be much that needs remaking. It will not be easy. But it seems to me the best thing to do."

The best thing to do. There would be no time to think about the disasters that had befallen them, since the alternative so moved her heart. She was a long time giving any answer, and he began to look anxious again.

"I know you were happy in Spain," he said hopefully, "and so was I. We could make something of it, I'm sure."

Across the coffee cups she smiled at him.

"When do we go?" she asked him.

He grinned, but he even had that one worked out.

"I have months' more chaos to clear up," he said, "and by that time the war will be over."

Joe will be back, she thought, with her mother in her mind.

"When we're ready, we'll take my father's big old Armstrong Siddeley and put everything we own into it. And by that time, my love, it may not be too much. Then we'll climb with it onto a cargo boat for Lisbon."

Her love for him shone in her eyes. If that was the solution to his problems, then God had blessed her with good fortune, for she would have done anything on earth he wished, no matter how hard. For better or for worse. The thing was, the worse seemed to also be the stuff that dreams were made of.

She took his hand again.

"And we'll drive singing," she said, "across Portugal and Spain."

He looked into the loving eyes.

"And drive, singing, across Portugal and Spain. Oh, Em, my darling Em, what would I do without you."

They talked all day and most of the night, until she really understood the magnitude of the disaster, and his wisdom in not trying to struggle with it. But she had no time to reflect on it all until the next unbearable parting was over, and she was alone in the train, going back to Darlowe.

She saw nothing of the gray scars of inner London, nor the endless rows of small shattered houses of the suburbs; nor the swell of the dark fields beyond them, hazed with the first green of the winter wheat.

Her mind was entirely on all they had talked about. As she had begun to realize their plan for the future, she had difficulty in remembering to look sad about Castle Keene. As she had told Marianna, there had been little time to think about it, but she would have felt small excitement at the idea of going to live in a corner of the great house that would have inevitably crumbled around them, with no money to keep it up.

She would have done her best to love it because it was Dermot's. No more. And she was comforted by a few things he had said that revealed that he thought himself no more than an interloper. Castle Keene and the estate belonged, in his mind, to Paul.

But now it would be Spain.

She closed her eyes and let her happiness invade her. A real life where they would have to work hard for what they got. A love, such love, as she once foolishly thought she had lost forever in Spain.

Light and color and the dark blue sea; days that seemed to go on forever. The smell of flowers on the wind at night.

And Dermot.

Make her peace with the ghost of Alejandro.

Make her peace with Remedios, whom she had loved once, and could love again.

She smiled to herself a little wickedly, her eyes still closed.

Two things she would like to see. Sam's face if she could tell him she had married a man with even less than he had. For Sam would be much too respectable to have a heap of debts.

And Remedios's face, when she told her she was married to an earl.